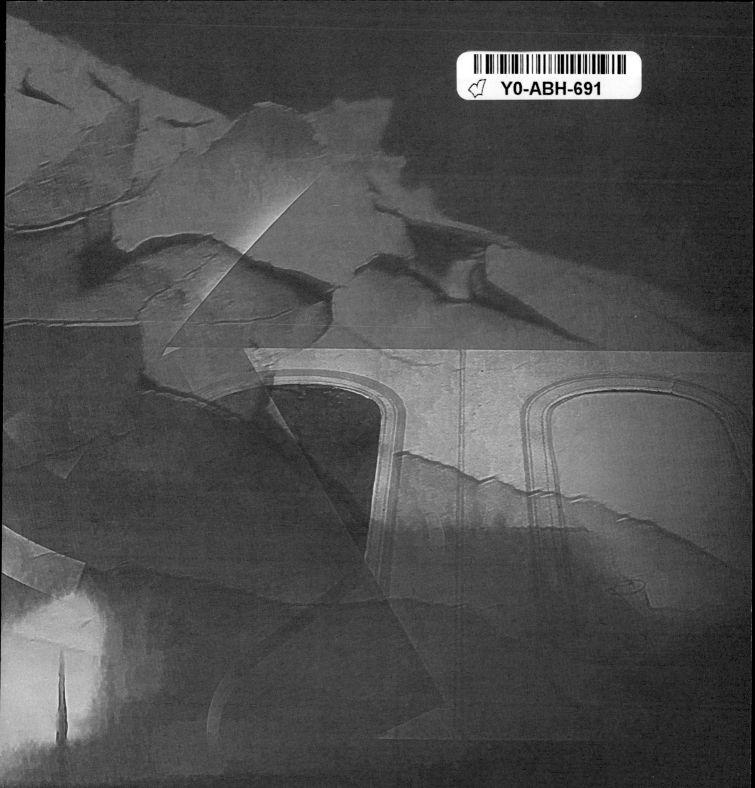

As Timeless As Infinity:

The Complete Twilight Zone Scripts of
Rod Serling

Edited by Tony Albarella

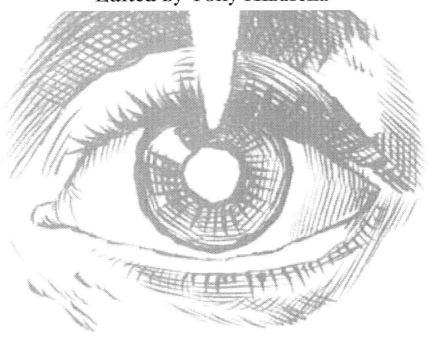

Carol Serling
Carol Serling

A Gauntlet Original

This signed numbered edition of

As Timeless As
Infinity

The Complete Twilight Zone
Scripts of Rod Serling

Volume 1

is limited to 750 copies.

This is copy ___162___

To Chris Conlon, who really knows
why this time.

As Timeless As INFINITY

The Complete Twilight Zone
Scripts of Rod Serling

Volume 1

Edited by Tony Albarella

GAUNTLET PUBLICATIONS
2004

GAUNTLET

FIRST EDITION
ISBN:1-887368-71-X
Copyright © 2004 by Tony Albarella
Jacket Art © 2004 by Harry O. Morris
Jacket and Text Design by Bill Walker

Gauntlet Publications
5307 Arroyo Street
Colorado Springs, CO 80922
United States of America
Phone: (719) 591-5566
e-mail: info@gauntletpress.com
Web site: www.gauntletpress.com

Some people looked at me with arched eyebrows when I announced my intention to go into a film series. To go from writing an occasional drama for *Playhouse 90*, a distinguished and certainly important series, to creating and writing a weekly, 30-minute television film, was like Stan Musial leaving St. Louis to coach third base in an American Legion little league.

But the half-hour film *can* probe effectively, dramatize and present a well-told and well-filmed story. The exciting thing about our medium is its potential, the fact that it doesn't have to be imitative. The horizons of what it can do and where it can go stretch out beyond vision. What it can produce in terms of novelty and ingenuity has barely been scratched. This is a medium that can spread out, delve deep, probe fully and reach out experimentally to whole new concepts.

And that's what we're trying to do with *The Twilight Zone*. We want to tell stories that are different. We want to prove that television, even in its half-hour form, can be both commercial and worthwhile. At the same time, perhaps only as a side effect, a point can be made that the fresh and the untried can carry more infinite appeal than a palpable imitation of the already proven.

Here's what *The Twilight Zone* is: It's an anthology series, half hour in length, that delves into the odd, the bizarre, the unexpected. It probes into the dimension of imagination but with a concern for taste and for an adult audience too long considered to have IQs in negative figures.

Each story is complete in itself. The audience will find itself standing on the bridge of a doomed ship at the elbow of a U-boat commander haunted by the knowledge of what will happen within a moment. Our viewers will walk a death march up a Western street with an aging gunman who clutches a magic potion, depending on it for his survival. And they'll visit an asteroid and watch a man fall in love with a woman robot.

The Twilight Zone is what it implies: that shadowy area of the almost-but-not-quite; the unbelievable told in terms that can be believed.

Here's what the program isn't: It's not a monster rally or a spook show. There will be nothing formula'd in it, nothing telegraphed, nothing so nostalgically familiar that an audience can usually join actors in duets. This anthology series is not an assembly-line operation. Each show is a carefully conceived and wrought piece of drama, cast with competent people; directed by creative, quality-conscious guys, and shot with an eye toward mood and reality.

October 2 was the date of departure. It capped eight months of shooting and a year and a half of planning. That was the night *The Twilight Zone* opened its gates and invited the viewer to take a journey into what we believe is a wondrous land of the very different. No luggage is required for this trip. All that the audience need bring is the imagination.

—Rod Serling
Excerpts from *"Seeking Far Horizons"*
TV Guide
November 7, 1959

CONTENTS

❧

Scripts by Rod Serling
Commentary by Tony Albarella

A MESSAGE FROM
CAROL SERLING

If you were born in the last century and had a TV set, chances are that you have heard of *The Twilight Zone*. And if you are holding this book right now the odds are pretty good that you have a real working knowledge of the *Zone* and know the place that the dictionary defines as "an indefinite boundary," a *Twilight Zone* between fantasy and reality. The phrase conjures up visions of the land of imagination and the unexpected and just a few notes of the *Twilight Zone* theme send one sailing into that other dimension of alternate realities "as vast as space and as timeless as infinity."

The Twilight Zone has become a crowded field over the years. The Secretary of State used the phrase to describe international relations some time back and almost every day one hears some reference to the phrase. There have been books written about *The Twilight Zone*, a movie made, a magazine published, wallpaper and greeting cards printed, games to play, a Disney theme park ride, a pinball game, a DVD release, a slot machine, audio cassettes, trading cards, play productions, short story adaptations and many critiques written.

But this book, this retrospective collection, is the first and only work to reproduce the *Twilight Zone* scripts in their original format as they were originally conceived and crafted by Rod Serling. The on-screen counterparts, while done with immense care and talent, were understandably altered along the way in minor but perceptible degrees by directors, actors and the countless others who were involved in the production of the series. In addition to the original shooting scripts in this book, we have included earlier versions of some

9

and various memorabilia that surrounded the productions (what I like to think of as important add-ons). As you can see this has taken the form of original reviews of the program written at the time of the original airing, telegrams and letters written to the author and others, essays and interviews and a detailed analysis of each episode, including unique commentary from some of the show's original actors and production people. All this compiled and collected with loving care by editor Tony Albarella.

When *The Twilight Zone* was first broadcast in 1959, it was an era of international conflict...Cold War, assassinations, civil rights battles, political scandals and domestic downturn. As someone said, "*Twilight Zone* defined the shadowy transition between the fabulous 50's and the psychedelic 60's. The best and most memorable of the episodes reflected, in the guise of fables, a mirror image of the passing parade of significant national events."

Rod felt strongly that any writer worthy of the name "artist" had a duty to address important issues and he found that through parable and illusion he could make social comment and confront these troubling issues of the day. *The Twilight Zone* gave him the vehicle to comment on sensitive social themes—bigotry, violence, the Cold War, prejudice, the Holocaust, witch-hunts, ethics, segregation, totalitarian societies, corruption—and he was not censored by sponsor interference, network timidity or the tyranny of ratings. In truth, these corporate entities very seldom understood the issues that he was addressing. (As Rod once said, "Things which couldn't be said by a Republican or Democrat could be said by a Martian.")

This is the first edition of what will be the complete collection of Rod's *Twilight Zone* scripts...ninety-two excursions into the alternate world of the *Zone*. The stories have proven to be of lasting quality; perhaps because of the staying power and timeliness of the underlying themes, or maybe because they are just really good stories, or as Buck Houghton, the show's producer called it, "the stinger in the tail" that jolted the viewer into examining their own prejudgments and attitudes. Whatever the reason, we invite you to come along for the ride. As Rod would have said:

"This highway leads to the shadowy tip of reality; you're on a
through route to the land of the different, the bizarre, the
unexplainable...Go as far as you like on this road. Its

limits are only those of the mind itself. Ladies and gentlemen, you're entering the wondrous dimension of imagination. Next stop—*THE TWILIGHT ZONE.*"

EDITOR'S PREFACE

To borrow from the grandiose ads of a bygone movie era, AS TIMELESS AS INFINITY has quite literally been "years in the making." The process of conducting interviews with those connected to Rod Serling and *The Twilight Zone* began in the waning years of the twentieth century and will continue throughout the production of this series. Participants include many of Serling's contemporaries—actors, directors, writers, production personnel, family, friends, colleagues—as well as current talents who never knew Serling personally, yet acknowledge his profound influence on their successful careers. Among these disparate personalities and experiences, I have found one common thread that binds them all: a deep admiration for Serling and a reverence for his work.

Still, these insider anecdotes and memories are simply icing on the proverbial cake. They frame the real works of art to be found within these pages: Rod Serling's original, unadulterated *Twilight Zone* scripts. His words, his creations, his voice, his vision. These classic teleplays are reprinted directly from Serling's personal collection and have never before been made accessible to the general public.

In most cases, the presented script is Rod's final version, which contains all revisions and was used as the shooting script. Earlier drafts may occasionally be supplied if they vary significantly in content or contain handwritten notations, and select variant scenes that meet these criteria may be highlighted. The goal here is to present Serling's finalized work while offering an exclusive peek at the evolution of these beloved stories.

It is my great privilege to research, document and produce this rare glimpse into Serling's creative process. The man was a true visionary and *The Twilight Zone* showcased some of his finest creations. AS TIMELESS AS INFINITY is designed to be a unique and definitive tribute to both Rod Serling and his considerable legacy.

APPRECIATION:

Richard Matheson

In 1959 my friend Charles (Chucky) Beaumont and I were invited to view the pilot film for a new half-hour anthology TV show to be called *The Twilight Zone*. Little did we know that this show would still be aired (and most successfully—even with its own July 4th marathon) forty-four years later, after its beginning! Why? When asked that my answer is that it has lasted because the stories are so *interesting*. Not to mention the A-class quality of the productions—the best directors, the best actors, the best crews. And not to mention (*my* wish to mention this) the fact that Rod, being the superlative writer that he was, had total respect for other quality writers so that our scripts were invariably filmed word-for-word. What a pleasure!

All of which serves as a nostalgic preamble to the truth that Rod's *Twilight Zone* scripts were so superb. How he maintained such creative quality when he had to write so *many TZ* scripts will always remain a mystery to me. I remember him as a charming, amusing man who was—with Buck Houghton—a delight and a writing education to work with. But Lord! Chuck Beaumont wrote twenty-two *TZ* scripts, I wrote fourteen. A handful of other writers—like Earl Hamner and George Clayton Johnson—contributed a small amount of scripts, but Rod did the rest! How on earth did he manage it? I know he dictated, but even so, the amount of work Rod had to accomplish is literally *staggering*. That he wrote such a huge amount of excellent scripts is even more staggering. Rod's specialty was the humanistic type of story. Chuck and I were, first and foremost, *storytellers* and, as such, did not even *attempt* to write the kind of stories Rod was so remarkably proficient at—character examinations, human beings adjusting to

Twilight Zone situations. He transferred his powerful skill from shows like *Playhouse 90* to the world of the offbeat, of fantasy, of science-fiction, always retaining his profound touch with people of every kind. *The Twilight Zone* was Rod's zone. I hope we helped to enhance it—but the true, lasting strength of the series came from the mind of a very talented writer named Rod Serling.

APPRECIATION

Rockne S. O'Bannon

od Serling taught me how to write.
I never met the man (like all of us, I damn well wish I had. Wish we'd hung out. Had long lunches to avoid writing, as I do now with my other writer friends. I wonder if Rod would have been into sushi? Come to think of it, I wonder if Rod ever actively avoided attacking the blank page, as my friends and I do. Considering his prodigious output, probably not).

So how did he teach me how to write?

Novelists often talk of the one seminal book that inspired them, that they read over and over until the spine came apart in their hands, the book that taught them about their craft, fueled their passion, more than anything else.

As an aspiring screenwriter, for me, that work was *The Twilight Zone*. I watched TZ over and over and over—the video equivalent of reading until the spine comes apart. (Considering that watching and re-watching the original TZ was my "classroom," it was especially gratifying that my first experience as a professional writer came on CBS's revival of the series in the mid-1980s.)

Television and films today are flagellated by an MTV-born need for speed. The prevailing wisdom is that contemporary audiences assimilate information faster, thus they demand their entertainment move at a dizzying techno-inspired pace. Problem is, too many filmmakers take this as a mandate to short-hand both story and character. The feeling seems to be that clichéd characters are more easily—more *quickly*—understood by the audience.

But four decades ago, TZ taught us that doesn't have to be the case.

Here is what the best episodes of *The Twilight Zone* did every week, *in half-*

17

an-hour's time (less, actually, when you consider the minutes given over to commercials): each introduced a fully-realized, flesh-and-blood protagonist, often with a character flaw that drove the theme of the tale, very quickly established and made clear this character's normal world, then—*spun this normal world entirely on its ear* in some highly original fashion. But no matter how unexpected or unfamiliar this new world was, it always remained absolutely crystal clear to the audience. And, in the end, the story was brought to a satisfying climax, often with a truly surprising twist at the fade out (a TZ specialty).

All of this, as I say, in under half-an-hour's time.

Nothing less than astonishing. And Rod Serling did it week after week after week (with a little help from his fellow Olympians, Matheson, Beaumont, et al).

Looking for a lesson in telling complex, emotional, riveting tales that both examine the human experience *and* tell an imagination-charged story—all with remarkable pace and economy? Have a look again at TZ episodes "Eye of the Beholder," "It's a Good Life," "To Serve Man."

Better yet, read them. Check out the *tour de force* visual misdirection of "Eye of the Beholder" included in this volume, or the taut claustrophobic atmosphere of "It's a Good Life" and the wholly convincing portrait of a world-wide alien invasion in "To Serve Man," both appearing in upcoming volumes. Notice how it was all on the page long before any director came aboard.

A better education in the craft of screenwriting can't be found anywhere.

I remember reading a Rod Serling quote where he said he considered the night his television play "Patterns" first aired on *Kraft Television Theater*—January 12, 1955—as the official beginning of his extraordinary career.

Happens to be the night that I was born.

Means nothing, really. Less than nothing. But it means a great deal to me, I'll tell you.

I'll seize on any kinship I can to the unparalleled Mr. Serling.

After all, unbeknownst to him, the man taught me how to write.

Tributes & Rarities

TRIBUTES

Because I worked with Rod on the first hundred or so episodes of *The Twilight Zone*, I often find myself standing in the reflected limelight, being asked what he was like. It's a comment on him, I guess, that I have never run out of words nor of points of view with which to answer. He was a man of great variety and of many parts, not the least of which was his resiliency, an important attribute in one who intends to please many masters...a public, a network, a budget, and one's self.

He evidently pleased the public, although that was not so evident when we were first on the air as it is now.

He didn't always please the network, but he took their displeasure with a grin and a growl.

He pleased the budget, for the series was never based on splendor but on ideas.

But, like most creators with any gusto, he seldom pleased himself. There was always an 'i' he wished dotted or a 't' he wished that I had crossed.

And here I come to my point: Serling never carried those displeasures for a minute longer than it took to express them. He was resilient, bouncing untarnished from a disappointment or an argument to the next item.

I well remember, for example, that when it was decided to go to series, Serling had a producer in mind; CBS felt strongly about me, a stranger, in the role. Rod and I met and I was never given to feel that he had wished for anyone else. He did not burden himself with might-have-beens. And that is a great quality to find in a friend/business associate: you're never hoist on yesterday's petard.

The Twilight Zone was, season by season, in peril of not being renewed. It was not a hit, rating-wise; *succes d'estime*, yes, but not the sort of series anyone could have predicted would be running so many years later. Serling's skill as a writer has a lot to do with that…also his compassion for the human race as he saw it around him, from day to day. His optimism about the human condition led to stories that made one feel good about the race and its chances for emotional triumph.

Serling was *The Twilight Zone*…irreplaceably. I had been approached about reviving the series or its like; tempting as it is, I always tell the inquirer that there is one missing ingredient in his plan…Rod Serling. It's been tried and made evident that he had a touch, a bond of communication with a certain idea quality that you don't crank out just because the pattern seems clear. It's clear until you try to do it! In whatever of the five dimensions Rod mentioned he now exists, I am sure he's gratified that people are still enjoying what he did, decades after he did it.

—Buck Houghton
Producer of *The Twilight Zone*

※   ※   ※

The qualities I remember most about Rod were childlikeness, enthusiasm and the pure joy felt by someone who had found his voice; who had struck a vein of gold in the 'Vast Wasteland' and had run with it. I have vivid memories of Rod hanging around like a kid on the set, radiating excitement, having fun.

He was generous to performers: he listened, he took suggestions, he gave everybody a free hand. If his directors or actors had ideas to contribute, bits of business, ideas for staging, Rod leaped on them in helping to realize his vision.

His wide-ranging imagination allowed him to experiment, to take chances, and this was unique. It still is. He was a fearless and enthusiastic trailblazer.

—Fritz Weaver
Actor

※   ※   ※

I, like most of the rest of the world, thought Rod was a genius.

—Ron Masak
Actor

✖ ✖ ✖

I remember Rod as being an easy and thoughtful man. And even today, after all these years, the show itself remains memorable. *The Twilight Zone* never dated itself in its concepts, language or style. It did not rely on 'in' jokes, jargon or people. Its time is always the present. It stayed away from the trite in plot and circumstance and portrayal. The word 'original' found a meaning in *The Twilight Zone*; it was entirely its own work. Even trapped by time into being black and white, it is remarkably current in its imaginative stories and situations. And it sweeps us up each time into a never-never land filled with provocation and irony and mystery and suspense and surprises. Forty years from now it will still be new.

—Shelley Berman
Actor/Comedian

✖ ✖ ✖

Rod Serling was a good friend of mine. He was very kind to actors. He would re-write any scene an actor was uncomfortable with…a real rarity in our business. Working with a Rod Serling script you felt that Laurence Olivier was right when he said, "Acting is an honorable profession."

—Robert Stack
Actor

✖ ✖ ✖

Rod Serling was the most wonderful person to meet. He was truly a person who was caring and you felt welcome. You felt as if you were a part of a family. It was truly a warm feeling.

—Kim Hamilton
Actress

✖ ✖ ✖

Serling—my God—I was such a fan. I remember meeting him; this very quiet, assured, very confident man, and you really felt his presence of work.

—George Murdock
Actor

⁂

I always admired Rod Serling enormously. Would that there were such as he around and working today. There really is little I could add to the justified praise that the man and his work earned during his lifetime. I simply echo it.

—Maxine Stuart
Actress

⁂

I was, and continue to be, such a fan of Rod Serling. He set the standards very high and his work resonates with a dedication to excellence. I have always been proud to say that I was in a *Twilight Zone*. I believe that any dramatic piece, done with intelligence, creativity and a dedication to doing the finest work possible will continue to entertain audiences. *The Twilight Zone* always epitomized these qualities and with a passion.

—Denise Alexander
Actress

⁂

Rod was a hell of a guy…a man's man, straightforward, very nice. He was a fine artist and a great writer. I think he handled that medium better than anyone. I don't think anybody quite understood it as well as he did or accomplished as much as he did. Witness the success of *The Twilight Zone*. The words were the thing. The things that made *The Twilight Zone* were the words, and Rod.

—William Reynolds
Actor

CBS TELEVISION PREMIERE

TELEVISION CITY • HOLLYWOOD, CALIF.

May 26, 1959

"THE TWILIGHT ZONE," UNUSUAL NEW SERIES BY ROD SERLING,
WILL BOW ON THE CBS TELEVISION NETWORK OCT. 2

Kimberly-Clark Corp. and General Foods Corporation Will Sponsor

"The Twilight Zone," an unusual new series of dramas dealing with the stranger-than fiction, with fantasy and at times the occult, with scripts by Rod Serling, will make its debut on the CBS Television Network, Friday, Oct. 2 (10:00-10:30 PM, PDT), under the sponsorship of Kimberly-Clark Corp. for Kleenex products and General Foods Corporation, it was announced today by Hubbell Robinson, Jr., CBS Television Network Executive Vice President in Charge of Network Programs.

Most of the scripts will be originals by Mr. Serling, one of television's most creative and most honored writers. Others, adaptations of current short stories, will be prepared by selected writers. Each production will be supervised by Mr. Serling. Executive producer of "The Twilight Zone" for the CBS Television Network is William Self.

"The Twilight Zone" will have no "green-headed monsters" or rattling skeletons and no fairy-tale atmosphere. Each story will have a provocative ending as a trademark; one which is set up in the context of the plot to be shocking, unexpected, but at the same time, in retrospect, valid and honest.

In defining "The Twilight Zone," Mr. Serling says:

An early CBS Press Release, which still includes "sixth dimension" reference.

"There is a sixth dimension beyond that which is known to man. It is a dimension as vast as space, and as timeless as infinity. It is the middle ground between light and shadow - between man's grasp and his reach; between science and superstition; between the pit of his fears and the sunlight of his knowledge. This is the dimension of imagination. It is an area that might be called 'the twilight zone'."

* Agencies for "The Twilight Zone" sponsors: Foote, Cone & Belding for Kimberly-Clark Corp.; and Young & Rubicam, Inc. for General ████████nka Coffee).

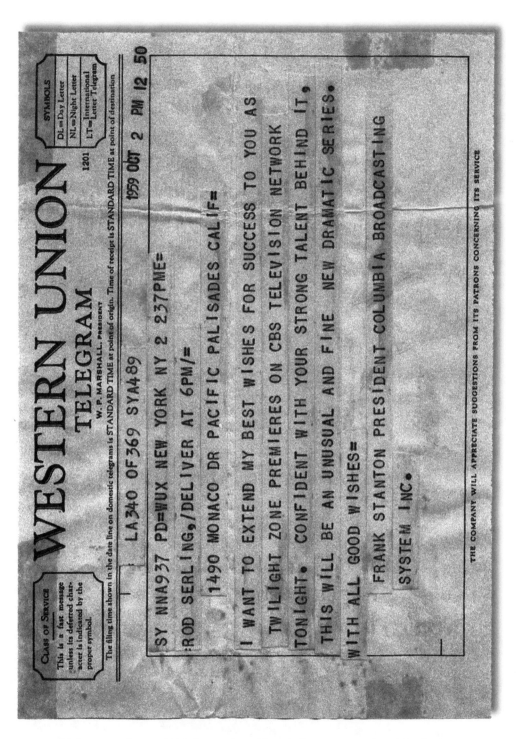

Telegram from CBS President Frank Stanton to Rod Serling.

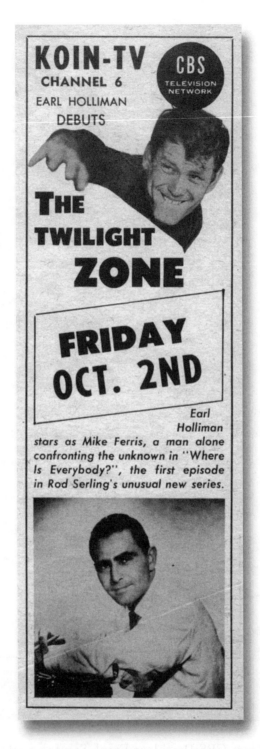

A regional ad announcing the premiere of *The Twilight Zone*.

DAILY VARIETY
D. 8,128
JUL 2 1959
JUL 2 1959

LIGHT and AIRY
by JACK HELLMAN

BILL SELF MUST BE THE ENVY OF HIS CRAFT. AS EXECU-
tive producer with Rod Serling of "Twilight Zone," he is not plagued
with a practice that has put many another of his opposite numbers
on a tranquilizer kick. Casting actors and directors for his anthology
series is the least of his worries. He's more concerned with filing away
all the calls that come to him from these selfsame actors and directors,
who offer their service. The cause of this reverse procedure is the
writer, who has won the respect of the industry with a record of
successes in dramatic finesse — Mr. Serling. "Next to his scripts, which
are automatically acceptable, the easiest part of my job is casting," says
Self. "Some of the best actors in town want to do the show but insist
that the script must be written by Serling. To them it represents a
perfect showcase for their talents. They're not concerned that the
writing may overshadow the acting."

To those confused by the title, "Twilight Zone," Self hastens to
correct the prevailing impression that it's a science-fiction series. He
best describes it as "Stories of the Imagination," with possibly one or
two in the realm of science-fiction. Serling will personally write nine
of the first 15 scripts, with six to be bought on the outside but with
Serling to adapt four of them. Self belies his youthful look. He got
into tv eight years ago as producer of the Schlitz dramatic series and
followed this with Frank Sinatra and assignments from CBS-TV. Buck
Houghton will produce the "Twilight" anthology and directors already
assigned are Jack Smight and Robert Stevens, both Emmy winners.
"Twilight" represents to Self the most exciting collection of plays he
has ever been associated with and with a Serling script to start with
he's completely satisfied that "we'll do them as well as they can be
done in television."

An article from Serling's files.

ACTORS TELEVISION MOTION PICTURE MINIMUM THREE-DAY CONTRACT
Continuous Employment—Three-day Basis—Three-day Salary—Three-day Minimum Employment

THIS AGREEMENT made __March 28__, 19 _61_ between CAYUGA PRODUCTIONS, INC.
a corporation, hereinafter called "Producer," and __JACK GRINNAGE__, hereinafter called "Player,"

WITNESSETH:

1. *Photoplay; Role and Guarantee.* Producer hereby engages Payer to render service as such in the role of __"HENRY"__,

in a photoplay produced primarily for exhibition over free television,the working title of which is now __"THE MIND & THE MATTER"__

Player accepts such engagement upon the terms herein specified. Producer guarantees that it will furnish Player not less than _____

_____days employment. (If this blank is not filled, the guarantee shall be three days.)

2. *Salary and Advances.* The Producer will pay to the Player, and the Player agrees to accept for three (3) days (and pro rata for each additional day beyond three (3) days) compensation as follows:

Three-day salary	($ _600.00_)
*Advance for television re-runs	($_____)
*Advance for theatrical use	($_____)
Three-day Total (including advances)	($ _600.00_)

3. Producer shall have the unlimited right throughout the world to re-run the film on television and exhibit the film theatrically.

4. If the motion picture is re-run on television in the United States or Canada and contains any of the results and proceeds of the Player's services, the Player will be paid the amounts entered in the blanks in this paragraph plus an amount equal to one-third (⅓rd) thereof for each day of employment in excess of three (3) days and if the blanks are not filled the Player will be paid the minimum additional compensation prescribed therefor by the 1960 Screen Actors Guild Television Agreement below mentioned, and the amount, if any, designated in Paragraph 2 as an advance for re-runs shall be applied against the additional compensation for re-runs payable under this Paragraph 4.

2nd run	3rd run	4th run	5th run	6th and all succeeding runs

5. If the motion picture is exhibited theatrically anywhere in the world and contains any of the results and proceeds of the Player's services, the Player will be paid $_____ plus an amount equal to one-third thereof for each day of employment in excess of three (3) days (but in any event the total shall not be less than the minimum required by the 1960 Screen Actors Guild Television Agreement). If this blank is not filled in, the Player will be paid the minimum additional compensation to which he would be entitled under such Television Agreement, and the amount, if any, designated in Paragraph 2 as an advance for theatrical use shall be applied against the additional compensation for the theatrical use payable under this Paragraph 5.

6. *Term.* The term of employment hereunder shall begin on __March 28, 1961__ on or about **_____ and shall continue thereafter until the completion of the photography and recordation of said role.

7. *Basic Contract.* Reference is made to the 1960 Screen Actors Guild Television Agreement and to the applicable provisions set forth in such Agreement. Player's employment shall include performance in non commercial openings, closings, bridges, etc., and no added compensation shall be payable to Player so long as such are used in the role(s) and episode(s) covered hereunder and in which Player appears; for other use, Player shall be paid the added minimum compensation, if any, required under the provisions of the Screen Actors Guild agreements with Producer. Player's employment shall be upon the terms, conditions and exceptions of said schedule applicable to the rate of salary and guarantee specified in Paragraphs 1 and 2 hereof.***

8. *Player's Address.* All notices which the Producer is required or may desire to give to the Player may be given either by mailing the same addressed to the Player at __6125 Glen Oaks Ave. L.A. 27__, California, or such notice may be given to the Player personally, either orally or in writing.

9. *Player's Telephone.* The Player must keep the Producer's casting office or the assistant director of said photoplay advised as to where the Player may be reached by telephone without unreasonable delay.

The current telephone number of the Player is __HO. 3-5007__

10. *Motion Picture Relief Fund.* The Player (does) (does not) hereby authorize the Producer to deduct from the compensation and advance hereinabove specified an amount equal to 1% of each installment of compensation and advances due the Player hereunder and payable during the employment, and to pay the amount so deducted to the Motion Picture Relief Fund of America, Inc.

11. *Furnishing of Wardrobe.* The Player agrees to furnish all modern wardrobe and wearing apparel reasonably necessary for the portrayal of said role; it being agreed, however, that should so-called "character" or "period" costumes be required, the Producer shall supply the same.

12. *Next Starting Date.* The starting date of Player's next engagement is _____

IN WITNESS WHEREOF, the parties have executed this agreement on the day and year first above written.

CAYUGA PRODUCTIONS, INC.

(signature)   By _(signature)_
Player   Producer

(The Player may not waive any provision of the foregoing contract without the written consent of Screen Actors Guild, Inc.)
*No advance for re-runs or theatrical use may be made unless the weekly salary prescribed above is at least $1,500.
**The "on or about clause" may only be used when the contract is delivered to the Player at least seven (7) days before the starting date.
***Producer shall own all rights in and to the results and proceeds of Player's services hereunder which the 1960 Television Agreement or Theatrical Agreement permits Producer to acquire; respecting all others rights thereto without limitation, Player grants same to Producer subject to Producer's obtaining requisite consent or waiver from Screen Actors Guild.

Enterprise Printers & Stationers • HOllywood 5-2540   27

Actor Jack Grinnage's contract to appear in "The Mind and The Matter."

William Bendix and Carolyn Kearney in *Westinghouse Desilu Playhouse's* production of "The Time Element," *Twilight Zone's* unofficial pilot.

Earl Holliman stars as Mike Ferris in the official *Twilight Zone* pilot, "Where Is Everybody."

Everybody's here: writer Rod Serling, actor Earl Holliman and producer William Self discuss the script during soundstage rehearsals.

In this series of proofs, Earl Holliman takes a "break" from filming to pose for potential publicity photos.

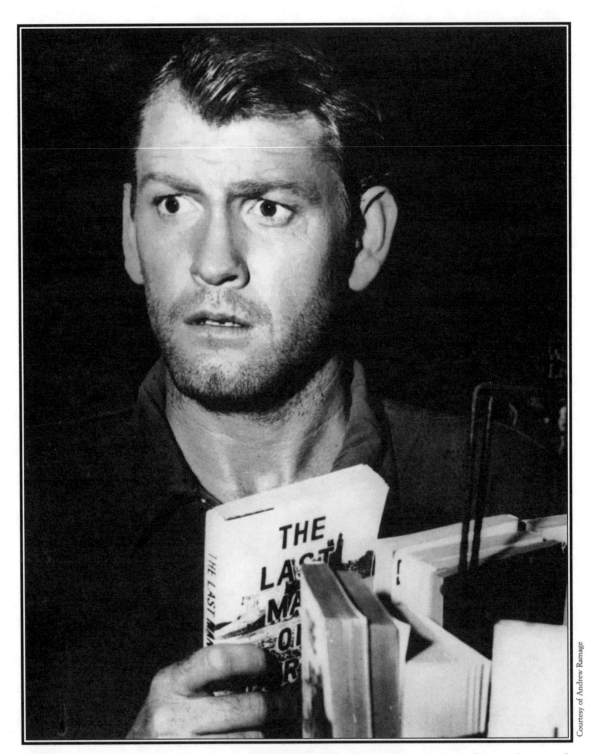

As sole resident of an eerily abandoned town, Mike Ferris contemplates his nightmarish existence.

EYE OF THE BEHOLDER

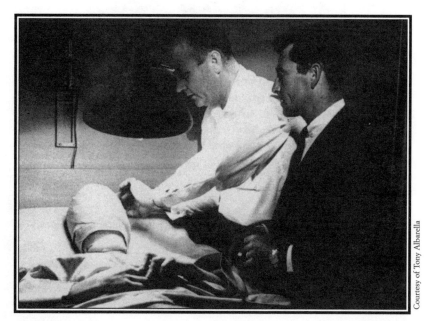

Courtesy of Tony Albarella

Rod Serling and director Douglas Heyes on the set.

Courtesy of Andrew Ramage

The Twilight Zone film crew lines up a scene.

William D. Gordon and Joanna Heyes
in full makeup.

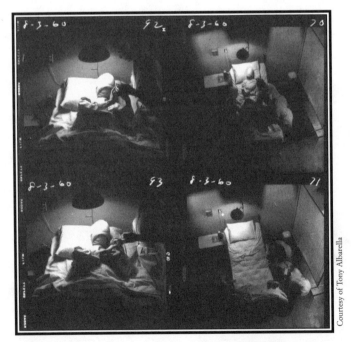

Maxine Stuart as a bandaged Janet Tyler.

Conceptual drawing by director Douglas Heyes.

Courtesy of Dwight Deskins

Donna Douglas as Janet Tyler, revealed.

THIRD FROM THE SUN

Courtesy of The Rod Serling Memorial Foundation

"Cat's-eye view" of Fritz Weaver, Edward Andrews, and Joe Maross in "Third From The Sun"

THE PURPLE TESTAMENT

Fitzgerald and Riker brief the platoon.

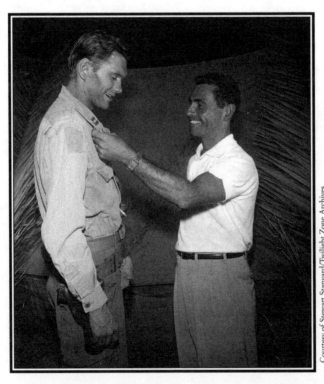

Rod Serling visits with Dick York on the set.

Captain Riker (Dick York) tries to help Lieutenant Fitzgerald (William Reynolds) cope with an unsolicited ability to predict the death of fellow soldier.

A Soundstage at MGM is transformed into a Phillipine jungle.

THE BIG, TALL WISH

Ivan Dixon, Steven Perry, and Kim Hamilton
pose on the set.

Bolie Jackson (Ivan Dixon) and Frances
Temple (Kim Hamilton) struggle with the
existence of childhood magic.

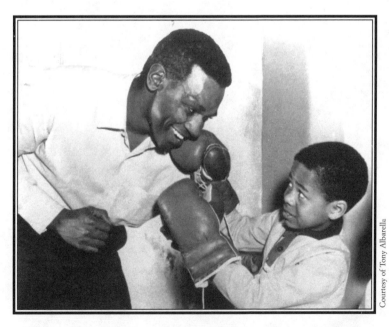

Henry Temple (Steven Perry) fights to keep the faith.

A MOST UNUSUAL CAMERA

Rod Serling introduces a most unusual episode.

Paula (Jean Carson), Chester (Fred Clark) and Woodward (Adam Williams) are in good spirits as an unscrupulous waiter (Marcel Hillaire) examines their prized posession.

Paula, Chester and Woodward enjoy a day at the races.

Paula relishes sole ownership of the camera, moments before taking the plunge.

THE MIND AND THE MATTER

Archibald Beechcroft (Shelley Berman) enjoys the ultimate self-help book.

Beechcroft endures another run-in with Henry (Jack Grinnage).

Shelley Berman suffers the company of masked men.

A world full of Beechcrofts proves to be a real drag.

THE DUMMY

Courtesy of Tony Albarella

Jerry Etherson (Cliff Robertson) lashes out at his alter ego, Willy.

Cliff Robertson spends quality time with his significant other...

...and introduces his pal, Willy, to friends on the set.

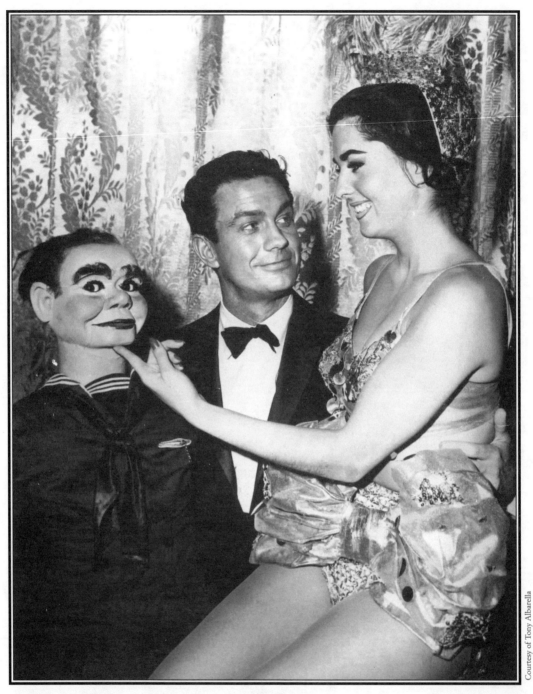

Jerry uses Willy to impress a chorus girl (Bethelynn Grey) when posing for photos...

...But onscreen, the ladies (Bethelynn Grey, Sandra Warner) prefer Goofy Goggles.

Desilu Playhouse

THE TIME ELEMENT

Airdate: 11-24-1958

Manuscript Date: 8-26-1958

First Draft

Dated 8-21-1958 with
revisions dated 8-26-1958

Revised 1st Draft
August 21, 1958

Desilu Playhouse

"THE TIME ELEMENT"

by

ROD SERLING

SETS

INTERIORS

NEW YORK BAR   (Exterior Door)

GILLESPIE'S OFFICE & ANTEROOM

HAWAIIAN HOTEL ROOM & CORRIDOR

HAWAIIAN BAR

BOQ OFFICERS' QUARTERS

ARMY DOCTOR'S OFFICE

ORDERLY ROOM

NAVAL STATION

STOCK

SCOFIELD BARRACKS

PROCESS

INT. FRENCH DOORS

CAST

PETER JENSON

DR. GILLESPIE

MAID

ENSIGN JANOSKI

MRS. JANOSKI

BARTENDER

COL. ABERNATHY

CAPT. FRANKLIN

LT. ORDWAY

ARMY DOCTOR

WAITER

LUSH

FELCH

ORDERLY BAILEY

ARMY C. Q.

ENSIGN #1

ENSIGN #2

N. Y. BARTENDER

HOTEL CLERK (voice o.s.)

MAN

NARRATOR

"THE TIME ELEMENT"

1   FADE IN: 1

INT. DR. GILLESPIE'S OFFICE - PAN SHOT ACROSS
THE ROOM

Moving from left to right taking in walls,
furniture, couch, and winding up on a shot
of venetian blinds over the window behind
the desk as at this moment a hand reaches
out and partially closes them, throwing the
room into a semi-darkness. Now the CAMERA
PULLS BACK for

2   SHOT - DR. GILLESPIE   2

walking back to his desk.

3   SHOT - PETER JENSON   3

sitting across from him. Throughout this,
we hear a voice in narration.

                        NARRATOR'S VOICE
        Once upon a time there was a
        psychiatrist named Arnold Gillespie
        and a patient whose name was Peter
        Jenson. Mr. Jenson walked into the
        office nine minutes ago. It is
        eleven o'clock, Saturday morning,
        October 5, 1958. It is perhaps
        chronologically trite to be so
        specific about the hour and the
        date...but involved in this story
        is...a time element.

4   TWO SHOT - DR. GILLESPIE AND JENSON   4

Gillespie smiles. He's got an open, pleasant face,
steel gray hair. He's a man in his early fifties.

                        GILLESPIE
        Now, Mr. Jenson, I think I have
        all the chronology down here.
        You're forty one years old. Un-
        married. No physical ailments of
        any serious nature. No previous
        visits to a psychiatrist.

                                        (CONTINUED)

CONTINUED:

Jenson is obviously very ill at ease, his face
tired, bordering on haggardness.

                    JENSON
          No previous arrests either. And
          the only time I ever saw a psychi-
          atrist before was in a cartoon.

                    GILLESPIE
               (chuckles)

          At best you'll find us helpful
          and at worst harmless.

He takes out a pack of cigarettes and offers one
to Jenson who shakes his head.

                    GILLESPIE
          Now. Your occupation?

                    JENSON
          Various. Part-time unsuccessful
          bookie. Card dealer. I tended
          bar once. Just down the street
          from here. Couple of doors. Andy's
          Place. I was also a butcher. High-
          ly successful. My thumbs weighed
          twelve pounds. Now how do I stack
          up? Normal, abnormal, subnormal or
          just a typical young American Lad.

                    GILLESPIE
               (grins again)
          Family?

                    JENSON
          Father and Mother. Both married.
          Scranton, Pennsylvania. He was
          a coal miner.

                    GILLESPIE
          Coal?

                    JENSON
          You know. Little black things
          people used to put in furnaces.

                    GILLESPIE
               (with a kind of
               professional smile)
          Sounds like interesting work.

                              (CONTINUED)

4   CONTINUED: - 2

                    JENSON
                (cocks an eye at him)
          It does? Then maybe you ought to
          go to a psychiatrist?
                (he wets his lips,
                becoming more nervous)
          I think I will take one of those
          cigarettes.

Gillespie gives him one, then lights it for him,
putting the lighter back down on the desk.

                    JENSON
          Do you want me to pull up a
          couch now.

                    GILLESPIE
          Not necessarily if your comfortable
          there. Let's begin right here.
          Start by telling me what your
          problem is.

There's a silence for a moment. Then Jenson
leans back.

                    JENSON
          All right.
                (he eyes the psychiatrist
                evenly and rather intently)
          Nothing shakes you up, does it?

                    GILLESPIE
          How do you mean?

                    JENSON
          Everything's all calm and cool and
          you're the boss. When I walked in
          here I could see you making an in-
          ventory. Check the cut of the
          clothes. Check the language. And
          up inside your head there - that's
          where you mark down all the results.
          And then later on you put it all in
          pigeon holes. This fits here and
          this fits there. You got me pegged,
          don't you?

                    GILLESPIE
          Not entirely.

                    JENSON
          You figure this is a kind of minor
          league horse player. Maybe a little
          hung over - maybe a little bugged -
                    (MORE)
                                    (CONTINUED)

> JENSON (cont'd)
> But either way - maybe about
> forty degrees tilt.

> GILLESPIE
>
> Go on.

> JENSON
> (looks at his cigarette)
> My cigarette went out.

He pats around for his lighter. Gillespie picks
up the lighter off the desk and lights his cigarette
again for him. Now Jenson leans back in the chair.

> JENSON
> All right. Pigeon hole this one.
> If said minor league horse play
> tells you a half-witted story -
> can you tell me in a very simple
> statement whether or not I'm off
> my rocker? Without trotting in
> Sigmund Freud and a lot of medical
> school language - can you tell me
> in English what's wrong with me?

> GILLESPIE
>
> I can try.

> JENSON
> I keep having a dream.

> GILLESPIE
>
> Go on.

He quietly takes a pencil from the drawer and begins
to jot down something. Jenson notices this and
points to the paper.

> JENSON
> You take all this down?

> GILLESPIE
> You keep on talking. I'll just
> make some notes on those things
> that seem pertinent.

> JENSON
> I don't know whether any of this
> will sound pertinent. But I will
> tell you that it'll probably sound
> nuts. It sounds nuts to me, but
> there it is.

(CONTINUED)

                        GILLESPIE
          Go on.

                        JENSON
          I've had this dream. I've had it
          ...Maybe, I don't know, maybe five
          or six times now.

There's another pause.

                        GILLESPIE
          What sort of dream?

Jenson leans back and shuts his eyes for a moment.

                        JENSON
          A real one. Have you ever had
          any wacky dreams that seem real?

                        GILLESPIE
          I guess we all have.

                        JENSON
          But have they happened over and
          over again?

                        GILLESPIE
          Recurred? The same dream?

                        JENSON
          The same dream. Identical. It
          doesn't change.

                        GILLESPIE
          Go on. Tell me about it.

                        JENSON
          It always begins the same way.
          I'm asleep. I'm sound asleep.

As he talks, the CAMERA begins a slow PAN AWAY from
him, over to the window, toward the closed blinds.
We HEAR Jenson's voice continuing o.c.

                    JENSON'S VOICE
          I'm lying in a bed and I wake up,
          sudden like. I open my eyes....
          I look around.

                               LAP DISSOLVE FROM
                               THE BLINDS TO:

5   FRENCH DOORS - HOTEL ROOM   5

6-8   OMITTED   6-8

                                  (CONTINUED)

9   INT. HOTEL ROOM

This is a medium sized, rather attractive hotel room.
Through the French doors we can see a waving palm
tree. Jenson is in bed, just opening his eyes. He
rubs them, takes a deep yawn and stretches, still
lying on his back, then his eyes slowly narrow in
thought. He looks up toward the ceiling, then
around the room. He gets up, sits on the bed.
Slowly the strangeness of the room becomes apparent
to him. He gets up off the bed, standing there in
pajamas, not looking at anything in particular -
but obviously trying to recollect how he got where
he is and where   (MORE)

                              (CONTINUED)

that is. He looks at a telephone on a night stand
near the bed, goes over and picks up the receiver.

                    VOICE (O.C.)
          Yes, sir?

                    JENSON
               (a little hesitantly)
          Tell me...I got in pretty late
          last night, didn't I?

                    VOICE
          I beg your pardon, sir?

                    JENSON
               (a little
                impatiently)
          I asked you if I got in late
          last night?

                    VOICE
           s this 206?

                    JENSON
          Yeah, yeah, this is 206.

As he says this he looks at a key and reads a number
off it. It's been lying near the phone.

                    VOICE
          I really don't know, Mr. Jenson.
          I wasn't on duty last night.

                    JENSON
          How about a morning paper?

                    VOICE
          It's probably at your door, sir.

                    JENSON
          Thanks.

                    VOICE
          That's perfectly all --

                    JENSON
               (interrupting)
          What do you call this place,
          anyway?

                    VOICE
          I beg your pardon, sir?

                                        (CONTINUED)

9   CONTINUED: - 2   9

                    JENSON
              (very impatient now)
         I asked you the name of the
         hotel. Tell me, Jack, do you
         work here or are you just
         inspecting the kitchen? I
         asked you what the
         name of the hotel was.

                    VOICE
         This is the Royal Hawaiian,
         sir.
              (a light laugh)
         Are you in the right hotel, Mr.
         Jenson?

10   CLOSE SHOT - HOTEL STATIONERY   10

         on a desk nearby. On the top of it in full view is
         the letterhead of the hotel: "Hotel Royal Hawaiian".

11   PAN SHOT - PAST THE DESK   11

         to the open French doors and palm trees.

12   MED. CLOSE SHOT - JENSON   12

         on telephone.

                    JENSON
         Yeah, yeah. I'm in the right
         hotel.

         He puts down the receiver, studying it thoughtfully.
         His face shows a constant question mark. He keeps
         scratching his head and running his hand over his
         face and jaw. Suddenly he looks toward the far wall
         of the room.

13   TIGHT CLOSE SHOT - PAD CALENDAR ON THE WALL   13

         The page on the top reads: "December 6".

                    JENSON
              (aloud)
         December 6th? What kind of
         crazy --

                                              (CONTINUED)

He is interrupted by a knock on the door.

                         JENSON
              Yeah?

                         MAID'S VOICE
                    (O.C.)
              Maid, sir. Do you want me to
              clean up now?

                         JENSON
              No.
                    (then suddenly)
              Wait a minute -- yes.

He looks around the room for his clothes and spies
a bathrobe hanging on a chair. He puts it on hurriedly, walks over to the door and opens it. The
maid, a middle-aged, pleasant-looking woman enters.

                         MAID
              Good morning, sir. Did you
              sleep well?

                         JENSON
              Mother, that's a moot question!
                    (then he points a
                    waggling finger
                    toward the wall
                    and the calendar)
              Do you want to explain the gag
              now?

                         MAID
                    (looking at him
                    blankly)
              Excuse me, sir?

                         JENSON
              I asked you if you wanted to
              explain the gag. You tell
              the guy who put you up to this
              that he's on the threshhold of
              a deep wound. You tell him
              that I'm going to take out his
              teeth one by one. This is
              October, isn't it?

The maid looks at him puzzled, completely bewildered
by him.

                         MAID
              October, sir? What's October?

                                          (CONTINUED)

                    JENSON
                (looking at her
                 for a long moment)
        Thirty days has October, April,
        June, and November. Remember?
        Am I getting through to you,
        Mama? This month. This is
        October, isn't it?

                    MAID
                (smiles at him)
        October, sir? I don't believe
        so, sir.

                    JENSON
        What do you mean, you don't
        believe so? Is it October or
        isn't it?

                    MAID
        It's December, sir. December
        sixth.

                    JENSON
        It's what?

                    MAID
        It's December sixth.

                    JENSON
        That's what I thought you said.

He turns away, rubbing his eyes, and then his fore-
head, then he looks toward the French doors, studying them thoughtfully and reflectively. Now the
curiosity is marred by a sense of disquiet and apprehension.

                    JENSON
                (repeating)
        December sixth.

                    MAID
        Are you all right, sir?

                    JENSON
        Yeah, yeah. I'm all right.
                (then he turns
                 toward her)
                    (MORE)

(CONTINUED)

                         JENSON (CONT.)
              Except that I have obviously
              just come down the homestretch
              of the biggest toot in the
              history of man! You tell me
              this is December sixth. Well,
              last night I was in New York
              City. It was October and it
              was New York City.

The maid starts to back away from him, a little
frightened now.

                         MAID
              You're probably over-tired, sir.
              Maybe you aren't feeling so well.
              Why don't I come back later --

Jenson takes a step forward and she's backed against
the door.

                         JENSON
              I'll tell you, honey, over-
              tired I'm not. Not feeling so
              good -- this is the champion,
              blue ribbon understatement of
              the year. A toot that takes two
              months and winds up in -- what's
              the name of the place?

                         MAID
              What the name of what place,
              sir?

                         JENSON
              This place!

                         MAID
                  (gulps)
              Royal Hawaiian Hotel.

                         JENSON
              That's what I mean. The Royal
              Hawaiian Hotel. Well, since
              when is there a Royal Hawaiian
              Hotel in New York City?

                         MAID
              It isn't in New York City, sir.
              It's in Honolulu.

                                        (CONTINUED)

                              JENSON
                    That figures. The Royal
                    Hawaiian Hotel is in Honolulu.

Then he looks around a little surreptitiously and
waggles a finger toward the woman. Her eyes go
wide. He waggles a finger again and motions with
his head. She takes a few steps toward him.

                              JENSON
                         (almost sotto)
                    Which leads me to the next
                    question. What am I doing in
                    Hawaii?

                              MAID
                    I'm sure I don't know, sir.

                              JENSON
                    That's what I thought you said.
                    There's just one other question.

                              MAID
                    Really, sir --

                              JENSON
                    Just one more. Commere.

The maid, almost numb with fear, takes another step
toward him.

                              JENSON
                         (continuing)
                    I'll never ask you again, I
                    promise.

                              MAID
                         (croaks)
                    What, sir?

                              JENSON
                    This hotel got a bar?

The maid nods relievedly.

                              MAID
                    Yes, sir. It's got a lovely
                    bar.

                              JENSON
                    Where is the lovely bar?

                                        (CONTINUED)

                    MAID
          Downstairs, sir. Off the lobby.

Jenson nods, pinches the woman's cheeks.

                    JENSON
          If I were ever to have another
          mother, I'd want it to be you!
          Come back later, honey, and
          we'll dance.

                    MAID
          Yes, sir. Absolutely, sir.

She backs out of the room and once outside makes a
mad sprint down the hall. Jenson slams the door behind her, walks over to the calendar on the wall,
taps the "December 6" with his finger, and keeps tapping it.

                                        DISSOLVE TO:

14   INT. BAR - DAY   14

There is the early afternoon weekend bar crowd in
evidence, a sprinkling of uniforms and Palm Beach
suits. There is a great deal of laughter, juke box
music in the b.g., and a general festive air. Facing
the door, on the opposite side of the room, is about
a thirty foot bar with every stool occupied. Jenson
enters, looks around. A waiter comes over to him,
sees him studying the bar.

                    WAITER
          Sorry, sir. The bar's crowded.
          There's a booth over here if
          you want.

                    JENSON
          I want to sit at the bar.

                    WAITER
                (a little more
                 sternly)
          There are no seats left at the
          bar, sir.

                    JENSON
          Look, if the President of the
          United States came in here and
          wanted a seat at the bar, you'd
          have one for him, wouldn't ya?

                                        (CONTINUED)

                        WAITER
                      (smiling)
              Well, of course, sir.

                        JENSON
                      (slaps him on
                       the back)
              Well, all right. I can give
              you my guarantee he's not
              coming, so I'll take his stool.

Just as he says this a man slides off a stool after
whispering a question to the bartender. The bartender points toward the far end of the room. The
man a little tipsily walks in that direction. Jenson immediately takes his seat and pushes his half-
filled drink out of the way. He sits between a
very attractive young Ensign and his girl on his
left and a far-gone lush on his right. The Ensign
and the girl intermittently nuzzle and coo and kiss.
Jenson studies them for a moment, looks at the bartender, motions with his head toward the couple, makes
a face.

                        BARTENDER
              That stool's occupied.

                        JENSON
              You know it. I want a Bloody
              Mary.
                      (he makes a big
                       size with his
                       fingers, indicating
                       a large drink)
              I want the tomato juice anemic
              but lots of vodka. Maybe five
              fingers, huh?

                        BARTENDER
              You're the boss.

He turns and starts to mix it. Jenson rubs his face
with his hands, takes another look at the Ensign who
is now kissing the girl all over her arm. He turns
away abruptly. The bartender puts the drink down in
front of him. Jenson immediately takes a large swig,
then breathes deeply and relievedly.

                        JENSON
              Better just keep 'em coming.
              I'm just on the last lap of the
              biggest binge in the world.

                                          (CONTINUED)

                         BARTENDER
          Rough night?

                         JENSON
          Thirty rough nights. Would
          you believe it? I fell asleep
          in New York City a month ago.
          I woke up here this morning.

The lush alongside looks at him sympathetically.

                         LUSH
          Dear boy, I know the feeling.
          Once I fell asleep at the Dublin
          Airport and I woke up on a
          British troop train going into
          Palestine. That's my record.
          Forty-three days in the arms of
          Morpheus.

                         JENSON
          Well bless you, bless you.

He looks around the room a little thoughtfully, happens to meet the Ensign's eyes. The Ensign kind of
grins at him sheepishly.

                         ENSIGN
                    (boyishly)
          My wife!

Jenson moves the Ensign's arm away from the bar.

                         JENSON
          My drink.

                         ENSIGN
                    (again very boyishly)
          I'm sorry.

                         JENSON
          Think nothing of it. It just
          disappeared for a minute, that's
          all. Ya been married long?

                         GIRL
          One day, six hours and twelve
          minutes.

                         JENSON
                    (clucks)
          No kidding? I'd **have** never
          guessed it.
                         (MORE)

(CONTINUED)

                         JENSON (CONT.)
                    (he winks at the
                    bartender and in
                    the process sees
                    a picture of
                    Fiorello LaGuardia,
                    points toward it)
          You from New York?

                         BARTENDER
          Born, bred and raised.

                         JENSON
                    (nods; points
                     to the picture)
          Good man.

                         BARTENDER
                    (moving away)
          Sure is.

Jenson takes a swig from his drink then looks a little
quizzically toward the bartender.

                         JENSON
          Was.

                         BARTENDER
          How's that?

                         JENSON
          Was a good man.

                         BARTENDER
          That's what I said.

                         JENSON
          You said he is a good man.

                         BARTENDER
          Well, isn't he?

                         JENSON
          He was. He's not here today.

                         BARTENDER
          Of course he isn't!

Jenson looks satisfied.

                         BARTENDER
          He's in New York where he should
          be.

                                        (CONTINUED)

Jenson slams down his drink.

> JENSON
> Did anybody ever tell you you
> had a nutsy sense of humor?

The bartender lays aside his various equipment,
leans forward on the bar.

> BARTENDER
> What are you, the argumentative
> type? You want to argue, buddy,
> is that it?

> JENSON
> I don't want to argue. I just
> want to tell you if you're
> trying to rib me I'm going to
> come back there for about seven
> minutes and you're going to be
> able to fix up all your Bloody
> Marys with your own blood.

> ENSIGN
> (interceding)
> Let me buy you a drink.

> JENSON
> No. Let me buy you one.
> (to the bartender)
> A round for the newlyweds.

> BARTENDER
> They're drinking champagne.

> JENSON
> What do I look like, a deadbeat?
> Give them champagne.

He turns on his stool to face the young couple, who
smile at him, and the smiles are so infectious and
so warm that Jenson is forced to grin back at them.
The bartender delivers the drinks.

> JENSON
> To the bride and groom.

They all drink.

> LUSH
> Long may she wave!

(CONTINUED)

They all chuckle at this.

                    JENSON
          You off a ship?

                    ENSIGN
          You bet your life. Best baby
          afloat.

                    THE GIRL
                 (bubbling)
          The Arizona.

                    JENSON
                 (looks at her wryly)
          The what?

                    ENSIGN
                 (his smile fading
                  ever so slightly)
          The Arizona.

                    JENSON
          The Arizona!
                 (he makes a wry
                  face toward the
                  bartender)
          When did they dredge her outta
          the mud?

The Ensign looks mad and his young wife puts a re-
straining warning hand on his arm. The Ensigh shakes
it off.

                    ENSIGN
          You're talking about my
          battle wagone and she's never
          been close to the mud.

                    JENSON
          She hasn't, huh?
                 (he again makes a
                  wise look toward
                  the bartender)
          Buddy boy, you got a lovely
          wife and a lousy memory. You
          trying to tell me she wasn't
          sunk?

                    ENSIGN
          I'm not trying to tell you, I'm
          telling you. The Arizona's never
          been sunk in her life.

                                   (CONTINUED)

14   CONTINUED: - 6   14

>   This time Jenson looks at the bartender with a big
>   shrug.

                    JENSON
          She's never been sunk in her
          life.
                    (he looks at the
                    Ensign for a
                    long moment)
          Never been sunk, huh?

                    ENSIGN
          You know it!

                    JENSON
                    (prods him in
                    the chest with
                    a finger)
          You know it. I don't know it.
          I say she got sunk on December
          7, 1941, and that's where she
          sits today, in the mud at Pearl
          Harbor. Now what do you think
          of that?

>   The bar is suddenly very quiet as Jenson's voice is
>   carried over and registered. The Ensign is looking
>   at him strangely.

                    ENSIGN
                    (in a strained voice)
          What'd you say?

15   PAN SHOT - DOWN THE BAR   15

>   past the suddenly sober faces, winding up on the
>   lush who is blinking a couple of times.

                    JENSON
          I said --

>   He stops dead, staring across at the far end of the
>   bar where a newspaper is propped up between the bar
>   top and the wall. The headline is big, black, and
>   very much in evidence. It reads: "JAP ENVOYS TO
>   FDR". Jenson gets off his seat, walks slowly past
>   the silent people over to where the paper is. He
>   picks it up and studies it for a moment. He looks
>   up over the top of the paper toward all of them, who
>   now collectively stare at him. Then he looks back to-
>   ward the paper and his eyes go wide.

16   EXTREMELY TIGHT CLOSE SHOT - MASTHEAD OF THE PAPER   16

It reads: "THE HONOLULU ADVERTISER", and under that in bold, black, sharp relief, the date line, "Saturday, December 6, 1941."

17-20   SERIES OF DIFFERENT ANGLE CLOSE-UPS - THE DATE LINE 17-20

each bigger and blacker than the last one, winding up with tight close shot, the newspaper being slammed down on the bar.

21   MED. SHOT   21

Jenson retraces his steps back to the stool. The other drunk is sitting there now. Jenson, with a single motion, grabs him and sends him flying off the stool. He then sits down in his place, takes a glass and drains it. Then he puts the glass down, turns to the Ensign.

                    JENSON
         It isn't 1941. It's 1958.
         You hear me? It's 1958.

Over his shoulder we see the lush suddenly throw his glass over his shoulder, get up and start to walk out of the bar. The CAMERA MOVES AROUND FOR:

22   MED. CLOSE SHOT - JENSON   22

Now he is staring straight ahead and he speaks to no one in particular.

                    JENSON
         How could it be 1941? How could
         it be? It's 1958!

23   INT. DR. GILLESPIE'S OFFICE - CLOSE-UP JENSON   23

                    JENSON
         How could it be 1941? It's
         1958.

CAMERA PULLS BACK for:

24   TWO SHOT - GILLESPIE AND JENSON   24

Gillespie is studying him pensively.

                                   (CONTINUED)

                         Dr. GILLESPIE
                    (nodding)
              Uh huh, uh huh. And the dream
              ends there?

                         JENSON
              No, it goes on.

                         DR. GILLESPIE
              I see. But to that point each
              dream is identical, you say?

                         JENSON
              Identical. I even remember
              going to the door of the bar
              and looking out in the street.
              I look at all the cars. 39's
              40's, 41's. No fins or any-
              thing.

                         DR. GILLESPIE
              Go on.

                         JENSON
              All right. Now get this. This
              is where you separate the men
              from the wacky.
                    (a long pause)
              I don't think this is a dream.

              Gillespie makes a note of something on the pad.
              Jenson sees him doing this and then rises.

                         JENSON
                    (continuing)
              You can make all the chicken
              tracks you want to. This is the
              goods here.

                         GILLESPIE
              I believe you.

                         JENSON
                    (sticks a cigarette
                    in his mouth)
              You do? All right, then call up
              the sanitarium and tell them
              we'll take a double room.

                         DR. GILLESPIE
              I mean I understand why you think
              it's real.
                         (MORE)

                                        (CONTINUED)

                         DR. GILLESPIE (CONT.)
                    Some dreams are extremely
                    realistic. As often as not
                    they're impossible to distinguish
                    from reality -- while you're
                    asleep.

Jenson blows the smoke out from his mouth, butts the
cigarette out in an ashtray, and sits on the desk.

                         JENSON
                    You don't get what I'm trying
                    to tell you, do you?
                         (now he turns to-
                         ward the doctor)
                    It isn't just that it's real
                    while I'm asleep, while I'm
                    telling you this... while I'm
                    sitting here telling you this
                    ...it's still real. Everything
                    that happens in those dreams --
                    that's real.

                         DR. GILLESPIE
                    Go on, Mr. Jenson.

                         JENSON
                    That spills the beans, doesn't
                    it?

                         DR. GILLESPIE
                    This is your problem, then?

                         JENSON
                    That's some problem, isn't it?
                    A guy who dreams things and
                    thinks they're real?

                         DR. GILLESPIE
                    I told you that some dreams are
                    very real.

                         JENSON
                    I've had dreams just like every-
                    gody else, but a couple of weeks
                    ago when these things started --
                    I knew they weren't dreams.
                    Understand? They're not dreams.

                         DR. GILLESPIE
                    If they're not dreams, Mr. Jenson
                    -- what do you suppose they are?

                                                  (CONTINUED)

                        JENSON
                   (leans back in the
                    chair, studying
                    the doctor for a
                    moment)
            What do you think they are?

                      DR. GILLESPIE
            Let's examine the alternatives.
            I can think of only one.

                        JENSON
            That's the one I'm thinking of.
            I wake up in a hotel room in
            Honolulu in 1941, but I mean I
            really wake up and it's really
            1941.

                      DR. GILLESPIE
            Going back in time.

Jenson nods, then after a long silence:

                        JENSON
            That's what I'm doing, Doc.
            I'm going back in time.

                      DR. GILLESPIE
                    (writes a little
                    something in the
                    pad)
            That's interesting.
                    (then he puts the
                    pencil down;
                    looks at him;
                    leans back in the
                    chair)
            Go on, Mr. Jenson, what happens
            then...when you're back in time?

The CAMERA starts a SLOW PAN back across the desk
over to Jenson who starts to lean forward as if to
speak.

                    WE CUT ABRUPTLY TO BLACK.

                  END ACT ONE

ACT II

FADE IN:

24A   INT. ROYAL HAWAIIAN HOTEL ROOM - DAY   24A

Jenson is sitting on the bed. There's a tall, cool
drink alongside on the bed stand, an open phone book
beside him, an ashtray full of cigarette butts. The
clock on the wall reads "2 o'clock". Jenson is on
the telephone.

JENSON
Yeah, yeah. Well, are you a
bookie or aren't you? All
right, then. This is the bet.
I take Joe Louis over Buddy
Baer. What kind of odds will
you give me if I pick Louis in
one round?
    (a pause)
What are you talking about,
they're not scheduled? They
will be. That's right.
They're going to fight on
January 9th.
    (impatiently)
Yeah. Yeah. Buddy Baer!
That's right. I pick Louis in
one round. Now what's the
quote? Thirty to one? Come
on, boy, come on, boy! That's
more like it.
    (he makes a little
    notation with a
    pencil)
How's that? What do you mean,
how do I know? I know it, that's
all. Did you get my name?
J E N S O N. That's right.
Jenson. Peter Jenson. I'm at
the Royal Hawaiian. Now wait a
minute, now. How about the All
Star game for next year? Well,
do you want to cover me or don't
you? I pick the American League.
What kind of odds will you give
me if I get the score? All right,
you got a bet. I say it's the
American League, three to one.
    (MORE)

(CONTINUED)

                         JENSON (CONT.)
          That's right. $500. That's
          right. Okay, now. Do you want
          to go to the Series? I'll take
          St. Louis in the National
          League, the Yankees in the
          American. And then I pick St.
          Louis in five games. $500.
          That's right.
                    (again he makes more
                     notations in the pad)

He continues to talk, but now unintelligibly as we
hear his voice in narration over.

                         JENSON'S VOICE
          I spent the next two and a half
          hours in a kind of paradise
          making bets on sure things.
          Every race, every prize fight,
          every football game I can
          remember happening after
          December of 1941. I got it
          figured out that if this crazy
          stuff goes on at least six more
          months, I'm a shoo-in to collect
          about $464,000 from a half a
          dozen soon to be impoverished
          bookies! I'm not scared, you
          understand. I don't have one
          idea what I'm doing back here
          but as long as I'm back -- I
          figure I'll put it all to good
          use!

Jenson now hangs up the phone, takes a long, satisfying drink from the glass alongside, is about to
rise when there's a KNOCK AT THE DOOR.

                         JENSON
          Come in!

The door opens and the Ensign stands there, hat in
hand, a little embarrassed, sheepish, but terribly,
terribly earnest.

                         ENSIGN
          How are you?

                         JENSON
          I'm fine. Come on in and have
          a drink.

                                        (CONTINUED)

The Ensign takes a step into the room.

                    ENSIGN
          My wife...my wife asked me to
          stop by -- and see how you felt.

                    JENSON
          That was nice of her. I feel
          great. How about a drink?

                    ENSIGN
               (shakes his head)
          No, thanks. We're going swim-
          ming. She was a little
          concerned -- my wife, I mean.

                    JENSON
          About what. About me?

                    ENSIGN
               (not wanting to
                actually say the
                things that are
                on his mind)
          Well, it's just that down at
          the bar -- after you saw the
          paper --

                    JENSON
          Oh, that?
               (makes a shrugging
                off gesture)
          Don't worry about that. As a
          matter of fact, I was going to
          ring you up and tell you I was
          sorry about the Arizona bit, you
          know the mud stuff and every-
          thing. I didn't mean anything
          personal, you understand.

                    ENSIGN
          Sure.
               (and now it comes
                out blurtingly)
          Are you sick?

                    JENSON
          No, I'm not sick.

                    ENSIGN
          Well, what made you say it was
          1958?

                                        (CONTINUED)

                         JENSON
          What made me say it? Nothing.
          I was a little whirley up there!
          That's all.

                         ENSIGN
          Sure. Well, look, we'll be back
          here about four or five. Maybe
          you'd like to have a drink with
          us then, if you feel okay.

                         JENSON
          You got yourself a deal.

                         ENSIGN
          Well, see you later then?

                         JENSON
          Sure thing.

25   CLOSE SHOT - JENSON   25

       as he studies the Ensign for a long moment. His
       face suddenly looks serious and a little grim.

                         JENSON
          Hey --

       The Ensign turns at the door.

                         ENSIGN
          Yeah?

                         JENSON
          What do you do on the Arizona?

                         ENSIGN
               (grins)
          I'm in the Engineering Section.

                         JENSON
          You work down below, huh?

                         ENSIGN
          Most of the time.

                         JENSON
               (nods and forces
                a smile)
          Good job, huh?

                                             (CONTINUED)

25   CONTINUED: 25

                         ENSIGN
          I like it.

                         JENSON
          Well, I'll see you later then?

                         ENSIGN
          We'll give you a call when we
          get in.

                         JENSON
          Fine.

The Ensign opens the door and starts out.

26   LONG SHOT   26

Jenson goes to the door and watches him as he walks
down the corridor. His wife stands near the
elevator at the far end.

27   TWO SHOT - ENSIGN AND WIFE   27

She holds out her hands to him.

                         GIRL
          How is he?

                         ENSIGN
          I think he's okay.

                         GIRL
          He seemes so...so lost in there -

                         ENSIGN
          He'll be okay. Said to give him
          a call when we get back.

                         GIRL
          Wonderful.

She looks up at him and they are lost in the secret
smile that young lovers have. Then they kiss.

28   CLOSE SHOT - JENSON   28

watching them from his door.

                              (CONTINUED)

28   CONTINUED: 28

                                    JENSON'S VOICE
                    I remember thinking right at
                    this given moment that these are
                    two nice lookin' kids obviously
                    so much in love that you could take
                    the looks they give one another and
                    spread it on pancakes. And while I'm
                    watchin' them - the thought hits me
                    that this boy works down deep in the
                    hold of the ship that has about four-
                    teen hours left to ride on the waves.
                    After that it goes under with about
                    a thousand men as I recall. And
                    suddenly...suddenly making bets on
                    things that I know will happen seems
                    about as interesting as catching
                    lake trout in a pop bottle. Somehow,
                    trying to help those two kids, is the
                    one thing in the whole world I've got
                    to do. So right at this moment...
                    I do the only thing I can do - I make
                    a jerk out of myself!

28A   INT. HOTEL ROOM   28A

      as Jenson goes back inside, picks up a phone book
      and starts to thumb through it. Then he picks up
      the receiver.

                                    JENSON
                    Operator, can you tell me how to
                    get to Scofield Barracks?

                                                    CUT TO:

28B   EXT. ARMY BARRACKS - CLOSE SHOT A SIGN   28B

      Which reads: "Scofield Barracks, United States
      Army".

                                                    DISSOLVE TO:

28C   INT. OFFICER'S QUARTERS - PAN SHOT   28C

      down a row of hangers, each with an officer's tunic
      on it with various insignias, from Captain on up.

29   FULL SHOT - THE ROOM   29

      Four officers are playing cards. There are a
      couple of Kibitzers hanging over. There's a
      knock on the door.
                                                    (CONTINUED)

29   CONTINUED: 29

                         COLONEL
              Come on in!

An orderly comes in.

                         COLONEL
                       (continuing)
              Spit it out, Bailey!

                         BAILEY
              Excuse me, sir, but that same
              guy is in the Orderly Room.

                         COLONEL
              What's he want?

                         BAILEY
              Same as before. Says he wants
              to see somebody in charge.

                         CAPTAIN
              Who's this?

                         COLONEL
              I don't know. Some gleep with
              a tambourine or something. I
              think this must be Soul Saving
              Saturday or something. What's
              his story, Corporal?

                         BAILEY
              I can't piece it all together,
              sir, but it's something about
              the Japanese bombing, or some-
              thing.

                         CAPTAIN
              This ought to be good.

                         COLONEL
              What do you say we give him a
              ride, shall we? Send him in.

The Colonel rises and puts on his coat. Another man
does the same thing.

                         COLONEL
              Keep it straight **now**, boys!

30   INT. HALLWAY   30

         as Jenson is led down the hall toward the room.

                                        (CONTINUED)

30   CONTINUED: 30

      They arrive at the door. The orderly knocks and
      then opens the door.

31   ANGLE SHOT - LOOKING OVER JENSON'S SHOULDER   31

      All the officers are framed in the open door, all
      dressed to the teeth now in uniform and looking
      somber and serious. Jenson comes in and is startled
      by the SOUND of the door slamming behind him. The
      Colonel rises.

                         COLONEL
                You're Mister --

                         JENSON
                Jenson. Pete Jenson.

                         COLONEL
                I'm Colonel Abernathy. Major
                Sloan. Major Henson. Captain
                Franklin. Lieutenant Ordway.
                What have you got on your mind,
                Mr. Jenson?

                         JENSON
                I can give it to you in about
                three paragraphs, but I want to
                guarantee before I do, I want
                to know for sure I'm not going
                to get stuck in any rubber room
                with a vest after I finish this
                story.

                         COLONEL
                Go on.

                         JENSON
                I happen to have information
                that the Japanese are going to
                bomb Pearl Harbor tomorrow morn-
                ing. Eight AM Honolulu time.

      There's a long silence.

                         COLONEL
                You know this to be a fact?

                         JENSON
                As sure as I know the good Lord
                made race horses.
                         (MORE)

                                          (CONTINUED)

31   CONTINUED: 31

                          JENSON (CONT.)
               They're going to come over here
               in about thirty waves off a
               bunch of carriers. They're
               going to plaster us while we're
               still in bed dreaming about the
               night before. Pearl Harbor,
               Oahu, the air field, and right
               here, too. Scofield Barracks.

The Colonel rises, scratches his jaw a little im-
periously.

                          COLONEL
               This is very serious. I think
               we'd better take immediate steps,
               gentlemen. All right you,
               Franklin, contact the Naval
               Station at Pearl. See that they
               have all personnel standing by,
               at least thirty PBY's ready to
               go up. You, Ordway, you'd better
               call the Commanding General.
               All troops will have to be on
               the beach.

He continues to spout out the orders like a machine
gun as the CAMERA moves over for a...

32   MED. CLOSE SHOT - JENSON   32

looking very pleased and satisfied, delighted with
all the action as the various officers to to and
fro, back and forth in front of him. He then looks
up to look at the Colonel's face just in time to
catch the Colonel wink at one of the other officers.
Jenson's features work, anger building. Suddenly
he shouts.

                          JENSON
               Awright, knock it off! Cut
               the gag!

At this moment the Colonel bursts out laughing as do
the rest of the officers. Jenson takes a step over
toward him and two other officers immediately step
in between them.

                          JENSON
               I'm going to tell you some-
               thing, you brass-covered hyena!
                          (MORE)

                                                    (CONTINUED)

                    JENSON (CONT.)
          Tomorrow morning you're going
          to be about four thousand miles
          away from any kind of laughing!
          Understand? And you're not
          going to be able to say nobody
          warned you! And this is no gag,
          believe me!

                    COLONEL
                  (very grimly)
          You're quite right. It's no
          gag. We've had about all of it
          we can take for one afternoon.
          Now you can leave peacefully,
          Mr. Jenson -- or I might see to
          it that you're escorted outside.

                    JENSON
          I can walk out by myself, and
          you stick people at my elbows --
          you're going to have to bring in
          the Medical Corps on the double.

                    CAPTAIN
          We don't appreciate that kind of
          talk, Jenson --

                    JENSON
          Is that a fact? You really
          don't? What do you appreciate,
          Captain? Maybe you'd appreciate
          getting punched right smack dab
          in the jaw -- something to pay
          me for my troubles getting over
          here, trying to get in to see you.

                    CAPTAIN
          Mr. Jenson, this is going to hurt
          me worse than it is you, believe
          me!

                    JENSON
                  (nods)
          I believe you!

          The Captain takes a step toward him, swings, misses,
          then winds up on his back after Jenson lets him have
          it right on the button.

33   INT. ARMY DOCTOR'S OFFICE - CLOSE SHOT - EYE   33
      REFLECTOR

      on Doctor's forehead.

                                        PULL BACK FOR:

34   FULL SHOT OF THE ROOM   34

35   CLOSE SHOT   35

      The Army Doctor pulling down the skin from beneath
      Jenson's eyes to more closely examine the eyes.
      Then he moves back.

36   MED. CLOSE SHOT - THE COLONEL   36

      as he motions toward the Doctor. Doctor steps over
      toward him.

                        COLONEL.
                       (whispering)
                  Is he out of his head?

                        DOCTOR
                  Appears to be sane enough.

      The Doctor again turns and looks pensively toward
      Jenson. Across the room we see the Captain with a
      large bandage around his jaw.

                        CAPTAIN
                  I think you ought to fit him
                  for a jacket --

      Jenson makes a move to get out of the chair.

                        JENSON
                  You walk on your lower lip one
                  more time, soldier boy, and I'll
                  get you out of the Army on a
                  Medical!

      The orderly pulls him back down in his chair. The
      Doctor walks back over to him, studying him. He
      taps his fingers together, rubs his jaw. Jenson
      eyes him quizzically.

                        DOCTOR
                  You don't have any reason to
                  doubt your sanity, do you?

                                        (CONTINUED)

                         JENSON
          Stop it! I'm as sane as any
          of the people in this room.
                    (he looks around)
          A more incriminating statement
          I'll probably never make the
          rest of my life!

Jenson looks at the kind of dubious look that crosses
the Army Doctor's face.

                         JENSON
          Go ahead. I could prove it to
          you. Ask me some questions.

                         DOCTOR
          I will. Suppose we start like
          this. What's the date today?

                         JENSON
          December 6th.

                         DOCTOR
          And we're?

                         JENSON
          We're what?

                         DOCTOR
          We're where?

                         JENSON
          Honolulu, Hawaii.

                         DOCTOR
          What have you had to eat today
          ...or drink?

                         JENSON
          Nothing. Nothing to eat and
          precious little to drink. Most
          of the afternoon I've spent
          wasting my time with these
          kooks!

The Doctor turns, walks slowly over toward the
venetian blinds. Suddenly he whirls around:

                         DOCTOR
          Who's the President of the
          United States?

(CONTINUED)

36   CONTINUED: -2   36

                              JENSON
                    Who's kiddin' who? And you're
                    supposed to be finding out
                    whether I'm nuts? President
                    Eisenhower. Who'd you think it
                    was -- U.S. Grant?

The other men in the room look at one another. The
Doctor's eyebrows raise.

                              DOCTOR
                    Who? Who did you say was the
                    President?

                              JENSON
                    Eisen--

He stops abruptly. Over the Doctor's shoulder he's
looking at a picture on the wall.

37   TIGHT CLOSE SHOT - PICTURE   36

It's a photograph of Franklin D. Roosevelt.

38   TIGHT CLOSE SHOT - JENSON   38

His eyes suddenly close, and his lips move.

                              JENSON
                         (whispers)
                    Of course. Of course. It's
                    1941.
                         (now he opens his
                          eyes and his voice
                          is much louder)
                    FDR is President. Franklin D.
                    Roosevelt.

                              DOCTOR
                    Who's the other person you
                    mentioned? Eisen-- something?

                              JENSON
                         (very defensively)
                    I was thinking about something
                    else. Franklin D. Roosevelt is
                    the President.

                                              (CONTINUED)

                          DOCTOR
                 (like a hound dog
                  on a scent)
             Who else did you mention?

                          COLONEL
                 (interrupting)
             Eisenhower. Dwight Eisenhower.
             He's a light colonel on the
             general staff in Washington.
             I was with him at the Point.
                 (he turns toward
                  Jenson)
             How did you know about Ike
             Eisenhower?

The Doctor waves him quiet.

                          DOCTOR
             Who's the Vice-President, Mr.
             Jenson?

                          JENSON
             The Vice-President?
                 (he wets his lips,
                  closes his eyes
                  for a moment)
             Let's see. That would be...
             that would be...John Nance
             Garner?

The men look at one another. The Colonel looks
pleased, the Captain just overjoyed that they caught
him in a mistake.

                          DOCTOR
             John Nance Garner was the Vice-
             President but he isn't any
             longer.

                          JENSON
             Wait a minute. Wait a minute.
             Let me think. Just a minute...
             just a minute. Truman? Harry
             Truman. It is Harry Truman.
             because he becomes President.

All three men look at one another for a moment.

                          DOCTOR
             How's that?

(CONTINUED)

                              JENSON
                    When Roosevelt dies then Truman
                    becomes the President. What's
                    the matter with you jerks?
                              (shouting)
                    What's the matter with you Jerks?!
                    Don't you know that Roosevelt dies
                    and then Truman takes over and then
                    Eisenhower becomes President? What's
                    the matter with you guys?

The Doctor steps away very reflectively, then he very
slowly nods toward the Colonel who acknowledges the
nods with an I-told-you-so look. Jenson is on his
feet and he backs toward the door.

                              JENSON
                    Uh, Uh! I take it back, boys.
                    You name the Vice-President -
                    and that's who it is. Forget
                    I even mentioned it.

Now he's at the door.

                              DOCTOR
                    Mr. Jenson, stick around a while.
                    We'll give you a nice little
                    sedative and you can sleep it off.

Jenson looks from face to face in the room, then
takes on a very wise look.

                              JENSON
                    Any of you guys know what a
                    sputnik is?

The men look at one another.

                              JENSON
                    How about Rock-N-Roll? Jet
                    propulsion? How about television?
                    Ever hear of a guy named Marciano?
                    How about a couple of horses named
                    Swaps or Citation? Needles.

He looks from face to face and they just stare at him
blankly. He nods, turns and walks toward the door,
the pauses.

                              JENSON
                    Atomic bombs?
                              (another pause)
                              (MORE)

                                        (CONTINUED)

                              JENSON (cont'd)
                    I didn't think so. So forget
                    about it. You got no worries.
                    There must be a couple of good
                    Officer's Club Dances you can
                    go to tonight - or a Polo Match
                    or two on the docket for the
                    afternoon. So why worry, boys,
                    Huh? Why worry.

                              COLONEL
                         (bursting at the seams now)
                    I could have told you, Doctor,
                    even before you looked at him.
                    This man is absolutely non compos
                    mentis!

                              CAPTAIN
                         (through hurt jaws)
                    A maniac! A raving maniac!

                              JENSON
                         (looking around)
                    But I'm harmless, boys. Very
                    harm-less. Well...
                         (he looks around again
                          then makes the V sign)
                    Buy bonds!

          He takes off out of the door. The Colonel takes
          after him, shouting.

                              COLONEL
                         (shouts)
                    Jenson! Jenson!

          Then he turns back toward the room.

                              DOCTOR
                    He's right. I think he is
                    harmless.

                              CAPTAIN
                         (massaging his jaw)
                    I respectfully take issue with
                    that conclusion.

                                             (CONTINUED)

                              COLONEL
                    Swaps, Rock-N-Roll, atomic
                    bombs, or something -- and you
                    think he's harmless, Doctor?

                              DOCTOR
                    Unless he's provoked.
                         (he slaps the
                          Colonel on the
                          back)
                    He's a civilian anyway, Jeff.
                    So why concern yourself with
                    him?

                              COLONEL
                    Because some of his cock and
                    bull stories involve the
                    military. Did you hear what he
                    told us?

                              DOCTOR
                         (laughing)
                    You mean about the Japanese
                    going to bomb Pearl Harbor?

                              COLONEL
                    Is that supposed to be an
                    observation in passing of a
                    normal man?

                              DOCTOR
                         (chuckles and turns
                          back into his office)
                    I've heard nuttier stories,
                    believe me! Why don't you go
                    back and finish your game and
                    forget about it? Captain,
                    before the dance tonight come
                    back and I'll give you another
                    dressing.

          He goes back to his desk as the other officers pre-
          pare to leave. They slowly go out of the room,
          leaving only a little second lieutenant. The Doctor
          looks up at him.

                              DOCTOR
                    Something on your mind,
                    Lieutenant?

                                        (CONTINUED)

> LIEUTENANT
> (rubs his jaw)
> Nothing, sir. Nothing, except -

> DOCTOR
> Except what?

> LIEUTENANT
> (looks at the Doctor a
> little strangley)
> There's nothing insane about
> that man.

> DOCTOR
> I didn't say there was.

> LIEUTENANT
> He knew what he was saying. And
> what's more he believed it!

> DOCTOR
> (shrugs)
> Well, that's his business.

> LIEUTENANT
> (very earnestly now)
> I don't know. It's just that...
> (then a long, thoughtful
> struggle within himself.
> He shrugs)
> Nothing. I guess it is his
> business.

The Docotr points to the pad of paper that the
Lieutenant has been doodling on, twists his head
so he can see it.

> DOCTOR
> You're quite an artist, Lieutenant.

> LIEUTENANT
> (embarrassed)
> Just a doodler, sir.

The Doctor picks up the sheet on top of the pad.

> DOCTOR
> Interesting.

> CUT TO:

39   TIGHT CLOSE SHOT - THE DOODLE   39

Shows a ship going down, and planes dropping bombs
from high up.   (CONTINUED)

>   DOCTOR
>   Planes are Japanese, I suppose?
>
>   LIEUTENANT
>   (laughing embarrassedly)
>   Not really. Just doodles, that's
>   all.

The Doctor laughs, crumples up the paper and throws it away.

>   DOCTOR
>   You'd best watch yourself! I'll
>   have you in front of a Board!

The Lieutenant joins in his laughter, turns and starts to walk out. The Doctor goes back and sits down at his desk and just for a brief moment turns to look down at the waste basket where the crumpled paper is in evidence.

>   DISSOLVE TO:

40   INT. BAR - LATE THAT AFTERNOON   40

41   EXTREMELY TIGHT CLOSE SHOT - JUKE BOX   41

Playing. The swirling lights drift lazily around the neon tubes. There is a soft ballad on of 1941 vintage. The CAMERA moves back for:

42   MED. CLOSE SHOT - THE BAR   42

Jenson sits there all alone over a drink. The bartender is wiping glasses, but intermittently looks over at him with a kind of half-smile playing on his face.

>   JENSON'S VOICE
>   (in narration)
>   Well...I'd struck a blow for law
>   and order - but it turned out to
>   be just a wild slap with a left
>   hand several thousand miles off
>   target. I was tabbed as some kind
>   of wild-eyed, meathead with a leak
>   in his attic and it was just left
>   at that. So I figured I'd just spend
>   the rest of the day drinking quietly,
>   feeling sorry for everybody else who
>   wasn't as bright as I was. I done
>   what I could and I figured that was
>   all that could be expected! The
>   (MORE)   (CONTINUED)

42   CONTINUED: 42

                          JENSON'S VOICE
                       (in narration) (cont'd)
                 next morning they'd probably all
                 come back and measure me for a
                 brass statue but it would be too
                 late. I didn't care any more.

Now Jenson looks around the bar at a couple of the
booths. There are several young soldiers and sailors
there. One couple dances near the juke box. They
look particularly young. Jenson turns back to study
his drink. His voice comes in again in narration.

                          JENSON'S VOICE
                 But it was kind of a crazy feel-
                 ing though to watch these kids
                 relax over their dates and their
                 drinks like all was well with
                 the world...when tomorrow morning
                 there'd be a couple of odd thousand
                 of them taking a miserable route
                 through hell to get to heaven.

43   MED. CLOSE SHOT - THE BARTENDER   43

as he walks slowly over toward Jenson, puts his elbow
on the bar.

> BARTENDER
> Hiya.

> JENSON
> (looks up)
> Likewise.

> BARTENDER
> (very confidentially)
> Hey - you know what you were
> talkin' about this morning?

> JENSON
> I got a vague recollection.

> BARTENDER
> You know - about the Arizona
> bein' sunk?

> JENSON
> Why don't you knock it off.
> You don't believe me! I feel
> no grief, pops! You don't see
> me bleeding, do ya?

> BARTENDER
> I'm not trying to drum up an
> argument. I just wanted to show
> you something.

He taps Jenson's shoulder over the bar and then points
toward the front of the saloon. Jenson turns on the
stool to look.

                              CUT TO:

44   FILM CLIP - AS SEEN THROUGH A BARWINDOW   44

of the mighty Arizona in anchorage several thousand
yards beyond.

> BARTENDER
> (again very surreptitiously)
> I just wanted to tell ya - that
> happens to be the Arizona. Some-
> body got the signals crossed. She's
> still afloat!

Then he gives out with a very low chuckle that starts
some place deep in the stomach, works its way out
till it becomes a roaring laugh which he can't control.

                              (CONTINUED)

He just leans against the back of the bar, hands over
his big stomach, laughing with tears rolling down his
eyes. Jenson looks disgustedly away. The lush from
before comes into the bar, comes over and sits a
couple of stools away from Jenson.

                    LUSH
              (without any build-up)
     I know how it is, pal, believe me,
     I know how it is. Once I tied
     one on in New Orleans around
     Mardi Gras time. I woke up
     outside of the bleacher section
     of Ebbets Field on St. Patrick's
     Day - still in costume! Believe
     me I know the problems of which
     you are exposed...to.

Jenson nods, sloughing him off, then he turns to see
the Ensign and his bride take a booth close by. They
both smile at him, and the girl waves. Jenson takes
his drink, walks across the bar over toward them.
The Ensign rises.

                    ENSIGN
     Hi. Have a drink with us.

                    JENSON
     Thanks. I'm a little ahead of you.

He sits down across from the two of them, notices
briefly that they are still holding hands.

                    JENSON
              (continuing)
     How was the swim?

                    GIRL
     Wonderful.

                    JENSON
              (grins)
     How many hours is it now?

They both laugh.

                    GIRL
     Thirty-one hours and fifteen minutes.

                    JENSON
              (wrily)
     And everybody said it wouldn't last!

Again the Ensign and his bride laugh. The girl's
smile now fades slightly and her voice is earnest.

                                        (CONTINUED)

                         GIRL
              Mr........is it Jenson?

                        JENSON
              Try Pete.

                         GIRL
              Pete - are you all right?

                        JENSON
              Yeah...I'm all right.   Why?

The girl takes a quick look toward the Ensign.

                         GIRL
              It's just that well...this morning
              ...you seemed so...so sure it was
              another year.

                        JENSON
              I did? Well, look, honey - today
              I wouldn't be sure if somebody
              pointed out the ocean to me and
              told me it was really glass I
              wouldn't be sure enough to call
              'em a liar! I'm kind of mixed up
              - but don't let it throw you.
              And I didn't mean anything
              personal about what I said about
              your ship.

                        ENSIGN
              I told you to forget that.

Jenson finishes his drink. The waiter comes over.

                        JENSON
              A round for all of us.

                         GIRL
              Tom Collins for me.

                        ENSIGN
              Same here. How about you, Mr.
              Jenson. What are you drinking?

                        JENSON
              Same thing.

                        WAITER
                   (nods)
              Double Scotch?

                                        (CONTINUED)

                          JENSON
Double Scotch.

                          WAITER
You sure like your scotch, don't
you?

                          JENSON
                    (looks up)
Why? You got a grandfather
in the bourbon business?

                          WAITER
I was just making an observation.

He looks a little hurt and goes away. Jenson turns
and suddenly stares at the two kids in front of him.
He looks from one to the other. The girl seems to
unconsciously grip her husband's arm a little tighter.

                          GIRL
What's the matter, Mr. Jenson?

                          JENSON
                    (after a long silence)
I wasn't kidding this morning.
I meant it. The Arizona's going
to get sunk tomorrow morning.

                          ENSIGN
                    (very deliberately
                     removes his wife's
                     hand)
Are we on that again?

                          JENSON
We're on that again! Look,
Lieutenant --

                          ENSIGN
Ensign.

                          JENSON
Lieutenant, Ensign, whatever you
are. I've got no axe to grind,
you understand? Tomorrow morning
I have every intention of going
down into the basement, cuddling
up to a furnace, and spending the
whole day listening to the sirens!
You tell me that you're an
engineering officer or something.
That means you're down there near
the boilers. Well, I'm telling
                    (more)

                                        (CONTINUED)

                    JENSON (cont'd)
You now - at about twenty minutes
past eight tomorrow morning there
won't be any boilers, there won't
be any decks, there won't be any
ship left. And that goes for a lot
of boilers, and a lot of decks, and
a lot of ships. Not to mention
handsome young ensigns with new
brides!

                    GIRL
               (biting her lips)
Please - don't talk like that -

                    JENSON
I gotta talk like that! Listen -
I want to tell you something that's
going to sound wacky to you.

The lush from the bar suddenly overhears Jensons'
voice growing louder, sidles over to stand near
their booth, a glass in his hand.

                    JENSON
This is the second half of the
story. Now get this. Listen to me.
I know what's going to happen tomorrow
morning because December 7, 1941 is
tomorrow for you people, but it happens
to be seventeen years ago for me. That's
right. Last night I was in New York
City and it was 1958. It was October.
It was seventeen years after what it
is this minute and I've lived through
those seventeen years and I know
what's going to happen!

45   CLOSE SHOT - THE DRUNK   45

The glass just drops right out of his hand and
breaks on the floor. He looks sick and walks
directly out of the room.

46   MED. SHOT - BOOTH   46

                              JENSON
                Look you're nice kids. You're nice
                young kids. I've got no reason in
                the world...no reason to give you
                any grief! Would you do me a favor
                and just listen to me. Just take
                a hundred to one shot that this
                weirdo in front of you might have
                at least one point. I'm telling
                you kids that tomorrow morning
                we're going to get attacked and
                if your're on that ship --

                              ENSIGN
                I'll be on that ship. Because
                that's my berth, and Mr. Jenson...
                you're a nice fellow and all that
                but if you keep saying crazy wild
                things like this and making Edna
                worried - I'm going to have to
                pop you!

Jenson takes a deep breath, puts his glass down, rises.

                                        CUT TO:

47   MED. CLOSE SHOT - THE BARTENDER   47

who puts both palms on the bar.

                              BARTENDER
                Hey - you! No more trouble, huh?
                You want trouble - go out and fight
                a lamp post!

                              JENSON
                You shut your mouth.

Several of the other people in the bar look over
toward Jenson to see the trouble. Jenson by this
time is getting drunk and it is quite obvious in
the way his voice is now loosening. He turns back
toward the young couple.

                              JENSON
                So what are you going to do about
                it? You gonna sit around holding
                hands and biting earlobes till he
                goes back to his ship? Because
                I'm here to tell you that if this
                boy goes back to the Arizona he
                may not be alive at nine o'clock
                tomorrow morning. Repeat! He may
                not be alive tomorrow morning!
                                        (CONTINUED)

47   CONTINUED: 47

The girl lets out a stifled cry.

                    ENSIGN
          Mr. Jenson -- you just won't learn,
          will you.

He then suddenly hauls off and socks Jenson flush in
the face. The blow catching Jenson by surprise, sends
Jenson reeling across the room to land backwards against
the juke box. There he sits, the swirling lights
playing over his face. He shakes his head. Opens and
closes his eyes, then looks through the haze to the
various people staring at him. He slowly inches his
way back onto his feet. He now looks haggard and
unshaven, a little wild. The ballad continues to
ooze out of the machine until finally Jenson can't
stand it. He turns and starts to punch buttons
indiscriminately. The bartender shouts:

                    BARTENDER
          Hey, buddy, I told you to watch
          it! I don't want no trouble --

Jenson whirls around, his eyes wide.

                    JENSON
          You don't want no trouble, huh?
          He doesn't want any trouble! I
          don't want to give you trouble. I
          want to give you music. I want
          to sing songs for you you've never
          heard before.

He begins to sing in a wavery, cracked voice.

                    JENSON
          "Let's remember Pearl Harbor as
          we go to meet the foe...."
          Do you want to hear another one?
                  (again he sings)
          "Praise the Lord and pass the
          ammunition. Praise the Lord and
          pass the ammunition. Praise the
          Lord and pass the ammunition, and
          we'll all stay free." Hear that?
          That's what you're going to be
          singing. You're going to start
          to sing that in about a week
          because...because the Japs are
          going to...want to hear another
          song?

                                        (CONTINUED)

47   CONTINUED: - 2   47

He wets his lips as his mind begins to probe back into
memory and he suddenly again begins to sing, loudly,
tunelessly in a screechy voice now.

                         JENSON
          "Let's Remember Pearl Harbor...
          Let's Remember Pearl Harbor..."

The bartender comes out from behind the bar and is
heading toward him. Jenson backs up against the juke
box and holds up his hands.

48   TIGHT CLOSE SHOT - THE BARTENDER'S FIST   48

          as it swings in an arc toward him. There is the
          resounding crash of furniture, tables, a woman's
          scream as we:

                                                 CUT TO:

49   INT. HOTEL ROOM   49

PAN SHOT ACROSS THE ROOM taking in various objects
like a newspaper lying on the bed, a coat crumpled
up on a chair, calendar page torn in half but the
letter "6" is visible, and finally a small clock
on a dresser which reads "4:30". We HEAR the click,
click, click of a receiver and finally take in a
SHOT of Jenson on the telephone. His face looks
somewhat bruised.

                         JENSON
          I know he's out. You told me he's
          out. But where is he? Where can I
          reach him? Listen...Will you listen
          ...Listen to me, please! This is
          urgent. I've got to talk to the
          general. If I can't talk to him
          give me somebody who can tell me
          where he is!
                    (screaming)
          Don't tell me he can't be reached.
          This is important!
                    (a pause, then screams)
          Buddy, he may not be alive to call
          me tomorrow! Now this is what you've
          got to do -- hello...hello?
                    (he jiggles the
                     receiver again)
          Hello?

                                           (CONTINUED)

49   CONTINUED: 49

He slowly puts the phone down. He's in his shirt
sleeves and looks desperately tired. He goes back
over to the bed where a phone book, obviously crumpled
from much recent and violent use, is open. He starts
to thumb through it again violently. Then he traces
the page with his finger and starts to murmur a number.
He goes to the phone, picks up the receiver.

                    JENSON
          I want to get Navy 7096. That's
          right.
                    (a pause in which he stands
                     there shifting from one foot
                     to another, takes a handkerchief
                     out of his pocket and mops his
                     face)
          Is this the Naval Station? Well, who
          do I talk to who's in charge?
                    (a pause)
          Don't give me that! Just put me on
          with somebody who's in charge. All
          right. All right. Now get this:
          The Japanese are going to attack
          Pearl Harbor tomorrow. I said the
          Japanese are --
                    (he jiggles the
                     receiver again)
          Hello. Hello.
                    (then his voice turns
                     down into a mumble)
          Hello. Hello. Hello. Hello.

He slowly replaces the receiver, staring down at it.
He turns and walks over to the French doors, puts his
face against them, closes his eyes.

                                        CUT TO:

50   REVERSE ANGLE SHOT   50

Looking from outside on the little balcony toward
the room. Jenson is seen through the glass, his face
pressed up against it. Now he turns, goes over, flings
himself on the bed. His head goes from side to side
in a mute remonstrance against the events of the day
and very slowly his eyes get heavy and he closes them,
then his breathing becomes regular and heavy, and
he's in deep sleep. The CAMERA starts a SLOW DOLLY IN
until the CAMERA is VERY TIGHT on him.

                                        DISSOLVE TO:

51   OUT OF FOCUS SHOT - JENSON'S FACE   51

DISSOLVE TO:

52   CLOSE SHOT - JENSON IN CLARITY   52

as he wakes up with a start. Sunlight beaming in on his face. He jumps up out of bed, then whirls around to look at the clock. It reads "8:00 AM". He then looks at the calendar on the wall which reads: "December 7". He rushes to the French doors and suddenly flings them open. There is the SOUND of aircraft engines, building up in a crescendo of noise.

CUT TO:

53   FILM CLIP OF R.S.P. IF POSSIBLE   53

of planes framed in the opening of the French doors. Mitsubishis and Zeros as they come in from the ocean and head straight for the CAMERA.

> JENSON
> I told you, didn't I? Didn't I
> tell you? Why wouldn't anybody
> listen to me? I told you they
> were coming! I told you, I told
> you, I told you --

There's the staccato drum-fire of aircraft machine guns and we --

CUT ABRUPTLY TO:

54   TIGHT CLOSE SHOT - DR. GILLESPIE'S PAD   54

as he's jotting down notes. PULL BACK FOR:

55   FULL SHOT - THE ROOM INT. HIS OFFICE   55

Jenson is lying on the couch. The room is in utter silence now in sharp and vivid contrast to the violent sounds of the previous moment.

> JENSON
> (in a quiet fury)
> I told you. I told you. I told
> you. Why wouldn't anybody listen
> to me?

Then he stops, the perspiration rolling down his face.

(CONTINUED)

He opens his eyes, takes a deep breath, looks toward
the desk where Dr. Gillespie is sitting. Gillespie
rises and walks over toward him.

                    DR. GILLESPIE
Then?

                    JENSON
Then I wake up. That's just where
I wake up every time. Standing
there by the doors and watching
those planes come in low. Bombs
dropping...strafing....all Hell
breaking loose. That's where I
wake up.

Gillespie sits down in a chair **very** near the couch.

                    DR. GILLESPIE
Realistic...and very frightening.
How long has it been going on
like this? How many times have
you dreamed this?

                    JENSON
Every night for a week.

                    DR. GILLESPIE
Everything always the same.
Chronologically the same, every-
thing, huh?

                    JENSON
                (nods)
Everything. The ensign and his
girl - the bar, in my room trying
to phone, the whole thing. And
the moment ...
                (he closes his eyes now)
The moment when I open up those
doors and see the planes coming
in, it's always the same.
                (then he **opens** his
                 eyes and looks at the
                 doctor)
And I know it's real. I know I'm
going back in time.

                    DR. GILLESPIE
                (nods thoughtfully;
                 gently)
I know. I know.
                (more)

(CONTINUED)

                         DR. GILLESPIE
                    (continuing;
                     he rises, lights a
                     cigarette, goes over
                     to the blinds)
          Mr. Jenson, I won't attempt now
          to analyze that dream.
                    (turns back toward
                     the patient)
          Except to say this. That very
          often you dream with a purpose.
          The dream is significant of some-
          thing very deeply rooted in a
          man's sub-conscious. But very
          often the things you dream about
          are not really the things that
          are bothering you. They're
          symbols of the things that bother
          you.

                         JENSON
                    (looks up at him)
          Don't try to out-logic me, Doctor.
          I'm not trying to pass this off as
          logic. I just know what I know.
          I can't give you any explanation.
          I thought maybe you could give them
          to me. I'm going back in time.
                    (he rises)
          And I'll tell you something else.
          In that dream when I'm standing
          by that door and the Jap planes
          are coming in - I always wake up
          then. But even as I'm lying in
          bed thinking about it, I know that
          the dream shouldn't have ended
          there. It should have gone on beyond
          that.
                    (he turns away now)
          One of these nights it will go on
          beyond that.

                         DR. GILLESPIE
          But you have no idea what might
          transpire in the moment...beyond
          that.

                         JENSON
                    (shakes his head)
          I don't have one idea.

                                        (CONTINUED)

                              DR. GILLESPIE
               That is as it may be. But let's
               approach it this way. Let's look
               at it as if this weren't a dream -
               let's looks at it very practically.
                         (he goes back to chair,
                         sits down)
               Assume now that it were possible to
               go back in time. We make that
               assumption now. You go back in
               time and you do something - say,
               you warn people about an accident
               that you know is going to happen
               so that the accident doesn't
               happen. But what do you do then,
               Mr. Jenson? By altering the past
               you change the future. For
               example.
                         (he picks up his lighter
                         that's on the desk)
               This is the present and my lighter
               is on my desk. Now! Go back in
               time and I pick up this lighter.
                         (he picks it up)
               And I put it in my pocket and I
               keep it there. Now.
                         (he looks back at the desk)
               We are now back in the present.
               I've returned from being back in
               time. Now by rights, having re-
               moved that lighter it should no
               longer be here in the present.
                         (then he puts lighter
                         back on desk)
               But there it is. You get my
               point?

                              JENSON
               Look, Doc. -

                              GILLESPIE
               This is important, Mr. Jenson.
               It's very important that you grasp
               this. Try this analogy. Supposing
               I were to go back in time, and I were
               to be hit, say, by a taxi. Now, it
               figures that if I went back in time
               and were killed - I shouldn't be
               living today. Not only that, but I
               think of the other lives affected.
               I wouldn't have children. I wouldn't
               have bought a house.
                         (MORE)

(CONTINUED)

                            DR. GILLESPIE
                          (continuing)
All these things wouldn't exist
as they do today because I changed
them in the past by being killed.

                            JENSON
                          (looks up at him)
So?

                            DR. GILLESPIE
                          (makes a gesture with
                            his hands)
So -- it's not possible to go back
in time. We must assume that this
is a dream.

                            JENSON
Try this then.

                            DR. GILLESPIE
Go on.

                            JENSON
I've never been in Honolulu in my
whole life -- except during that
dream.

                            DR. GILLESPIE
Go on.

                            JENSON
So after the first couple of times
I dreamed this -- I ...

He wets his lips.

                            DR. GILLESPIE
Take your time.

                            JENSON
I decided I ... well, I'd put it to
a test. I remembered the Ensign's
last name. It was kind of an odd
one. Janoski. He told me that he
and his girl had come from a little
town called White Oak, Wisconsin.
I placed a call there. There was
only one Janoski in the book. Some
woman answered. She said it was
his mother. I told her I was a
good friend of his from Honolulu --
was he there?

There's a long silence.

                                  (CONTINUED)

                                DR. GILLESPIE
            And then?

                                JENSON
            And then she told me that both her
            son and his wife were killed in
            Honolulu on December 7, 1941. He
            went down with the Arizona. She
            was shot down near King Street by
            a plane strafing.

There's a long, long silence now as Gillespie lets
this one sink in. He's obviously affected by it.
He looks away very, very thoughtfully, and then rubs
his jaw.

                                JENSON
                          (after a pause)
            Well, Doctor?

                                DR. GILLESPIE
                          (looks at him for a
                           long moment)
            You sure you've never been in
            Honolulu?

                                JENSON
                          (shakes his head)
            Yeah -- I was there once.

                                GILLESPIE
                          (his eyes going wide)
            When?

                                JENSON
                          (takes a deep breath)
            When I'm supposedly having that
            dream -- which isn't a dream at
            all.
                          (a pause)
            All right, Doc -- tell me.

Dr. Gillespie just stares at him open-mouthed for a
long, long moment.

                                JENSON
            I don't hear you talkin'!

                                DR. GILLESPIE
                          (shakes his head back
                           and forth)
            At the moment...I don't quite
            know what to say!

                                                FADE OUT:

                        END OF ACT TWO

FADE IN:

56   LONG ANGLE SHOT LOOKING DOWN AT JENSON   56

He's lying on the couch. The smoke from Gillespie's
cigarette curls into the frame. CAMERA PULLS BACK
for SHOT of Dr. Gillespie's back as he stares down
at the patient.

                    GILLESPIE'S VOICE
          My patient lay on the couch almost
          in a stupor. We'd been talking for
          hours. It was Saturday and I'd plan-
          ned to close early and go play golf.
          At that moment I'd forgotten golf. I
          was concerned only with the fascinating
          and unbelievable story that this man
          in front of me had told me. And then
          as I looked at him lying there on the
          couch I knew he was falling asleep.
          But it was not a deep sleep. You
          could tell by the look on the face
          that Mr. Jenson was far from resting,
          though his eyes were closed and he
          was no longer aware of me.

Gillespie rises, goes over to the couch, bends low
over it.

                    GILLESPIE
          Mr. Jenson? Are you asleep, Mr. Jenson?

There is no response. Gillespie sits back down in
his chair, butts out the cigarette, lights another
one, exhales the smoke from the cigarette, stares up
at it as it curls up toward the ceiling, then he leans
back in the chair and very thoughtfully looks over at
the patient. The CAMERA STARTS A SLOW DOLLY over to
him until we're on a VERY CLOSE PROFILE SHOT of Jenson
then down toward his hands as they suddenly convulse
and his fingers clench and reclench. Gillespie notices
this, looks back toward the sleeping face. It begins
to work. The CAMERA again PANS DOWN to the hands.

                              ` WE LAP DISSOLVE TO:

57   CLOSE SHOT JENSON'S HANDS   57

on the door frame of his hotel room. We're looking
over his shoulder at the fleeing chambermaid on a
reverse angle of the same scene played earlier. He
turns back into his room now, closing the door.

58   SUPERIMPOSE SHOT OF JENSON SLEEPING ON THE COUCH   58

over the shot of Jenson standing in the middle of the
room thoughtfully, then going over to the French doors
exactly as earlier. We play the next few moments in
pantomime with Jenson performing the same actions in
the hotel room as he did before. THE SUPERIMPOSED SHOT
OF HIM LYING ON THE COUCH DREAMING REMAINS THE SAME.
                              DISSOLVE TO:

59   INT. THE BAR   59

    A few moments of a pantomime scene with Jenson
    talking and then walking across the bar to the news-
    paper and staring at it.

                         DISSOLVE TO:

60   INT. HOTEL ROOM   60

    again as he lies on the bed phoning with the scratch
    pad and the phone book and a drink.

                         DISSOLVE TO:

61   INT. OFFICERS' QUARTERS   61

    as Jenson talks to them, again in pantomime, winding
    up with his hitting the captain.

                         DISSOLVE TO:

62   INT. ARMY DOCTOR'S OFFICE   62

    Again in pantomime as Jenson is talking to him. Then
    Jenson rises and goes to the door.

                         DISSOLVE TO:

63   INT. BAR   63

    A few moments of the second bar scene in which the
    Naval officer has just hit him and he's fallen back
    against the juke box. CAMERA SLOWLY DOLLIES IN for
    TIGHT CLOSE SHOT of his face with the neon lights
    playing on him.

                         DISSOLVE TO:

64   INT. HOTEL CORRIDOR   64

    WE NOW CLEAR THE SUPER OF JENSON SLEEPING, as Jenson
    himself gets out of an elevator, starts to walk
    steadily toward his room, his jaws bruised in a couple
    of places from where the Ensign and the bartender have
    worked on him. From behind the camera walks the
    Ensign and his girl. They pass Jenson without looking
    at him, heading toward the elevator. Jenson stops,
    turns toward them as they stand by the elevator.

                    (CONTINUED)

64   CONTINUED:

                    JENSON
        Hey, Janoski --

The Ensign turns.

                    JENSON
                  (continuing)
        Where are you going?

                    ENSIGN
        Why don't you just sleep it off,
        Pete?

                    JENSON
        Do me one favor, will ya?
                  (a pause)
        Play hokey tomorrow morning.

                    ENSIGN
        You're outa your head!

                    JENSON
        If you never do anything for the
        rest of your life -- do this, will
        ya? Stay off that ship of yours.
        Take this little lady and get away
        from Pearl Harbor! I don't care
        where you go! -- Get on a Pan Am
        and go to the Canal Zone, but
        get out of here.

The Ensign starts to take a step toward him.

                    GIRL
        Jimmie, forget it, will you!

The Ensign throws her arm off and points a finger
at Jenson.

                    ENSIGN
        That's a great plan. And you
        know what that would cost me,
        don't you? Only my commission
        in the Navy, that's all.

                    JENSON
        If you don't go -- have you any
        idea what it's going to cost you?
        Just a little item like your life
        and her life, too!

                    ENSIGN
        I've had it with you, I swear!
        This time I'm going to shut that
        mouth of yours --

                              (CONTINUED)

64   CONTINUED: - 2   64

The elevator doors suddenly go up. The girl grabs
his arm.

                         GIRL
              Come on, Jimmie. Please!

He lets himself be led over to the elevator and they
walk inside.   Jenson runs over to the elevator door
just as it's closing.

                       JENSON
              Please -- what have you got to
              lose by just --

65   LONG ANGLE SHOT - LOOKING UP THE SHAFT TOWARD THE   65
      FLOOR THE ELEVATOR HAS JUST LEFT

We HEAR Jenson's fists pounding on door and his voice
echoing hollowly down the shaft.

                    JENSON'S VOICE
              You crazy kids, I'm only trying
              to save your lives, that's all!
              You dumb, balmy, twisted, kids --

                                              CUT TO:

66   MED. CLOSE SHOT - JENSON   66

Standing by the door. The CAMERA PANS UP for a SHOT
of the floor indicator as it reaches lobby.

67   TRACK CLOSE SHOT - JENSON   67

as he walks slowly back toward his room. Tears are in
his eyes.

                                              CUT TO:

68   INT. HOTEL BEDROOM   68

PAN SHOT ACROSS THE ROOM, taking in various objects
like newspaper lying on the bed, a coat crumpled up on
a chair, a calendar page torn in half but the letter "6"
is visible, and finally a small clock on a dresser which
reads: "4:30". We HEAR the click, click, click of a
receiver and finally take in a SHOT of Jenson on the
telephone.

                                         (CONTINUED)

68   CONTINUED: 68

                              JENSON
                  I know he's out. You told me
                  he's out. But where is he?
                  Where can I reach him?

                                        CUT TO:

69   INT. ORDERLY ROOM - ARMY POST   69

A bored C.Q. is on the switchboard.

                              C.Q.
                           (boredly)
                  Look, Mac, I told you once, I
                  told you twice and now three
                  times and it's out. I don't
                  know where the General is. He
                  don't tell me where he's goin'.
                  His wife don't tell me where he's
                  goin'. The adjutant don't tell
                  me where he's goin'. And it's
                  Saturday night. Who cares where
                  he's goin'! And all I'm tellin'
                  you now is that he can't be
                  reached!

                                        CUT TO:

70   JENSON - ON THE TELEPHONE   70

                              JENSON
                  Don't tell me he can't be
                  reached. This is important.
                           (a pause)
                  Buddy, he may not be alive to
                  call me tomorrow. This is what
                  you got to do -- hello ... hello?
                           (he jibbles the
                            receiver again)
                  Hello?

He slowly puts the phone down. He's in his shirt
sleeves and looks desperately tired. He goes back
over to the bed where a phone book, obviously
crumpled from much recent and violent use, is open.
He starts to thumb through it again violently. Then
he traces the page with his finger and starts to
murmur a number. He goes to the phone, picks up
the receiver.

                                        (CONTINUED)

CONTINUED:

                              JENSON
                 I want to get Navy 7096. That's
                 right.
                              (a pause in which he
                              stands shifting from
                              one foot to another,
                              takes a handkerchief
                              out of his pocket and
                              mops his face)
                 Is this the Naval Station? Well
                 who do I talk to who's in charge?

                                        CUT TO:

71   INT. NAVAL STATION   71

A young Ensign on the telephone.

                              ENSIGN
                 This is Ensign Lammers. It's
                 my watch and it's your nickel
                 so go ahead. What'd you got on
                 your mind? The what? The who?
                 What are they gonna do?

Another Ensign across the room, looks up from playing
solitaire.

                              ENSIGN TWO
                 Who is it?

                              ENSIGN ONE
                 Some wino - I dunno.
                              (back into the phone)
                 I'll tell you what, buddy. Take
                 a nice shower and then dive into
                 a percolator! And a good good-
                 night to you!

                                        CUT TO:

72   JENSON - ON THE TELEPHONE   72

                              JENSON
                              (jiggling the receiver)
                 Hello -- Hello.
                              (then his voice turns
                              down into a mumble)
                 Hello -- hello -- hello.

He slowly replaces the receiver, staring down at it.
He turns and walks over to the French doors, puts his
face against them, closes his eyes.

                                        CUT TO:

73   REVERSE ANGLE SHOT   73

    looking from outside on the little balcony toward the
room. Jenson is seen through the glass, his face
pressed up against it. Now he turns, goes over,
flings himself on the bed. His head goes from side
to side in a mute remonstance against the events of
the day and very slowly his eyes get heavy and he
closes them, then his breathing becomes regular and
heavy, and he's in deep sleep. The CAMERA starts
a SLOW DOLLY in until the CAMERA is very tight on him.

                         DISSOLVE TO:

74   OUT OF FOCUS SHOT - JENSON'S FACE   74

                         DISSOLVE TO:

75   CLOSE SHOT - JENSON IN CLARITY   75

    as he wakes up with a start. Sunlight beaming on his
face. He jumps out of bed, then whirls around to look
at the clock. It reads: "8:00 AM". He then looks at
the calendar on the wall which reads "December 7".
He rushes to the French doors and suddenly flings them
open. There is the SOUND of aircraft engines, building
up in a crescendo of noise.

                         CUT TO:

76   FILM CLIP OR R.S.P. IF POSSIBLE   76

    of planes framed in the opening of the French doors.
Mitsubishis and Zeros as they come in from the ocean
and head straight for the CAMERA.

                 JENSON
         I told you, didn't I? Didn't I
         tell you? Why wouldn't anybody
         listen to me? I told you they
         were coming! I told you, I told
         you, I told you --

There's the staccato drum-fire of aircraft machine guns
and we:

                         CUT TO:

77   REVERSE ANGLE - LOOKING FROM THE BALCONY INTO THE ROOM 77

    as the French doors suddenly disintegrate with a crash
of broken glass. Jenson staggers back, smashed by the

                   (CONTINUED)

77   CONTINUED: 77

impact of bullets, clutching his stomach, then slowly
sinking to the ground on his knees, then pitching
forward on his face. The CAMERA MOVES over for a
tableau of his still body, the engine ROAR persisting
in the b.g.

                              CUT ABRUPTLY TO:

78   SHOT PSYCHIATRIST'S COUCH   78

in Gillespie's office. The room is in utter silence
and Gillespie is sitting there alone. There is no
one on the couch. He has his head in one hand, his
fingers on his eyes. He suddenly looks up, blinks,
takes his hand away, looks over toward the empty
couch, frowns for a moment, looks around the room
briefly. He looks puzzled as if trying to grasp something that has eluded him momentarily, but something
that he should know. Then he shakes his head, giving
up. He walks around the room briefly, staring at
things. Then he stops, looking down at his desk.

79   TIGHT CLOSE SHOT   LIGHTER   79

on his desk. He picks it up. Fingers it for a
moment, then puts it down. Then he turns and walks
out of the room.

80   PAN SHOT   GILLESPIE   80

as he goes into the ante room. There's no one out
there. He looks down at his secretary's desk, at
the appointment pad. He stares at it.

81   CLOSE SHOT   RECEPTION PAD   81

There, written in a dainty, feminine hand, and
standing out in bold relief is the line "No
patients today".

82   CLOSE SHOT GILLESPIE   82

as he frowns, rubs his head, continuing to stare
down at the pad. He retraces his steps back into
his office, standing there motionlessly in the
center of the room, looking at the empty couch.

83   MED. CLOSE SHOT   THE COUCH   83

Then we hear Gillespie's filtered voice as he recalls
something he knows he's said just a few hours ago.
                              (CONTINUED)

83 CONTINUED: 83

                              GILLESPIE'S VOICE
                                (filtered)
                    Try this analogy, Mr. Jenson.
                    Supposing I were to go back in
                    time, and I were to be hit, say,
                    by a taxi. Now it figures if I went
                    back in time and were killed I
                    shouldn't be living today.

Gillespie shuts his eyes tightly as if by this overt
act he could force out of his mind a picture containing
a missing link of his consciousness. He takes one more
look around the room, turns, walks back into the anteroom and then out the door.

                                        DISSOLVE TO:

84   EXT. BAR   84

        Shooting through the front door. A sign on the glass
        reads Andy's Place.

                                        CUT TO:

85   INT. BAR   85

        Gillespie is just entering. CAMERA PANS WITH him
        over to a bar. There's a juke box playing and the
        sound of quiet, day drinkers. There's something
        free and warm about the room.

86   CLOSE SHOT - GILLESPIE   86

        We see on his face, a gradual but perceptible relaxing.
        He's obviously responding to the flesh and blood
        realism of what now surrounds him. The bartender
        comes over to him.

                              BARTENDER
                    Sir?

                              GILLESPIE
                    Bourbon on the rocks, please.

        He reaches in his pocket and takes out a cigarette then
        gets his lighter out of his coat pocket. He lights
        the cigarette in an automatic, unreflective motion.
        He's about to put the lighter back when he suddenly
        stops and stares at it for a moment. He smiles a
        secret smile as if at last he's been able to satisfy
        his sense of disquiet and as if he somehow rationally
        explained away his questions inside of himself. Still
        smiling, he puts the lighter back on the counter as
        the bartender brings over his drink.

86   TWO SHOT - BARTENDER AND GILLESPIE   86

                         BARTENDER
                   (putting the drink down
                    in front of him)
              Bourbon on the rocks.

Gillespie takes the glass, holds it up, grins at the
bartender.

                         GILLESPIE
                   Happy dreams, huh?

                         BARTENDER
                   (grins back)
              Whatever you like! Drink hearty!

                                        CUT TO:

87   SHOT THROUGH THE CURVE SURFACE OF THE GALSS   87

      of a group of blown up snapshots pasted on the
      bar, most of them of men in uniform. One in
      particular stands out in relief. The glass comes
      down and the CAMERA CONTINUES to shoot toward the
      picture, this time in clarity.

88   ZOMAR INTO CLOSE SHOT OF SNAPSHOT   88

      of Peter Jenson in a bartender's apron.

89   CLOSE SHOT - GILLESPIE   89

      as he stares wide-eyes at the picture.

90   FLASH SHOT OF PICTURE   90

91   FLASH SHOT - GILLESPIE   91

      continuing to react.

92   MED. CLOSE SHOT - BARTENDER   92

      as he looks from the picture to Gillespie.

                         BARTENDER
                   Problem, Mister?

93   CLOSE SHOT - GILLESPIE   93

His face looks somehow at this moment very wan
and his voice is too obviously matter of fact.

               GILLESPIE
    No, no, no. Nothing wrong.
        (He waggles a finger toward
          the picture)
    The guy in that picture.

The bartender points to one of them.

               GILLESPIE
    No, the one on the bottom. He...
    he looks familiar.

               BARTENDER
      (nods)
    Pete Jenson. Used to tend bar here.

               GILLESPIE
      (repeating the name more
      for himself than as a
      response)
    Jenson?
      (then after a long moment's
      pause, he slowly shakes hi
      head)
    No...I don't recollect the name.
    He looked familiar, that's all.
      (another silence as he stares
      down in his drink and
      averting the bartender's
      glance, talking into his
      glass)
    Where is he now?

94   CLOSE ANGLE SHOT   94

Looking up from the bar top toward the bent head of
Gillespie. He slowly raises his eyes to meet the
bartender's. The bartender is wiping a glass.

               BARTENDER
      (matter of factly)
    He's dead. Got killed at Pearl
    Harbor.

A man at the other end of the bar holds up his hand.

               MAN
    Two more, Huh?

               BARTENDER
    Yes, sir.

95   MED. CLOSE SHOT - BARTENDER   95

He walks out of the frame toward the end of the
bar and the CAMERA REMAINS on the reflection of
Gillespie in the mirror. A SLOW PAN DOWN to his
fingers as he taps them on the top of the bar, one
after another, until it sounds like the rythmic
ticking of a clock. CAMERA SLOWLY PANS UP to a
ANGLE SHOT of the clock over the bar as the ticking
seques into the sound of Gillespie's fingers
tapping.

96   LONG ANGLE SHOT   96

Looking down at Gillespie as he sits at the bar.

> NARRATOR'S VOICE
> (over the ticking)
> It is October 5, 1958, Saturday,
> twelve ten P.M. if anyone is
> remotely interested in the ele-
> ment of time!

                         SLOW FADE TO BLACK:

THE END

TWILIGHT TIME

Given *The Twilight Zone*'s innovative format and deservedly landmark status in television history, one might well assume that the series began with a flash of inspired revelation. This was not the case. The conceptual roots of the show reach far back into Rod Serling's life and professional career. The seeds of *The Twilight Zone* were planted several years before it premiered, and were cultivated by the rigid standards and controlled chaos of early television. "The Time Element," generally considered the unofficial *Twilight Zone* pilot, played a critical role in the show's development and evolution.

Rod Serling sold his first script to the fledgling television medium in 1950. He soon wrote for many of television's live anthology shows and amassed an extensive collection of produced teleplays. It was, however, Serling's Emmy Award-winning breakthrough script "Patterns" for *Kraft Television Theater* in early 1955 that firmly established the writer as a major creative force. His teleplays became synonymous with dramatic quality, and Serling was chosen to launch a new prestige show at CBS: the celebrated live anthology *Playhouse 90*.

Rod Serling's second teleplay for *Playhouse 90*, 1956's "Requiem for a Heavyweight," garnered unprecedented critical and public acclaim and earned him the second of an eventual six Emmy Awards. But as time wore on, live anthology broadcasts began a gradual decline in the wake of shows captured on film. Unlike early dramas, which were broadcast live from coast to coast and then forever lost, a filmed show could be repeated and was quicker and cheaper to produce. *Playhouse 90* and a small group of anthologies continued until the end of the decade, but as they waned, television clearly shifted its focus to the filmed series.

127

Eager to involve their esteemed writer in this trend, CBS approached Serling in 1957 and asked for his ideas on a potential series. He proposed a concept that he had considered for some time: a fantasy-oriented weekly anthology. Serling had always been fond of stories that delved into fantasy and science fiction. In fact, several years prior, he had written a time-travel yarn entitled "The Time Element." It told the tale of a man who is whisked back to the Hawaii of 1941— on December 6th, one day before the attack on Pearl Harbor—and his futile attempts to warn locals of the impending doom.

While Serling was in college and working at WLW in Cincinnati as a contributing writer, this earlier incarnation of "The Time Element" was produced on the station's primitive live television show, *The Storm*. Encouraged now by William Dozier, CBS's vice president of West Coast programming, Serling doubled the length of the half-hour script, added the series title *The Twilight Zone*, and submitted it to CBS. The network purchased the script as a possible future pilot.

By this time Serling had enjoyed abundant success but not without complications. His reputation for tackling controversial themes and complex social and political issues often put him at odds with a television industry ruled by network censors and product sponsors.

The censors would veto any language or topic that could conceivably offend viewers, and Serling's work was permeated with issues that they labeled contentious. Product sponsors, fearful that any controversy would cause a backlash that would rob them of consumers, also wielded enormous power over program content. Counterproductive to any exploration of adult drama, these restraints hampered the work of the writer, and Serling's battles with network interference are legendary.

These incessant assaults on creativity often forced Serling and his fellow writers to compromise quality and grudgingly allow heavy censorship of their work. "Sponsor interference is a stultifying, often destructive and inexcusable by-product of our mass media system," Serling said in a 1963 interview with *Gamma* magazine. "Ideally, a sponsor should have no more interference rights than an advertiser in a magazine. At one time the networks could have demanded and received creative prerogatives. They could have demanded some kind of cleavage between the commercial and the artistic aspects of a program.

But they gave this prerogative away. And after a while, when you're told things like troops can't *ford* a river if Chevy is the sponsor, you just don't give a damn."

This took a heavy toll on writers, and many eventually abandoned television for the creative freedom of the stage and film. Serling chose to stay and fight, utilizing a slightly different tactic than before. He was now hopeful that a series dealing in fantasy would allow him to camouflage, and thereby adequately address, controversial themes and topics.

"The strength of *Twilight Zone*," the writer commented in the *Gamma* interview, "is that through parable, through placing a social problem or controversial theme against a fantasy background you can make a point which, if more blatantly stated in a realistic frame, wouldn't be acceptable. Because of this, from time to time, we've been able to make some pertinent social comments on conformity, on prejudice, on political ideologies, without sponsor interference. It offered a whole new outlet, a new approach."

In 1957, however, the television industry was not yet ready to provide Serling with his otherworldly platform. Science fiction and fantasy, reasoned CBS, was for pulp magazines and Saturday morning fare, not major network commercial television. "The Time Element" was shelved and forgotten.

Bert Granet would be the man to rescue the script in 1958. Granet was the producer of *Westinghouse Desilu Playhouse*, which featured Desi Arnaz and Lucille Ball. The popular couple only appeared in one show out of four, and Granet was on the hunt for quality material to fill the remaining three weeks. He sought out Rod Serling. "He gives the story a reason for being," Granet explained of Serling's talent. "He is literate and he doesn't talk down to audiences."

Granet met with Serling to find out if the writer had anything to contribute to *Desilu Playhouse*. Serling mentioned that "The Time Element" was in limbo at CBS and Granet pursued the matter. "I found out what it was," Granet said, "and bought it for what was a lot of money at that time – ten thousand dollars."

The battle to get "The Time Element" on the air, however, was far from over. McCann-Erickson—the advertising agency for Westinghouse—had script approval, and voiced the same reservations about the fantastic plot that had caused CBS to abandon the teleplay a year earlier.

"The network people and the agency people didn't like unfinished stories, like 'The Time Element,' which left the audience hanging," recalled Granet. "I

TONY ALBARELLA

can't tell you how much they didn't want to do it. They liked their stories neat and wrapped with a bow."

Granet battled for the script and Desi Arnaz stood behind his producer. McCann-Erickson relented, but insisted that conditions be met both in front of and behind the cameras. They required of Bert Granet that he promise never to pursue a similar type of story for the show. And they demanded a change in the script itself.

As the script in this book illustrates, Serling's first draft has Pete Jenson approach the Army about the imminent Japanese attack. His ranting is met, of course, with predictable incredulity and skepticism. Jenson's premonition, however, ultimately proves true, and the Army had done nothing to heed his warning. Westinghouse was involved in a number of government contracts and feared that audience members might draw a parallel between Army incompetence and the Pearl Harbor attack. Unable to risk any negative connotations in the minds of the viewers, McCann-Erickson demanded that the scene be cut or changed.

Serling chose to have Jenson meet instead with members of a Honolulu newspaper. This alteration doesn't influence the outcome of the scene as the newspapermen also ridicule Jenson's seemingly fantastic claim. But the character has to pursue some course of action and this plausible alternative serves that purpose.

Wryly, Serling did manage to work a reference to the Army into his final draft, by having the editor query Jenson about pleading his case to a newspaper instead of to the military. Jenson's reply, that "There isn't enough time to go through a lot of brass, trying to be heard," works on two levels. It demonstrates the character's aversion to military red tape yet also gives voice to the writer's frustration with sponsor interference.

Flexibility, in this case, spared the final production from any real impact due to censorship. Nevertheless, this example illustrates how the whim of sponsor demand could handicap a writer.

Filming commenced with a budget of $135,000. Cast in the lead was William Bendix, an accomplished film actor known for roles both comedic and deadly serious. He was most popular as the bumbling, affable Chester A. Riley in all three mass media incarnations (radio, television and film) of *The Life of Riley*.

Bendix was a smart choice to portray Pete Jenson, a wisecracking New York who is a bit abrasive and confrontational. At first Jenson selfishly trades on his predicament by placing bets on all the completed sporting events he can remember, a plot device that again surfaced in *The Twilight Zone* and in later productions such as the BACK TO THE FUTURE movie trilogy. However, Jenson's basic good nature eclipses his greed when he befriends a doomed young couple and realizes that his information would be put to better use in the saving of lives.

A solid group of actors round out the cast: Jesse White, Martin Balsam, Dwayne Hickman (of *Dobie Gillis* fame) and Carolyn Kearney. The performances are capable yet not outstanding and this serves the story well. It is essential that the audience identify with ordinary and believable characters in a work of imaginative fiction. Serling's writing also fits this mold of gritty realism. Certain scenes, such as an impromptu fistfight with the newspaper editor, ring false and this is not Serling at his absolute finest. However, authentic characters and the writer's choice of a framing technique (flashbacks while telling the story to a psychiatrist) inject necessary realism into the fantastic plot.

Numerous other television shows—*The Time Tunnel, Quantum Leap* and *Early Edition,* for example—would later use an ability to change the past as a series premise. Owing much to "The Time Element" is the 1980 movie THE FINAL COUNTDOWN, in which a modern-day nuclear submarine hits a time warp and is transported to Pearl Harbor on December 6th, 1941. The crew then wrestles with the dilemma of whether to use their firepower to prevent the attack and thereby change the course of history.

It's not surprising that "The Time Element" met so much resistance in the conservative era of the late fifties. Aside from the time-travel plot is an ending that is not only ambiguous but extremely gloomy; for all his efforts, Pete Jenson is killed, as are both members of the young newlywed couple. The death and destruction at Pearl Harbor (and in the war to follow) transpires just as history records. And although a slight residue of Pete's existence still haunts Dr. Gillespie, all seventeen years of Jenson's post-Pearl Harbor life are wiped away.

Serling himself tried to soften the blow, describing the script as a kind of exercise in cosmic déjà vu. "I'm not making any supernatural claims in this story," he said in a CBS press release. "What my central character experiences is just an extension of something that's happened to all of us. For example, who hasn't had that chilling moment of recall in which a new occurrence seems to be something that's happened before?"

To further appease Westinghouse, Desi Arnaz appeared in an epilogue to offer this "explanation" for potentially confused viewers: "We wonder if Pete Jenson did go back in time or if he ever existed. My personal answer is that the doctor has seen Jenson's picture at the bar sometime before and had a dream. Any of you out there have any other answers? Let me know."

"The Time Element" premiered on November 24, 1958. Reaction from critics and the public was instantaneous and enormously positive. The network was bombarded with phone calls, telegrams and more mail from excited viewers than *Desilu Playhouse* had received all year.

"Rod Serling is one of the pioneer television writers who still stays in the medium, even though he is as articulate as video's expatriates about TV's limitations," noted critic Jack Gould in his influential *New York Times* review. "The humor and sincerity of Mr. Serling's dialogue made 'The Time Element' consistently arresting. And Mr. Serling wisely left the individual viewer to work out for himself whether the play's meaning was that even with fresh knowledge of the past no one will heed its lesson, that to be out of step with the crowd is to only invite ridicule.

"Mr. Serling had his troubles in Hollywood over script censorship," continued Gould. "But where other dramatists either capitulate or retire, he manages to achieve a great deal through the subtlety of his approach. What he might do with no shackles could be most exciting."

The executives at CBS were most impressed by this reception. They quickly decided to give Serling another crack at a *Twilight Zone* pilot. The time-travel concept—a staple of science fiction and fantasy literature—had been granted one of its earliest tests in adult, mass-audience network television. It passed with flying colors and earned a place in history.

✖   ✖   ✖

Next Stop...*The Twilight Zone*!
Eager to begin production on a series pilot, CBS handed the reigns to

producer William Self. "I had never worked at a network," explains Self, "and I was hired by Bill Dozier to come to CBS and be in the Development Department. He assigned four projects to me. One was *The Twilight Zone* and with my good fortune that was the first one I produced.

"I had never met Rod Serling. Bill Dozier set up a meeting and Rod came into my office. He was very pleasant and we had a nice chat. He expressed enthusiasm for my being on the show and I expressed my admiration for his work and we were just having a great time. And he left a script with me, which was called 'The Happy Place.'"

Serling's script told of a futuristic dystopia in which people are whisked away to "The Happy Place" upon reaching the age of sixty. There they discover how the societal problems of old age and overpopulation are solved: senior citizens are exterminated in government-run death camps.

"I read it," says Self, "and I hated it. I didn't know what to do, because Dozier had told me that they were very high on the script at CBS, they were very high on Rod Serling and they thought this was a terrific project. I was a little naïve and I didn't tell Dozier my reaction, which I probably should have. Rod came back to learn my reaction and I said, 'Rod, I hate it, and I'll tell you why. It's well-written as usual and it would make a great show somewhere along the line, but we're making a pilot that will be shown to advertisers and I don't think you can sell a series when the opening episode is about the euthanasia of old people.'"

Serling vehemently disagreed, and in light of these early creative differences, wondered if Bill Self was the right man for the job. "I thought I was off the show," Self admits. "I said, 'Well, I'm sorry, because I'm confident that the series is a good idea, I just think that this pilot would be a bad sales tool for the show.'"

Rather than demand a producer who would acquiesce to his demands, Serling contemplated the discussion and soon realized the wisdom in Self's opinion. "Only a few days later," the producer continues, "Rod showed up unannounced at my office and gave me a different script called 'Where is Everybody?' He just went home and wrote it. Rod could do that, he dictated and he could write a script in two or three days. In general, when you got a Rod Serling script you could just shoot it. There may be suggestions made but he was very prolific and he was very solid. He said, 'I agree with you' and we were off and running. And of course the show was a very big success."

The Twilight Zone

WHERE IS EVERYBODY?

Airdate: 10-2-1959

Manuscript Date: N/A

First draft

Script One

Episode One

THE TWILIGHT ZONE

Script One

"WHERE IS EVERYBODY"

by

ROD SERLING

FIRST DRAFT

Transferring
Pl. to oth., though rails

FADE IN:

1. EXT. SKY NIGHT   1.

    Shot of the sky...the various nebulae, and planet bodies
    stand out in sharp sparkling relief. As the CAMERA begins
    a SLOW PAN across the Heavens:

                        NARRATOR'S VOICE (O.S.)
                    There is a sixth dimension beyond
                    that which is known to man. It is
                    a dimension as vast as space, and as
                    timeless as infinity. It is the
                    middle ground between light and
                    shadow - between man's grasp and
                    his reach; between science and
                    superstition; between the pit of
                    his fears and the sunlight of his
                    knowledge. This is the dimension
                    of imagination. It is an area that
                    might be called the Twilight Zone.

    The CAMERA has begun to PAN DOWN until it passes the horizon
    and is flush on the OPENING SHOT (EACH WEEK THE OPENING
    SHOT OF THE PLAY.)   _director T_

    We are now looking down the small, two lane asphalt highway.
    It is dawn and the road is deserted save for a small diner
    on the left hand side. A broken neon light flashes on and
    off over the front door and from inside the sound of a
    rock-n-roll record that lends a strange, raucous dissonance
    to the silence of the early morning. Then the CAMERA SWEEPS
    right for a

2. LONG SHOT MIKE FERRIS   2.

    Who suddenly appears walking down the road. His step is
    tentative, unsure. He's a tall man in his thirties. His
    dress is nondescript. The only identifiable garment being
    army pants. There's an indecisiveness - a puzzlement, in
    his features as he comes closer to the CAMERA, sees the
    diner, stops, rubs his knuckles over the side of his face
    and feels his beard stubble. Then he pats in his pocket,
    unsure, reaches in and pulls out a couple of dollar bills.
    For some reason this buoys him up. He looks a little more
    resolved now as he walks up the steps and into the diner.

3. INT. DINER   3.

    It is a small, nondescript, typical eatery with a row of
    small booths alongside the outside window, a counter, and
    a kitchen beyond. The room is empty.

4. PAN SHOT MIKE   4.

    As he walks over to a stool and sits down at the counter,
    reaches over, takes a menu, studies it for a moment, then
    turns and looks over toward the juke box.

3. INT. DINER   3.

    It is a small, nondescript, typical eatery with a row of
    small booths alongside the outside window, a counter, and
    a kitchen beyond. The room is empty.

4. PAN SHOT MIKE   4.

    As he walks over to a stool and sits down at the counter,
    reaches over, takes a menu, studies it for a moment, then
    turns and looks over toward the juke box.

5. MED. CLOSE SHOT JUKE BOX   5.

    Garish, multi-colored, still blaring out the music.

6. MED. SHOT ROOM   6.

    He turns on his stool to look toward the opening to the
    kitchen.

7. CLOSE SHOT AN OVEN INSIDE KITCHEN   7.

    Through the glass we can see a row of six or seven pies
    baking and browned almost fully.

8. MED. SHOT ROOM   8.

    Mike calls out.

                    MIKE
            Can you lower this thing out
            here? It's awful loud.

    There's no answer. He turns and again looks at the juke
    box. He rises, gets off his stool, goes over to the
    juke box, looks all around it, pushes it away from the
    wall a few inches, reaches back, fiddles with a knob.
    The music goes much lower. Then satisfied he pushes the
    machine against the wall, goes back over to the counter.

                    MIKE
            Kind of early for that kind of
            music, isn't it?

    There's still silence.

                    MIKE
            I noticed the sign Oakwood out
            there. Where is Oakwood?

                                        CONTINUED

8.   CONTINUED   8.

Again silence. Mike puts the menu down, peers through
the little opening into the kitchen.

                    MIKE
          Hey, I asked you a question in
          there. Where's Oakwood?

Mike gets off the stool, goes around the counter, and
through a swinging door that leads into the kitchen.

9.   INT. KITCHEN   9.

A small room with a couple of stoves, et cetera. He
goes over to the stove and turns down the oven and looks
around the room again. He goes over to a back door,
tries it and it swings open. He steps back as it creaks
to a full opening and reveals the outdoors to the back.

                    MIKE
                 (calls out)
          Hey? You got a customer out
          front! Hey! Customer here.

Still no answer. Mike turns, retraces his steps back
to the lunch counter.

10.   MED. SHOT ROOM   10.

Mike still shows no real emotion beyond a puzzlement.
There's no real concern and no fright as yet. He again
picks up the menu and studies it and he talks out loud
now.

                    MIKE
          I think ham and eggs. Eggs up
          and soft. Hash browns. Coffee.
          Black.
                 (looks up, calls out again)
          Customer! Got a customer out
          front.
                 (he rises again from the
                  stool - sticks his head
                  in the kitchen)
          Ham and eggs. Hash browns.
          Coffee black.

He stands there by the open swinging door staring into
the empty kitchen. His eyes dart around now and for
the first time we see something beyond puzzlement on
his features. The hint....the suggestion of concern.
He feels in his shirt pocket, takes out a crumpled pack
of cigarettes,

                                              CONTINUED

12. CONTINUED   12.

He goes back to the lunch counter. Now he scratches his
head, sits down on the stool for a long moment. Suddenly
the music stops on the juke box. The sudden cessation of
noise brings with it a silence even more obvious. Mike
turns and stares at the juke box then looks up at the
clock which reads:

13. CLOSE- SHOT CLOCK   13.

It reads a quarter to six

14. MED CLOSE SHOT MIKE   14.

His fingers tap a nervous staccato on the counter top,
the silence now is beginning to be oppressive and nerve
wracking. Suddenly as if an afterthought he reaches into
his pocket and pulls out the money, looks at it in his
hand, then he reaches in all his other pockets to reveal
nothing. He rubs at his face again. Mike speaks aloud
but obviously to no one in an attempt to make noise or
sound or just to end the stillness by some means.

                    MIKE
          Cash customer here. Hungry cash
          customer.
               (he rubs his face again)
          I got two dollars and eighty five
          cents.
               (then his voice seems to
               crack a little and is much
               lower)
          I got two dollars and eighty
          five cents.

He looks at the clock again, and into the opening to the
kitchen and the swinging doors, then at the silent juke
box, and back at the money in his hand.

                    MIKE
          I don't know who I am or where I
          am, but I got two dollars and
          eighty five cents and I'm hungry.

He gets up off the stool and suddenly slams both palms
down hard on the counter, making all the salt shakers and
catsup bottles quiver and rattle.

                    MIKE
               (shouts)
          I got two dollars and eighty five
          cents and I'm hungry!

He stops dead now, listening to the silence that enfolds and
surrounds him. Then he looks around, bites his lip, takes
a drag on his cigarette, then butts it out, rises, goes to
the front door and stares out.

15. EXT. LUNCH ROOM   (still picture?) 15.

The long road that leads away from the lunch counter
without a sign of traffic, people, or anything. He
whirls around to look back into the lunch room.

                    MIKE
               (aloud)
          I'm gonna wake up in a minute.
          I know I'm gonna wake up. I
          wish...I wish there'd be a
          noise or something to wake me
          up.
               (then his voice rises)
          I wish there'd be a noise.
               (then he shouts)
          Somebody make a noise!   (Echo?)

Then he stops dead and listens to the silence. Now he
goes back into the lunch counter.

16. INT. LUNCH ROOM   16.

He sits down, buries his face in his hands, rubbing his
eyes, massaging his temples as if trying to force out
with his fingers some connective link...some reassurance
of existence......some knowledge. Over this tableau
of a frightened, tired, desperate man the title "WHERE
IS EVERYBODY" is superimposed, followed by the credits.
Clear the credits.

                                        DISSOLVE TO:

17. EXT. TOWN STREET   17.

Still early morning.

18. LONG SHOT MIKE FERRIS   18.

As he walks down the sidewalk looking from one side of
the street to the other.

19. TRACK SHOT   19.

Past stores as Mike goes by them. Drugstore, grocery,
soda bar. Most of the doors are open and there are
lights on inside, but there are no people. There's an
odd, indefinable feeling that permeates the scene, a
sense of activity and yet coming with no players, and
no people, as if it was a place full of motion and
movement suddenly stripped of the people performing it.

20. LONG SHOT DOWN THE STREET   (*bell* picture?)   20.

From Mike's P.O.V. It is devoid of any kind of movement
whatsoever. It is absolutely quiet.

21. CLOSE SHOT MIKE   21.

As he stops and looks around. He is suddenly startled
by the sound of chimes. He whirls around and looks up.

22. LONG SHOT CHURCH STEEPLE BELL   22.

As it rings.   (do we _see_ the bell swinging??)

23. CLOSE SHOT MIKE   23.

As he begins to perspire. He wipes at his face with his
shirt then looks around again. Suddenly his eyes go
wide.

24. LONG SHOT ACROSS THE STREET   24.

    A little clothing store. A human figure can be seen
    behind the counter through the front window.

25. LONG ANGLE SHOT   25.

    Looking down, as Mike races across the road to the store.
    It is half ajar and he wrenches it open, and thunders
    inside into the room.

26. INT. STORE   26.

    As Mike slams the door behind him and leans against it.
    Men's and women's clothing are on racks on either side.
    The figure, now unseen, is behind the counter. We are
    on Mike's face as the words pour out.

                        MIKE
          Oh, thank God. Miss, you got
          to help me. I don't want you
          to think I'm nuts or anything
          because I'm not. Really. I
          guess I'm just...sick or
          something. That must be it.
          I'm...I'm sick. Because I don't
          know who I am or where I am and
          I haven't seen anybody. I
          looked all around and I didn't
          see anybody around. I...I
          guess it's just early or
          something -
                (he closes his eyes
                and shakes his head)
          Please, I'm sorry. I'm not
          dangerous - I won't hurt you, I
          promise you. I'm just...I'm
          scared. I'm really very scared.
          You know I woke up this morning -
                (then he stops, closes
                his eyes again)
          I didn't exactly wake up. I
          just sort of found myself on the
          road walking.
                (then suddenly)
          Amnesia! That's what they call
          it, isn't it? Amnesia? Well,
          that must be what I got. I
          just don't remember a thing...
          I can't find anybody to ask.
          You're the first person --

    His voice continues to run on as the CAMERA TAKES A SLOW
    PAN over to the figure behind the counter. It's back
    remains to the camera. We can see now that it is a female
    figure. Mike takes a step across the room.

                                        CONTINUED

26. CONTINUED   26.

                           MIKE
              Please, Miss, I don't want to
              scare you, honest. I was just
              wondering if maybe you could
              just tell me where I am. Get
              a doctor or something. I think
              that's probably what I need -
              a doctor. You see I went to
              this lunch counter and I tried
              to get breakfast and it was the
              craziest thing - water running,
              music on, nobody there. I
              came into town. There isn't a
              soul around except you. You're
              the first person -

He stops abruptly.

27.   CLOSE SHOT BACK OF THE FEMALE HEAD   27.

28.   FLASH CLOSE SHOT MIKE'S EYES   28.

      As they suddenly go wide, dilating.

29.   FLASH SHOT FEMALE FIGURE'S SHOULDERS   29.

      And then a SLOW PAN DOWN until we stop at the elbows. There
      are no arms extending beyond. Mike suddenly reaches over,
      grabs at the hair of the figure, pulls it around to stare
      into the wooden face of a mannequin. With a sob, almost
      of horror he lets loose and the mannequin tumbles down.

30.   CLOSE SHOT FLOOR   30.

      There are several arms and legs of mannequins lying around,
      all jumbled together, looking up with glassy, manufactured
      eyes.

31.   MED. SHOT ROOM   31.

      Mike whirls around again to stare up and down at the little
      store. There are men's and women's clothes but the store
      is absolutely empty. Again his eyes dart around the room
      and suddenly he stops short again seeing something on the
      wall.

32.   CLOSE SHOT TELEPHONE   32.

33.   MED. SHOT ROOM   33.

      Mike stumbles across the room over to the telephone,
      upsetting a counter in the middle of the floor which he
      pushes aside. He goes over to the phone, takes the phone
      off the hook without even waiting for a dial tone or operator
      or anything and starts to spew into it.

                                             CONTINUED

33. CONTINUED   33.

floor which he pushes aside. He goes over to the phone,
takes the phone off the hook without even waiting for a
dial tone or operator or anything and starts to spew
into it.

                    MIKE
          Hello. Listen. I don't know
          who I am. I'm a...I'm a sick
          man or something and I need
          help. Operator could you get
          a doctor here or something?
          Operator. Operator. What in
          the hell's the matter here?
          Don't you even have an operator?

He pounds on the phone and then just sort of
indiscriminately dials. He's about to throw down the
phone in disgust when suddenly at the other end of the
line he hears a dial tone ringing. Timorous, almost
frightened to listen, he picks up the phone and at this
moment hears a voice filtered at the other end.

                    VOICE
                 (filtered)
          This is the special operator.
          The number you have reached is
          not a working number. Please
          make sure you have the right
          number and are dialing it
          correctly.

                    MIKE
                 (starts to scream into
                  the phone)
          Operator, listen to me. Listen,
          operator --

Then she repeats all she's just said as Mike listens to
her, excited beyond words that he has found someone
alive. When she finished repeating the message he
grabs the phone and is about to speak when suddenly he
hears the operator's voice again)

                    OPERATOR'S VOICE
          This is a recording.

Again a fear cluthces him.

                    MIKE
          A recording?
                 (he pounds on the receiver
                  hook and shouts)
          Operator! Look, all I want to
          know is where I am. I just
          want to know the name of this
          place -

                                        CONTINUED

33. CONTINUED   33.

    Then he slowly lets loose of the receiver and it hangs
down from the phone box. Mike's hand touches and then
grasps a telephone book, a narrow thin one that he grabs
and looks at hungrily.

34. CLOSE SHOT TELEPHONE COVER   34.

    On it is written "Oakwood"

35. MED. SHOT MIKE   35.

    He rips open the cover, looks down at the first page.

>   MIKE
> "A". Abel. Adams. Ackerman.
> Allenby. Arnold. All these
> people - where are you all?
>   (he screams)
> Where are you all?
>   (then he rips the page
>   open)
> Baker. Beldon. Biltmore.
> Botsford. All these people,
> all these names. Well, where
> are you? Where are all the
> people in the phone book? Why
> aren't you on the street? Why
> aren't you in the stores?

CONTINUED

(Still Picture ?)

36. EXT. STREET   36.

It is still absolutely empty and tomblike.

37. CLOSE SHOT MIKE   37.

As once again he stares at something that catches his
eye. CAMERA SWEEPS ACROSS the street to a

38. SHOT RADIO REPAIR STORE   38.

A loudspeaker has been placed over the door and suddenly
Mike is aware of music playing through it.

39. LONG ANGLE SHOT THE STREET   39.

As Mike runs across the street toward the radio store.
He slams up against the front door, pulls it open, stares
inside.

40. MED. LONG SHOT THE RADIO STORE   *natural interior*   40.

Absolutely empty. Mike backs out of the store then stares
up at the loudspeaker from which the music emanates. He
keeps shaking his head back and forth. He starts to turn
away and then stops, staring at a neon sign that is inside
the store window. It's a clock and over it the call letters
"WGBN 1060 on the dial". And underneath the clock is the
lettering, "Voice of the Midwest. Offices and studios at
16 Main Street."

41. SHOT THROUGH GLASS   41.

Looking out at Mike as he presses his face against the glass
staring at it.

42. MED. SHOT MIKE   42.

He turns away from the window, stares up at a street sign
which reads "Main Street," looks at the number on the door
front. It reads "24".

43. LONG ANGLE SHOT   *chance for unusual camera treatment ?*   43.

Looking across at Mike as he starts to walk down the
street. PAN SHOT as over his shoulder we see the numbers
on the various door fronts as they read "22", "20", "18", "16"
and finally

Subliminal effects experiment ?

44. LOW ANGLE SHOT   44.

Looking up from the sidewalk at the front of a small
building with the letters "WGBN" over the front door.
He hurriedly enters the building.

45. INT. BUILDING   *Perhaps natural exteriors*   45.

46. LONG ANGLE SHOT   46.

Looking down a flight of stairs. Mike starts to race up
them. He arrives at the top of the landing, opens the
door and is in a small reception room.

47. INT. RECEPTION ROOM   47.

Beyond the receptionist's desk you can see the glass
enclosed, small broadcasting studio and beyond that a
control room.

                         MIKE
                    (shouts)
               Hello! Who's here? I heard
               the music! I heard your
               broadcast!

He runs past the reception desk and on into the studio.

48. INT. STUDIO   48.

It's completely empty save for a small table and a couple
of microphones not in use. He whirls around and almost
bumps head first into the small glass that separates the
room from the control room. He looks through the glass.

49. MED. CLOSE SHOT   TURNTABLE   49.

As seen from Mike's P.O.V. It continues to slowly revolve
at 33 1/3 RPMS playing music on a long playing record.
There's no one to be seen.

50. SHOT   MIKE   50.

Mike illogically pounds his fist on the glass.

                         MIKE
               Who's playing the music? Who
               put the record on? Who's around
               here?

He turns, seems to grope his way across the room, stumbling
against the door. Then he goes on out into the reception
office.

51. INT. RECEPTION ROOM   *set*   51.

Behind it he sees a large window overlooking the town. He
goes over to it, tries to open the window and is unable to.
He grabs a heavy book off the receptionist's desk and
suddenly flings it through the window.

                              CUT ABRUPTLY TO:

52. OUTSIDE LOOKING IN   52.

     Toward the jagged hole of the window at Mike Ferris who
     stands there framed. He looks out at the absolute silence
     and emptiness of what surrounds him.

                         MIKE
                    (screams)
               Where is everybody?   WHERE IS
               EVERYBODY!?

     WE TAKE A SLOW FADE TO BLACK on the anguished features of
     the man.

     END ACT ONE

ACT TWO

FADE ON:

(optical effect?)
for heat shimmer?

53. FILM CLIP A HOT AND HIGH AFTERNOON SUN   53.

Shimmering in a sea of heatwaves. The CAMERA SWEEPS DOWN
until it is level with the street and a

opt. effect off

54. LONG SHOT MIKE FERRIS   54.

As he sits on a curb, staring dully and numbly across at
nothing. The church steeple clock sounds "two." He looks
up, listens to it, but is no longer shocked by it. He just
lets the sound of the chimes play along the edges of his
consciousness without really being aware of them. Now he
rises and walks slowly, methodically, without much apparent
purpose across the street. He looks up to see a sign
reading "Pool Hall." He enters.

55. INT. POOL HALL *natural interiors? or set*   55.

The place is entirely lit. There is a cigar counter in
front, a couple of pool tables at the far end of the room.
He reaches into a box of cigars behind the counter, takes
out a couple of them, unwraps one, sticks it in his mouth,
lights it, takes a couple of draws, butts it out, reaches
in another box, takes one of these, looks at the box.

                    MIKE
          Two for a dollar. Now that's
          more like it. I always liked
          an expensive cigar.
               (then he turns with a half-
               smile, says to nobody)
          How about you guys - any of you
          want a cigar?

56. SERIES OF SHOTS OF EMPTY POOL TABLES   56.

And empty clothes racks, empty seats along the wall.

57. MED CLOSE SHOT MIKE   57.

As he laughs a low, mirthless, chuckle. He sticks the
cigar in his mouth, lights it. Then he goes over to one
of the tables, takes out a cue, chalks it, sends a few
balls on the table, then proceeds to go around the table
shooting.

58. CLOSE SHOT BALLS   58.

Hitting one another, going into the pocket or bouncing off
the sides. Each time one ball hits another the sound seems
to magnify until pretty soon the effect is that of thunder
bowling balls, that keeps rising in a crescendo of sound
until -

58.. CLOSE SHOT   BALLS   58.

    Hitting one another, going into the pocket or bouncing
    off the sides. Each time one ball hits another the
    sound seems to magnify until pretty soon the effect is
    that of thunder bowling balls, that keeps rising in a
    crescendo of sound until -

59. MED. SHOT MIKE   59.

    He suddenly throws down the stick. closes his eyes and
    slams his fist against his ears until the noise suddenly
    dies out and there's an absolute silence. He begins to
    breathe irregularly and deeply, wetting his lips, opening
    and closing his eyes, wiping the perspiration away from
    his forehead. All of a sudden he hears another sound
    like the trickling of water. It grows a little louder.
    Now he knows he hears it and he almost lurches in the
    direction of the sound toward a door at the back of the
    room. He grabs at the doorknob and throws it open.

59X1.CLOSE SHOT A SINK   59X1.

    With water running in it. A shaving brush still lathered,
    a razor alongside. CAMERA PANS RIGHT for

59X2.SHOT TOWEL RACK   59X2

    A crumpled towel hangs there.

59X3. MED. SHOT MIKE   59X3

    As he picks up the towel and feels of its dampness and
    shakes his head, perplexed. Then he turns, walks through
    the store and back out into the street.

60. MED. SHOT STREET   (Heat effect ?)   60.

    Mike pauses to blink against the hot, glimmering orb of
    sun. He wets his lips, wipes the back of his hand against
    his mouth and looks down the street again on the same
    side.
                                        (still ...)
61. LONG SHOT SIGN "DRUGSTORE"   61.

62. TRACK SHOT MIKE   62.

    As he walks toward the drugstore. He enters.

63.   INT. DRUGSTORE   *set*   3.

It is light and cheerful inside. On the left hand side
is the soda bar with a big mirror behind it full of
stickers advertising various concoctions, soft drinks,
ice cream, sandwiches. He gets up on a stool.

                    MIKE
          I'll take a chocolate soda with
          chocolate ice cream.

He starts to laugh, but the laugh is checked almost
immediately as he sees his reflection in the mirror
behind the counter. His fingers run exploringly across
his face, taking in the beard stubble, the hollowness
beneath the eyes, the strange, haunted frightened look
that is obvious there. He looks at himself again for a
long moment.

                    MIKE
          You'll forgive me old pal, but
          I don't recollect the name.
          The face seems vaguely familiar...
          but it's the name that escapes me.
                    (a pause)

                                        CONTINUED

63. CONTINUED   63.

He rises now and goes behind the counter. He starts to
fix himself a chocolate soda, experimenting with some of
the cupboards until he finds the right ingredients, the
ice cream, the milk, et cetera. Then he mixes himself a
soda, tall, frosty, delicious. He starts to sip it with
a straw as he walks around the drug store. He stops by a
poster of a high school football schedule.

64. CLOSE SHOT CARDBOARD SIGN   64.

It reads, "Oakwood High School, 1958 Schedule," then a
list of teams and dates to be played.

65. MED CLOSE SHOT MIKE   65.

As he takes it in one hand and reads it as he sips the
soda. But the normality of it suddenly points out the
incongruity of what he's living through. He puts the
poster back on the counter, shaking his head. He turns,
stares across at a big magazine rack near the front window
of the store. He crosses over to it, stares down at some
of the magazines, then he kneels down, interested and
begins to trace the dates on each one of the magazines.
The majority of them say October 1958 and his mouth forms
that phrase, October 1958. Then he bites his lips, shakes
his head again, rises, looks down at the group of comic
books, each with a lurid title having to do with horror
themes, spook themes, et cetera. Then suddenly he stops
and looks down at one, the cover of which is peeping out
from behind the others and the title is visible. He
reaches down and pulls it out just a few inches farther
so that he can read the entire title.

66. TIGHT CLOSE SHOT COVER   66.

It reads, "The Last Man on Earth."

67. MED SHOT MIKE   67.

He picks it up and stares at the cover, then flings it
down on the floor. He turns rapidly away and heads back
to the counter where he puts the soda down. He is suddenly
gripped by another spasm of such utter loneliness that it
forces him out onto the street.

68. EXT STREET   68.

CAMERA FOLLOWS him out of the store. As he gets out on
the street he suddenly shouts, shrilly, illogically.

                    MIKE
                 (shouting)
        Hey! Hey, anybody! Anybody
        hear me? Anybody hear me?

                                        CONTINUED

67. MED SHOT MIKE   67.

He picks it up and stares at the cover, then flings it
down on the floor. He turns rapidly away and heads
back to the counter where he puts the soda down. He is
suddenly gripped by another spasm of such utter
loneliness that it forces him out onto the street.

68. EXT. STREET   68.

CAMERA FOLLOWS him out of the store. As he gets out
on the street he suddenly shouts, shrilly, illogically.

                         MIKE
                      (shouting)
            Hey! Hey, anybody! Anybody hear
            me? Anybody hear me?

He almost lurches to the other side of the street where
he buries his face against the window of a building.
When his head goes back he sees the letters U.S. Post
Office and he starts to laugh again.

                         MIKE
            Any mail for me? Anybody write
            me a letter? I don't know what
            my name is but maybe you can tell
            me in there, huh? Will you tell
            me what my name is?

He pounds his fist against the glass and then is
suddenly wracked by sobs as he gives in to loneliness,
to the unknown, to the pulsating, gnawing fear that
envelopes him. Then he turns away from the window,
struggling for composure.

69. CLOSE SHOT MIKE   69.

As his eyes go wide again. CAMERA SWEEPS WIDE until
it stops on --

70. MED LONG SHOT THEATRE MARQUEE   70.

With the sign "Twelve Cartoons for the Kiddies. 3PM
this afternoon."

71. TRACK SHOT MIKE   71.

He walks across the street, stops by the ticket window,
and then almost dreamlike speaks.

                         MIKE
                I'd like one tick-

                         CONTINUED

71.   CONTINUED   71.

    Then he stops, shakes his head, closes his eyes, realizing
how ludicrous this is. He is about to go in when he
suddenly stops and stares through the grill just under
the peephole in the ticket taker's window.

71X1 TIGHT CLOSE SHOT ASHTRAY   71X1

    Inside the booth. A cigarette is burning in it with
lipstick stain on the end. It's about three quarters
length.

71X2 MED SHOT MIKE   71X2

    Mike slowly shakes his head, backs away from it and
heads toward the lobby.

73. CONTINUED   73.

A long beam of white light shines from the projection
booth and suddenly on the screen appears a big introductory
title "Cartoon Parade" with appropriate march music. Mike
leaps to his feet, looks from the projection booth down to
the screen. He suddenly starts to run down the aisle,
shouting.

                    MIKE
          Hey! Hey, somebody up there?

He stops in front of the projectionist's light so that we
get the almost nightmarish picture of the cartoons partially
showing on his face and body as he screams.

                    MIKE
          Hey, somebody up there? Who's
          running the pictures? Can you
          see me? Can you see me up there?
          Hey!

Then he races back up the aisle, arriving at the rear of
the theatre. He looks wildly around, then he sees a door
with a glass window, steps visible on the other side.

74. LONG ANGLE SHOT STAIRS   74.

As he races up them.

75. INT. PROJECTION BOOTH   75.

As he bursts inside. The picture is running from one of
the two projectors, but the room is absolutely empty.
Mike races over to the machine, bends down and peers at
it as the film goes through and you hear the sound of the
cartoon music and voices. This is too much for him. He
throws himself against the wall, peering out of the small,
circular hole that the picture shoots through.

76. LONG ANGLE SHOT THROUGH THE HOLE   76.

Of the vast, empty theatre.

77. INT PROJECTION BOOTH   77.

He turns away, goes out the door, stumbling down the steps.

78. ANGLE SHOT DOWN STAIRS   78.

He continues down the steps and out into the lobby again.

79. INT LOBBY   79.

He stops for a moment and looks across the lobby.

80.   MED LONG SHOT POPCORN MACHINE   80.

That is at this moment making popcorn.

81.   CLOSE SHOT MIKE   *at lens*   81.

As he closes his eyes, shakes his head. Then he opens
them, his eyes go wide. He starts to run toward the
CAMERA, coming up very close and almost at the point of
impact we

                                   CUT AWAY TO

82.   TIGHT TWO SHOT   82.

Of Mike and a mirror as he smashes his face and hands
against it and then recoils from the reflection, backs
off a few feet, and then looks at the mirror on the
opposite side of the room. The combination throws off
reflections almost to infinity. He looks from left to
right staring at the hundreds of Mike Ferrises who ape
him in his every movement. Then he stops and looks across
at the refreshment stand where the popcorn continues to
pop in the big container. This, too, is more than he can
stand. His face screws up like a small child about to
cry, and then he shouts.

                      MIKE
          Oh my God. Oh my dear God!

He stumbles through the lobby and out into the street.

83.   EXT STREET   83.

He stumbles down the street, tears rolling down his face,
not crying loudly now, but just the slow, deep-rooted
sobs that come out intermittently. He stops and sits down
on the curb again, burying his face in his hands, his
shoulders shaking convulsively. Then he looks up with
a tear-stained face to once again find himself looking
through the drug store window. The magazine that he's
been reading lies on the floor, face up.

84.   HIGH ANGLE SHOT   *(Optical)*   84.

Looking down through the window, distorting the cover of
the magazine in such a manner as to make the lettering
appear big and irregular. Once again the title slaps
at him across the face. "The Last Man on Earth." He
rises slowly, backing away from the window, shaking his
head. He turns and races across the street when suddenly
he stops abruptly as the light on the corner changes to red
and he instinctively comes to a halt.

                             CONTINUED

83. CONTINUED   83.

He stops and sits down on the curb again, burying his face
in his hands, his shoulders shaking convulsively. Then he
looks up with a tear-stained face to once again find
himself looking through the drug store window. The
magazine that he'd been reading lies on the floor, face up.

84. HIGH ANGLE SHOT   84.

Looking down through the window, distorting the cover of
the magazine in such a manner as to make the lettering
appear big and irregular. Once again the title stars at
him across the face. "The Last Man on Earth." He rises
slowly, backing away from the window, shaking his head.
He turns and races across the street when suddenly he stops
abruptly as the light on the corner changes to red and
he instinctively comes to a halt. And then he stops dead
realizing once again the ludicrousness of it and begins to
laugh, now the laughter is convulsive, wild and all the way
across the street he continues it until he reaches a
building next to the Post Office. He looks up to stare at
the sign over the front door.

84X1 CLOSE SHOT SIGN   84X1

"City Bank"

84X2 MED SHOT MIKE   84X1

Again he begins to laugh as he enters the bank.

84X3 INT. BANK   (Material Shots)   84X3

TRACK SHOT Mike as he walks past all the teller's cages.
He stops at the end of the line, presses his face against
the bars.

84X4 CLOSE SHOT ROW AFTER ROW OF STACKED BILLS   84X4

84X5 MED SHOT MIKE   84X5

                         MIKE
          I'd like to borrow about eight
          hundred thousand dollars. How
          about it?
               (then he nods and grins)
          Thanks. I think that's generous
          of you. I think that's really
          generous.

He pulls the bars up, reaches in and takes two packages of
money. Then he starts to retrace his steps toward the
front door. He's about to leave when he looks toward the
first teller's window.

84X6 MED SHOT ROWS OF COINS ON TOP OF THE COUNTER   84X6

84X7 MED SHOT MIKE   84X7

He takes out part of the bills that he's crammed into
his shirt pocket, throws them away.

                    MIKE
          Gotta make room for some silver.

He goes behind the teller's window and starts to cram rolls
of coins in his pockets and then with coins and money
trailing from him he heads back out into the street.

84X8 EXT. STREET   84X8

He sits down on the curb again, pulls out a fistful of
bills, stares at them, then he laughs again.

                    MIKE
          This is something I've always wanted
          to do. Always wanted to do!

He takes out a match and lights one of the bills. Then
he takes the cigar, half smoked, out of his pocket,
lights it with the bill, then holds out the burning paper
and lets it flutter to the ground. He looks once again up
and down the street, and then down at the burning paper.

                    MIKE
          Big deal. So what? Big deal.

He lets his head hang a moment and then looks at the sign
in front of the Post Office next door.

85. CLOSE SHOT SIGN   85.

Which reads, "Join The Air Force."

86. MED CLOSE SHOT MIKE   86.

He looks down at it for a long moment.

                    MIKE
          Air Force. Air Force.
             (then he whirls around,
              looks up toward the sky)
          Air Force. I'm Air Force.
             (he looks down at his
              trousers, feels them,
              grabs at them)
          Air Force. I'm in the Air Force.

                                        CONTINUED

86. CONTINUED   86.

                         MIKE (CONT'D)
                (and then suddenly shouting)
                Hey, everybody -- I'm in the
                Air Force. I remember that much.
                I'm in the Air Force. Does
                anybody hear me? I'm in the
                Air Force.
                     (and then once again he
                     rubs his eyes, runs a hand
                     wildly across his face)

                                        CONTINUED

86. CONTINUED   86.

                          MIKE (CONT'D)
            What does that mean? Was there
            a bomb or something? Is that
            what happened? That must have
            been it, a bomb. But if there
            was a bomb -
                   (He looks up and down
                    the empty street)
            It would have destroyed everything
            and nothing is destroyed.

Then he starts to take a slow, shuffling walk down
the middle of the street.

87. TRACK SHOT   87.

As he goes by all the stores that we've been introduced
to. As he goes by each one a sound emanates from them
but a sound way out of proportion to what it actually
should be. When he passes the pool hall we hear the mammoth
bowling alley sound echoing from it. From in front of
the picture theatre is a cacaphony of music and laughter.
The drug store there is a fizzling, bubbling sound of
drinks. The record store, the dissonant, blaring sound
of music, as each noise joins in it becomes jumbled and
part of a big morass of noise. Gradually the very
dimension of it so frightens and shocks Mike he begins
to back away from each store as he passes it as if being
assaulted on all sides. He stumbles against a street
post, whirls around frightened, stares at it, and then
suddenly, almost supplicatingly, throws his arms around
it, buries his face against it and he starts to sob.

                          MIKE
            Please, somebody. Please, somebody
            help me, please. Please, somebody,
            anybody. Please....

And then he looks down. His hands have touched a button.
He looks down at it.

88. TIGHT CLOSE SHOT   A BUTTON   88.

With a sign over it "Push to turn green."

89. MED. SHOT   MIKE   89.

As he looks away toward the light.

90. CLOSE SHOT - THE LIGHT   90.

91. MED. SHOT   91.

And then suddenly Mike slams the palm of his hand
against the button and then punches it over and over
again.

91. CONTINUED   91.

                          MIKE
               Somebody help me. Help me.
               Help me.

92. CLOSE SHOT THE LIGHT   92.

     As it flashes from red to green. from green to red,
     from red to green, over and over again.

93. CLOSE SHOT MIKE'S HAND   93.

     As he keeps pushing the button. His voice, sobbing,
     screeching, plaintive, frightened.

                          MIKE
               Somebody help me. Please.
               Please, help me -

                                        DISSOLVE TO:

94. OUT OF FOCUS ON HIS HAND   94.

95. CLOSE SHOT IN FOCUS HIS HAND   95.

     Pushing a button on an instument panel. The CAMERA
     DOLLIES AWAY until both the back of the panel and Mike's
     face are on a small television screen.

96. LONG ANGLE SHOT   96.

     Down a line of officers in a viewing room as they
     watch intently the screen. We hear Mike's voice as
     it coincides with a red light that flashes brilliantly
     on and off over the viewing screen.

                       MIKE'S VOICE
               Please. Please, help me. Help
               me.

     A General, obviously in command, turns to his Aide
     on his right.

                          GENERAL
               Clock him!
                    (And then turning to his
                    left says to the officer
                    alongside)
               Get him out of there quick!

     Officer Two reaches over for a hand mike, pushes
     the button.

                       OFFICER TWO
               Release the subject! On the double!

97.   INT. LARGE HANGAR-LIKE ROOM   97.

In the center of it, illuminated by a couple of spots
in an otherwise dark room, is a small, hermetically
sealed metal box about six by five feet and about five
feet high. A sliding panel is pushed back. Several
Air Force men reach down and start unstrapping Mike and
then carefully lift him through the hole. A ~~white-clad~~
medical officer begins to remove electrods that have
been taped to his body at various points. By this time
Mike has stopped speaking. His eyes are half closed.
He breathes deeply and irregularly.

98.   LONG SHOT GENERAL AND STAFF   98.

As they hurriedly approach the scene, their footsteps
ringing hollowly on the concrete floor.

                    MEDICAL OFFICER
          He's all right, sir.   Delusions
          of some sort. I guess that's it.
          He's coming out of it now.

                    GENERAL
               (nods)
          Fine. You get all your data
          recorded?

                    MEDICAL OFFICER
          Yes, sir. Every bit of it.

                    GENERAL
               (to Officer One who
               comes up from behind)
          Did you get him clocked?

                    OFFICER ONE
          Yes, sir. Four hundred and
          eighty four hours, thirty six
          minutes.

                    GENERAL
          Good. I'd like to get a look at
          all the data when they're
          compiled. I'd like the reaction
          chart on him, too.

                    OFFICER TWO
               (sotto)
          The press, sir. You said you'd
          see them.

                    GENERAL
          Oh, yes. Can I make it brief?

                    CONTINUED

                          OFFICER TWO
              I told them you'd have to
              cut it short, sir.

                          GENERAL
                    (nods)
              All right.

Officer Two nods toward the far end of the room and
then accompanies the General as he walks toward the
group of newsmen standing in a group.

                          GENERAL
              How are you, gentlemen?

                          REPORTERS
                    (ad libs)
              Hello, General.
              Etc.

                          REPORTER ONE
              Consider it a success, sir?

                          GENERAL
              Very much so. Something in the
              neighborhood of four hundred
              and eighty four hours all alone
              in that box which is roughly
              equivalent to a couple of trips
              to the moon and back.

                          REPORTER TWO
              What about the wires attached
              to him?

                          GENERAL
              Electrodes. All of his reactions
              were charted and graphed.
              Respiration, heart action, blood
              pressure.

                          REPORTER THREE
              How is he?

                          GENERAL
              The Doctor says he'll be all
              right.

                          REPORTER ONE
              What about toward the end -
              What was the matter with him?
              Just before he pushed the button -

                              CONTINUED

                         GENERAL
        Delusions of some sort. He
        cracked then. But I'll tell you
        something, gentlemen -- you
        spend two and a half weeks all
        by your lonesome without ever
        being able to hear a human voice
        other than your own...I'll give
        you especially good odds that
        your imagination would run away
        with you too just as his obviously
        did. However, he's in good shape.
        Captain Grant here will have a press
        release drawn up for you. It should
        be ready in an hour or so, shouldn't
        it, Captain?

                         CAPTAIN
        Yes, sir.

                         REPORTER ONE
        Last question, General. How
        did you know he was ready to
        come out?

                         GENERAL
                (with a tight grin)
        He asked out. There were several
        levers and buttons inside. Each
        one controlled a simulated
        mechanism for a moon flight.
        Oxygen, fuel, temperature, that
        sort of thing. And the last
        button --

                         REPORTER ONE
        Which was?

                         GENERAL
        The "want out" button. When he
        had all he could take, when he
        had to get out. That was the
        last button. That's what he
        pushed.

                         REPORTERS
        (Ad Lib Reactions)

                         REPORTER ONE
        What about a trip to the moon?
        We haven't got it licked yet,
        have we?

                                         CONTINUED

> GENERAL
> (shakes his head)
> Not this hour we don't. Maybe
> not this day. But we will have
> it licked and I think maybe
> while we're all alive. There's
> a lot we don't know yet. A lot
> of problems.

> REPORTER ONE
> I can imagine. Did you find
> any special ones with that thing?

He points toward the metal box in the middle of the room.
At this point the doctor comes up. He's overheard the last
question.

> GENERAL
> How about it, Doc? Any new
> problems? Not classified?

The doctor looks toward the box.

> DOCTOR
> Maybe one more that we'd already
> given some thought to, but we
> saw it demonstrated very vividly.

> REPORTER ONE
> What's that?

The CAMERA STARTS A SLOW PAN OVER toward the empty box
that now sits alone in the giant room.

> DOCTOR
> (O.C.)
> The barrier of loneliness. We
> can feed stomachs with concentrates.
> We can supply microfilms for
> recreation, reading. We can
> pump oxygen in, waste material out.

The CAMERA NOW MOVES AROUND so that it is looking at the
box in the foreground and the group of men far off in
the distance just on the periphery of the light.

> DOCTOR
> There's one thing we can't simulate.
> And that's a pretty basic need -
> man's hunger for companionship.
> The barrier of loneliness. That's
> one we haven't licked yet.

CONTINUED

98. CONTINUED   *Boom Shot* 98.

Now the voices become unintelligible as they echo off
the walls of the giant room. The CAMERA STARTS A SLOW
DOLLY AWAY, higher and higher, until it is shooting down
at the lone box in the middle of the room.

                    NARRATOR'S VOICE
            The barrier of loneliness. The
            palpable, desperate need of the
            human animal to be with his
            fellow man.

                                          Dissolve To transfer roll

Now the CAMERA TILTS UPWARDS until it is shooting
toward the sky, a night sky full of stars.

                    NARRATOR'S VOICE
                     (continuing)
            For up there..up there in the
            vastness of space, in the void
            that is sky, is an enemy known
            as isolation. It sits there in
            the stars waiting, forever waiting...
            in The Twilight Zone.

                                    FADE TO BLACK

                    THE END

TOWN WITHOUT PITY

Rod Serling's official pilot script—entitled "Where is Everybody?"—showcased many of the elements that were to become synonymous with *The Twilight Zone* series. It captured a mood of isolation and fear, a loss of place and self. It examined the human condition and illustrated both the power and the horror of imagination. It featured stunning cinematography, fine acting, skillful direction and top-notch production on all levels.

One thing the pilot script did *not* do was display any sign of the fantastic trappings that would later characterize the series. The stories of Martians and angels and androids, all the staggering shock conclusions, these would come later. What was needed to sell a unique speculative-fiction anthology in the conservative era of the late fifties was a finely-crafted story that spirited viewers away to a strange new place...yet, more crucially, explained how and why the journey took place. This first, tentative exploration of *The Twilight Zone* gingerly probed the boundaries of the imagination but safely returned to reality.

Director Robert Stevens, a veteran of esteemed productions such as *Alfred Hitchcock Presents* and *Playhouse 90*, was chosen to helm the pilot based on his experience and reputation for employing innovative camera work. Celebrated cinematographer Joseph La Shelle—whose work included MARTY (1955), LAURA (1944), and HANGOVER SQUARE (1945)—assumed the position of director of photography. Together, Stevens and La Shelle captured the script's atmosphere of claustrophobic bewilderment. The show established an ambience of disorientation that blends well with later *Twilight Zone* classics.

The lead role of amnesiac Mike Ferris went to Earl Holliman, who had worked with a Serling script the year before in the *Playhouse 90* production "The

Dark Side of the Earth." Initially reluctant to tackle a fantasy story, Holliman read Serling's teleplay and was captivated.

"I thought I would just kind of peruse it, but I couldn't stop turning the pages," Holliman told Serling biographer Joel Engel. "It was fascinating. The goose pimples stood up on my flesh. First of all, there was nobody in it but me, plus I was fascinated with this guy who went from place and place and constantly just missed somebody who was there—but there was never anybody there. I was so pleased with the script. Just delighted. I called [Serling] the next morning and said, 'Yes, yes, yes.'"

Production of the pilot commenced on a chilly December morning in 1958, at the backlot of Universal-International studios. Budgeted at $75,000, a princely sum at the time, "Where is Everybody?" took a total of nine days to shoot. Driving up the cost and length of production was a technical snafu that occurred on the first day of filming. As evening approached and the second-to-last shot of the day was being organized, the assistant cameraman realized that his camera had malfunctioned. Every frame of film shot that day had been lost.

"A costly little mistake," chuckles producer William Self. "I was there for everything, out in Universal where we shot it, there in charge of the director. It was my first project at CBS so I was anxious."

The professional crew overcame this early hurdle to fashion a riveting show. "I remember walking into the jail," Holliman related in an NPR broadcast, "and the door starts closing behind me and the water's running in the sink. I mean, I remember feeling a sense of the fear of not understanding, and what the hell is going on here?"

Serling's inspiration for the pilot came not only from articles about astronaut training but from an incident in which the writer found himself strolling through an eerily quiet and abandoned town. "I got the idea while walking through an empty lot of a movie studio. There were all the evidences of a community—but with no people. I felt at the time a kind of encroaching loneliness and desolation, a feeling of how nightmarish it would be to wind up in a city with no inhabitants."

When the time came to create the musical score—an area critical in setting mood and tone—the production added another stellar artisan to its impressive roster of talent. Academy Award winner Bernard Herrmann, one of the most distinctive composers to ever work in film, lent his characteristic sound to *The Twilight Zone*. Herrmann's score for the pilot weaves a subtle web of loneliness and disquiet as Ferris explores his abandoned surroundings, and rises to a fever pitch in key scenes of panic and frustration. The music perfectly complements the direction and camerawork; working in unison they set quite an effective atmosphere for "Where is Everybody?"

Herrmann would score a total of seven episodes for the series, and he supplied the mesmerizing, understated theme music used throughout *Twilight Zone*'s inaugural season. This passage was later replaced by Marius Constant's catchy four-note cue, which became a hallmark of the series.

Earl Holliman describes the challenge of acting solo, with his character single-handedly carrying the majority of the show. "You have to remember that even though I was alone, there were about fifty people there with me. You didn't see them but they were all on the other side of the camera. It's hard to divorce yourself totally from that. An actor has to; I had to just rub them out, but it was never like really being totally alone. The difficult thing was just talking to myself. Now that I'm of a different age I talk to myself anyway. I could be wonderful in that part today!"

At a time when the Soviet Union had launched a Sputnik satellite—as well as an international space race fueled by Cold War paranoia—the subject matter was topical and fresh. Yet the revelation that Ferris was an astronaut who had hallucinated the entire ordeal does not pack the wallop of later *Twilight Zone* twists. Interestingly, Earl Holliman suggested an ending that was on par with the enigmatic conclusions of forthcoming teleplays, but at this critical juncture Serling and company simply could not take the risk.

"My suggestion to Rod was, 'Wouldn't it be interesting if he tears a page out of the phone book and sticks it in his pocket, and at the end of the show, when they discover this whole thing took place in his mind, if this page of paper falls out of his pocket?' That would have been ambiguous. Rod said, 'No, they won't go for it.'"

In April of 1960, when *The Twilight Zone* had established its footing as a fantasy series, Serling released FROM THE TWILIGHT ZONE, his first collection of script adaptations for Bantam Books. "Where is Everybody?" was one of the teleplays Serling chose to adapt; he took the opportunity to incorporate Holliman's suggestion and insert an ending that better fit the *Twilight Zone* format. In this version of the story, Ferris awakens from his ordeal to find a ticket stub in his pocket…a stub that he himself had put there while visiting the movie theater during his "hallucination."

Immediately following the nine-day shoot, the pilot was scored, edited and shown to William Paley, the influential Chief Executive Officer of CBS. "I had the pleasure," recalls William Self, "of flying to New York with the pilot film and screening it for Bill Paley. I was there just to make sure that nothing went wrong and of course, something went wrong.

"We were screening it for Paley and the projectionist got so caught up in the film that he forgot to change reels. The acts were on individual reels before we finalized it, and when Earl Holliman went crashing into the mirror, which was a shocking shot, that was the changeover and the projectionist should have gone over to reel three. He missed the changeover, the screen went blank, and Paley said, 'What happened?' I nearly had a heart attack! But the projectionist came around, turned on the other machine and we finished the screening." Ironically, the "shattering mirror" scene that Self describes takes place as Ferris races down a flight of theater stairs, immediately after discovering that the projection booth is abandoned and the projector left unattended.

Unfazed by the delay and distraction, William Paley quickly expressed his enthusiasm about the production. "Paley was extremely high on it," Self concludes. "He was a big supporter of it. Strangely enough, some of the other executives at CBS were not; they didn't know what it was, they didn't quite get it. But Paley did and that was all that counted at CBS in those days."

※　※　※

You've Just Crossed Over…into *The Twilight Zone*

Following the success of the pilot, Serling was given the green light to begin production on the first twenty-six episodes of *The Twilight Zone*. Under the banner of Cayuga Productions (named after the upstate New York lake where the writer and his family vacationed), Serling began the hunt for a production crew by approaching William Self.

"When the pilot turned out so well," says Self, "Rod Serling offered me the job to produce the series for Cayuga Productions. I said, 'Rod, you know I'm flattered, but I have a wife and two kids and I don't know if the show's going to make it. I think it will, but the steady job is what I need.' He said, 'I understand that' and he asked if I knew somebody who could produce it."

Self recommended the services of a highly competent production team with which he was familiar. "I had just had an organization producing *The Frank Sinatra Show* which consisted of Buck Houghton as my story editor, George T. Clemens as a cameraman, Ralph Nelson as the production manager and others. I said to Rod, 'Look, here's a unit that I have worked with on *The Schlitz Playhouse of Stars* and then on the *Sinatra* show, and they're well acquainted with each other and how they work. Take them over.'"

Serling accepted Self's advice. "I think most of the crew on *The Twilight Zone*," Self recalls, "came over from *Schlitz Playhouse* and *Sinatra*. If you compared the crew list on *The Twilight Zone* with *Schlitz Playhouse* you would be amazed at how many people did both shows." Indeed, several *Schlitz Playhouse* crew members, with duties ranging from casting director to production manager, made the transition to Rod Serling's new series. And no fewer than six directors—Justus Addiss, John Brahm, Robert Florey, Bernard Gerald, Ted Post and Don Weis—helmed episodes of both shows.

Beyond his involvement with the pilot and the production crew, William Self contributed to the evolution of *The Twilight Zone* in several other ways. Originally, as evidenced by the early press release featured in this book, Serling planned to open each show with following line: "There is a sixth dimension, beyond that which is known to man." Self caught the flub in Serling's now-famous opening narration.

"I said to Rod, 'Please explain to me what the sixth dimension is.' He looked at me and said, 'Oh, aren't there six?'" The men soon realized that modern science recognized only height, width, depth and time, so the opening was rewritten and rerecorded to tag *Twilight Zone* as the fifth dimension.

Self also played a role in choosing Serling as the show's narrator, a task that was important in bringing a sense of continuity to the anthology format. "All the CBS people wanted a big voice, a dramatic narrator," Self relates. "We explored the possibly of getting Orson Welles and Westbrook Van Vorhees, who had done

The March of Time. We actually put some of these people on tape. And Rod kept saying, 'They sound pompous. They kind of talk down to my audience and I don't like it.'" The famed narrators were also too expensive for the proposed budget.

Serling suggested that he himself take a crack at the narration. The idea did not meet with a great deal of enthusiasm, but Self admits that all doubts were soon assuaged. "We taped some tests of Rod and he was terrific. I think it was a major factor in the success of the show." Paid considerably less than any "professional" spokesman, Serling voiced the opening and closing narration for every episode of the first season. Starting with the second season, the show's creator further cemented his iconic status as the embodiment of *The Twilight Zone* by moving in front of the camera to deliver his introductions.

William Self is proud of his association with Rod Serling and *The Twilight Zone*. "I stayed on the show for a while, as CBS's representative. But then I got an offer elsewhere as a direct result of *Twilight Zone*. I went to Fox—it was a good company, more money, and a good title—and stayed there for fifteen years. Yet I had a lot of regrets about it because I liked *Twilight Zone* and I loved working with Serling. He was enthusiastic and full of ideas."

The Twilight Zone

THIRD FROM THE SUN

Airdate: 1-8-1960

Manuscript Date: 8-6-1959

Story by Richard Matheson

Dated 7-16-1959 with revisions
dated 8-4-1959 and 8-6-1959

Episode Fourteen

THE TWILIGHT ZONE

"THIRD FROM THE SUN"

Teleplay by
ROD SERLING

Story by
RICHARD MATHESON

July 16, 1959

FADE IN:

1.   EXT. SKY NIGHT   1.

Shot of the sky...the various nebulae, and planet bodies
stand out in sharp, sparkling relief. As the CAMERA
begins a SLOW PAN across the Heavens --

                    NARRATOR'S VOICE (O.S.)
          There is a fifth dimension beyond
          that which is known to man. It is
          a dimension as vast as space, and
          as timeless as infinity. It is the
          middle ground between light and
          shadow -- between science and
          superstition. And it lies between
          the pit of man's fears and the
          summit of his knowledge. This is
          the dimension of imagination. It
          is an area which we call The
          Twilight Zone.

The CAMERA has begun to PAN DOWN until it passes the
horizon and is flush on the OPENING SHOT (EACH WEEK
THE OPENING SHOT OF THE PLAY)

2.   EXT. FACTORY GATE DAY   2.

There is a sign at the gate: SECURITY GATE. Men are
filing out, as if at the end of the day. One guard checks
each man's credentials; another guard puts a check mark
down on his list as the name is called. DOLLY IN for
medium close group shot of the entrance.

                    GUARD
          Parkison, Chemical Warfare.

The second guard checks off that name as another man
presents his credentials.

                    GUARD
          Amberly, Hydrogen Armament.

And he's checked off the list. Another man and his
credentials.

                    GUARD
          Mills, Germ Warfare Research.

Check. Now we're close on WILLIAM STURKA, a tall man in
his late thirties, early forties. The guard routinely
checks his card.

                                        CONTINUED

2.   CONTINUED   2.

                              GUARD
                    Sturka. Hydrogen Armament.

And Sturka is checked off the list.

                              GUARD
                    You guys are busy up there,
                    aren't you?

                              STURKA
                         (nods)
                    Very.

                              GUARD
                    Okay, keep moving.

3.   TRACK SHOT WITH STURKA   3.

As he goes down the steps of the building, pauses, takes
out a pack of cigarettes and lights one. The match is
held out ready to be shaken out when a hand comes into
the frame and grabs his wrist. CAMERA PULLS BACK for
two shot of Sturka and Ed Carling, a heavy, gross
looking man with small, piggish eyes.

                              CARLING
                    Hold the light will you, Sturka?
                         (he guides Sturka's
                         hand to his own
                         cigarette, lights it,
                         then blows out the
                         match)
                    Long days, huh?

                              STURKA
                         (nods)
                    Very long.

                              CARLING
                    Your department's going full
                    blast, isn't it?

                                               CONTINUED

3. CONTINUED

Sturka nods noncommittally.

                         CARLING
             It's coming, boy. It's really
             coming. And a big one too. I
             betcha that while we're talking
             here the military's getting all
             set. Got it all mapped out I'll
             bet.
                  (and then sidling in
                   closer, very
                   confidentially)
             Talk is -- forty eight hours.
             Wait and see if I'm not right.
             Forty eight hours and we'll have
             'em aloft.
                  (he makes a motion with
                   his hand imitating
                   a rocket going off)
             Whoosh. Up, over and whammo! And
             there goes the enemy. Obliterated.
             Finished.

4. CLOSE SHOT   STURKA   4.

His face is grim and a little sick.

                         STURKA
             What are they doing in the
             meantime?

5. TWO SHOT   5.

                         CARLING
             What do you mean what are they
             doing? They're probably
             retaliating as best they can.
             Just a big waste of time let me
             tell you. We get the first licks.
                  (he shakes his head)
             So they can't do much.

                         STURKA
             They can go whoosh, up, over and
             whommo!

                         CARLING
                  (as if this were the
                   meat of the logic)
             Absolutely. But not so many.
             Not so properly aimed. Not so
             efficiently carried out.

                                        CONTINUED

5. CONTINUED   5.

                         STURKA
                (laughs but there's no
                 mirth in the laughter)
             So instead of losing fifty million
             people we may lose only thirty
             five huh?

6. CLOSE SHOT   CARLING   6.

    His little pig eyes narrow accusingly.

                         CARLING
             You a defeatist, Sturka? That's
             dangerous thinking. You better
             mind what you say.   '

7. TWO SHOT   7.

                         STURKA
             And what I think too.

                         CARLING
                (nods)
             Yeah and what you think.

                         STURKA
             Good night, Carling. See you
             tomorrow.

    He turns and starts to walk away. Carling watches him
    leave, his face a mask suggesting thought -- deep,
    menacing thought. The CAMERA PANS BACK UP the steps
    to the line of men who pass the guards and we hear
    little shreds of conversation. "Hydrogen". "Germ".
    "Bomb". "Armament". Over this we hear the Narrator's
    Voice.

                         NARRATOR'S VOICE
             Five thirty PM...quitting time at
             the plant...time for supper now.
             Time for families. Time for a
             cool drink on a porch. Time for
             summer birds and crickets and the
             noises of the warm time of year.
             Time for the quiet rustle of leaf
             laden trees that screen out the
             moon and project odd shadows on
             cooling sidewalks.

                         (MORE)

                                   CONTINUED

7. CONTINUED   7.

                        NARRATOR'S VOICE (CONT'D)
              (a pause)
          And underneath it all, behind the
          eyes of the men...hanging invisible
          over the summer night is a horror
          without words. For this is the
          stillness before storm; this is
          the eve of the end!

                                           FADE OUT:

OPENING BILLBOARD
FIRST COMMERCIAL

FADE ON:

8. INT. STURKA'S HOUSE   MOVING SHOT   STURKA   8.

    As he enters through the entrance hall with the front
    porch visible through the screen door. Dining room on
    the right, living room on the left. A stairway that
    leads to the second floor. It's medium sized, comfortably
    furnished, modern but not stark, quality but not
    expensive. Records play on a phonograph, a swing tune
    not identifiable but pleasant, with a beat.

9.- DIFFERENT SHOTS OF ROOMS AND FURNITURE   9.-
12. STURKA'S P.O.V.   12.

    As he walks from room to room. He seems to dwell on each
    object in turn as if testing its reality.

13. INT. LIVING ROOM   13.

    As he walks over to the phonograph, looks down at it.
    Behind him we see his daughter, Jody, coming down the
    steps three at a time. She's sixteen and beautiful.
    She stops seeing her father in the living room.

                    JODY
          Hi, Dad.

    He turns, smiling at her.

                    STURKA
          Hello, baby. Where's your Mom?

                                           CONTINUED

13. CONTINUED   13.

                              JODY
                    Out in back trying to urge
                    radishes out of the ground or
                    something.
                         (she enters the
                          living room now)
                    And I'm here waiting for you to
                    invite me to dance.

                              STURKA
                         (forces a smile, goes
                          over to the phonograph
                          and shuts it off, stares
                          at it for a moment)
                    Some other time, huh, honey?

She stares at him intently. He goes over to the window
his back to her.

                              JODY
                         (her voice quiet)
                    Dad?

                              STURKA
                    What, Jody?

                              JODY
                         (takes a step toward
                          him)
                    What's the matter?

                              STURKA
                         (forces a smile again)
                    Nothing serious. I'm just feeling
                    my years. And you, my dear,
                    with your beautiful face and your
                    maturing ways suddenly remind
                    me that my youth is up in the
                    attic spread out over a few
                    photo albums.

                              JODY
                    Is that all?

                              STURKA
                         (laughs)
                    All? That's quite enough.

14.   TRACK SHOT JODY   14.

As she walks over to her father, her face very
thoughtful, filled suddenly with a maturity that seems
to suddenly come with the moment. She looks up at
him.

                    JODY
          Dad -- you like your job? Is
          that the problem?

                    STURKA
               (stares at her for a
                moment)
          My job?
               (he shrugs, forces
                a smile)
          It's all right.
               (he makes a gesture)
          It's a job.

                    JODY
          I mean having to work on the
          kind of things you do. Fever
          bombs and hydrogen bombs and
          gas and things like that --

                    STURKA
               (looks away)
          I'm only a...a cog in a wheel,
          Jody. I mean...look at it this
          way...in one bomb there are
          perhaps...a thousand parts and
          each part requires a team of
          fifty, sixty, seventy men.
               (he turns back to
                her)
          Looking at it that way I'm not
          quite as responsible as --

He stops abruptly.

15. PAN SHOT ACROSS THE ROOM TO EVE   15.

     Who stands there. A strikingly attractive woman in
     her late thirties. She's overheard the conversation
     and is staring at Sturka expectantly.

16. FULL SHOT   THE ROOM   16.

     As Sturka turns away. Jody looks from one to the other
     and finally.

                         JODY
                Everyone I've talked to lately...
                they've been noticing it.

                         EVE
                    (a smile)
                Noticing what, Jo?

                         JODY
                    (with a look at her
                    father)
                That something's wrong. That
                something's in...something's in
                the air. Something's going to
                happen. Everyone's afraid, mother.
                    (then turns to her
                    father)
                Everyone, Dad. Why?

                         STURKA
                    (turns, walks a few
                    feet over to her, goes
                    down on his knees,
                    grips her shoulders
                    very tightly)
                People are afraid because they
                make themselves afraid. They are
                afraid because they subvert every
                great thing that's ever discovered -
                every fine idea ever thought, every
                marvelous invention ever conceived.
                They subvert it, Jody. They dirty
                it up. They make it crooked and
                devious and too late...far too late
                they ask the question - "Why"?
                Sitting in their own rubble...in
                their own tears...they ask the
                question - why?
                    (he shakes his head)
                And then it's too late. Far too
                late!

     He touches his daughter's face very gently, rises and
     looks at Eve.

                                        CONTINUED

16. CONTINUED   16.

There's a silence now that hangs heavy over the room.
Sturka lights a cigarette.

                          STURKA
              Invite Jerry Riden and his wife
              over tonight, will you, Eve? We'll
              play some cards or something.

                          EVE
              Tonight?

                          STURKA
                   (nods)
              Yes. Call them up. Ask them to
              come over around seven or so.

                          EVE
              Isn't Jerry out of town? Wasn't he
              testing some kind of aircraft up
              North?

                          STURKA
              He's back. He came back this
              morning. I told him we'd phone
              them.
                   (then he turns to
                   Jody)
              You'll be here won't you, Jody?
              They'd like to see you.

                          JODY
              Can't. I've got a date, Dad. But
              maybe I can get in early.

                          STURKA
                   (in an attempt at
                   matter of factness)
              Break it, Jody, will you? I'd
              like you home tonight.

                          JODY
              Dad -
                   (she stops and then
                   quietly)
              All right, Dad.

He turns and starts out of the room.

                          STURKA
              You know Jerry has some interesting
              stories. He has a very interesting
              job you know...he...

                                        CONTINUED

16. CONTINUED   16.

His voice sort of trails off, as he stares back at
Eve. She grabs his hand as if preparatory to asking
a question. He smiles, touches her face.

                    STURKA
          I thought maybe you'd like some
          cards tonight. Get your mind off
          things.

Now he has to turn his eyes away from her. He walks
out of the room.

                                        CUT TO:

17. INT. BEDROOM   17.

As Sturka enters, goes over to the dresser, empties
his pockets, takes off his coat, stands there for a
moment, his head down. We see the reflection of his
wife in the morror as she comes in after him. She
stands there for a moment silently.

                    EVE
          Bill?

He looks at her reflection and nods.

                    EVE
          What is it? What's happening?

                    STURKA
          What do you feel is happening?

                    EVE
          I have so much fear inside me that...
          I can't give it words.

He turns to her now.

                    STURKA
          Eve, it's too late for subterfuge
          now. It's too late to hide anything.
               (he walks over to
               her and grabs her)
          Eve, it's coming. It's coming
          probably within forty eight hours.

Her hand goes to her mouth.

                    EVE
          Will it...will it be bad?

                                        CONTINUED

17. CONTINUED   17.

                         STURKA
                    (simply, quietly)
               It'll be a holacaust. It'll be
               hell. It'll mean the end of
               everything we know. People,
               places, ideas, everything. It'll
               all be wiped out.

                         EVE
                    (in a whisper)
               In forty eight hours?

                         STURKA
                    (he nods)
               Maybe sooner.

                         EVE
               What can we do, Bill?

                         STURKA
                    (steps away from her)
               Sit down on the bed, Eve. I've
               got something to tell you.

She takes a step toward him, hand outstretched.

                         EVE
               Bill -

                         STURKA
               Sit down on the bed.

She crosses over and sits.

                         STURKA
               We're leaving. You and I and the
               kids. Jerry and his wife. We're
               leaving tonight.

                         EVE
               Leaving? Leaving for where?

                         STURKA
               I can't tell you that. I can only
               tell you that sometime between
               midnight and one - we've got to be
               out of here and gone.
                    (he takes a few
                    steps over toward
                    her, looking down at
                    her on the bed)
               And no one is to know. I mean no
               one. Not the neighbors. Not
               relatives...not even Jody. She
               isn't to know. And we won't
               be able to tell her until we're
               already on our way.

                                             CONTINUED

17.   CONTINUED   17.

At this moment Jody's voice is heard from down in the
foyer, calling.

                    JODY'S VOICE
          Dad? Jerry Riden's down here. He'd
          like to see you.

                    STURKA
          I'm coming down, Jody -

                    EVE
               (jumps up, grabs him
                as he passes)
          What's it mean? Why is he here
          now?

                    STURKA
          That's what I want to find out.

18.   LONG ANGLE SHOT   LOOKING DOWN STAIRS   18.

As Sturka goes down. At the foot we see Jerry Riden
standing there. He looks up expectantly, a grimness
on his face that he tries to hide. He nods.

                    JERRY
          Hello, Bill.

19.   TWO SHOT   THE FOOT OF THE STAIRS   19.

As Sturka shakes his hand.

                    STURKA
          How are you, old friend? Now if
          you've come to tell us you can't
          make it for cards tonight -

He smiles the kind of smile that looks like it could be
chipped off with a chisel and Jerry's answering smile
has the same kind of almost painted on look.

                    JERRY
          Are you kidding? It's a dollar a
          point tonight because I've been very
          hot at cards the last couple of weeks.
               (he scratches his jaw
                in a nervous gesture)
          No, I just dropped by to talk to
          you about that...that...

He obviously searches in his mind, aware that Jody is
staring at him.

                                        CONTINUED

19. CONTINUED   19.

                              STURKA
                         (throwing this out
                         abruptly)
                    Your watch giving you trouble again?
                    Probably that mainspring. Jerry,
                    remember I told you it looked like
                    it had some rust on it. Come on
                    into the garage. We'll look it over.

          He starts to walk Jerry toward the front door. Jerry
          smiles and winks at Jody as they pass her. Jody doesn't
          return the smile. Instead she looks frightened. The
          two men exit. Jody looks up the steps.

20. LONG SHOT   LOOKING UP TOWARD   EVE   20.

          Who stands there at the top of the stairs. Jody's
          look calls for an answer or at least a statement and
          Eve can only stand there and shake her head.

                                             DISSOLVE TO:

21. INT. GARAGE   DAY   21.

          This is a typical frame building with a large overhead
          door which is now shut. Two or three high windows in
          the opposite wall. On the left wall is a large, well
          equipped tool bench. Sturka and Jerry enter.

                              STURKA
                         (in a loud voice)
                    Let's see the watch now.

                              JERRY
                         (with a look around
                         hands it to him and
                         then as if bursting
                         this gets spilled out)
                    Bill, I've had to change plans -

                              STURKA
                         (through his teeth)
                    Not now, not now! Wait a minute.
                         (he turns on one
                         of the small electric
                         machines and then in
                         a loud voice)
                    Here's your trouble right here, Jerry.
                    Look.

22. CLOSE TWO SHOT   22.

          As the two men's faces are close together over the
          bench.

                                             CONTINUED

22. CONTINUED   22.

                         STURKA
                    (over the machine)
               All right now. Tell me. And keep
               looking at the watch. For Heavens
               sake keep looking at the watch. Smile
               occasionally too.

Jerry starts to look toward the windows. Sturka grabs
him.

                         STURKA
               That's the point. You never know
               who's looking...or listening. Just
               keep looking at the watch. Now what's
               happened, Jerry? Tell me.

                         JERRY
               They've put a different guard on the
               ship. On the one AM shift. The one
               I know...the one I've paid gets off
               at eleven.

                         STURKA
               Then we must leave at eleven.

                         JERRY
               It'll be a lot tougher. There's a
               fuller complement of personnel on the
               field then. There's an extra tier
               of searchlights on too.

                         STURKA
               That doesn't have to make any
               difference. We're gonna tell them
               the same story anyway.

                         JERRY
               You're relatives of mine and you've
               got Government clearance to look
               .at the new ship.

                         STURKA
               That's right. Now have you told Ann?

                         JERRY
               Not everything. Only that we're in
               danger and we've got to get out. I
               didn't tell her where or when. What
               about Eve and Jody?

                                        CONTINUED

22. CONTINUED   22.

                              STURKA
              Eve knows now. Jody'll stay home
              tonight. I told her you were coming
              over to play cards. You and Ann.
              You can come around seven can't you?

                              JERRY
                    (nods)
              Yeah.

Now Sturka bends over and flicks off the machine, in
a very loud voice hands the watch back.

                              STURKA
              I think that does it, Jerry. Just a
              little mainspring trouble. You might
              want to have it checked over by a
              jeweler or something in a month or
              so. I couldn't get all the rust out.

                              JERRY
              Thanks, Bill, very much.

23. CLOSE SHOT   STURKA   23.

As he smiles, handing the watch over. His eyes go up
and the smile freezes.

24. FLASH SHOT   CARLING'S FACE   24.

Staring at them through the high window in the
opposite wall.

                                        FADE TO BLACK:

                        END ACT ONE

ACToverride ACT TWO

FADE ON:

25. INT. STURKA HOUSE NIGHT   25.

SLOW PAN SHOT from foyer toward living room. There are
low voices in the b.g. Then the CAMERA is inside the
living room shooting toward the card table where Sturka
and Eve play cards with Jerry and Ann Riden. The voices
are unintelligible and low.

26. MED. CLOSE SHOT TABLE   26.

As the cards change hands and the game goes on. PAN SHOT
around their faces. Each shows the strain of playing a
role. On occasion Jerry will look at his watch. Sturka
and Eve's eyes lock then Eve looks over her shoulder at
Jody who stands in the partial darkness at the far end
of the room. When she turns back to look at Sturka he
nods, barely perceptibly. Eve's face brightens with a
make believe hostess smile.

                         EVE
            How about some lemonade and
            home made cake?

                         ANN
            Sounds wonderful. I didn't
            even give Jerry dessert tonight.

                         JERRY
                 (the smile that
                 never quite reaches
                 the eyes)
            You see what the rigors are of a
            test pilot's life?

                         EVE
                 (gets up from the table)
            Let me get a tray.

                         ANN
            I'll help you, Eve.

                         EVE
                 (over her shoulder
                 at Jody)
            Come on, young woman. Lend a hand.

Jody follows the two women into the kitchen.

                                        CUT TO:

27. ANGLE SHOT LOOKING DOWN AT STURKA AND JERRY   27.

Alone at the table.

                    JERRY
          What about that guy in your office -
          what's his name - Carling? Still
          asking questions?

                    STURKA
               (nods)
          Still. Questions, hints and innuendoes.
          He's the last of the unsubtle informers.

                    JERRY
          Pity we can't be sure about him.
          Subtle or unsubtle - he could fix
          our wagon!
               (he looks at his watch
               again)
          I've got ten minutes to ten.
          That right?

                    STURKA
               (checks his watch)
          Yeah.

Now Sturka looks across the room toward the front window.

28. CLOSE SHOT WINDOW   28.

With blinds drawn.

29. CLOSE SHOT STURKA

As he looks in the opposite direction toward the windows
on either side of the fireplace.

30. CLOSE SHOT WINDOWS   30.

Both covered by drapes.

31. TWO SHOT STURKA AND JERRY   31.

                    STURKA
               (leans over)
          Jerry - what about our destination?

Jerry reaches into his vest pocket, takes out a folded
sheet of paper, looks around surreptitiously, puts it down
in front of him.

                    JERRY
               (pointing toward it)
          Right there.

32.   CLOSE SHOT STURKA   32.

As he looks and then looks up toward Jerry.

                          STURKA
          How far?

                          JERRY
                    (quietly)
          Eleven million miles.

                          STURKA
                    (closes his eyes,
                     whispers)
          Eleven million miles. In a
          ship we don't even know will
          leave the atmosphere.

                          JERRY
          Or whether or not its pilot can
          either take off or get you down
          in one piece, but that's the risk,
          Bill. That's the risk we've been
          talking about for months now.

                          STURKA
                    (nods)
          It's not a bad risk when you
          consider the alternatives.
                    (a pause)
          And the place we're going - ?

                          JERRY
          It's populated, Bill. It has
          people on it. We've picked up
          radio waves. Even some snatches
          of a language not dissimilar to
          ours. We've been able to decipher
          a lot of it.
                    (a pause)
          With a little help...a couple of
          breaks...and God -
                    (he nods)
          We might even make it there.

At this moment we hear Eve's voice as it cuts into the
ensuing silence. It carries with it an odd tone. PAN
SHOT OVER to kitchen door. Eve stands there.

                          EVE
          Bill? Mr. Carling's here.

Carling comes in behind her from the kitchen on into
the living room.

                          CARLING
          Well! How goes it, Sturka?
          Little cards tonight?

                                        CONTINUED

32.   CONTINUED   32.

Sturka has to catch his breath when he first sees him,
then rises.

                         STURKA
                   Little cards, Carling. We're
                   about to cut into a cake. Care
                   to join us?

                         CARLING
                   Thank you. Just a little lemonade
                   for me. I was just telling your
                   wife that she makes wonderful
                   lemonade.
                         (he runs a finger
                         through his collar)
                   Hot night, too.
                         (he goes over and
                         sits in a chair
                         facing the table)
                   This is a night for a front porch
                   or sleep...but nothing else.

                         JERRY
                   How right you are.
                         (he looks at his watch)
                   We'll be leaving in a couple of
                   minutes. I've been up North
                   testing an aircraft. I haven't
                   had much sleep the last couple
                   of weeks.

                         CARLING
                   I know the aircraft. They say
                   it's capable of leaving our
                   atmosphere. Talk is it could
                   go to another planet if the right
                   man flew her.

33.   CLOSE SHOT STURKA   33.

Reacting.

34.   CLOSE SHOT JERRY   34.

As his face looks grim.

                         JERRY
                         (forcing a smile)
                   Not for a while yet. Needs a
                   lot more testing.

35. CLOSE SHOT CARLING   35.

As he looks from one to the other.

                         CARLING
                 Got a cigarette, Sturka?

Sturka pats his pockets. He looks across the room at a
package that sits on a table near the entrance.

                         CARLING
                     (rises)
                 Don't bother. I'll get them.

36. TRACK SHOT CARLING   36.

As he walks past the table.

37. CLOSE SHOT   37.

As he looks toward the table.

38. CLOSE SHOT MAP   38.

That lies there near Jerry's hand.

39. CLOSE SHOT CARLING   39.

As he looks.

40. CLOSE SHOT STURKA   40.

His face twisted with fear.

41. MED CLOSE SHOT JERRY   41.

As he swiftly turns the paper over and starts to write
down some numbers.

                         JERRY
                 Way I figure it, Mr. Sturka -
                 you owe Ann and I a little money
                 here.
                     (then with a grin
                     toward Carling)
                 Marvelous scientist - very bad
                 card player.

Carling has gotten the cigarettes now, takes one, puts
them down, lights it. In the glow of the match his face
suddenly takes on a menacing look.

                         CARLING
                 Now I wouldn't have believed that.
                 I'd have guessed that Sturka here
                 was a good gambler. I'd have guessed
                 he'd gamble on most anything.

                                     CONTINUED

41. CONTINUED   41.

At this moment the two women come out with the tray,
glasses, a pitcher and a cake on the plate.

                         EVE
                (her voice shaking
                 ever so slightly)
            Here we are. Lemonade for everyone?

                         ANN
            I'll cut the cake, Eve.

42. MED CLOSE SHOT EVE   42.

As she picks up the pitcher and starts to pour. Her hand
shakes spasmodically, lemonade running over the rims of
the glasses. Carling walks over to her and takes the
pitcher from her hand.

                         CARLING
            You're a little nervous, Mrs.
            Sturka. Very nervous.

Eve looks at him wanting to say something, anything, but
nothing comes out. Carling pours the last glass and
puts the pitcher down and seems to hover over the table.
He looks down at it.

43. CLOSE SHOT JERRY'S HAND   43.

On top of the paper. Carling reaches over and pulls the
paper out. Jerry makes a gesture but it's too late.

44. MED CLOSE SHOT CARLING   44.

The paper in his hand. We can see the diagram on the
side facing the camera.

                         CARLING
                    (looks up)
            You've lost a lot of money
            according to this, Sturka.

45. CLOSE SHOT STURKA   45.

He can only nod now. He can't say anything.

46. GROUP SHOT   46.

Carling starts to turn the paper over just as Jerry yanks
it from his hand.

                         JERRY
            We won't settle tonight. Next
            week - next week we'll give you
            another chance.

                                        CONTINUED

46. CONTINUED   46.

Carling is just swigging down his lemonade. He puts the
glass down.

                    CARLING
          Next week? You plan ahead. You
          plan way ahead.

                    JERRY
          A week?

                    CARLING
          A lot can happen in a week. A
          lot can happen in forty-eight
          hours. Well, I'll go on back
          home now. I like to take walks
          on warm evenings. Makes me sleep
          better.

                    STURKA
          I'll show you to the door,
          Carling.

                    CARLING
              (looks at him for
              a long moment)
          Thanks. I'll probably see you
          at the office tomorrow.

                    STURKA
          Sure.

47. TRACK SHOT WITH THEM   47.

As they leave the living room and go to the foyer. They
pause at the front door. Sturka opens the screen door
for him. Carling takes a step out and stands there
looking up.

                    CARLING
          Pretty night. Clear as a bell.
          Nothing but stars.
              (pause)
          Ever think, Sturka, that those
          stars may have people on them too?
          Maybe people like us?

                    STURKA
              (quietly)
          That thought's crossed my mind.

                    CARLING
              (whirls around toward him)
          Ever think...maybe you'd be happier
          on one of those than you are here?

                    CONTINUED

47. CONTINUED   47.

                              STURKA
                    That thought's crossed my mind,
                    too.

                              CARLING
                         (with a smile)
                    I have no doubt.

He turns and walks out into the night. Sturka closes the
screen door and then slams the regular door behind it.
He leans against it, his eyes closed, for a moment in
relief. A low chime sounds on the mantel. He looks up
and across toward the living room.

48. MED CLOSE SHOT CLOCK ON MANTEL   48.

It reads "10:30."

49. MOVING SHOT STURKA   49.

As he walks back into the living room. The others stare
at him.

                              STURKA
                    Jody...I've got something to
                    tell you now. We're leaving here
                    tonight. There's a ship over at
                    the Government field. We're
                    all going to get in the car and
                    drive there. We've bribed a lot
                    of people and the ship's loaded
                    with supplies. Enought to last
                    for a long time.

                              JODY
                    Where are we going, Dad?

                              STURKA
                    A long way from here. A long,
                    long way. Your mother has one
                    suitcase packed. It's in the
                    basement. Jody. Under the stairs.
                    Go get it.

                              JODY
                         (in amazement)
                    You've been planning this -

                                        CONTINUED

49.   CONTINUED   49.

                              JERRY
                    For three months now. But tonight
                    has to be it, Jody. Tonight's the
                    last chance. We've got to leave
                    here tonight.

                              ANN
                    (rises, biting her lip)
                    Jerry...I'm so frightened...

                              JODY
                    Why tonight, Jerry?

                              STURKA
                    Because this world as we know it,
                    Jody, won't exist very much longer.
                    It's about to blow itself up. And
                    that may happen by morning.

                              JODY
                    And by morning...where will we be?

                              STURKA
                    (with a strange gentleness)
                    We'll be out in space, Jody. Far
                    out in space. We'll be on an
                    adventure by then. The biggest
                    adventure.
                    (then a pause)
                    All right, everybody. Let's get
                    ready. I'll back the car out of the
                    garage. Ann, is your bag ready?

                              EVE
                    It's in our bedroom. I'll get it.

                              STURKA
                    Then let's get going.

        At this moment the phone rings. All stop dead, staring
        at it.

50.   CLOSE SHOT   PHONE   50.

        As it rings persistently at intervals.

51.   MED SHOT   51.

                              EVE
                    Bill - ?

                                             CONTINUED

                              STURKA
                    I've got to answer it.
                         (he walks over to
                         the phone, picks
                         it up)
                    Yes?

                              VOICE
                         (filtered)
                    Sturka? This is Evans. I'm afraid
                    I'm going to have to ask you to
                    come back to the lab tonight.

                              STURKA
                    Tonight?

                              VOICE
                         (filtered)
                    That's right. Some things are
                    happening. We're asking all the
                    crews to report in. We're sending
                    a car for you. It's on its way now.

                                        CONTINUED

51. CONTINUED   51.

                              STURKA
                         (close into the phone)
                    I'm....I'm in bed.

                              VOICE
                         (filtered)
                    So was practically everyone else
                    I called. Get out of bed and get
                    your clothes on. The car will be
                    there in just a few minutes.

                              STURKA
                    You don't...you don't understand.
                    I'm...I'm ill.

                              VOICE
                         (filtered)
                    How ill?

                              STURKA
                    Bad cold. Fever.

                              VOICE
                    That's too bad. But this is urgent.
                    Top priority. I'm afraid nothing
                    less than rigor mortis would excuse
                    you tonight. The car'll be there
                    in a few minutes.

There's the click of a distant receiver being replaced.
Sturka turns towards the others who stare at him.

52. ANGLE SHOT   OVER HIS SHOULDER   52.

At them.

                              STURKA
                    That was my Division head. They're
                    working tonight. They're sending a
                    car for me.

                              JERRY
                    Then we'd better get out of here
                    right now.

                              JODY
                    I'll get the bags.

She races out of the room.

                              ANN
                    I'll get ours.

                                        CONTINUED

52. CONTINUED   52.

She goes out of the foyer and starts up the steps. Eve
goes over to the tray and starts to put glasses on it.

                    STURKA
              (shouts)
         Eve!
              (he goes over to her
               and grabs her wrist
               looks down at her)
         Leave it, honey. Leave everything.
              (softly)
         We're not coming back here.

                                        DISSOLVE TO:

53.- EXT HIGHWAY DIFFERENT ANGLES   THE CAR   53.-
56.   56.
     As it speeds through the night.

                                        DISSOLVE TO:

57. EXT FIELD NIGHT MESH FENCE   57.

     As the car pulls up to it. Sturka and Jerry get out.
     The others remain in the car.

58. MOVING SHOT   WITH THEM   58.

     As they go to the fence and stare through it toward the
     field.

59. LONG ANGLE SHOT   LOOKING ACROSS THE FIELD   59.

     At a saucer which sits there illuminated by the moonlight.

60. TWO SHOT   THROUGH THE FENCE   60.

     Looking toward Jerry and Sturka.

                    STURKA
              (obviously impressed,
               his tone almost
               reverent)
         That's our transportation, huh?

                    JERRY
              (nods)
         That's it.

His eyes scan the field back and forth across the fence.

61. LONG SHOT THROUGH FENCE   61.

Of a figure walking toward them, a swinging flashlight in
his hand.

62. CLOSE SHOT JERRY AND STURKA   62.

                         STURKA
              Is that our contact?

                         JERRY
              That's him.

63. REVERSE ANGLE LOOKING THROUGH FENCE   63.

As the man with the flashlight gets closer and closer.

                         JERRY
                 (looking back toward car)
              Eve, flash the lights just once!

64. ANGLE SHOT LOOKING TOWARD CAR   64.

The lights go on and off once.

65. MED CLOSE SHOT STURKA AND JERRY   65.

As they wait. The lights from the approaching flashlight
now catching the face and flashing on them. Sturka smiles
and holds up his hand. Now the flashlight comes very
close. The person holding it is right at the fence. The
light goes from Sturka's face to Jerry's. The man holding
it is unrecognizeable in the darkness.

                    CARLING'S VOICE
              Good evening, Sturka. You're a
              long way from home, aren't you?

The flashlight slowly turns toward himself and we see
Carling's smiling face. We also see a gun in his free
hand. Jerry and Sturka stand stock still. Carling holds
the gun up.

                         CARLING
              Just stay there quietly you two
              and breath through your nose.
              Very, very quietly.

He takes a step away from the fence, walks down just a
few feet to the locked gate, unlocks it, pushes it open,
then he comes out walking toward them. He brandishes the
gun.

                         CARLING
              Now would you mind getting back
              in the car?

                                        CONTINUED

65. CONTINUED   65.

The two men turn slowly and walk toward the car, Carling
behind them.

66. MED CLOSE SHOT CAR   66.

As they get to it.

                    CARLING
          Get in the front seat, please.
          Would you three ladies be so kind
          as to get out? The two gentlemen
          and I have an engagement with the
          authorities.

67. MED CLOSE SHOT JODY   67.

Seen from outside one of the rear windows. She suddenly
opens the rear door. It smashes against Carling, sends
the flashlight tumbling to the ground. Sturka is on him
in a moment, hits him two thudding, smashing blows in the
face, wrenches the gun out of his hand. Carling is knocked
back against the car and then down on the ground. He makes
a motion as if to rise at which point Sturka brings the
gun down heavily on his head.

                    STURKA
               (half out of breath)
          Get in the car, Jerry. Let's go.

68. ANGLE SHOT LOOKING DOWN   68.

As they meet in the car. The car starts and screeches
ahead through the open gate and onto the field.

69- DIFFERENT ANGLES   69-
71.   71.

As it heads toward the saucer.

                                        CUT TO:

72. LOUD SPEAKER ON A POST IN THE FIELD   72.

                    VOICE ON LOUDSPEAKER
          Unauthorized vehicle on field.
          Unauthorized vehicle on field.
          Guard unit seven approach
          unauthorized vehicle. Approach
          unauthorized vehicle and request
          it to halt.

73. DIFFERENT ANGLE STURKA'S CAR   73.

As it screeches to a halt. They rush out, start to run the
hundred or so yards toward the saucer. Sturka pushes,
propels, urges them from behind.

74.   MED CLOSE SHOT   METAL LADDER   74.

Leading up to ship as the group arrives there and each in
turn hurries up to disappear inside the ship. Sturka is
the last man there and is half way up the ladder when a
uniformed guard lurches up toward him, catches his leg.
Sturka kicks himself free then lets the guard have it in
the face. Another guard replaces him just as the metal
door shuts and Sturka disappears inside.

75.   DIFFERENT ANGLE   THE SAUCER   75.

As the engines start and it slowly leaves the earth.

76.   DIFFERENT ANGLE   THE SAUCER   76.

As it heads up into the night sky.

                                        DISSOLVE TO:

77.   INT SPACE SHIP   77.

Jerry is at the controls in a small pilot's cabin. Sturka
enters, goes over and sits next to him.

                        JERRY
             Everybody all right?

                        STURKA
                  (nods)
             Twelve o'clock and all is well.
                  (he looks out toward
                   the giant screen that
                   sits on top of the
                   control panel,
                   thoughtfully)
             The stars look far away.

                        JERRY
                  (nods)
             They are far away.
                  (a pause)
             But the one we want...that's not
             so far, Bill. See it there? It's
             the shiny one. The bright one
             over on the right.

78.   CLOSE SHOT   SCREEN   78.

One star particularly luminous.

79.   ANGLE SHOT   THE TWO MEN   79.

As they stare toward the screen.

                        STURKA
             And there are people on it?
             People like us?

                                        CONTINUED

79. CONTINUED   79.

                         JERRY
                    (nods)
          People like us. It's the third
          planet from the sun, Bill. It's
          called Earth. That's where we're
          going. A place called Earth!

The CAMERA PANS UP to the screen as the star seems to
grow brighter and larger.

                    NARRATOR'S VOICE
          Behind a tiny ship heading into
          space is a doomed planet on the
          verge of suicide.
                    (a pause)
          Ahead lies a place called Earth.
          The third planet from the sun
          and for William Sturka and the
          men and women with him...it's
          the eve of the beginning in
          The Twilight Zone.

                                        FADE TO BLACK:

                    THE   END

EARTHBOUND

In 1959, Richard Matheson—already the respected author of several novels, scores of short stories and the screenplay for 1957's THE INCREDIBLE SHRINKING MAN—was invited (along with the legendary Charles Beaumont) to a screening of the *Twilight Zone* pilot "Where is Everybody?" Both writers would eventually play major roles in the shaping of this breakthrough series.

Richard Matheson went on to pen fourteen scripts, but his first two excursions into *The Twilight Zone* took the form of short stories that were adapted by Rod Serling: "Disappearing Act" and "Third from the Sun." The latter story originally appeared in the October 1950 issue of *Galaxy* magazine and tells a clean, edgy tale that is light on specifics but heavy on the emotional anxiety of its characters.

Serling's adaptation retains the tense mood but fleshes out the main characters, who in the short story are purposely left ambiguous to mislead the reader into assuming that they are contemporary human beings. These changes were necessary in easing the transition from page to screen. The addition of a villain—in the form of an overzealous government lackey named Carling—may seem a bit superfluous when compared to the short story, as the impending destruction of civilization is sufficient enough motivation to drive a hurried evacuation. But expansion was Serling's task and he achieved it without disrupting the flow of the story. The oily Carling provides momentary tension and fills out a half-hour script by padding the brisk but skeletal story.

Serling also raises the anxiety factor by truncating the holocaust's estimated time of arrival. Matheson's original mentions a time frame of two years but

Serling's script expects the devastating missile attack to take place within forty-eight hours. Early dialogue between Sturka and Carling, as they discuss the first-strike casualty rate, depicts the men as political and philosophical opposites. Sturka regards the attack as a mad and futile exercise in war-mongering while Carling sees the staggering death toll as a necessary loss in the pursuit of victory over a faceless enemy. The influence of both writers is showcased; the scene is an example of Matheson's dynamic plot stimulus as seen through the prism of Serling's anti-war stance.

"It was the episode which marks the point at which many occasional tuners-in became addicts," wrote prolific author Stephen King in his 1981 book DANSE MACABRE. "The gimmick [of the plot]—that the group of protagonists is fleeing not from Earth but *to* it—is one that has been utterly beaten to death by now (most notably by that deep-space turkey *Battlestar Galactica*), but most viewers can remember the snap of that ending to this day. Here, for once, was something Completely New and Different."

One notable deviation from the short story involves the survival of the species and a suggestion that the tale's characters are the ancestors of mankind. In Matheson's story, the neighbors are allowed to make the trip primarily because they have a son who can breed with the main couple's daughter, and no mention is made of life on the destination planet of Earth. While some readers may interpret this as a creation tale, Richard Matheson did not intend it as such.

"The point to the end of 'Third from the Sun,'" says Matheson, "was simply that the father thought they were escaping a dangerous planet, not realizing that they were headed for an equally dangerous planet." The propagation subtext is rendered moot in Serling's version, which nullifies it with a quick reference to a pre-existing population of people "just like us."

The performances of the cast are uniformly first-rate. Edward Andrews brings an insidious and treacherous quality to Carling, the sort of role that Andrews perfected over a long and distinguished career. Fritz Weaver as William Sturka and Joe Maross as Jerry Riden capture the tense atmosphere of the script and convey the nervous solemnity of men in possession of a horrible secret.

Prior to his foray into *The Twilight Zone*, Fritz Weaver's television experience had been limited to a handful of live broadcasts. "'Third from the Sun' was my first film ever, of any kind," reveals Weaver. "I didn't know a thing about it. I had some small success on the stage that year and I guess the casting people paid attention, dumb luck for me. In my naiveté, I thought all filming was going to be like that: wild, improvisational, with imaginative texts that took you out of the ordinary. Alas, it did not turn out that way."

In his trial by fire, Weaver recalls a frustrating introduction to the concept of continuity. "I thought I might smoke a cigarette as 'business' in one scene. It went well on the first take but when they moved in for the second take, the medium shot, the script girl stopped it to remind me that I had inhaled just before the fifth word and blown the smoke seven words later. I also had tapped out the ashes when I got up and stubbed the cigarette out when I sat down."

Duplicating this pedestrian task proved harder than the rookie actor could have imagined. "Many, many takes later I was still trying to remember all the cigarette business and making a perfect mess of the scene. When the nightmare was over and some sort of acceptable version was mercifully achieved, Eddie Andrews took me aside and said, 'Now you know why Gary Cooper keeps his hands in his pockets.' Lesson learned!"

"'Third from the Sun' was a delight," says Denise Alexander, who portrayed Jody Sturka. "Doing the show as an actor was great fun. The cast was all so caring about the project. We took great pleasure in the twist at the end of the tale, and felt we were making something truly unique that would engage the audience. As a teenager, it felt even more special, as I was entrusted with the secret of the 'twist' and treated as an equal by my fellow actors."

Alexander recalls a fascination with the "futuristic" set dressings. "Even though they were all contemporary pieces, we had such fun with the props that took us into the future. I remember the telephone—what an odd shape it was— and the director explaining that it was new and so odd in style that it would look futuristic without the audience realizing it." (The functional telephone, a product of the L.M. Ericsson Company of Sweden, was a one-piece, ultramodern design called *The Ericofon*.)

"I also remember how insistent the director and producer were that we play things as realistically as possible, very everyday normal, and not try to 'act the future.' It seemed strange at the time but I really get it now. They took great delight in using odd camera angles and subtle ways to suggest that this was not of the current time, but in a way that the audience would only see later."

Indeed, director Richard L. Bare went to great lengths to achieve this effect. "The sudden twist at the end is what made the film," Bare states, "and the objective in the scenes that led up to the climax was to avoid betraying Serling's secret that we were actually watching members of another planet preparing to come to ours. It was decided to use conventional-looking, -acting and -sounding players, living in conventional Earth-like surroundings; but they would be treated differently with the camera.

"I ordered the widest-angle lens that Metro-Goldwyn-Mayer Studios had, a 17.5mm 'bug eye.' I told the cameraman that I wanted this lens used exclusively, even on the close-ups. I explained I wanted the distortion that this lens gave everything and suggested that the cameraman work out unorthodox sources for the lighting, sources that would bring an unusual aura to the film. In addition to this, every camera setup was cocked to one side or the other, which further served to take away the feeling of normalcy. What I was striving to do was protect Serling's surprise ending and yet give the feeling of oddness so that when the picture was over, the audience would understand why the 'kooky' camera treatment was used."

Bare further explains how he manipulated the conventional scene of a bridge game with this unconventional approach. "Since the results of the game had no story value, and the scene itself was only one to denote the passing of time, I pondered how to make it interesting. The first angle I set up was from below the glass-topped table, showing the cards and faces of the players as the cat might view them. The second, and the one that demonstrates the complete scope of the camera, was made by placing the camera in the center of the table and panning it from the face of the leading man, across the faces of the other players as they made their bids, and right on around through 360 degrees until the leading man came into a close-up again.

"Although this shot took a little doing, it was accomplished by first enclosing the open side of the set with walls to make a four-wall room, and then removing all the lights and grip equipment from around the camera. All crew members were obliged to leave the set and the scene was lighted by lamps suspended from above. As the camera was panned from face to face, only the operator and myself walked around behind it, keeping out of its view."

The result is wonderfully effective. It captures the apprehension of each cast member in real time and never breaks the tension by stopping the camera. The dizzying effect also plays into the otherworldly feel of the camerawork.

Denise Alexander regards her appearance in the episode as a highlight in her career. "I loved watching *The Twilight Zone* as a kid but I had no idea how big the audience was, how well-regarded the show was in our profession and the extent to which it was lauded. 'Third from the Sun' was such a terrific show and everyone I knew loved it, so to be a part of it was a thrill. As I matured, I became more and more proud to have been in that episode. I still love telling the story to people and springing the last line on them!"

The Twilight Zone

THE PURPLE TESTAMENT

Airdate: 2-12-1960*

Manuscript Date: 8-18-1959

Script Nineteen

Episode Nineteen

* Scheduled airdate—episode was
pre-empted

THE TWILIGHT ZONE

SCRIPT NINETEEN

"THE PURPLE TESTAMENT"

by

ROD SERLING

August 18, 1959

FADE IN:

1.   EXT   SKY   NIGHT   1.

Shot of the sky...the various nebulae, and planet bodies
stand out in sharp, sparkling relief. As the CAMERA begins
a SLOW PAN across the Heavens -

                         NARRATOR'S VOICE (o.s.)
                    There is a fifth dimension beyond
                    that which is known to man. It is
                    a dimension as vast as space and as
                    timeless as infinity. It is the
                    middle ground between light and
                    shadow - between science and super-
                    stition. And it lies between the *pit of his fears*
      and the summit of his knowledge. This is
                    the dimension of imagination. It is
                    an area which we call The Twilight
                    Zone.

The CAMERA has begun to PAN DOWN until it passes the horizon
and is flush on the OPENING SHOT (EACH WEEK, THE OPENING SHOT
OF T HE PLAY)

2.   EXT DIRT ROAD   THE PHILLIPINES   NIGHT   2.
     LONG SHOT   EYE LEVEL   LOOKING TOWARD COLUMN OF
     APPROACHING G.I. TRUCKS

As they rumble slowly down the road toward the camera and
then past it. Each is loaded with infantrymen being
brought back from combat.

3.   DIFFERENT ANGLE   LOOKING TOWARD THE DESTINATION OF   3.
     THE TRUCKS

A tent encampment that is a regimental rear echelon. Super
over this scene the legend, "LUZON, PHILLIPINE ISLANDS, 1944".

4.   LOW ANGLE SHOT   LOOKING UP   4.

Toward a truck tail gate as the truck stops and the driver
comes out to put the gate down. The CAMERA NOW MOVES UP
so that it's looking down a line of the faces of the men as
they slowly rise, ready to file off the truck. There is
an element of brutal sameness about these faces. They're
dirty, desperately tired, hollow eyed, each showing the
aftermath of shock and violence; each creviced with lines
of desperate fatigue and the back wash of fear.

                                        CONTINUED

4.   CONTINUED   4.

                         NARRATOR'S VOICE
                Infantry platoon, U.S. Army. Phillipine
                Islands, 1944. These are the faces
                of the young men who fight, as if
                some omniscient painter had mixed a
                tube of oils that were at one time
                earth brown, dust gray, blood red,
                beard black and fear yellow-white.
                And these men were the models. For
                this is the province of combat, and
                these are the faces of war.

Now each man in turn moves in close to the camera as he
gets off the truck and we see face after face, young men,
as they climb off the truck.
                                              FADE OUT:

OPENING BILLBOARD
FIRST COMMERCIAL

FADE ON:

5.   EXT ROAD NIGHT SHOT OFF SIDE OF ROAD   5.

Where Riker, the Company Commander, stands looking at the
four trucks, his eyes darting from one to the other.

6.   TRACK SHOT WITH HIM   6.

As he walks toward the trucks. A Sergeant is helping a
wounded man off the truck. He turns now to see the Captain.

                         SERGEANT
                Evening, Captain. Ain't it a crummy
                night?

                         RIKER
                Rough?

The Sergeant reaches into his pocket and takes out a badly
bent cigarette which he has obviously been saving. He
smooths it out, puts it in his mouth. Riker lights it for
him. The Sergeant nods his thanks.

                         SERGEANT
                We got the bridge - whatever they
                wanted it for. Japs got naval guns
                stuck in the ground and they're
                zeroed in on the town. That bridge.
                         (MORE)
                                              CONTINUED

6. CONTINUED   6.

                         SERGEANT (cont)
              gets it every three minutes.
                   (He takes out the
                   cigarette, breathes
                   deeply of the smoke)
              If the General wants to know where
              the Jap fleet is - it's dug in on
              the road to Manila.

He turns and is about to leave.

                         RIKER
              Sergeant?

A pause as the Sergeant turns back.

                         RIKER
              Who'd we lose?

                         SERGEANT
              Lotsa wounded. Maybe ten, twelve.
              men. Four dead.

At this moment Lt. Fitzgerald comes into the frame, a
tall, rather gaunt looking second Looie platoon leader.

                         FITZGERALD
                   (in a kind of dead
                   voice)
              Hibbard, Horton, Morgan and Levy.
                   (then he turns toward
                   the Sergeant)
              Bed them down. Check with the Mess
              Sergeant. Make sure there's hot
              coffee and a meal. And if they're
              not hungry - eat anyway.

                         SERGEANT
              Yes, sir.
                   (then turning toward
                   trucks)
              A Company, First Platoon. Let's go.

And a straggly column of men follow him away from the trucks
toward the tents. Then the trucks pull ahead and disappear, leaving the Company Commander and the Lieutenat
standing alone on the road.

7. CLOSE SHOT CAPTAIN   7.

As he stares toward the Lieutenat.

8. CLOSE SHOT LIEUTENANT   8.

His face is indistinct in the night.

9. TWO SHOT   9.

                         RIKER
          Fitz?

                         FITZGERALD
                    (looks up at him)
          Sir?

                         RIKER
          I got me a bottle of Phillipine Tuba
          in my tent. It isn't Johnny Walker,
          but you'd be surprised what it does
          to a man's outlook.
                    (he walks over, puts
                    his hand on Fitzgerald's
                    shoulder)
          C'mon.

The two men start down the road toward the tents.

                                             DISSOLVE TO:

10. INT TENT NIGHT   10.

There's a big wooden crate that serves as a desk for the
Company Commander. An army cot is in the corner on a
tent floor. A Coleman lantern burns brightly on an orange
crate. A large map board has been set up close to the desk.
Riker sits on the bed, the bottle between his knees. He
holds it up toward Fitzgerald who stands near the opening of
the tent.

                         RIKER
          Give me your cup.

Fitzgerald turns, brings it over. Riker pours from the
bottle then holds the bottle up.

                         RIKER
          Cheers.

                                             CONTINUED

10. CONTINUED   10.

Fitzgerald nods briefly and drinks. Riker drinks from the
bottle but his eyes never leave Fitzgerald. He puts the
bottle down, wipes his mouth.

                         RIKER
              Bum day, huh, Fitz?

                         FITZGERALD
                   (nods tersely)
              Twelve wounded. Four dead. All in
              two and a half hours.
                   (he shakes his head
                   again)
              Twelve wounded. Four dead.

11. CLOSE SHOT RIKER   11.

The thin, intelligent face is probing.

                         RIKER
              Anything special about the four men?

12. TWO SHOT   12.

                         FITZGERALD
                   (turns toward him)
              Anything special? What do you mean?

                         RIKER
              We've lost four men before. We've
              lost eight and ten. You're taking
              this one a little harder than usual.
              I thought it might have been a little
              special.

                         FITZGERALD
                   (his voice edgey)
              They were four kids under twenty two -
              does it   have to be more special than
              that?

                         RIKER
                   (shakes his head,
                   quietly)
              No, it doesn't.
                   (a pause)
              But this has gotten to you. More than
              I've ever seen. I'd like to know why.

                                        CONTINUED

                    FITZGERALD
               (turns toward him,
               the shadows from the
               lamp play on his
               face, grimly)
          You're a perceptive man. It's the
          mark of a good officer, isn't it?
          To ward off trouble - by anticipating
          it.

                    RIKER
          You gonna give me trouble?
               (he grins and shakes
               his head)
          I don't think so, Fitz. You're a
          good officer. You've got guts and
          brains.
               (another pause)
          But something's gotten to you. I
          told you I'd like to know what it is.

                    FITZGERALD
               (takes a step toward
               him)
          Would you?

He reaches in his fatigue shirt pocket, takes out a slip
of paper all crumbled up. He unfolds it, takes it over to
Riker and hands it to him. Riker looks at it then reads
from it.

                    RIKER
          "Hibbard, Horton, Morgan and Levy."
               (he looks up from
               the paper)
          So?

                    FITZGERALD
          So who are they?

                    RIKER
          Four K.I.A.'s

                    FITZGERALD
          Yeah, that's what they are. Killed
          in action. Luzon, P.I., 13 June 1944.
          But you want to know what it is that's
          gotten to me. I'll tell you, Captain.
          What's gotten to me is that...I...I-

                                        CONTINUED

                          RIKER
You what?

                          FITZGERALD
I wrote those names down yesterday.
I wrote them down before we went up.

There's a long silence between the two men. Riker stares
at the younger man.

                          RIKER
Why'd you write their names down,
Fitz?

                          FITZGERALD
We were having a weapons check. I
looked into their faces - these four
men -

A pause as he suddenly seems to shake, his voice getting
unsteady. Riker gets up, goes over to him, pours from the
bottle into his mess cup, then points at him.

                          RIKER
Go ahead.

Fitzgerald takes a long swig from the cup and then in a sudden,
compulsive gesture, flings the cup against the desk, the
noise of it jarring the silence of the room. He stands there,
his head down, hands to his side.

                          RIKER
You feel better?

                          FITZGERALD
                 (looks up at him)
I looked at forty four faces yesterday
morning but when I got to these four -
it was a special look like a ...like a
light almost. I can't describe it to
you. It doesn't have any description. I
Just looked into their faces and I
knew.
                 (a pause)
I knew this was their last day. I
knew they'd get it.
                 (he holds up his hands
                 in a gesture)
I just <u>knew</u>. There wasn't any doubt.
Then driving up the highway this morning
                 (MORE)

                         FITZGERALD (cont)
          I was in their truck. All four of
          them were sitting across from me.
          Same thing, Captain. Same funny...
          odd look. Completely set apart from
          the others. As if somebody had a
          searchlight and had picked out those
          four faces. And again I knew.

                         RIKER
               (very toughtfully
               rubs his beard
               stubble)
          That's funny. That's sure funny.

                         FITZGERALD
          I haven't slept much. I've been
          wondering. Is this the way it's gonna
          be? If everytime I stand in front
          of a platoon ready to take them up -
          am I gonna be able to look down the
          line and tell which ones aren't
          coming back?
               (he shakes his head)
          Thanks but no thanks. This is lousy
          stuff. This can make you sick.
               (he turns away,
               his eyes closed)
          This can drive you out of your ever
          lovin' mind.
               (he turns back toward
               the Captain)
          We're not supposed to know these things.
          We're not supposed to be able to tell.
               (a pause)
          Captain, why can I tell? Why?

     Riker bends over and picks up the slip of paper off the cot,
     looks at it for a long, pensive moment.

                         RIKER
          Fitz - when did you write these names
          down? You sure it was yesterday? You
          sure it wasn't today? On the way back?
          In the truck?

                         FITZGERALD
               (walks back to him)
          Yesterday. Yesterday morning. That's
          when I wrote them down. I swear!
          That's when I wrote them down!

                                        DISSOLVE TO:

13. EXT STATION HOSPITAL DAY   13.

This is an old beat up schoolhouse comandeered by theU.S.
Army and utilized as a hospital. An ambulance is just
pulling away as we start to dolly in toward its entrance.

                                             DISSOLVE TO:

14. INT MEDICAL OFFICER'S OFFICE   14.

This is a make shift room formerly a classroom. The
Medical Officer in charge is Captain Gunther, a lean man in
his forties. At this moment he's alone in the room with
Riker.

                         RIKER
          Well?

                         GUNTHER
                    (from behind his desk,
                    looks up, shrugs)
          I can't tell, Captain. Stuff you've
          given me is perfunctory at best. It's
          obviously illusory. I looked up his
          records. Never been wounded. Pretty
          steady customer. No evidence of battle
          fatigue or anything at any time. Why
          all of a sudden he should get this
          weird idea - that's hard to say. I
          think we better pull him in. Run some
          checks.

                         RIKER
          The thing of it is - he believes it.
          You hear him tell it - you almost
          believe yourself.
                    (he shakes his head,
                    lights a cigarette then
                    rises from off the
                    school desk he's been
                    sitting on)
          I'd appreciate your checking him over
          though. He's a good man. He came in
          as cadre while we were still back in
          the States. He's one of the best
          officers we've got.

                         GUNTHER
          I'll do all I can, Captain. He's here
          now you know.

                         RIKER
                    (looking up quickly)
          No, I didn't know.

                                             CONTINUED

14. CONTINUED   14.

                          GUNTHER
          Yes, he's up in the ward visiting
          one of the boys from his platoon.

                          RIKER
          Well, when you see him, Doc, I'd
          appreciate your going at him a little
          subtly. I wouldn't like to have him
          think that I'd -

                          GUNTHER
                    (a little tiredly)
          I understand. I'll do it as subtly
          as I can.

     Riker heads toward the door.

                                              DISSOLVE TO:

15. INT WARD DAY   15.

     There are perhaps seven or eight men in the room, mostly
     bandaged cases. An Army nurse goes from bed to bed and a
     couple of ward attendants go on about their duties. We see
     the back of Fitzgerald as he stands over one of the beds.

16. DOLLY IN TO THE BED   16.

     The boy lying there is about nineteen. His arm is in a
     suspended cast. He looks pale and drawn. This is Smitty.

                          SMITTY
          How's the rest of the boys, Lieutenant?

                          FITZGERALD
          They're all fine. Porkie got a little
          piece of shrapnel in his finger but
          you know Porkie. That's about as
          bad as he's ever got.

                          SMITTY
                    (with a kind of weak
                     laugh)
          This is a lucky kid.

                          FITZGERALD
          That he is. And you didn't come out
          so bad. Get that all patched up,
          you'll be heading home and that's
          not hard to take, is it?

                                              CONTINUED

16. CONTINUED   16.

                              SMITTY
                    No, sir. Sure isn't.

His eyes go down to the cigarette in his mouth. It's gone
out. Fitzgerald takes out a book of matches, starts to
light it.

                              SMITTY
                         (shakes his head)
                    No, thank you, sir.
                         (with a free hand
                         he takes the cigarette
                         out)
                    Could you lay it down there for
                    me? I won't be needing it for a
                    while.

                              FITZGERALD
                    Sure.

He takes the cigarette, puts it in an ashtray alongside the
bed.

17. TWO SHOT FITZGERALD AND THE BOY   17.

                              FITZGERALD
                    I have a lot of stuff to do, Smitty.
                    I'll come in in the morning. You
                    take it easy - hear?

                              SMITTY
                         (nods)
                    Yes, sir.

                              FITZGERALD
                    Anything you need? You got stuff
                    to read?

                              SMITTY
                         (nods)
                    All I need.

18. CLOSE SHOT THE BOY   18.

As he stares up at the Lieutenant.

19. CLOSE SHOT FITZGERALD   19.

As he forces a smile.

                                        CONTINUED

19. CONTINUED   19.

                         FITZGERALD
                  Then take care, Smitty.

He turns and starts to go.

20. MED LONG SHOT THE BED   20.

Smitty tries to prop himself up.

                         SMITTY
                  Thanks for comin', Lieutenant.
                  Goodbye.

21. CLOSE SHOT FITZGERALD   21.

As he turns back toward the bed.

                         FITZGERALD
                      (in a strangely
                       quiet voice)
                  Goodbye, Smitty.

He turns and continues toward the camera. He's got a pack
of cigarettes in his hand which suddenly accidentally slip
out of his hand.

22. CLOSE SHOT CIGARETTES   22.

Landing on the floor.

23. DIFFERENT ANGLE FITZGERALD   23.

As he bends over to pick them up. In doing so his profile
is to the bed and he suddenly turns to look toward it.

24. LONG SHOT THE BED   24.

Suddenly we can see a light play on Smitty's face.

25. REVERSE ANGLE OF FITZGERALD   25.

As suddenly he reacts, slowly rising, staring bug eyed toward
the bed, his head involuntarily shaking back and forth. His
mouth forming a word, "no", but with no sound emitted. Then
eyes closed, he seems to sway on his feet and then turn in a
lurch toward the camera.

26. ANGLE SHOT LOOKING TOWARD THE FAR WALL   26.

And then PANNING UP TOWARD CEILING then DOWN ANOTHER WALL.

                                                ABRUPT CUT TO:

27. MED CLOSE SHOT   THE FLOOR   27.

As Fitzgerald's head lands on it in a faint.

                                                    CUT TO:

28. LONG ANGLE SHOT   LOOKING UP TOWARD CEILING   28.
FITZGERALD'S P.O.V.

It goes in and out of focus for a moment and then into the
frame comes the out of focus face of an Orderly which finally
takes on a clarity.

                         ORDERLY
                        (concerned)
                 You okay, Lieutenant?

29. REVERSE ANGLE   LOOKING TOWARD FITZGERALD   29.

Lying on the floor. He opens his eyes, blinks them several
times, forces himself up on an elbow.

                        FITZGERALD
                 Yeah. Yeah, I'm okay.

30. FULL SHOT THE ROOM   30.

As Fitzgerald gets to his feet.

31. MED. CLOSE SHOT   FITZGERALD   31.

As he seems to force himself to look toward the bed. The
attendant alongside hovers near him and then lets his eyes
follow Fitzgerald's.

32. CLOSE SHOT   ATTENDANT   32.

Reacting.

33. DIFFERENT ANGLE   THE BED   33.

As the Orderly rushes toward it, followed by Fitzgerald who
stops a few feet away.

34. CLOSE SHOT THE BED   34.

As the Orderly leans over the now lifeless body of Smith.
He touches the boy's head then the side of his face. Then
his fingers go down to the one free hand that lies motionless
on the bed. He feels its pulse then looks up toward
Fitzgerald.

                                                    CONTINUED

34.   CONTINUED   34.

                          ORDERLY
              He's dead. Just like that. They
              go awful quick sometimes. Awful quick.

He slowly removes the buckle holding up the arm in traction
and then carries the wounded hand and arm gently down to the
bed. Then he reaches for the fringe of the sheet and pulls
it up over the boy's face.

35.   MOVING SHOT FITZGERALD   35.

As he turns and slowly walks out of the room.

                                                CUT TO:

36.   INT HALLWAY AND STAIRS   36.

As Fitzgerald walks slowly down the steps to the foot.
The CAMERA FOLLOWS HIM as he makes the descent, stops at the
foot of the steps.

37.   REVERSE ANGLE LOOKING DOWN THE HALL TOWARD RIKER   37.

Who stands smoking a cigarette outside of Gunther's office.
Riker looks up, grins, and then the grin is wiped off when
he sees the expression on Fitzgerald's face. He takes a
couple of anxious steps toward him and stops a few feet away.

                          RIKER
              Fitz?

                          FITZGERALD
              I was up seeing Smitty.

                          RIKER
                    (nods)
              I know. I read his tag. Doc says
              he's gonna be okay now.

                          FITZGERALD
                    (shakes his head
                    slowly from side to
                    side, very quietly)
              No he isn't. I took a look at his
              face.
                    (a pause)
              I took a look at his face. I knew.
              And then a minute later...he's gone.

38.   CLOSE TWO SHOT   THE TWO MEN   38.

                    RIKER
               (in almost a whisper)
          Same thing?

                    FITZGERALD
               (nods)
          Same thing. The look...the funny...
          the funny light or whatever it is.
          But I knew. I knew, Captain.

39.   CLOSE SHOT   RIKER   39.

As he stares at the other man. His eyes narrow, surveying,
weighing, trying to give this thing a label of understanding,
trying to come up with some kind of meaning that he can
relate to reality. Finally he puts an arm on Fitzgerald's
shoulder.

                    RIKER
          Fitz, I can't explain this but -

                    FITZGERALD
          I don't want you to explain it. How
          can you explain it? How can anybody
          explain it?
               (and then almost
               supplicating)
          I want you to believe it, Captain.
          That's all I want from you. I want
          you to believe it.

40.   LONG SHOT   LOOKING DOWN THE CORRIDOR   40.

As Gunther comes out and starts toward the steps.

                                        CUT TO:

41.   LONG SHOT   UP THE STEPS   41.

As the Attendant comes down. He passes Fitzgerald and Riker
and meets Gunther a few feet from the foot of the steps.

                    ATTENDANT
          Bed five, sir. Smith. He just died.

                    GUNTHER
               (nods, softly)
          I'll go up and have a look.

                                        CONTINUED

41. CONTINUED   41.

                         FITZGERALD
          For what?

Gunther and the Attendant turn toward him.

                         FITZGERALD
          There's nothing to look at...except
          a body. He's dead. And I knew he
          was going to die. I read it on his
          face. I read it as if somebody had
          painted it there.

                         GUNTHER
                    (very disturbed, to
                    the Attendant)
          Go on back up. I'll be right
          there.

The Attendant nods, looking wide eyed at Fitzgerald, then goes
back on up the steps. Gunther walks over toward Fitzgerald
and exchanges a look with Riker as he does so.

                         GUNTHER
          You knew huh, Lieutenant?

                         FITZGERALD
                    (nods)
          You bet I knew. I tabbed four men
          yesterday too. I knew they were
          going to get it too.

                         GUNTHER
                    (takes a deep breath)
          Odd, don't you think, Lieutenant?

                         FITZGERALD
                    (lets out a laugh
                    that is not too far
                    from hysteria)
          Odd? It's not odd. Odd is when you
          go thirty days on the line and not
          lose a man. That's odd. Odd is
          when you walk twenty five miles and
          don't get a blister. Now you're
          talking odd. This isn't odd, Captain.
          This is...this is nightmare. This is
          a lousy dog face line officer who
          can see death on people's faces. A
                         (MORE)

                                              CONTINUED

41. CONTINUED   41.

                    FITZGERALD (cont)
          lousy dog face line officer who'd
          like to give back the power to who-
          ever gave it to him.

                    GUNTHER
                 (very quietly)
          Or a dog face line officer who's
          cracking under the strain from having
          done too much and felt too much and
          finally having to...to succumb to it.

                    FITZGERALD
                 (with a crooked grin)
          I'm five for five now, Captain. How
          many coincidences add up to a fact?
          How many men do I have to tab as the
          least likely to succeed? How many
          more faces do I have to look into?
                 (he turns away)
          What I'd like to know is - what's
          it take before you guys realize
          that somewhere along the line I
          picked up a talent they don't teach
          at O.C.S.
                 (he turns to look
                 from face to face)
          I'm kind of a...kind of a recording
          clerk for the grim reaper now.

42. CLOSE SHOT FITZGERALD   42.

                    FITZGERALD
                 (his voice trembling)
          There is one thing you might do in
          the interim...while you're waiting
          and scratching your heads and
          calling in a psychiatrist.
                 (he takes a step
                 toward them his voice
                 bordering on a night-
                 marish fear and a plead-
                 ing supplication)
          Put tape over my eyes, will you?
          Or poke them out. Or do something
          so I won't be able to see!
                 (MORE)

CONTINUED

42. CONTINUED   42.

                    FITZGERALD (cont)
                 (he closes his eyes
                 tightly, his hands
                 move up to grab at
                 his face, in almost
                 a whisper now and a
                 half sob)
            So I won't have to look at any more
            faces!

Now he turns and starts slowly down the hall as we take a

                                    SLOW FADE TO BLACK

                    END ACT ONE

ACT TWO

FADE ON:

43. EXT TENT STREET NIGHT   43.

PAN SHOT ACROSS AREA. There are a row of G.I. trucks, the
tail gates down, obviously in preparation for a move. The
CAMERA CONTINUES to PAN across the tents where inside by the
light of Coleman lanterns we can see men packing up gear and
getting ready for a jump off.

                                           DISSOLVE TO:

44. INT RIKER'S TENT NIGHT   44.

He stands there in front of a map board. In front of him are
four Lieutenants. Fitzgerald is one of them. All men are in
fatigues, helmets, side arms and ready to move. Riker's
dressed identically. He makes a mark on a map then turns to
face them.

                         RIKER
            All right. I'll give it to you just
            as I got it from Regiment. We spearhead
            the attack. We go to a point exactly
            four miles.north of the bridge.
            That's right here.
                 (taps the map)
            That's the Pasig River. At this point
            on the highway the bridge is out but
            over here to the East...the army's
            sticking across a Bailey. It should
            be done by 0200. We'll spearhead the
            operation and move across the bridge
            as the point. Baker and Charlie company
            follow us. Now up here some Filipino
            guerrillas will be crossing by boat.
            We hope unobserved. Their job will
            be to take any and all guns the Japs
            have on the other side so we should
            be able to get across that bridge
            against only small arms. Any questions?

There's a silence in the tent.

                         RIKER
            All right then, that's it. We've got
            about twenty two minutes before we
            load up on the trucks. Give each one   -20
            of your platoons a good briefing.
            Belts, five grenades a piece, six clips
            of ammo, no back packs. That's it.
            Good luck.

                                           CONTINUED

44. CONTINUED   44.

There's a mumble of voices as the three officers start to
leave the tent. Fitzgerald stands there motionless staring
toward Riker at the map board. Riker looks at him a little
perfunctorily then rips down the map, folds it up, goes over
to the makeshift desk, shoves the map in a drawer then just
sits there for a long silent moment staring down at it, only
the top of his head visible. PAN SHOT OVER to Fitzgerald
who now stares at him.

45. REVERSE ANGLE LOOKING TOWARD FITZGERALD   45.

As Riker slowly raises his head. We're on the back of it
looking directly into Fitzgerald's face as once again his
eyes go wide.

46. A SLOW SEMI-CIRCULAR PAN   46.

Until we can see part of the front of Riker's face. It's bathed
in the odd light just as Smith's in the previous act.

                                                    CUT TO:

47. CLOSE SHOT FITZGERALD   47.

As he takes a step toward him.
                                                    CUT TO:

48. FULL SHOT THE TENT   48.

As Riker slowly gets to his feet, his voice strained.

                          RIKER
                What's the matter, Fitz?

                          FITZGERALD
                    (in a whisper)
                Nothing.

                          RIKER
                Do you still think you're well
                enough to take the platoon?

Fitzgerald doesn't answer.

                          RIKER
                Gunther thinks you'd be better off
                with three weeks back at Division.
                I agree with him too. This one
                probably won't take but a few hours -
                but it'll be messy!

49.   CLOSE SHOT RIKER   49.

As he looks intently at Fitzgerald.

                    RIKER
                 (softly)
            What's the matter, Fitz?
                 (then slowly his features
                 change, the tone of his
                 voice changes, it's edged
                 now with an alarm)
            What are you looking at? Fitz -

                                              CUT TO:

50.   CLOSE SHOT FITZGERALD   50.

                    FITZGERALD
            Captain...you'd better not go!

51.   TWO SHOT THE TWO MEN   51.

                    RIKER
                 (his eyes narrow)
            Why, Fitz?

There's a silence. Riker reaches up to touch his face.

                    RIKER
            Do you see something, Fitz, is that
            it?

Fitzgerald nods.

                    RIKER
            Do you see something...like with the
            others.

                    FITZGERALD
            It's on your face. If you go...
                 (he shakes his head)
            You won't be coming back.

52.   CLOSE SHOT RIKER   52.

He stares at Fitzgerald for a long moment and then has to
turn his eyes away. Then he turns and faces the map board.
The CAMERA MOVES OVER for a CLOSE PROFILE SHOT of him as he
thinks this one out. There's a long, long silence.

                    RIKER
                 (tersely but quietly)
            Get your platoon set, Fitz. You've
            only got about fifteen minutes.

53. TWO SHOT   *Retype*   53.

Fitzgerald takes a step toward him.

                    FITZGERALD
          What about -

He leaves the rest unsaid. Riker takes a deep breath.

                    RIKER
          I tell you what we'll do about that.
          We'll talk about it when we get back.
          We'll have a drink on it. We'll drink
          to an illusion - a couple of coincidences.
                    (a pause)
          That's it, Fitz. I'll see you at the
          trucks.

He turns now to stare at Fitzgerald who continues to study
him.

                    FITZGERALD
                    (shaking his head)
          You won't drink to anything. You
          aren't coming back.

He turns, walks out of the tent. CAMERA PANS BACK OVER for
a MED CLOSE SHOT of Riker whose eyes go down pensively,
deep in thought. He looks at his watch then goes over to
his cot, picks up a gunbelt, hooks it on, sticks a couple
of grenades through the belt, reaches for his helmet, sticks
it on, takes out a forty five from the holster, spins the
cartridges, then puts it back in the holster. Then he looks
at his watch again, very, very pensively, then toward the
flap opening of the tent. Then he slowly rubs the watch,
then puts the hand down at his side. Now he takes his wallet
out, looks at some of the pictures. He's about to put it back
in his pocket when he stops, looks at it again, takes the
pictures out, lays them on the makeshift desk and leaves them
there. He looks at the ring on his finger. He takes that off
too and puts it alongside the pictures. He looks grimly down
at all of it, then, as if driven, he walks across the tent
and exits.

                                        DISSOLVE TO:

54. EXT COMPANY STREET NIGHT   54.

Long lines of men quietly get on the trucks. The only sound
is that of metal hitting metal, equipment rattling, etc.

55. LONG. SHOT   LOOKING ACROSS TOWARD. THE STREET   OF   55.
Retype FITZGERALD

As he walks toward the trucks.

56. REVERSE ANGLE   FITZGERALD'S P.O.V.   56.

Looking toward a squad of men who await his arrival. He
slowly approaches them.

57. TRACK SHOT WITH HIM   57.

As he passes them, studying face after face. The men look
at him and then turn their faces away uneasily. He finally
reaches one particularly young soldier who continually bites
his lower lip. This is a nineteen year old named Freeman.

                    FREEMAN
               (blurting this out)
          Lieutenant, what about it? Everybody
          says you can tell. Everybody says
          you know who's gonna get it and who
          isn't. Well, how about it, Lieutenant?
          Give us a break.
               (now his voice raises
               several octaves and
               becomes uncontrollable)
          Come one, Lieutenant, please - it
          ain't fair you knowin' and not
          tellin' us who - |

He's cut off by Riker's voice, sharp, loud, incisive. He
enters the frame from the left.

                    RIKER
          Freeman, knock it off|

58. GROUP SHOT THE MEN   58.

As they look from Riker to Fitzgerald.

                    RIKER
               (now his voice is
               quieter with a kind
               of half-hearted and yet
               compulsive attempt at
               lightness)
          Somebody started a wild gag - and
          that somebody's gonna get burned
          for it. Nobody in this company's a
          mind reader - including Lieutenant
          Fitzgerald.
                    (MORE)

                                              CONTINUED

58. CONTINUED   58.

                          RIKER (cont)
                    (then his eyes slowly
                    traverse until he's
                    staring directly at
                    Fitzgerald)
               How 'bout that, Lieutenant?

59. CLOSE SHOT FITZGERALD   59.

60.. PAN SHOT AROUND THE FACES OF THE MEN   60.

     As they stare ending up again on Fitzgerald. His eyes drop.

                         FITZGERALD
               That's right, sir.

61. CLOSE SHOT RIKER   61.

                           RIKER
               Okay, boys. Let's hop!

     The men start to clamber on the trucks.

                           VOICE
                    (shouting)
               Let's get the troops out of the hot
               sun!

62. DIFFERENT ANGLE LOOKING DOWN THE ROAD   62.

     As the trucks one by one pull away loaded with soldiers and
     head down the road into the night.
                                             FADE TO BLACK:

     FADE ON:

63. EXT COMPANY STREET DAY   63.

     It's early morning and the tents are quiet.

64. PAN SHOT DOWN THE STREET   64.

     Past the empty tents until in front of one we see a soldier
     with his arm in a sling playing a harmonica. The sound of it
     is like a frail girl singing over the silence. The soldier
     suddenly looks up as off in the distance we hear the sound of
     trucks, first from far off then gradually getting closer and
     louder.

65.　ANGLE SHOT　LOOKING DOWN THE ROAD　　　　　65.

Toward the trucks as they once again head into the area.

66.- DIFFERENT SHOTS　OF THE SOLDIERS　　　　66.-
68.　　　　　　　　　　　　　　　　　　　　　　68.

As the trucks stop and the soldiers start to file off. There's
low conversation, an occasional laugh. This is obviously the
aftermath of a comparatively easy time. The CAMERA PICKS UP
a LONG SHOT of Fitzgerald as he says a few unintelligible words
to a sergeant and then slowly turns and walks toward the
camera, the CAMERA DOLLYING BACK to keep the approaching
Fitzgerald in frame It DOLLIES BACK until we're abreast of
Riker's tent. Then the CAMERA PANS OVER TO THE LEFT for a
shot of Fitzgerald as he walks into the tent.

　　　　　　　　　　　　　　　　　　　　CUT TO:

69.　INT RIKER'S TENT　DAY　　　　　　　　　　69.

He looks briefly around the room and then very slowly walks
over to the makeshift desk. He looks down at the pictures
and the wallet on it. Then the ring.

70.　CLOSE SHOT　DESK　　　　　　　　　　　　70.

71.　CLOSE SHOT　FITZGERALD　　　　　　　　　71.

As he reaches into his pocket and takes out a chain with two
dog tags on it. This he slowly lays on the desk top. Then he
sits down and stares at it.

72.　MED CLOSE SHOT ╴ TENT FLAP　　　　　　　72.

As it opens and the Colonel enters. The Colonel nods. Fitzgerald comes to his feet. The Colonel waves him back.

　　　　　　　　　COLONEL
　　　　At ease, Fitz. I just came around
　　　　to congratulate you boys on a good
　　　　job.

　　　　　　　　　FITZGERALD
　　　　(nods a little numbly)
　　　　Thank you, sir.

The Colonel takes out a cigar, lights it, takes the cigar out
of his mouth, looks across at Fitzgerald.

　　　　　　　　　COLONEL
　　　　All the odds fell in on our side.
　　　　Those guerrillas did a right handly
　　　　job on the guns. You walked right
　　　　across didn't you.

　　　　　　　　　　　　　　　　　　CONTINUED

72.   CONTINUED   72.

                         FITZGERALD
                    (nods)
               Right across.

                         COLONEL
               That's fortunate. There must have
               been at least six or seven .25's that
               the Air Force picked out. If those
               guns had been operating - that would
               probably have been the longest bridge
               you'd ever been on!
                    (a pause)
               Or the shortest! Sniper fire -
               that's all you had, wasn't it?

                         FITZGERALD
               Yes, sir. Sniper fire. We lost one
               man.

He looks down at the desk at the dog tags.

73.   EXTREMELY TIGHT CLOSE SHOT DOG TAGS   73.

Then the CAMERA PANS up for shot of the Colonel who suddenly
looks grim.

                         COLONEL
               That's   a pity.
                    (he points toward
                    the desk)
               There was a good man. You were good
               friends weren't you, Fitzgerald?

Fitzgerald nods and doesn't say anything. The Colonel walks
over toward the desk, reaches over and picks up the dog tags,
jingles them in his hand.

                         COLONEL
               And so much for Mrs. Riker's very
               lovely wedding and seven happy years
               and two fine sons.
                    (he lays the dog tags
                    slowly on the desk)
               God, but war stinks!

He turns and walks out of the tent. The CAMERA PANS back over
to a tight close shot of Fitzgerald.

                         FITZGERALD
               It stinks...but it stinks worse when
               you know. Much worse when you know!

                                             CONTINUED

73. CONTINUED   73.

At this moment the tent opens again and the Medical Officer,
Captain Gunther stands there.

                    GUNTHER
          Lieutenant?

Fitzgerald looks up.

                    GUNTHER
          Some orders have come through on
          you. You're to go back to Division.

                    FITZGERALD
               (looks up, his voice
                a little numb and very
                quiet)
          Back to Division?

                    GUNTHER
               (nods)
          That's right. They'd like to look
          you over. It'll be a nice coupla
             weeks rest for you. You better
          pack up your gear. Take it with
          you.

                    FITZGERALD
               (after a pause)
          Okay. Thank you, Captain.

He walks past Gunther and outside as we
                                        DISSOLVE TO:

74. INT FITZGERALD'S TENT DAY FULL SHOT   74.

An almost filled barracks bag lies near the cot. Fitzgerald
is in the process of shoving the last few items into it then
he pushes down and around its apex then buckles it with the
strap buckle. CAMERA FOLLOWS HIM as he crosses the tent over
to what is obviously a home made wash stand. A helmet lies
there half filled with soapy water, a brush and a razor.
Fitzgerald throws the water on the ground, sticks a helmet
liner inside the helmet, then he takes the brush and razor
and puts them in a leather over night kit and then by rote,
with little thought, he reaches up to a glass mirror that hangs
on a nail.

75. EXTREMELY TIGHT CLOSE SHOT MIRROR IN HIS HAND   75.

Of his reflection as suddenly the strange light again
appears this time on his reflection.

76. EXTREME TIGHT FLASH CLOSE SHOT FITZGERALD'S FACE   76.

As he reacts.

77. CLOSE SHOT GROUND   77.

As the mirror falls, breaking into a hundred pieces on the
ground. The light persists on the fragments of Fitzgerald's
reflection as he looks down on it.

                    VOICE
               (off)
          Lieutenant Fitzgerald? Ambulance
          is leaving now, sir, for Division.
          You set?

Fitzgerald remains standing stock still, staring down at
the broken mirror.
                                             CUT TO:

78. AMBULANCE DRIVER   78.

Standing by the opening of the tent.

                    DRIVER
          Lieutenant Fitzgerald? This your bag,
          sir?

Fitzgerald turns to look at him.

                    FITZGERALD
          What? Yes, yes, that's my bag.

                    DRIVER
          Can I put it in the ambulance for
          you, sir?

                    FITZGERALD
               (nods)
          Thank you. Thank you, very much.

                    DRIVER
          Whenever you're ready, sir, we're all
          set.

He picks Fitzgerald's bag up and goes out. Fitzgerald bends
down, picks up a couple of pieces of glass, stares at them
and tosses them back on the ground. He rises, picks up the
over night kit, looks at it, then throws it aside and exits.

                                             CUT TO:

79. EXT COMPANY STREET DAY   79.

The ambulance driver is just closing the doors of the
ambulance as Fitzgerald comes up alongside.

                    DRIVER
               (grins)
          You can ride up front with me, sir.
          Plenty of room.

                    FITZGERALD
               (stares at him for
               a moment)
          Thank you.

He climbs in the passenger's seat. The CAMERA MOVES BACK
until it is on a tableau of him sitting there stoically
staring out the front windshield.

80. DIFFERENT ANGLE THE TRUCK   80.

As the Driver comes around to his side and opens the door.
A Lieutenant walks up to him.

                    LIEUTENANT
          You going back to Division?

                    DRIVER
          Yes, sir.

                    LIEUTENANT
          You taking the Cavite Road?

                    DRIVER
          I got to, sir. The bridge is out on
          the highway.

                    LIEUTENANT
          That's what I figured. Some Engineers
          think they got some mines spotted
          just a mile up the road. They haven't
          had a chance to dig them out so take
          her careful and stay close to the
          shoulders.

                    DRIVER
          Yes, sir. Thank you, sir.

81. INT CAB   81.

As the Driver gets in. He grins sideways toward Fitzgerald.

                                        CONTINUED

81. CONTINUED   81.

                            DRIVER
                Get nice and comfy, Lieutenant.
                It's about a four hour ride.

 82. CLOSE SHOT   FITZGERALD   82.

     As he turns toward the driver.

83. CLOSE SHOT   DRIVER   FITZGERALD'S P.O.V.   83.

     His face too is bathed in the strange light.

84. CLOSE SHOT   FITZGERALD   84.

                          FITZGERALD
                Is it?
                        (then he turns and
                        stares out the wind-
                        shield again)
                I doubt it.

                                          DISSOLVE TO:

85. EXT COMPANY STREET   ANGLE SHOT LOOKING DOWN ON   85.
     AMBULANCE

     As it pulls away.

86. FULL SHOT   THE AREA   86.

     There are little groups of soldiers lying around reading
     mail. The boy in the sling begins to play the harmonica
     again. There's a feeling of repose, of peace, if only
     momentary, of quiet and rest.

87. MED CLOSE SHOT LIEUTENANT   87.

     As he walks over to the soldier with the harmonica.

                          LIEUTENANT
                You play that pretty good.

     The soldier looks up and grins and continues to play.

88. CLOSE SHOT   LIEUTENANT   88.

     As he hap hazardly, hands in his hip pockets, takes a
     stroll down the tents. He suddenly stops, stares off in
     the distance as there's the sound of a very distant clap
     of thunder.

89.   ANGLE SHOT LOOKING AT HIM FROM THE GROUND   89.

Where the soldier playing the harmonica sits.

                    LIEUTENANT
              (turns to him)
          You hear that?

                    SOLDIER
              (puts the harmonica
              down)
          Thunder?

                    LIEUTENANT
          I don't think so. That sounded
          like an explosion.

90.   CLOSE SHOT LIEUTENANT   90.

As he rubs his jaw pensively.

                    LIEUTENANT
          But maybe it was thunder. Yeah.
          Yeah, that's what it was. Probably
          thunder.

He turns and continues to walk.

91.   TRACK SHOT WITH HIM   91.

As he walks. When he passes the opening of Lieutenant
Fitzgerald's tent he continues on past the frame while the
CAMERA DOLLIES INTO the INT then takes a SLOW PAN down to the
ground for a SHOT of the cracked pieces of glass mirror.

                    NARRATOR'S VOICE
          From William Shakespeare, "Richard the
          Third", a small excerpt. The line
          reads, "He has come to open the
          purple testament of bleeding war".
          And for Lieutenant William Fitzgerald,
          A Company, First Platoon...the testa-
          ment is closed.
              (a pause)
          Lieutenant Fitzgerald has found The
          Twilight Zone!
                                        FADE TO BLACK:

                    THE END

WHEN DEATH HAS A FACE

There is a measure of irony in the fact that Rod Serling launched a remarkably successful science fiction/fantasy-based television series. His proven and primary strength was not in the realms of pure fantasy or hard science; rather, his writing expertise was rooted in character-driven drama. In "The Purple Testament," Serling fuses reality and the preternatural with precision, and demonstrates how a talented writer can adapt his skills and excel in any given format or genre.

First and foremost, this teleplay is about the dread and the anguish that is warfare. It is so grounded in reality, and populated by such authentic characters, that the introduction of a supernatural element does nothing to rob it of credibility. The focus is placed on the ubiquitous, hour-by-hour battle for survival that defines the tenuous existence of a soldier in combat. In this arena, Rod Serling operated from his home turf and it is quite evident that he was familiar with every inch of its bloodstained soil.

The setting of this episode is the Philippine Islands, where Serling himself endured many grueling months of brutal combat as a World War II paratrooper. Like so many other war-scarred authors, Serling sought refuge and catharsis in the telling of tales. "I was traumatized into writing by war events," Serling later said, "by going through a war in a combat situation and feeling the desperate sense of—the terrible need for some sort of therapy, get it out of my gut, write it down. This is the way it began for me."

Serling imbues the script with a sense of immediacy and desperation. His opening narration sets the tone with eloquence, and introduces a platoon of young soldiers who have lived with the specter of death for so long that they have become desensitized to it. We see exhaustion and apathy in the lethargic, zombie-like movements of the infantry; we hear the dispirited dialogue of officers who have carried burdens of responsibility for far too long. These are men who live moment to moment. The realization that a fatal bullet or piece of shrapnel can arrive swiftly and unannounced is brought home with every body of a fallen comrade.

Because Serling and his crew capture this illusion of reality, the episode is not hampered by the use of stock-footage battles or the utilization of a single soundstage dressed to simulate the dense Philippine jungle of Luzon. "They made good use of the sets," says lead actor William Reynolds. "They were simple but we had everything we needed. This project was so unique. No battle scenes, and somebody coming in and dropping dog tags on the table is much more telling than firefights. Today they wouldn't do it like that."

"It was like really being in World War II," adds actor Ron Masak, who portrayed a member of the company. "The actors, the set...it was a learning experience. *The Twilight Zone* was my first film credit and allowed me to get my Screen Actors Guild card. [Director] Richard Bare was a delight, and [producer] Buck Houghton was on the set often. I feel it was one of the best."

Reynolds does a fine job as the tortured Lt. Fitzgerald, as does Dick York as his sympathetic commanding officer. Reynolds would later star in *The FBI* while York would go on to gain fame as the bumbling Darren Stevens in *Bewitched*. Character actor Barney Phillips lends his usual stability in a supporting role, and a young Warren Oates makes a cameo as a doomed driver. "I had seen York on Broadway," says Ron Masak, "and he was a wonderful actor."

William Reynolds remembers his audition as a surprisingly casual meeting with Rod Serling. "I wasn't the initial selection, it was a last minute thing. I was at Metro doing a pilot for an adventure series, which I did later that year, and I got word that Rod was interested in seeing me. I went down to meet him and it was a very nice experience. It was a very painless kind of interview. I don't know what he'd seen me in. I'd done some things but I wasn't a household name. We just sat and talked for a while and as I recall, I remember feeling, 'Gee, this is good. I'd like auditions if they'd all be like this.'

"In those days I didn't do auditions very much, being a contract actor for the most part. You were assigned to things and you did them...or didn't do them, and suffered the consequences. I never felt more comfortable in an interview, before or since. I didn't read from the script or anything, we just talked about the part and about me. I was in the Army during the Korean War as a rear-echelon type; I was a staff sergeant in Japan for a year and a half. I understood the military."

Serling's writing lends believability to the relationship between Lt. Fitzgerald and his commanding officer, Captain Riker. The characters rely on each other for survival and have developed a strong bond of trust. Riker worries about his friend's visions but never totally discounts Fitzgerald's sincerity or sanity. In fact, when the lieutenant sees death on Riker's face and implores his captain to abandon the mission, Riker scoffs…but privately believes in the inevitability of the premonition. In a touching scene, Riker leaves behind his wedding band and pictures of his children—proof that he is aware of his impending sacrifice, yet unwilling to shirk his duty.

"We did it so fast," says William Reynolds, while discussing the inherent deadlines of episodic television. "Those circumstances are sometimes better. It's not that I was disadvantaged by the lack of time because the words carried themselves. All you had to do was try to set your emotional tone and let the words come. The only thing you don't have is the time to go back and reprise what it might be. One of the things about *The Twilight Zone* that I think is so interesting is that the actors were allowed to present various colors."

Indeed, Reynolds makes use of a full palette in his portrayal of a man teetering on the edge of sanity. In spite of this, he is not totally satisfied with his performance. "I got the script the day before we shot and there were a couple of scenes that I think I could have done somewhat better. With an actor's reticence, I could have found more interesting ways to play them. But I've never done anything that I didn't think I could improve on. However, I've had nothing but compliments on it."

This script about a soldier who could foretell the future would turn out to have a special significance for actor Ron Masak. "I was so good at playing a G.I.," he laughs, "that I was drafted two weeks later! I was in basic training when it aired and watched it with a sergeant. He kept looking at me and saying, 'Man, you really look like you had been to Luzon.' In a way, I had been."

William Reynolds tells of a far more ironic experience that befell him and director Richard L. Bare. "'The Purple Testament' was scheduled to be shown on the twelfth of February, 1960. Dick and I were doing this adventure show called *The Islanders* and we were doing background shots down in Jamaica. My son had just been born on the thirtieth of January so they postponed shooting a week or so. We were coming back into Miami to see if we could catch *The Twilight Zone*, flying across the island, and we crashed about three miles or so out. We nosed into the water pretty bad. The cameraman bled to death."

Reynolds himself sustained several lacerations and a broken leg. "We swam around for a while before heading in. Dick had two broken legs and was trying to paddle on this board. I had cuts; there was blood in the water, and my thoughts were of sharks. A canoe came out to the crash site to see what they could get in the way of salvage, so I got hold of the bow and told them that they weren't going anyplace without me and Dick!

"We were taken to this clinic kind of thing—they called it a hospital—and I was out of it for a while with the anesthesia, which was morphine and cognac. I woke up and here's this woman—a seamstress, not a physician. I was cut pretty badly across the hand and up the arm, and she was stitching my hand with a needle and thread."

The accident led to a pre-emption of the episode's broadcast. "It went out on the air that the plane had crashed, and they didn't know the disposition of anybody. Rod and Buck Houghton took [the episode] off the air. That's a gutsy thing from two men who were sensitive to my situation. My wife had a two-week-old baby and out of consideration for her they took it off the air, especially since the show was about somebody seeing their own death. I don't know whether those kind of sensibilities would have been visited on the people at ABC, for instance, who were doing my show, *The Islanders*. I was always grateful. I thought that was a singularly wonderful thing to do."

The harrowing crash failed to taint Reynolds' memories of his visit to *The Twilight Zone*. "I've done a lot of things over the years, but this half-hour TV show is one of the most memorable. I'm very proud of it."

The Twilight Zone

THE BIG, TALL WISH

Airdate: 4-8-1960

Manuscript Date: 2-22-1960

Dated 12-21-1959
with revisions dated 1-12-1960,
2-12-1960 and 2-22-1960

Script Twenty-Eight

Episode Twenty-Seven

"THE TWILIGHT ZONE"

Script Twenty-Eight

THE BIG, TALL WISH

by

ROD SERLING

December 21, 1959

"THE BIG, TALL WISH"

CAST

Bolie Jackson - 35 year old Negro prize-fighter.

Henry - 10 year old Negro boy

Frances - Henry's attractive mother

Mizell - vinegar-faced ring second who has seen them
all come and go

Thomas - fat and conscience-less fight manager.

Fat man - blood-thirsty ringsider

Floozie - blood-thirsty ringsider

Announcer - at ringside and for Voice-Over

Referee -

Man One - pg 20 & pg 26

Woman - pg 20

Teenager - pg 20

Voice - pg 11 & pg 13 - cast as young ring punk in case
director wants to see him at door

Bolie's opponent - bit stunt

THE TWILIGHT ZONE - "The Big, Tall Wish" - 1/12/60

"THE BIG, TALL WISH"

SETS

Exterior -

    Tenement Street - 1 3/4 pgs. - should be done night for
                            night without tarping on Lot 2.

    Tenement Roof - lit by city lights and roof signs nearby.
                    Have bare-bulb overhead for dissolve
                    effect at #81.

Interior -

    Bolie Jackson's Bedroom - a poor, rented room.
                            (door to hall, backed)

    Apartment Hall, stairs and Street Door (backed - tenement
                            style)

    Frances' Apartment Living Room and Henry's Bedroom -
                            suggest all in one with above set

    Prize Fight Dressing Room (Door to hall, backed) -
                            down beat. Walls of concrete.

    Prize Ring and First Six Rows of Seats - Need overheads
                            for shots #54 and #82. Consider
                            black backing with rear "Exit"
                            signs or ? to give depth past
                            two rows.

1. EXT. NEW YORK STREET - NIGHT - LONG ANGLE SHOT LOOKING   1.
    DOWN

    At a row of tenements. It's a typical street scene, hot
    summer night, people sitting out on curbstones and front
    porches, but almost motionless except for desultory fanning
    and the movement of rocking babies.

2. MED. CLOSE SHOT - STEPS OF A BROWNSTONE   2.

    An evening newspaper lies spread out over a sleeping man's
    face. The paper is open to the sports page. We see the
    headline, "Bolie Jackson tries Comeback Tonight."

3. MOVING SHOT - UP THE STEPS   3.

    Toward the front door as we

                                              DISSOLVE TO:

4. INT. BOLIE JACKSON'S BEDROOM   4.

    He's dressing in front of a bureau mirror, a stocky
    muscular thirty five year old Negro just putting on his
    shirt. We see the muscles ripple on an athlete's back and
    shoulders; the sense of grace with which he stands examining
    himself in the mirror. Behind him is the same newspaper
    seen outdoors with his name in the headlines.

5. DIFFERENT ANGLE - HIS REFLECTION IN THE MIRROR   5.

    As he studies himself, touches little scars that can be
    dimly seen over his eyes, his temples, one near his chin;
    then the lump on the bridge of his nose where bones have
    been shattered and then shattered again.

                         NARRATOR'S VOICE
              In this corner of the universe, a
              prize fighter named Bolie Jackson,
              one hundred and sixty three pounds
              and an hour and a half away from a
              comeback at St. Nick's Arena. Mr.
              Bolie Jackson, who by the standards
              of his profession, is an aging,
              over-the-hill relic of what was and
              who now sees a reflection of a man
              who has left too many pieces of his
              youth in too many stadiums for too
              many years before too many screaming
              people.
                    (pause)
              Mr. Bolie Jackson who might do well to
              look for some gentle magic in the hard
              surfaced glass that stares back at him.

6. PAN SHOT TO THE CORNER OF THE MIRROR   6.

Where we see the reflection of little Henry Temple, a
ten year old Negro boy who sits on the bed and stares
at the fighter.

                                          THEN FADE TO BLACK:

OPENING BILLBOARD
FIRST COMMERCIAL

FADE IN:

7. INT. OF ROOM - NIGHT   7.

Henry continues to sit on the bed watching Bolie button
up his shirt.

                        HENRY
              You feelin' good, Bolie?
                   (he folds out his
                    little fists)
              Feelin' sharp? Take a tiger
              tonight, huh, Bolie?

Bolie smiles gently at the little boy's reflection in
the mirror and he apes the little boy's gesture.

                        BOLIE
              Take a tiger, Henry. Gonna
              take me a tiger. Left, right,
              one in the stomach, then lift
              him up by the tail and throw 'im
              out to the ninth row.

The little boy grins, gets up off the bed, walks over to
the dresser.

                        HENRY
              You're lookin' good, Bolie. You're
              lookin' sharp.

Bolie's smile fades ever so slightly. He turns to look
at the little boy, reaches down and cups his little chin,
presses it gently.

                        BOLIE
              You gonna watch?

                                          CONTINUED

7.   CONTINUED   7.

                         HENRY
              You foolin'? I'll yell so loud
              you'll hear me all the way to
              St. Nicks.

Bolie has to laugh in spite of himself. He rubs the boy's
hair and goes back to buttoning his shirt in the mirror.

8.   CLOSE SHOT - HIS REFLECTION   8.

As he stares at himself intensely again. He touches one
or two of the scars.

                         BOLIE
                  (softly, reflectively)
              Fighter don't need a scrapbook,
              Henry. Want to know about what
              he's done? Where he's fought?
              Read it on his face. He's got
              the whole story cut into his
              flesh.
                  (he touches the scar
                   over one of his eyes)
              St. Louis, 1949. Guy named
              Sailor Levitt. Real fast boy.
                  (touches the
                   bridge of the nose)
              That was Memorial Stadium, Syracuse,
              New York. Italian boy, fought like
              Henry Armstrong. All hands and arms
              just like a windmill all over you.
              First time I ever had my nose broken
              twice in one fight.
                  (now he touches the
                   thin scar near his
                   ear)
              Move south, Henry. Miami, Florida.
              Boy got me up against a ring post.
              Did this with his laces.

He turns to look down at the little boy who stares at
him grimly and unhappily and with a vast, abiding concern.

                                           CONTINUED

                         BOLIE
          On the face, Henry, that's where
          you read it. Start in 1947
          then move across. Pittsburg,
          Boston, Syracuse.
                 (he touches each
                  scar then closes his
                  eyes and keeps two
                  fingers pressed against
                  them and then very,
                  very softly)
          Tired old man, Henry. Tired old
          man tryin' to catch a bus. But the
          bus already gone. Left a coupla
          years ago.
                 (he opens his eyes
                  and looks down at the
                  boy)
          Hands all heavy. Legs all rubbery.
          Short breath. One eye not so good.
          And there I go running down the
          street tryin' to catch this bus to
          glory.

The little boy compulsively grabs Bolie's arm.

                         HENRY
                 (with the quiet intensity
                  of a boy)
          Bolie, you gonna catch a tiger
          tonight. I'm gonna make a wish.
          I'm gonna make a big, tall
          wish. And you ain't gonna get
          hurt none either. I'm gonna
          make a wish that you don't get
          hurt none either. You hear,
          Bolie? I don't want you gettin'
          hurt none. You've been hurt
          enough already and you're my
          friend, Bolie. You're my good and
          close friend.

                                   CONTINUED

8. CONTINUED   8.

    Bolie turns from the mirror to kneel down in front of the
    boy. He holds him by the shoulders and stares at him and
    then very gently and quietly he kisses the boy on the side
    of the face, rises, goes over to the bed, takes an overnight
    bag from it, crosses the room and starts out.

9. EXT. HALL AND STAIRS - LONG SHOT - LOOKING DOWN THE   9.
    STEPS

    As Bolie, carrying his over-night bag, walks down
    toward the foot of the steps. Henry's mother, an
    attractive thirty year old woman, comes out of her
    apartment and smiles at Bolie as he walks down to
    her. Then she looks up toward the top of the steps
    where Henry leans against the banister.

                         BOLIE
                    (grins)
            You got quite a boy there, Frances.
            You got quite a boy.
                    (he looks over his
                     shoulder at him
                     briefly then back
                     to the mother)
            Talks like a little old man, you
            know? I'm his "good and close
            friend", that's what he says.
            Real...real intense. I'm his
            good and close friend.

                         FRANCES
            You're good to him, Bolie.
            You're real good to him. Takin'
            him to ballgames all the time.
            Takin' him out for walks.
                    (she looks up the
                     steps toward the
                     little boy and in
                     a soft voice)
            Hard for a boy not to have a
            father. He never did know his.

10.   TWO SHOT - FRANCES AND BOLIE   10.

As she instinctively touches his arm.

                        FRANCES
            He won't be goin' to bed tonight
            till you get back. Take care of
            yourself, Bolie. Don't get hurt none.

                        BOLIE
                   (with a crooked
                    little smile)
            I'll work hard on it.

He turns, looks up the steps again.

11.   CLOSE SHOT - HENRY   11.

He walks half way down the steps and stands there, his
little face intense.

                        HENRY
            I'm gonna make a wish, Bolie. I'm
            gonna make a wish nothin' happens
            to you. So don't you be afraid,
            Bolie. Understand? Don't you
            be afraid.

The little boy continues down the steps, into his
apartment, shutting the door.

12.   TWO SHOT - FRANCES AND BOLIE   12.

                        FRANCES
                   (softly)
            You're his friend, Bolie. He's
            got you in a shrine.

13.   CLOSE SHOT - BOLIE   13.

                        BOLIE
            Scared old man who don't remember
            nothin' except how to bleed.
                   (he shakes his head)
            I don't fit in no shrine, Frances..
                   (a pause, softly)
            But you tell him, Frances...
            you tell him how I'm obliged for
            his wish. That's what I need
            right now.

                        (MORE)

CONTINUED

13.   CONTINUED   13.

                              BOLIE (CONT'D)
                         (he looks down at
                         his hands, clenches
                         and unclenches his
                         fists)
                    A little magic.

                              FRANCES
                    He's been talkin' about makin'
                    a wish all night. He's all
                    the time makin' wishes, Bolie.
                    I see him standin' there in
                    his bedroom in the dark lookin'
                    out the window. I come in real
                    quiet and I say, "Henry, boy
                    why don't you go to sleep?" And
                    he turns to me with that serious
                    little face of his and he says,
                    "Makin' a wish, mama." Makin'
                    a wish for this. Makin' a wish
                    for that. Oh, he's all the time
                    wishin'. Why just the other
                    night -

14.   CLOSE SHOT - FRANCES   14.

      As she turns away, a very reflective, puzzled look on
      her face as she recollects something.

                              BOLIE
                    What?

                              FRANCES
                         (with a kind of lightly
                         scoffing at herself
                         laughter)
                    I needed fifteen dollars for the
                    rent. Henry said he was gonna
                    make the big, tall wish. That's
                    his biggest kind, the big, tall
                    wish. He don't waste that wish
                    on just anything. That's what
                    he calls the most important one.
                         (she pauses for a
                         moment, again thoughtful)
                    That was last Friday, and a woman
                    I did some nursing for out on the
                    Island sent me a check.
                         (she looks at Bolie
                         closely)
                    A check for fifteen dollars.

15.   TWO SHOT - FRANCES AND BOLIE   15.

As they stand there for a moment silently.

> BOLIE
> (shakes his head)
> Little boys. Little boys with
> their heads full up with dreams.
> And when does it happen, Frances?
> When do they suddenly know there
> ain't any magic? When does
> somebody push their face down on
> the sidewalk and say to 'em - "Hey,
> little boy - it's concrete. That's
> what the world is made out of.
> Concrete and gutters and dirty old
> buildings and tears for every
> minute you're alive."

16.   DIFFERENT ANGLE - BOLIE   16.

His face is twisted and contorted.

> BOLIE
> When do they find out that you
> can wish your life away?

17.   TWO SHOT - BOLIE AND FRANCES   17.

She shakes her head slowly from side to side.

> FRANCES
> (very gently)
> Good luck tonight, Bolie. We'll
> be waitin' for you.

> BOLIE
> (nods)
> Sure. Sure, Frances.
> (he nods toward
> the closed door of
> the apartment)
> Kiss him goodnight for me.

Then he turns and walks out.

18.   EXT. BROWNSTONE - NIGHT   18.

As Bolie comes down the steps. Several people call out
to him and wish him luck. He responds with a wave of
his hand and then continues down to the foot of the
steps, and down the sidewalk.

19.   TRACK SHOT WITH HIM AS HE WALKS   19.

a few feet, then stops, turns

20.   LONG SHOT - HENRY   20.

Staring out at him from the window.

21.   CLOSE SHOT - BOLIE   21.

He returns the stare, forces a smile, holds up his hand
in a kind of partial wave, then turns and continues down
the side walk as we

DISSOLVE TO:

22.   INT. DRESSING ROOM - ARENA - PAN SHOT ACROSS ROOM   22.

This is a typical second rate sweat and liniment room
with a smelly dressing table, a shower room flanked by
a dirty canvas, a big towel container oozing with some
bloody remnants of the card to that hour. A battered
fighter is just being led out of the room as we pick
up Bolie now in his trunks sitting on the rubbing table.
A thin, pigeon chested, vinegar faced old cut-man named
Mizell is finishing the process of wrapping the bandages
around his hands. Across the room Bolie's manager of
that evening leans against the wall smoking a big cheap
billowing cigar. This is a fat, obese, greasy, incredibly
dirty looking man named Thomas. Mizell finishes the
wrapping, holds up both his palms.

                    MIZELL
          Try it, Bolie.

Bolie flexes his knuckles, hits Mizell's palms several
times, then nods.

                    BOLIE
          Feels okay. Feels good, Joe.
          Thanks.

Mizell nods, touches them up once again, then turns to
Thomas.

                    MIZELL
          He's all ready.

Thomas pours out a long stream of cigar smoke and nods
disinterestedly. Bolie waves his hands through the
smoke.

                    BOLIE
          Butt it out, will you, Thomas?
          I want to breathe.

22. CONTINUED   22.

                         THOMAS
                 (deliberately takes
                  another big deep drag)
            You hired me for the night, Bolie.
            It's a package deal - me and the
            cigar.

                         BOLIE
                 (takes a step toward
                  him)
            I told you to butt it out!

23. CLOSE SHOT - THOMAS   23.

     As he studies him.

24. CLOSE SHOT - BOLIE   24.

     His face a mask.

25. DIFFERENT ANGLE - ALL THREE MEN   25.

     As Thomas takes the cigar out, butts it against the wall
     then crimps the end of it with his fingers and sticks
     it in his pocket.

                         THOMAS
            Feisty little old man. Older
            they get -- the louder they talk.
            The more they want --
                 (and then he spits
                  this out)
            And the less chance they got to
            get it.

                         BOLIE
            How'd I get you tonight?

                         THOMAS
            I'm a bargain, Bolie. I'm the
            expert on has-beens.

                         BOLIE
                 (shakes his head)
            I've seen your boys. Catchers,
            aren't they? Guarantee two rounds
            each. Shovel them in, shovel
            them out. Then sew them together
            for the next time.

                                        CONTINUED

25.   CONTINUED   25.

                              THOMAS
                         (laughs)
                    That's the only way to do it.
                    Month or so from now maybe I'll
                    sign you at the back door. Why
                    not? You're long gone, Bolie.
                    You've had it. Wait'll after
                    tonight. You'll want to get in
                    the stable too. All you have to
                    do is guarantee two rounds. Two,
                    three prelims every month. Do
                    that standing on your head, can't
                    you?

                              BOLIE
                         (takes a step toward
                          him)
                    I thought the smell came with
                    the cigar.
                         (he shakes his head)
                    You wear it all over yuh. You
                    stink, Thomas.

                              THOMAS
                    You tell 'em, champ. You tell
                    'em.

There's a knock on the door and a muffled voice calls
out.

                              VOICE
                    Jackson, ten minutes.

                              THOMAS
                    He'll be there.

Bolie goes back over to sit on the dressing table.
Mizell starts to knead his shoulders and arms. Thomas
stares at him from across the room.

                              BOLIE
                    What about tonight? What should
                    I look out for? I only seen this
                    boy fight once. That was a coupla
                    years ago.

                              THOMAS
                         (shrugs)
                    I ain't never seen him.

26.   CLOSE SHOT - MIZELL   26.

As he looks over Bolie's shoulder sharply, recognizing
the lie. Then he goes back to deliberately kneading
Bolie's shoulders.

27.   FULL SHOT   27.

Bolie looks from one to the other, deliberately takes
Mizell's hands off of him, rises again and walks over
to Thomas, lashes out with his bandaged hands, pulls
Thomas to him.

                         BOLIE
               You've watched him fight. You've
               seen him six times the past year.
               You piece of garbage you, Thomas.
               You're bettin' on him, aren't you?

He hauls off and backhands Thomas across the face.

                         MIZELL
                    (shouts)
               Bolie!

                         BOLIE
                    (still hanging tight on
                    Thomas's shirt front)
               It ain't enough he sells wrecks
               by the pound. He comes in here
               for a dirty twenty bucks supposed
               to help me and then bets on the
               other guy. I may be a bum
               upstairs in another ten minutes
               -- but I'm gonna fight a beautiful
               first round right here.

                         THOMAS
                    (squirming)
               Bolie, you touch me again and
               I'll have you up for ten years.
               I swear to you, Bolie -- I'll fix
               your wagon good --

Bolie backhands him again.

28.   CLOSE SHOT - BOLIE'S FACE   28.

Distorted, angry, perspiring with emotion, with hate.

29.   CLOSE SHOT - THOMAS'S FACE   29.

Fat, big pored, frightened.

                         THOMAS
                    (screeching)
               Lay off me, Bolie. Lay off me.
               You crummy tanker you --

30. TWO SHOT   30.

   Bolie hauls off and swings and at that moment Thomas
   lurches from his grasp.

31. DIFFERENT ANGLE   31.

   As Bolie's hand hits the concrete wall and there's a
   loud, horrifying crack. Bolie leans against the wall,
   eyes closed, and very slowly lets his right hand drop.
   Mizell scurries over to him to grab it and examine it.
   Thomas exits the room like a minute miler.

32. CLOSE TWO SHOT - MIZELL AND BOLIE   32.

   Mizell looks up with aged compassion and very wise eyes.

                         MIZELL
                      (gently)
               It wasn't enough you had to spot
               him all those years, Bolie. It
               wasn't enough, huh? Now you got
               to walk in with four busted
               knuckles.

   There's a knock on the door.

                         VOICE
               Okay, Jackson, you're on!

                         MIZELL
                      (takes a step away)
               Well?

                         BOLIE
                      (turns from the wall,
                       holds his hands up)
               Well nothing. Let's do it.

   Mizell takes the gloves hanging on the end of the
   rubbing table and starts to put them on, looking up
   intermittently into Bolie's numb, emotionless face.

33. CLOSE ANGLE SHOT - THE TWO MEN   33.

   Their faces close together.

                         BOLIE
               Poor little Henry Temple. I'm
               putting two strikes on all his
               magic. Two strikes.

                                        CONTINUED

33. CONTINUED   33.

                           MIZELL
                    (looks up, frowns)
               Whose?

                           BOLIE
                    (shakes his head,
                     softly)
               Nothing. Nothing, Joe. There
               ain't no such thing as magic.

                                        FADE TO BLACK:

                    END ACT ONE

ACT TWO

FADE ON:

34. INT. STADIUM - PAN SHOT ACROSS FRONT ROW OF SPECTATORS   34.

As seen through a smokey din of a cheap fight card. These
are the faces of a mob who want blood, violence, action.
Jaws go up and down in unison with the blows landed in the
ring a few feet in front of them. There's a cigar, a plug
of tobacco, the scream of excitement from a floozie at the
arm of a checkered suited cheap dandy. They all share one
thing in common. An intense desire to see some flesh
stripped off and have it come with pain. They suddenly
jump to their feet screaming as we:

                                                   CUT TO:

35. INT. RING - ANGLE SHOT LOOKING OVER FIGHTER'S SHOULDER   35.
     AT BOLIE

On the ropes. He's being pounded with lefts and rights.
At the fourth smash his mouthpiece flies out.

36. TILT ANGLE - FAT MAN   36.

Screaming through his clenched cigar.

37. CLOSE SHOT - BOLIE   37.

As he's pounded again in the face.

38. ANGLE SHOT - FLOOZIE   38.

Making frantic punching gestures.

39. CLOSE SHOT - FIGHTER   39.

As, arm weary, he continues to pound Bolie.

40. TILT SHOT - TEEN AGE BOY   40;

Eating popcorn, his eyes wide, agape as he stares at the
blood letting in the ring, eating fistfuls of popcorn
totally unconsciously.

41. CLOSE SHOT - HEAVILY RINGED HAND OF FAT MAN   41.

As he keeps pounding his fist into his palm in unison
with the blows in the ring.

                                                   CUT TO:

42. INT. HENRY'S APARTMENT - CLOSE SHOT THE BOY   42.

Standing several feet away from a television screen in
a tiny, darkened living room. Beyond him we can see
the screen and a vague moving picture of two men in the
ring. The crowd noises up and down intermittently and
over it we can hear a ringside announcer's voice.

                    ANNOUNCER'S VOICE
            Another left, another right, and
            Jackson's knees are very wobbly.
            He's hurt. Bolie Jackson is
            definitely hurt. Simmons moves in
            on him again. There goes one to
            the side of the head. One to the
            breadbasket. A left and right
            to the head again. Oh, is that
            boy hurt. Is that boy hurt.

43. CLOSE SHOT - HENRY   43.

As he whirls around, his back to the set, hands to the
side of his face, clutching at his cheeks.

44. DIFFERENT ANGLE - HENRY   44.

Frances can be seen in another part of the room now
staring at her son, shaking her head from side to side
and finally closing her eyes.

45. DIFFERENT ANGLE AGAIN - HENRY   45.

His little face contorting, tears in his eyes as he turns.

46. MOVING SHOT WITH HIM   46.

As he races to the set, almost buries his face against
the screen and screams into it.

                    HENRY
            Bolie! Bolie! Bolie!

                                    ABRUPT CUT TO:

47. CANVAS OF THE RING   47.

As Bolie's head falls into the frame and lands with a
dull thud as he's knocked down.

48. EXTREME TIGHT CLOSE SHOT - HIS FACE   48.

As he looks up toward the referee.

49. ANGLE SHOT - LOOKING UP - BOLIE'S P.O.V.   49.

The referee stands over him strangely out of focus, the
central ring light over his shoulder highlighting him in
an odd haze as his arm goes up and down beginning the
count. His voice seems hollow and distant as he counts
out.

                              REFEREE
              One.   Two.   Three.

                                              CUT TO:

50-   50-
52. SEVERAL DIFFERENT ANGLES OF THE SPECTATORS   52.

As they watch with rapt attention, chewing, smoking,
fidgeting like nervous animals at a stock yard.

53. ANGLE SHOT LOOKING DOWN FROM OVER THE REFEREE'S SHOULDER 53.

As he continues to bring his arm down.

                                          ABRUPT CUT TO:

54. CLOSE SHOT - CENTRAL RING LIGHT   54.

As it suddenly goes in and out of focus and there's an
absolute cecession of noises and gradually the crowd
noise comes up again. The CAMERA PANS DOWN to a back of
a fighter standing there with his arm being raised by
the referee. Beyond him we see handlers, cops,
spectators scrambling over the ring ropes. The CAMERA
MOVES AROUND IN AN ARC until we're looking at Bolie
standing on his feet with an arm raised. He looks
right and left, up and down, then suddenly turns to
stare at something beyond the camera.

55. MOVING SHOT ACROSS THE RING   55.

Until we're close on the other fighter in exactly the
same position Bolie was, lying on his back, his handlers
have just reached him and are now pulling him to his
feet.

56. MOVING SHOT BOLIE   56.

As he starts out of the ring. He looks dazed, totally
out of touch with reality.

                                          DISSOLVE TO:

57.   INT. DRESSING ROOM   57.

      Bolie sits on the dressing table now fully clothed, with
      his coat hanging over his arm. He continues to look
      dazed and unsure. Mizell comes in with a load of dirty
      towels which he dumps in the container. Then he looks
      across at Bolie.

58.   TRACK SHOT WITH HIM   58.

      As he walks over to the fighter, grins in his vinegar
      way, chuckles at him.

                          MIZELL
                You done dandy.

59.   CLOSE SHOT - BOLIE   59.

      As he stares at him.

                          BOLIE
                Joe.
                     (he holds up his right
                      hand and flexes his
                      wrist)
                You were wrong. Just bruised I
                guess, huh? Hurt like anything,
                but somebody said I got him with
                it. Couldn't have been broken
                after all.

                          MIZELL
                Who said it was?

                          BOLIE
                     (an odd look)
                You said. And it felt like it
                too. I could feel the knuckles
                coming up through the bandages.
                I coulda sworn it was busted.
                And when he knocked me down --

60.   CLOSE SHOT - MIZELL   60.

      As he whirls around to stare at Bolie.

                          MIZELL
                What? He did what?

      Bolie gets up off the table, takes a few steps over to
      him.

                          BOLIE
                Knocked me down, Joe. When he
                knocked me down. I don't even
                remember getting up. Next thing
                I knew there he was at my feet.

61. CLOSE SHOT - BOLIE   61.

As he stands there waiting, his eyes asking a question.

62. CLOSE SHOT - MIZELL   62.

As his eyes narrow and he frowns.

>   MIZELL
>   We was in different arenas
>   tonight together.
>   (he shakes his head)
>   You didn't get knocked down,
>   Bolie. You was never off your
>   feet.

63. DIFFERENT ANGLE - BOLIE   63.

As his head cocks to one side.

>   BOLIE
>   I wasn't?

64. REVERSE ANGLE - LOOKING TOWARD MIZELL - BOLIE'S P.O.V. 64.

>   MIZELL
>   No, you sure wasn't. This one
>   you carried all the way, baby.

He goes to the door and opens it.

65. REVERSE ANGLE - LOOKING TOWARD BOLIE   65.

>   BOLIE
>   Joe?
>   (then intensely)
>   I wasn't off my feet? I didn't
>   go down?

>   MIZELL
>   Not once. Good night, old timer.
>   I'm proud of yuh!

He turns and shuffles out of the room.

                                             DISSOLVE TO:

66. EXT. STREET - NIGHT - TRACK SHOT BOLIE   66.

As he walks down the sidewalk.

67. DIFFERENT ANGLE OVER HIS SHOULDER   67.

As we see him approaching the front steps of his
brownstone.

68. GROUP SHOT - PEOPLE ON THE STEPS   68.

As they get up and greet him.

                    MAN ONE
          Beautiful, Bolie. Beautiful.

                    WOMAN
          Oh, you were great, Bolie. We
          seen you on television. You
          was real great.

                    TEEN AGER
               (feeling Bolie's muscle)
          Oh you clobbered him, Bolie.
          That was a right! That was a
          real right!

69. MOVING SHOT - BOLIE - CLOSE ON HIS FACE   69.

As he goes through the crowd. The plaudits, the
backslaps, the handshakes. Continues up the steps. He
leaves them outside and enters the hallway.

70. INT. HALLWAY   70.

He's about to start up the steps when he looks toward
the closed door of Henry's apartment. He stands there
indecisively for a moment, then goes to the door and
knocks on it softly. The door opens and Frances stands
there. She smiles at him.

                    FRANCES
          You shoulda seen him, Bolie. He'd
          like to go out of his mind he was
          so happy. Whole building was
          shaking -- you'd never believe it!

Bolie looks over her shoulder questioningly into the room.

                    FRANCES
               (as if in answer to his
                inquiring look)
          He's up on the roof waiting for
          you.

Bolie nods, turns to start up the steps.

                    FRANCES
          Send him down soon, Bolie. It's
          real late.

Bolie nods, starts up the steps.

71. EXT. ROOF - NIGHT   71.

Just as Bolie comes outside.

72.   PAN SHOT ACROSS THE ROOF TO HENRY   72.

Who is standing at the ledge. The last diminishing neon
of the late night flashes on and off illuminating the
boy as he turns and walks over to the fighter. Bolie
kneels down, grips the boy's shoulders.

                    BOLIE
          What do you say, Henry Temple?

                    HENRY
          You were a tiger, Bolie. You
          were a real tiger.

                    BOLIE
               (grins)
          Look okay?

                    HENRY
          Sharp. Sharp like a champ. You
          was Louis and Armstrong and
          everybody all wrapped up into one.

Bolie starts to laugh, warm, rich laughter that floods
out of him and the boy joins him and they hug one
another. Then Bolie rises to his feet, takes a step
away from the boy, pounding his fist into his palm,
shaking his head at the sheer delight of it.

                    BOLIE
          Hey, you know somethin'? That
          boy musta hit me so hard he
          knocked the hurt right outa me!
               (he laughs, shakes his
                head with bewilderment)
          I don't remember a doggone thing,
          Henry. I must have really been
          punchy for a second because I
          thought he had me on my back. And
          there I was lookin' up at the old
          ref waving his arm down on me and
          I was staring up at the light,
          blinkin' my eyes. It must have
          been some kind of a dream or
          something --

He stops abruptly, staring at the little boy's face.

73. CLOSE SHOT - HENRY   73.

    As he turns away.

74. CLOSE SHOT - BOLIE   74.

    As he stares intensely at the boy. He takes a step over
    to him and turns him around to face him. His voice is
    strained and different.

                         BOLIE
                Henry? I was never off my feet.
                I never got knocked down.

    The little boy doesn't answer. He just looks down at his
    feet. Bolie grips him tighter, shoves his face close to
    him searching into the boy's face.

                         BOLIE
                Henry!
                    (he grips him
                     tighter)
                Henry, I was never off my feet.

    There's a long, long silence and still the boy doesn't
    respond.

75. ANGLE SHOT - LOOKING UP TOWARD BOLIE   75.

    As he rises looking down at the boy.

                         BOLIE
                   (in a still voice)
                Henry, was I? Was I lyin' on my
                back and on the way out?

76. CLOSE SHOT - HENRY   76.

    He slowly nods.

77. CLOSE SHOT - BOLIE   77.

                         BOLIE
                But nobody remembers it. Nobody
                at all. 'Cept me. I thought it
                happened...but it didn't. I thought
                I was lyin' there on my back gettin'
                counted out, but everybody tells me -

78. CLOSE SHOT - HENRY   78.

    As he moves very close to the man, looks up.

                                      CONTINUED

78. CONTINUED   78.

                         HENRY
            Bolie, I made the big wish then.
            I had to make the big wish. I
            wished you was never knocked down.
            I just shut my eyes and I...I
            wished real hard. It was magic,
            Bolie. We had to have magic then.

79. CLOSE SHOT - BOLIE   79.

As he shakes his head back and forth. His mouth forms
the word "no". He takes a step away from the boy. Henry
follows him.

                         HENRY
            Had to, Bolie. Nothing left for
            us then. Had to make a wish.

Bolie's head goes back and forth disbelieving, rejecting,
beyond any kind of understanding or logic. Then suddenly
he grabs the boy in a fury.

                         BOLIE
            Crazy kid. You crazy, kookie kid.
                 (he shakes the boy
                  furiously)
            Don't you know there ain't no
            magic? There ain't no magic or
            wishing or nothin' like that.
            You're too big to have nutsy
            thoughts like that. You're too
            big to believe in fairy tales.

                         HENRY
                 (tears beginning to
                  roll down his face)
            If you wish hard enough, Bolie,
            it'll come true. If you wish hard
            enough...and then believe - it'll
            stay that way -

                         BOLIE
                 (continuing to shake
                  the boy)
            Somebody got to knock it out of
            you, don't they? Somebody got to
            take you by the hair and rub your
            face in the world and give you a
            taste and smell of the way things
            are, don't they? Listen, boy, I've
            been wishin' all my life.
                      (MORE)

                                        CONTINUED

79. CONTINUED   79.

                    BOLIE (CONT'D)
          You understand, Henry? I got a
          gut ache from wishin' and all I
          got to show for it is a face full
          of scars and a head full of
          memories of all the hurt and all
          the misery I've had to eat with
          and sleep with all my miserable
          life. You crazy kid you.
              (he shakes his head)
          You tellin' me you wished me into
          a knock out. You tellin' me it
          was magic that got me off my back.
              (gripping the boy
               tightly)
          Little kook, that's what you are,
          Henry. How come I get mixed up
          with you? Ain't I got enough
          trouble without gettin' mixed up
          with some dopey kid that -

80. CLOSE SHOT - HENRY   80.

     As he stands there, the tears rolling down his face.

                    HENRY
          If you don't believe, Bolie, it
          won't be true. That's the way
          magic works.
              (he grabs the man
               tightly)
          Bolie, you got to believe. Please.
          Please believe.

                    BOLIE
          Now listen, boy, there ain't no
          magic - no magic, Henry. I had
          that fight comin' and goin'. I
          had it in my pocket. I was the
          number one out there. And it was
          me who done it. Me, Henry. It
          was old Bolie Jackson, full of
          moxie, movin' around and jabbin',
          and hookin' and winnin', Henry.
          I was the number one.

     Suddenly he stops. The man and the boy look at one another
     and then he sweeps the boy into his arms and holds him very
     tightly and closely, closing his eyes against the boy's
     cheek.

                                        CONTINUED

80.   CONTINUED   80.

                         BOLIE (CONT'D)
I was the winner(very, very softly)
               Henry, I can't believe. I'm
               too old and I'm hurt to believe.
               I can't boy. I just can't. Henry,
               Henry, there ain't no such thing as
               magic. God help us both, I wish
               there were -

                         HENRY
               Bolie, you got to believe.

                         BOLIE
                    (shakes his head)
               I can't.

                         HENRY
                    (his voice rising
                     in a cry)
               You got to, Bolie. You got to
               believe or else -

81.   MOVING SHOT AWAY FROM THEM   81.

      As we hear the boy's voice over and over again and Bolie's
      voice rejecting The CAMERA MOVES UP to a light hanging
      over the roof then DOLLIES IN VERY CLOSE to it, bringing
      it in and out of focus. Bolie's and Henry's voices
      gradually fade off into a dissonance as we

                                                   DISSOLVE TO:

82.   THE BRIGHT RING LIGHT SHINING INTO THE CAMERA   82.

      PAN SHOT DOWN to Bolie on his back.

83.   REVERSE ANGLE LOOKING UP TOWARD REFEREE   83.

      Who is bringing his arm down.

                         REFEREE
               Eight. Nine...Ten.

      He swipes hands out in opposite directons indicating a
      knock out.

84.   DIFFERENT ANGLE - THE RING   84.

      As the winning fighter is engulfed by well wishers who
      scramble up over the ropes. Mizell is a lone figure
      walking tiredly over toward Bolie who, like some kind of
      stricken animal, has risen to his hands and knees and
      looks around blindly through the lights and smoke. He
      allows Mizell to help him to his feet then he starts a
      beaten, stiff-legged walk to his corner.

                                                   DISSOLVE TO:

85.   EXT. STREET - NIGHT   85.

Identical walking shot of Bolie as he heads back toward
the Brownstone. This time the three people are there as
before, but the teenager and the woman merely look at him
with cold, accusative looks. The man sits on the steps
half sleeping, he opens up one eye, looks up at Bolie as
he starts up the steps.

                        MAN
            You shoulda stood in bed. How's
            come you didn't use your right?

Bolie looks down at a misshapen, bandaged right hand and
doesn't say anything. He continues up the steps and goes
on inside.

                                          DISSOLVE TO:

86.   INT. HENRY'S APARTMENT   .   86.

As Frances has just opened the door and Bolie enters.

                        FRANCES
            He's in bed, Bolie. That's a
            sad little boy in there.

                        BOLIE
              (nods)
            Can I see him?

                        FRANCES
            Sure. I expect he's waiting for
            you.

Bolie nods and starts across the room.

                        FRANCES
            Bolie?

He turns to her.

                        FRANCES
            I'm real sorry.

Bolie nods and doesn't say anything. He continues into
the bedroom.

87.   INT. BEDROOM   87

Henry lies in bed, his eyes wide open staring at the
ceiling. He looks toward the door when he hears it open,
rises in bed as Bolie enters.

88.   TRACK SHOT - BOLIE   88.

As he goes over to the bed and sits down next to the boy.
Nothing is said for a moment. Bolie finally clears
his throat, holds up his right hand.

                    BOLIE
          Pulled a rock, Henry. Threw a
          punch before I should have. Hit the
          wall. Busted my knuckles. I went
          in with half my artillery gone.

The little boy nods through the darkness, reaches over
and touches the fighter's shoulder.

                    HENRY
          You looked like a tiger even so. You
          looked like a real tiger. I was
          proud of you. I was real proud.

Bolie leans over and kisses the boy, gets off the bed
and starts out, opens the door.

89.   REVERSE ANGLE LOOKING TOWARD BOY IN BED   89.

                    HENRY
          Bolie?

                    BOLIE
          You go to sleep. Tomorrow we'll
          go to the hockey game and we'll
          get some hot dogs in the park,
          you and me.

                    HENRY
          Sure thing, Bolie. That'll
          be nice.

Another pause as Bolie is about to start out the door.

                    HENRY
          Bolie?

Bolie stops, turns to him.

                    HENRY
          I ain't gonna make no more wishes,
          Bolie. I'm too old for wishes.
          There ain't no such thing as magic
          is there?

90.   CLOSE SHOT - BOLIE   90.

Silhouetted in the darkness of the room from the lights
of outside.

                    BOLIE
              (very softly)
         I guess not, Henry. Or maybe...
         maybe there is magic. Maybe there's
         wishes too. I guess the trouble is...
         I guess the trouble is, there's
         not enough people around to believe.
         Goodnight, boy.

                    HENRY
         Good night, Bolie.

He quietly goes out of the room and closes the door, as
the CAMERA PANS OVER TO THE WINDOW and outdoors into
the night to begin a SLOW PAN UP TO THE STARS.

                    NARRATOR'S VOICE
         Mr. Bolie Jackson, a hundred and
         sixty three pounds, who left a
         second chance lying in a heap on
         a rosin spattered canvas at St.
         Nick's arena. Mr. Bolie Jackson
         who shares the most common ailment
         of all men...the strange and perverse
         disinclination to believe in a
         miracle. The kind of miracle to
         come from the mind of a little
         boy perhaps only to be found...
         in The Twilight Zone.

                              FADE TO BLACK:

                    THE END

A FIGHT TO KEEP THE FAITH

When the creative format of *The Twilight Zone* freed Rod Serling to pursue more unconventional story lines, he often returned to a favorite theme: the miraculous redemption of a downtrodden character. Serling's work is rife with social outcasts who are granted, by divine or otherwise mystical intervention, a chance to recapture lost opportunities or set right the mistakes of the past. "The Big, Tall Wish" results in one of the writer's most poignant yet ultimately disheartening stories of this type.

A callous world has so completely beaten down Bolie Jackson's spirit that he cannot accept magic even when faced with irrefutable proof of its existence. Perhaps Serling meant the story as a metaphor for man's reluctance to accept God, or as a cautionary tale about the danger of relinquishing one's hopes and dreams in the wake of unremitting defeat. Whatever the intent, Serling's mastery of character is on display whenever Bolie utters a line.

The burnt-out fighter's dialogue is laden with despair and an acceptance of pain and humiliation. Serling revisits here the same basic character he created in "Requiem for a Heavyweight"—an aging, sympathetic boxer discarded by a profession and a world that no longer has any use for him—and elevates him to the status of demigod in the eyes of a child. Henry's love and trust in a power greater than himself grants the broken boxer a miracle, a new beginning; a magical opportunity to forge an unlikely comeback. In return, Bolie stubbornly rails against the improbable and ultimately squanders his second chance.

Acting as a counterbalance to the negativity of the world-weary fighter is the character of young Henry Thomas. Untainted and accepting, Henry personifies the youthful vigor and unlimited potential that is utterly absent in Bolie. Raised with few prospects for a bright future in a depressed urban environment, and lacking a father figure to guide him, the boy latches onto Bolie in a complete and desperate act of hero worship. But Henry has chosen a poor teacher. Bolie can only impart knowledge of the bitter and brutal lessons of life. Cognizant of this, Bolie is apologetic, remorseful; he wishes he could believe, but he cannot.

The full impact of the fighter's cynicism is painfully evident at the conclusion of the story. Bolie's unrelenting denial of the magic generated by Henry's faith ultimately unravels the boy's own power of belief. When Henry proclaims that he's too old to believe in magic and gives up on wishing, his loss of innocence is sadly palpable. He is every child who has sacrificed a belief in Santa Claus to embrace the harsh reality of the adult world. In emulating his tragic role model, Henry not only forsakes a wondrous gift but also takes his first steps toward becoming another Bolie Jackson.

Serling's decision to populate his story with an African-American cast is indicative of the writer's well-known position on race and tolerance. "Television, like its big sister, the motion picture, has been guilty of a sin of omission," Serling commented about his casting decision. "Hungry for talent, desperate for the so-called 'new face,' constantly searching for a transfusion of blood, it has overlooked a source of wondrous talent that resides under its nose. This is the Negro actor."

While it could be argued that an inner-city setting of near poverty is a far cry from racial equality, Serling stayed true to the social conditions of the time and balked the status quo of his industry. Television, up to that point, had used African-American actors almost exclusively in dramas that dealt specifically with racial concerns. In contrast, "The Big, Tall Wish" dramatizes a universal problem and does not necessarily require a minority cast to drive the story. Yet Serling shows that *The Twilight Zone* does not discriminate; it visits redemption (or punishment) upon deserving people of any race, color or creed.

Sadly, the very fact that an all-black cast in a non-racial script was notable in 1960 ran counter to the image Serling sought to project. "Quite obviously, we've yet to reach that marvelously unselfconscious plateau where we can view men as men and not as colors," the writer remarked. "Hopefully that'll be the next chapter of American social progress."

As Bolie Jackson, Ivan Dixon does a marvelous job conveying the pain and hopelessness of his character. In the hands of a lesser actor the role could easily have slipped too far towards utter pathos or schmaltzy sentiment. Ivan Dixon walks this line with poise and skill. He has fond memories of both the episode and the creator of *The Twilight Zone*.

"I met Rod quite a few times," Dixon recalls. "I even met him on the street in Beverly Hills. A nice guy, a regular guy. Very astute. I was of course very familiar with his work. It was fun working for Rod. It was really exciting to be a part of it. He was extraordinary."

One minor drawback accompanies the portrayal of an aging boxer, and Dixon laughs off the years of pugilistic abuse that were applied to his handsome face. "*I thought,*" he quips, "that the makeup was a little distorted! But anyway, it turned out very well. It was a good show."

Despite limited screen time, Kim Hamilton embodies the character of Frances, Henry's mother, with ease. The actress is quick to reveal her delight at working with a marvelous cast and a respected writer. "I was excited to be able to get the job because of Rod Serling," she says. "I first met Rod prior to the shoot. He was there because it was a rehearsal period as if you were doing a play, before we actually went to camera. He really made me feel welcome."

Still active in television today, Hamilton considers this early part one of the finest in her long career. "It was a wonderful time to be in the business as far as feeling like you were talented and that you were important. My agent knew the casting director but also did what an agent does. He submitted me for the part and in those days agents really did wonderful things like go with you on the interview."

The task of capturing a warm chemistry between Bolie and Francis was virtually effortless for Ivan Dixon and Kim Hamilton. They first met while shooting the 1957 feature SOMETHING OF VALUE and would often appear together in television. "Ivan is wonderful," says Hamilton. "I am in touch with him all the time. In fact, I had lunch with Ivan the other day." The actress later met and married actor Werner Klemperer, who starred with Ivan Dixon in the television series *Hogan's Heroes*. "Kim is lovely," adds Dixon. "She played my wife several times and is just a lovely person."

Steven Perry does a remarkable job as Henry Temple. The role is demanding as well as crucial to maintaining the dramatic tone of the story. Perry does far more than simply recite his lines and hit his marks, the best that can be expected of many actors at such a tender age. His plaintive, repeated demands that Bolie surrender to the magic are heartrending and his overall performance is thoroughly believable.

"He was wonderful," remarks Ivan Dixon. "Steven was a cute little kid and a very active young man. My son was very jealous of him because on the set I took Steven out for hot dogs afterwards. My son, who was just about the same age at the time, got very angry. Now he's forty-six and he still remembers that moment!"

As is the case with many child actors, Perry abandoned the profession as an adult. He traded show business for the culinary business and has enjoyed much success. "I later saw him as an adult, many times," recalls Dixon. "He became the owner of a restaurant." Kim Hamilton also remembers a real-life encounter with her fully-grown co-star. "I saw him on the street a few years ago," she says, "in this really fancy car, all dressed up. He's not acting anymore. He's an entrepreneur."

"We just had a wonderful time," offers Kim Hamilton. "It went smoothly. The rehearsal period went extremely well. It was like being in the theater. When we did the show, it was all set, because we had rehearsed it as if it were a play. But everything went smoothly and it was wonderful. We felt like a family and the rehearsal period made it feel like we'd been together forever."

Composer Jerry Goldsmith, at a very early stage in his celebrated career, contributes a soulful score that perfectly compliments the mood of the episode. The soundtrack, guided by an expressive harmonica, gives voice to the awe of Henry's magic and the seediness of the craft of professional boxing. The score is particularly adept at capturing Bolie's anguish and resignation.

Subtle direction and meticulous photography allow the audience to focus on the power of Serling's story and the performances that bring it to life. The tenement rooms and the front stoop of the building are rendered in shadow, moody and bleak. A shift to the St. Nick's Arena set brings no respite from the gloom of Bolie Jackson's existence; the ring is starkly lit and a voracious, bloodthirsty crowd is simulated by a handful of extras and some deft camerawork. One brief shot, taken from Bolie's point-of-view as he sprawls on the canvas, shows him looking up at the ring lights and the referee who counts him out. A complex setup was required to place the huge camera rig below a mockup of the ring, demonstrating the level of attention to craft that went into every aspect of the show.

Asked if he is surprised at the longevity of *The Twilight Zone* in general and "The Big, Tall Wish" in particular, Dixon is quick to respond. "No, because it was Rod Serling. It was Rod Serling's writing that made it memorable."

"I thought it turned out very well," summarizes Kim Hamilton, "because Mr. Serling was so involved in it himself. It was wonderful to see him there all the time. I've been in the business a long time and you go through all kinds of experiences. This was one of those jewels that you could put on the map and say, 'This was special.' That will always be there."

The Twilight Zone

EYE OF THE BEHOLDER

Airdate: 11-11-1960

Manuscript Date: 8-1-1960

Date from revisions

Episode Forty-Two

THE TWILIGHT ZONE

"The Eye Of The Beholder"

CAST

Note: Voices and action convey the characterizations here,
        for faces are only seen for a moment.

Janet Tyler -   a young woman who alternates between deep
                    despair and a wistful hope about a better
                    life for herself.

Nurse -   firm first, kindly second

Nurse Two

Doctor -   he should impress us with his similarity to
                    the average.-- nothing unusual

Orderly

Announcer -   off-camera

Leader -   a big lump of bombast

Walter Smith -   a handsome young man

Narrator and host -   Rod Serling

THE TWILIGHT ZONE

"The Eye of the Beholder"

<u>SETS</u>

INT. Hospital Room, Corridor, Floor Nurses' Alcove and desk,
        elevator -- Night only

INT. Hospital Waiting Room, Double Doors, and Corridor -
        Night only

        Notes: Doubling of corridors required.
                  Floor Nurses' alcove and desk requires a
                  room-bell indicator and T.V. set; TV sets
                  should be black-faced for optical printing.
                  If stage space permits, let's try for one
                  composite set which includes the picture's
                  total needs.

A desk with flag-hung drape behind for the Leader to speak
    from. These shots will, in every case, be optically
    printed onto various T.V. sets.

THE TWILIGHT ZONE - "Eye of the Beholder" - 8/1/60

REVISED
-A

TO BE USED FOR "THE LEADER'S VOICE" THROUGHOUT ACT TWO

                    LEADER'S VOICE
          Good evening, ladies and gentlemen.
          Tonight I shall talk to you about
          glorious conformity...about the
          delight and the ultimate pleasure of
          our unified society...you recall, of
          course, that directionless, unproductive,
          over-sentimentalized era of mans' history
          when it was assumed that dissent was
          some kind of natural and healthy adjunct
          to society. We also recall that during
          this period of time there was a strange
          over-sentimentalized concept that it
          mattered not that people were different,
          that ideas were at variance with one
          another, that a world could exist
          in some kind of crazy, patch-work
          kind of make up, with foreign elements
          glued together in a crazy quilt.
          We realize, of course, now, that....

(This covers the Leader's Voice from P.15 through the
bandage removal scene.)

(The following covers Janet's running through the corridor
on Page 22.)

                    LEADER'S VOICE
          I say to you now...I say to you now
          that there is no such thing as a permissive
          society, because such a society
          cannot exist! They will scream at you
          and rant and rave and conjure up some
          dead and decadent picture of an ancient
          time when they said that all men are
          created equal! But to them equality
          was an equality of opportunity, an
          equality of status, an equality of
          aspiration! And then in what must
          surely be the pinnacle of insanity;
          the absolute in inconsistency, they
          would have had us believe that this
          equality did not apply to form, to
          color, to creed. They permitted a
          polygot, accident-bred, mongol-like mass
                    (MORE)

REVISED

LEADER'S VOICE (cont)
of diversification to blanket the
earth, to infiltrate and weaken!
(now he shrieks)
Well we know now that there must be
a single purpose! A single norm!
A single approach! A single entity
of peoples! A single virtue! A
single morality! A single frame of
reference! A single philosopjy of
government!
(shrieking again)
We cannot permit...we must not permit
the encroaching sentimentality of a
past age to weaken our resolve. We
must cut out all that is different
like a cancerous growth!

FADE ON:

1.   STANDARD OPENING   1.

      With human eye changing into setting sun. PAN DOWN TO
      OPENING SCENE OF PLAY.

2.   INT HOSPITAL ROOM   NIGHT   2.

      (Production note: Throughout the play until otherwise
      indicated, all characters with the exception of Janet
      are played either in the shadows or the camera is on
      their back, but never are actually seen face first.)

      The CAMERA STARTS A SLOW DOLLY in over toward a bed which,
      besides a bedstand, is the only furniture in an otherwise
      bare and antiseptic looking room. CAMERA STOPS on an
      ANGLE SHOT LOOKING DOWN at Janet Tyler whose face is
      entirely swathed in a bandaged mask, with only a little
      slit left open for the mouth. She remains motionless.
      Even her hands are limp, unprotesting extensions of
      herself, as if they too were resigned to a life of silent
      darkness. There's the noise of a door swinging open and
      then the very slight sound of glass medicine bottles
      rattling on a tray. The bandaged face burns toward the
      sound:

                                                   CUT TO:

3.   MED LONG SHOT   ACROSS THE ROOM   3.

      A nurse has just entered and is placing the tray down
      near the door. The position of the bedlight throws the
      far end of the room in shadows so that all we can see of
      the nurse is that of an angular, tall silhouette, her
      face invisible. Her voice, when she speaks, has a brittle
      and professional quality, unemotional and with a suggestion
      of boredom.

                          JANET
            Nurse?

                          NURSE
            Brought you your sleeping medicine,
            honey.

                          JANET
            Is it night already?

                          NURSE
            It's nine thirty.

4. DIFFERENT ANGLE - JANET   4.

    As her head turns to look up toward the ceiling.

                          JANET
              What about the day?

                          NURSE
              What about it?

                          JANET
              Was it a beautiful day? Was the
              sun out? Was it warm?

5. MOVING SHOT THE NURSE   5.

    As seen from behind her as she walks over to the bed,
    administers to the bandaged woman. The camera remains
    on her back.

                          NURSE
              Kinda warm.

                          JANET
              Clouds? Were there clouds in
              the sky?

    We can see the nurse shrug. Her voice becomes even
    duller.

                          NURSE
              I suppose there were. I never
              was much for staring up at the
              sky all the time.

    Now the nurse screws back the top on a medicine bottle,
    puts it in her pocket, shakes down a thermometer.

                          JANET
              I used to look at clouds a lot.
              If you stare at them long enough
              they become "things". Do you
              know what I mean? Ships, people,
              pastoral scenes...anything you want
              really, if you stare at them long
              enough.

                          NURSE
              Time to take your temperature now.

    She moves the thermometer toward Janet's mouth.

                          JANET
              Just one other thing - ?

                                            CONTINUED

5.   CONTINUED   5,

                          NURSE
               Well?

                          JANET
               When....when will they take
               the bandages off?

6.   CLOSE SHOT   THERMOMETER   6.

     It stops, poised in mid air, then travels in an arc back
     toward the nurse's side.

7.   DIFFERENT LONG ANGLE   7.

     As seen from above. The nurse has turned away, obviously
     reacting to the question. Janet's head follows her.

                          JANET
               How long?

                          NURSE
               Until....until they decide whether
               they can fix up your face or not.

                          JANET
                        (very softly)
               Oh. I guess it's....I guess it's
               pretty bad, isn't it?

8.   DIFFERENT ANGLE   SHOOTING OVER THE NURSE'S SHOULDER   8.
     TOWARD JANET

                          NURSE
               I've seen worse.

                          JANET
               But it's pretty bad, isn't it?
               I know it's pretty bad. Ever
               since I can remember...ever since
               I was a little girl...people have
               turned away from me. The very
               first thing I can remember is a
               little child screaming when she
               looked at me.

9.   EXTREMELY TIGHT PROFILE SHOT OF HER BANDAGED FACE   9.

     As she once again turns away. Her voice is soft, but
     there is a sense of desperation, of misery, of anguish
     that creeps in.

                                        CONTINUED

9.   CONTINUED   9.

                              JANET
               I never wanted to be beautiful
               I never wanted to look like a
               painting. I never even wanted
               to be loved.
                    (a pause)
               I just wanted...I just wanted
               people not to scream when they
               looked at me.
                    (now the bandaged
                    face turns once again
                    toward the nurse)
               When, nurse? When will they take
               the bandages off this time?

10.   DIFFERENT ANGLE   THE BACK OF THE NURSE   10.

      As she once again leans over, puts the thermometer in
      Janet's mouth, then turns, but so close to the camera
      that we are shooting her body below her face. She passes
      the camera and moves again to the opposite side of the
      room and into the shadows. The camera remains on this
      shot.

                              NURSE
               Maybe tomorrow. Maybe the next
               day. You've been waiting so long
               now...it really doesn't make too
               much difference whether it's two
               days or weeks now, does it?

11.   REVERSE ANGLE   LOOKING BACK OVER TO THE BED   11.

      Janet's head moves from side to side shaking her head "no".
      The nurse looks down at her watch then once again moves
      away from the camera over to the bed, takes the thermometer
      out, shakes it, then in identical fashion to before, passes
      the camera and goes out of the room.

                                             CUT TO:

12.   INT HOSPITAL CORRIDOR   NIGHT   12.

      This is a long, bare, almost cavernous tunnel-like hallway.
      The lights are dim and once again the people who pass under
      them, a doctor, another nurse, a patient, are in shadows
      and we cannot see their faces. A few doors down from
      Janet's room is a kind of reception desk. A nurse sits
      there, her back to camera.

13.   LONG SHOT   DOWN THE CORRIDOR   LOOKING TOWARD   13.
      RECEPTION DESK

      As Janet's nurse comes from behind the camera and starts
      walking toward the desk.

14.   MED LONG SHOT   INTER-COM   14.

On the reception desk as the CAMERA MOVES TOWARD IT,
staying on the back of Janet's nurse.

15.   CLOSE SHOT NURSE'S HAND   15.

As she flicks a button on the inter-com.

                    NURSE
          Dr. Bernadi. Evening report on
          Patient 307. Resting comfortably.
          No temperature change.

                    DOCTOR'S VOICE
               (over inter-com)
          Thank you, nurse. I'll be down
          later.

The nurse flicks off the button.

                    NURSE TWO
          Ever see her face? 307?

                    NURSE
          Indeed I have. If it were mine,
          I'd bury myself in a grave someplace.
          Some people want to live no matter
          what!
               (a pause)
          Got a cigarette?

A pack of cigarettes passes in front of the camera.
Janet's nurse's hand moves toward the pack and takes out
a cigarette, then moves out of the frame. There's the
sound of match being struck o.c., then a cloud of smoke
exhaled into the air. The CAMERA MOVES AROUND so that it
is SHOOTING THROUGH THE SMOKE across the desk, down toward
the corridor and Janet's room. At this moment we FREEZE
FRAME. Two nurses walking down the corridor away from the
camera stop and become immobile and over this tableau we
hear Serling's voice.

                    SERLING'S VOICE
          Suspended in time and space for
          a moment.
               (a pause)
          Year, place, circumstances...all
          indeterminate, because this is a
          story about beauty and about
          ugliness...and it is not dependent
          on a clock or a calendar.

                              CONTINUED

15. CONTINUED   15.

Out of Janet Tyler's room now walks Serling. Behind him we
still see the stationery figures of the nurses.

                        SERLING
            You have been introduced to Miss
            Janet Tyler who lives in a very
            private world of darkness; a
            universe whose dimensions are
            the size, thickness, length of
            a swathe of bandages that cover
            her face. In a moment we'll go
            back into this room and also
            in a moment we'll look under the
            bandages.
                 (a pause)
            Keeping in mind, of course, that
            we're not to be surprised by what
            we see because this isn't just a
            hospital. And this Patient 307
            is not just a woman. This happens
            to be The Twilight Zone...and Miss
            Janet Tyler, Patient number 307...
            with you, is about to enter it!

                                        FADE TO BLACK:

OPENING BILLBOARD
FIRST COMMERCIAL

FADE ON:

16.   INT HOSPITAL ROOM   NIGHT   EXTREMELY TIGHT PROFILE SHOT   16.
BANDAGED FACE OF JANET TYLER

Beyond at the far end of the room are the shadowy figures
of the doctor and the nurse. We hear them indistinctly
and muffled. Occasionally words like "temperature",
"pressure", "thyroid", "injection" can be heard above
the general indistinct rumble of their voices. Finally
the doctor takes a step toward the camera and the bed, his
face still in the shadows.

                    DOCTOR
               (over his shoulder)
          Come back about eleven, nurse.
          Give her the usual sedative then.

                    NURSE
          All right, doctor.

The CAMERA ARCS AROUND so that is is shooting behind
the doctor as he approaches the bed. He reaches it,
picks up Janet's arm, briefly checks her pulse while he
looks down at her.

                    DOCTOR
          Warm this evening, Miss Tyler.

                    JANET
          I thought it was. I couldn't
          be sure though.

                    DOCTOR
               (running a hand
                through his collar)
          Very warm. You can take my word
          for it. We'll have those bandages
          off you very shortly. I expect
          you're uncomfortable.

                    JANET
          I'm used to bandages on my face.

                    DOCTOR
          I've no doubt. This is your...
          ninth visit here? Is it the
          ninth?

                    JANET
          The eleventh.
               (a pause as she
                turns her bandaged
                face toward him)

               (MORE)

                              CONTINUED

16.   CONTINUED   16.

                         JANET (CONT'D)
          Sometimes I think I've lived my
          whole life inside a dark cave.
          The walls are gauze. And the
          wind that blows in from the
          mouth of the cave always smells
          of ether and disinfectant.
               (a pause)
          There's kind of a comfort though,
          doctor, to living in this cave.
          It's so wonderfully private.
               (she turns her head
               away)
          No one can ever see me.
               (another pause)
          It's hopeless, isn't it, doctor?
          I'll never look any different.

                         DOCTOR
               (putting her wrist
               down)
          That's hard to say. Up to now
          you haven't responded to the
          medication or to the shots or
          any of the proven techniques.
          Frankly, you've stumped us, Miss
          Tyler. Nothing we've done so far
          has made any difference at all.
          But we're hopeful of what this last
          treatment may have accomplished.
          There's no telling, of course--
          not till we get the bandages off.
          Unfortunately your case is one
          that can't be handled with plastic
          surgery. Bone structure, flesh
          type...many factors prohibit this
          kind of approach.

He turns away. The CAMERA ARCS AROUND with him so that
he's never full on camera.

                         DOCTOR
               (continuing thoughtfully)
          Your eleventh visit.

A pause. He moves over to the table, taps on it
tentatively.

17.   CLOSE SHOT - HIS FINGERS   17.

      As they tap.

18.   ANGLE SHOT - LOOKING ACROSS JANET TOWARD THE SLOUCHED   18.
      FIGURE OF THE DOCTOR

      There's a silence and finally Janet breaks it.

                                             CONTINUED

18. CONTINUED   18.

                         JANET
            No more after this, are there?
            No more tries.

                         DOCTOR
            Eleven is the mandatory number
            of experiments.
                    (he shrugs)
            No more are permitted after eleven.

                         JANET
            Now what?

                         DOCTOR
            Well you're kind of jumping the
            gun, Miss Tyler. You may very
            well have responded to these last
            injections. There's no way of
            telling till we get those bandages
            off.

                         JANET
            But if I haven't responded - then
            what?

                         DOCTOR
            There are alternatives.

                         JANET
            Like?

      The doctor starts to turn. WE CUT ABRUPTLY BEFORE HE
      GETS TO FACE THE CAMERA TO:

19. DOCTOR'S BACK   19.

      looking across to Janet.

                         DOCTOR
            Don't you know?

                         JANET
                    (very softly)
            I know.

                         DOCTOR
                    (approaching the bed)
            You realize, of course, Miss Tyler,
            why these rules are in effect?
            Each of us is afforded as much
            opportunity as possible to fit
            in with society. In your case
            think of the time and money and
            effort expended to make you look -

                                                 CONTINUED

19. CONTINUED   19.

He stops abruptly. His head goes down as if searching for
a word.

                    JANET
          To make me look like <u>what</u>?

                    DOCTOR
               (with a gesture)
          Normal. The way you'd <u>like</u> to
          look.

20. DIFFERENT ANGLE   JANET   20.

As she rises in bed, supporting herself on her elbows.

                    JANET
          Doctor? May I walk outdoors?
          May I sit out on the lawn. Just
          for a little while. Just to smell
          the flowers. Just to...just to
          feel the air. Just for....just
          for...
               (she bolts upright
               in bed now. Her
               voice takes on a
               different tone, a
               strained, tight,
               close-to-breaking
               harshness)
          To make believe, doctor! To
          make believe that I am normal.
          If I sit outside in <u>the</u>
          darkness then I know the
          whole world is dark. I'm
          more a part of it that way.
          Not just one grotesque, ugly,
          deformed woman with a bandage
          around her face...with a special
          darkness that belongs just to
          her.

The CAMERA MOVES IN for a VERY CLOSE SHOT of her bandaged
face and now her voice is high, shrill and unsteady.

                    JANET
          <u>I want to belong</u>! I want to be
          like other people. Please help
          me, doctor.
               (now her voice
               catches in a sob)
          Please help me.

                                        CONTINUED

20.   CONTINUED   20.

The CAMERA MOVES AROUND so that it is SHOOTING TOWARD THE
DOCTOR who stands in the shadows. He is silent for a
moment and then his voice is soft.

                         DOCTOR
                You're not alone, Miss Tyler.
                You realize that, don't you?
                You're hardly alone. There are many
                others who share your misfortune.
                People who look much as you do.
                One of the alternatives...should
                this last treatment prove
                unsuccessful...well this is
                simply to allow you to move into
                a special area in which people
                of your own kind have been
                congregated.

                         JANET
                    (bitterly)
                People of my own kind!
                    (a pause)
                Congregated, doctor? You don't
                mean congregated, you mean
                segregated. You mean imprisoned.
                You're talking about a ghetto
                now.
                    (and then plaintive,
                    anguished and more
                    as a cry, she shrieks
                    this out)
                A ghetto designed for freaks!

                         DOCTOR
                    (shouting over her)
                Miss Tyler! The State is not
                unsympathetic. Your presence
                here in this hospital attests
                to this. It's doing all it
                can for you. But you're not
                being rational, Miss Tyler.
                You can't expect to live any
                kind of life amongst...
                    (again he gropes,
                    but picks it up
                    quickly)
                Amongst normal people.

                                          CUT TO:

21.   CLOSE SHOT   JANET   21.

The bandages twitch as if underneath, her face were
contorting.

                                          CONTINUED

21. CONTINUED   21.

                          JANET
              I could try. I could wear a
              mask or this bandage. I
              wouldn't bother anyone. I'd
              just go my own way. I'd take
              a job. Any job.
                      (her voice
                      breaks again)
              Who are you people anyway? What
              is this State? Who makes up all
              the rules and the statutes and
              the traditions? The people who
              are different have to stay away
              from other people who are normal.
              The State isn't God, doctor.

                          DOCTOR
                      (firmly and obviously
                      concerned)
              Miss Tyler, please!

                          JANET
              The State is not God. It hasn't
              the right to penalize people for
              an accident of birth. It hasn't
              the right to make ugliness a
              crime -

                          DOCTOR
                      (now shouting)
              Miss Tyler, I must ask you to
              stop this kind of talk immediately!
              Now, Miss Tyler, now!

The CAMERA MOVES BACK over to a SHOT OF JANET who gets
out of bed and stands there for a moment motionlessly with
her head down, then very slowly, a hand out in front of her,
she moves across the room over to a window. She touches
it then puts her bandaged cheek against it.

                                          CUT TO:

22. REVERSE ANGLE LOOKING AT HER THROUGH THE GLASS   22.

One hand moves down the pane until it reaches the open
section at the bottom. She moves her hand back and forth.

                          JANET
                      (softly)
              I feel the night out there. I
              feel the air. I can smell the
              flowers.

                          (MORE)

22.   CONTINUED   22.

                          JANET (CONT'D)
                    (she turns slowly
                    to face the doctor.
                    Both hands go up to
                    touch the bandage,
                    in a very small still
                    voice)
               Please take this off me. Please
               take this off me.
                    (then screaming)
               Take this off me!

She starts to clutch and scrabble at the bandage, screaming
as she does so.

                                        ABRUPT CUT TO:

23.   INT. CORRIDOR - ROOM INDICATOR ON WALL OVER RECEPTION   23.
      DESK

A light "307" flashes over and over again. In the b.g.
we hear Janet's screaming voice pleading for the removal
of the bandage. The nurse passes the camera hurriedly.
CAMERA PANS AROUND SO THAT IT IS LOOKING at her as she
races down the corridor toward Janet's room.

                                        ABRUPT CUT TO:

24.   INT. HOSPITAL ROOM - AS SEEN THROUGH THE WINDOW FROM   24.
      OUTSIDE

The doctor is holding a fighting, squirming Janet as
the nurse barges in, takes her other arm and the two of
them move her back over to the bed. The scene is played
in pantomime and finally Janet quiets down. We then see
the nurse walk back over to the door and exit.

                                        CUT TO:

25.   INT. CORRIDOR - MED. SHOT - RECEPTION NURSE   25.

Reading a magazine that covers up her face. Janet's nurse
walks in front of camera so that we see most of her back and
and part of the nurse sitting behind the magazine.

                          JANET'S NURSE

               The doctor's decided to remove
               the bandages in 307. He wants
               to have the anesthetist stand by.

                                        CONTINUED

26.   DIFFERENT ANGLE - THE RECEPTION NURSE   26.

She turns just at the moment of the CAMERA CUT so that we
actually don't see her face.

                    NURSE TWO
          Of course it's not for me to say,
          but I think they spend an awful
          lot of time and trouble on some
          of these face cases--these
          throwbacks: Why not ship them
          out in the beginning?

She reaches for her magazine again and starts to
turn in her chair at which point THE CAMERA AGAIN
CUTS TO:

27.   SHOT OF HER BACK   27.

Looking over her shoulder.

                    JANET'S NURSE
          Is that what you'd want? If it
          were you?

The second nurse flicks the intercom impatiently.

                    NURSE TWO
          Anesthesia, please. Wanted
          for 307. Yes. She may get
          violent.

                              FADE TO BLACK

                              END ACT ONE

ACT TWO

FADE ON:

28. INT CORRIDOR RECEPTION DESK NIGHT   28.

A nurse and an orderly lounge around, backs to camera. The
orderly looks at his watch then across at a large television
set perched on the far end of the counter which fronts the
reception desk.

                    ORDERLY
          Leader's speaking tonight. Goes
          on in just a few minutes.

He rises, flicks on the set, then lights a cigarette.

29. TOP HAT SHOT THE MATCH   29.

As it goes into the ash tray. Directly across on a direct
line is the front of the television set which shows an
extremely long shot of a desk with an official seal behind
it. A man sits behind it, too far off to distinguish
clearly beyond a general outline. An off camera voice
announces portentously.

                    ANNOUNCER
          And now, ladies and gentlemen, our
          Leader.

There is cheering and off stage applause and we now hear
the stentorian tones of the gentleman just announced.

                    LEADER
          Good evening, ladies and gentlemen.
          Tonight I shall talk to you about
          glorious conformity...about the
          delight and the ultimate pleasure
          of our unified society...

His voice continues underneath as the CAMERA MOVES AWAY
from him and SHOOTS DOWN THE HALL.

30. DIFFERENT ANGLE THE DOOR OF JANET'S ROOM   30.

                                        DISSOLVE TO:

31. INT HOSPITAL ROOM NIGHT   31.

Janet now sits in a chair in the center of the room. A
single over-head light has been turned on so that she alone
is illuminated almost as if by a spotlight.

                                        CONTINUED

31. CONTINUED   31.

There's a low murmur of voices underneath as other shadowy
figures in the room walk back and forth in front of her,
their shadows playing briefly on her bandaged face as
they move. Behind this scene intermittently, we can
hear the voice of the Leader on the television set
outside. Then the voices of the doctor and the people
in the room die off. The doctor's body steps in front
of the camera. CAMERA PANS DOWN to a SHOT OF HIS RIGHT
HAND. It holds a scissors.

                         DOCTOR
               Now I have to ask you once
               again, Miss Tyler. I must insist
               that you promise to remain
               rational. No tantrums. No
               temperament. And no violence. You
               understand?

Janet nods.

                         DOCTOR
               Now I'll tell you precisely what
               I'm going to do. I'm going to
               cut the bandage at a point on the
               left side of your head. I'll
               start to unwind the bandage very
               gradually. The process has to
               be slow so that you can become
               accustomed to the light. As you
               know, the injections may have had
               an effect on your vision. Now as
               I unwrap I want you to keep your
               eyes open and I want you to describe
               to me the different shading of light
               as you perceive it as each layer of
               bandage comes off.

                         JANET
                    (softly)
               All right.

32. DIFFERENT ANGLE - PROFILE SHOT - JANET   32.

We see the doctor's body from the neck down, the scissors
now held in front of him.

                         DOCTOR
               Now if you make any movement or
               if you start getting emotional
               on us, Miss Tyler, I'm going to
               have to have the nurses hold you
               down and have the anesthetist put
               you under sedation. Is that
               understood?

                                                         CONTINUED

32. CONTINUED   32.

                              JANET
                          (falteringly)
                   I promise...I won't.

                              DOCTOR
                   All right then.

The scissors come out in front of him and move toward the
camera. From this angle they are disproportionately large
and almost fill the screen. We see them perform some
movement and the bandages start to move in sections across
the screen as if being unwound from a head.

                              DOCTOR
                   Do you see any light now, Miss
                   Tyler?

                              JANET
                   Just a little. It looks...it
                   looks gray.

                              DOCTOR
                   All right now, just be very
                   quiet.

Again bandage swirls across the screen and then stops.

                              DOCTOR
                   Now, Miss Tyler?

                              JANET
                   Much brighter. Very bright.

                              DOCTOR
                   Look up toward the light.

                                             CUT TO:

33. ANGLE SHOT LOOKING UP TOWARD LIGHT   33.

    A diffuse sun as seen through layers of bandage.

34. REVERSE ANGLE OVER THE DOCTOR'S SHOULDER LOOKING DOWN   34.
    TOWARD JANET'S FACE

    As once again he starts to unwrap bandage.

                              DOCTOR
                   How about now, Miss Tyler?

                              JANET
                   It's bright. It's very bright.

                                             CONTINUED

34.   CONTINUED   34.

                          DOCTOR
                Good.
                      (he continues to unwrap
                       then stops)
                I'm at the last layer now, Miss
                Tyler.

Janet's face goes up.

                          JANET
                I can...I can just distinguish your
                outline. Just vaguely...but I can
                see you.

                          DOCTOR
                Now I'm going to remove the
                last bandage, Miss Tyler. Now
                do you want a mirror.

There's a silence.

                          JANET
                No. No, thank you. No mirror.

Again she looks up as if trying to scan the faces of the
others in the room.

35.   PAN SHOT PAST THE FACES   35.

Of the anesthetist, and two nurses in the shadows as they
watch motionlessly and tensely.

36.   DIFFERENT ANGLE JANET   36.

As seen from the back of her head. The doctor once again
reaches for the last of the bandages.

                          DOCTOR
                Now I'm going to remove the
                last bandage, Miss Tyler. And
                I want you to remember this
                please. Miss Tyler? Are you
                listening?

                          JANET
                Yes, I'm listening.

                                        CONTINUED

36. CONTINUED   36.

                         DOCTOR
          We have done all we could. If
          we were successful --all well
          and good. There are no problems.
          If, however, this final treatment
          has not achieved the desired
          results, keep in mind that you
          can still live a long and fruitful
          life among people of your own
          kind. As soon as we discover
          these results, we'll either
          release you...or --

He pauses for a moment.

37. ANOTHER PAN SHOT PAST THE SHADOWY FACES   37.

Of the other people in the room, winding up on a SHOT OF
JANET'S thinly bandaged face through which we can now see
the outline of her features, eyes, nose, mouth, but no
definitive portrait of a face.

                         JANET
          Doctor?

                         DOCTOR
          Yes?

                         JANET
          If I'm still...if I'm still
          terribly ugly, is there any other
          alternative? Could I...could I
          be put away?

                         DOCTOR
          Under certain circumstances, Miss
          Tyler...the State does provide for
          extermination of undesirables.
          There are many factors to be
          considered though that bear on
          the decision. Under the
          circumstances considering your
          age...your general physical
          condition...I doubt very much
          if we could permit anything but
          your transfer to a communal group
          of people with your...your
          disability.

                         JANET
          You'll make me go then?

                                        CONTINUED

37.   CONTINUED   37.

                          DOCTOR
                That will probably be the case.
                All right, Miss Tyler. Remain
                very quiet please. Keep your
                eyes open.

38.   DIFFERENT ANGLE FROM BEHIND THE DOCTOR   38.

      As he reaches forward and starts to unwind the last
      bandage. The first strip of bandage comes off the top
      of her forehead, another layer falls revealing her
      forehead, another layer uncovering just the upper part
      of her eyebrows and eyes.

                          DOCTOR
                All right, Miss Tyler. Now here
                comes the last of it. I wish you
                every good luck!

      Again he reaches over and starts to unwind as we

                                              CUT TO:

39.   SHADOWY FACES OF THE OTHER PEOPLE IN THE ROOM   39.

      There's a moment's absolute silence, then one of the
      nurses lets out a gasp. Another involuntarily throws a
      hand and arm across her face to blot out what is
      obviously an incredible spectacle.

40.   FLASH CLOSE SHOT - DOCTOR'S HAND   40.

      As he drops the scissors and they land on the floor. He
      then steps back into the shadows to stand close to the
      others.

                       DOCTOR'S VOICE
                No change! No change at all!

40A. CLOSEUP - JANET   40A.

      She raises her head. If she is not startlingly
      beautiful, we have missed our point entirely.

41.   DIFFERENT ANGLE FROM BEHIND JANET   41.

      As she slowly rises. Her hands come up from her side to
      touch her face, then remain there as her head bends over
      and she buries her face in her hands. In the silence we
      hear one rasping sob that is finally and painfully
      controlled. Then she looks up, scanning the faces that
      confront her, then suddenly she breaks away and races
      toward the door. The doctor hurriedly and expertly steps
      in front of her way and grabs her.

                                              CONTINUED

41. CONTINUED   41.

                              DOCTOR
                         (curtly to the
                          other man in the
                          room)
                    Needle, please. I was afraid
                    of this.
                         (then to the nurse)
                    Turn on the lights!

                                        CONTINUED

41. CONTINUED   41.

The shadowy form of the nurse moves over to the light
switch.

42. CLOSE SHOT   HER HAND   42.

As she turns on the switch.

43.- ABRUPT FLASH CLOSE UPS OF THE TWO NURSES, THE   43.-
46. ANESTHETIST, AND THEN THE DOCTOR   46.

Each face is more grotesque than the other. Noses, eyes,
mouths, ears, everything, almost as if they were cartoons;
almost as if they were some caricature drawings come to
life.

47. MED. CLOSE SHOT   THE ANESTHETIST   47.

A syringe in his hand, as he walks slowly toward the
struggling girl whose face is buried against the doctor.
He holds up the needle and at this moment Janet breaks
free, opens the door wildly and races out into the corridor.

48. LONG SHOT AS SHE RACES DOWN THE CORRIDOR   48.

Past amazed nurses and doctors, each of whom has the same
odd ugliness of those we have already seen.

49. CLOSE SHOT DOOR OF JANET'S ROOM   49.

As the doctor barges out.

                         DOCTOR
                    (shouts)
            Stop that patient! Stop her!

50.- SERIES OF SHOTS OF JANET   50.-
52.   52.
     As she races down empty corridors.

53. CLOSE SHOT   ELEVATOR OPERATOR   53.

He opens the doors to the elevator just as Janet passes.
He, like all the others, is a cartoon-like looking character.

54. CLOSE SHOT DOCTOR   54.

Coming out of operating room, removing his mask just as
Janet runs by him. His face is like that of the elevator
operator.

55. RUNNING SHOT JANET   55.

As she races down the corridor.

56.- DIFFERENT ANGLES   TELEVISION SCREENS   56.-
58.   58.

As she runs by them. Each with a different angle of the
face of the Leader as he continues to speak, his voice
droning, unintelligible, but persistent and gradually
taking on a build of excitement.

59. DIFFERENT ANGLE JANET   59.

As she stops in the middle of an empty hall and looks
left, right, in front and then back.

                                    CUT TO:

60.- INTERSPERSED SHOTS OF THE TELEVISION SCREEN   60.-
62.   62.

As each shot shows it in larger and larger perspective.
The face of the Leader incredibly ugly as it shouts down
at her.

63. ZOOM IN TO CLOSE SHOT JANET'S BACK   63.

As her hands go to the sides of her head as if trying to
shut out the noises.

64. LONG ANGLE SHOT LOOKING DOWN   64.

As she races down the last corridor and turns a corner
then stops dead. WHIP PAN UP TO GIANT TELEVISION SCREEN.
The Leader's face fills it up entirely, screaming, ranting,
contorting.

65. CLOSE SHOT JANET'S HAND   65.

As she instinctively reaches for an ash tray near a bench
which is against one wall.

66. DIFFERENT ANGLE   66.

As she picks it up and flings it across the corridor.

67. EXTREMELY TIGHT CLOSE SHOT TELEVISION SCREEN   67.

The ash tray hits the face of the Leader head on and
splinters the set and from the broken, smoking remnant
of the machine, we hear the voice of the leader.

                                    CONTINUED

67.   CONTINUED   67.

                         LEADER'S VOICE
                It is essential in this society
                that we not only have a norm, but
                that we conform to that norm.
                Differences weaken us. Variations
                destroy us. An incredible
                permissiveness to deviation from
                this norm is what has ended nations
                and brought them to their knees.
                Conformity we must worship and
                hold sacred. Conformity is the
                key to survival.

     The voice persists as we

                                              CUT TO:

68.   DIFFERENT ANGLE - JANET   68.

     As she races down the corridor past the screen.

69.   CLOSE SHOT - DOUBLE DOORS   69.

     Unlabeled, as Janet runs in and smashes through them.

69A. INT. ROOM - MED. SHOT   69A.

     Janet bursts in an recoils in shock and horror at
     something she sees o.s. She shrieks and slides slowly
     down to the ground in a huddled heap and begins to cry.
     The CAMERA MOVES DOWN. The legs and feet of whatever
     monstrosity she has seen move into f.g. Janet is
     terrified. Then the doctor enters from another direction
     and bends down to her soothingly.

                         DOCTOR
                Don't be afraid, Miss Tyler. This is
                a representative of the group you're
                to live with. Oddly enough, you've
                come right to him. Come on now -- he
                won't hurt you.

     He lifts the terrified girl to her feet.

70.   CLOSEUP - JANET   70.

     Forces herself to look at the newcomer, her face full
     of revulsion.

71.   FULL SHOT   71.

Walter Smith steps into the light. We see a youthful,
tremendously attractive young man, dressed plainly in
simple trousers and shirt.

                    DOCTOR
           This is Mr. Smith, Janet. Walter
           Smith. He's in charge of the village
           group in the North. He'll take
           you there tonight. You can live
           among your own kind now.

72.   DIFFERENT ANGLE - SMITH   72.

As he walks over to Janet. We're looking across her back
and up into Smith's face. In addition to being attractive,
it's a gentle face, a compassionate face, an infinitely
kind face. He smiles, his voice is gentle and soft.

                    SMITH
           Miss Tyler?

The girl's head is raised.

                    'SMITH
           We have a lovely village and
           wonderful people. I think you'll
           like it where I'm going to take
           you. You'll be with your own
           kind and after a little while...
           you'd be amazed how little a
           while...you'll feel a sense of
           great belonging. You'll feel a
           sense of being loved. And you
           will be loved, Miss Tyler.

The girl remains motionless now. Smith looks up and
gestures with his head.

73. DIFFERENT ANGLE THE ROOM   73.

As the doctor leaves and shuts the door behind him.

74. CLOSE SHOT SMITH   74.

                              SMITH
          Miss Tyler? Would you get your
          things now? We can leave any
          time.

The CAMERA STARTS A VERY, VERY SLOW ARC until finally it
is shooting directly into the face of Janet Tyler. She's
like a beautiful living portrait. A face carved into the
mould of all things woman. Gentle, beautiful, feminine
and young.

                              JANET
          Mr. Smith?

                              SMITH
          Yes?

                              JANET
          Why...why are some of us born so
          ugly?

                              SMITH
                (smiles sadly)
          I don't know, Miss Tyler. I
          really don't know.
                (a pause)
          But do you know something? It
          doesn't really matter. There's
          an old saying...a very, very old
          saying...beauty is in the eye of
          the beholder. When we leave
          here...when we go to the village..
          keep that in mind. Try, Miss
          Tyler. Say it over and over in
          your mind. Beauty is in the
          eye of the beholder.
                (a pause as he
                 takes her hand)
          Come on now. We'll get your things
          and we'll leave.

The two of them walk to the double doors. He opens them
for her and they walk out into the corridor, a vast,
empty passageway that stretches out almost to infinity.
The CAMERA REMAINS STATIONARY as they walk away from it
down the corridor.

                                        CONTINUED

74. CONTINUED

                         SERLING'S VOICE
              Now the questions that come to
              mind...where is this place and
              when is it. What kind of world
              where ugliness is the norm and
              beauty the deviation from that
              norm. You want an answer? The
              answer is...it doesn't make any
              difference. Because the old
              saying happens to be true. Beauty
              is in the eye of the beholder. In
              this year or a hundred years hence.
                   (a pause)
              On this planet...or wherever
              there is human life perhaps out
              amongst the stars.
                   (a pause)
              Beauty is in the eye of the
              beholder. Lesson to be learned...
              in The Twilight Zone.

                                   FADE TO BLACK:

                    THE END

TRUTH IN BEAUTY

As one of the most memorable, shocking and popular installments of the entire series, "Eye of the Beholder" might well be described as the prototypical *Twilight Zone* episode. Brilliantly conceived and flawlessly executed, this compelling parable confronts the dangers of conformity with innovation and style.

Injustice and prejudice are themes that fuel many of Rod Serling's more powerful scripts. In this teleplay, shades of those topics are applied sparingly to add layers of texture and depth. Serling more directly tackles a trio of weighty issues—segregation, the importance of the individual, and the curious human hunger to blend in and be accepted by peers and society—without grand-standing or resorting to sanctimonious asides. The writer's approach is far from subtle but he expertly weaves his message into the fabric of the story.

Serling is careful to avoid any suggestion of vanity in his sympathetic lead character, and Janet Tyler's desire to simply appear "normal" is made clear within the script. The doctors and nurses who surround her maintain the careful balance of humane caregivers; they pity Janet and try to comfort her, but struggle to remain remote and professional. The camera's deliberate avoidance of faces is perplexing to viewers, and plants seeds of doubt that are cultivated when the hospital staff demonstrates a slavish devotion to speeches broadcast by their mysterious "Leader." These factors combine to enthrall the audience and set up a staggering conclusion that does not disappoint.

The setting of a totalitarian society (another of Serling's favorite targets) is a wise choice that lends credence to the story. The mistrust of this Kafkaesque State and its harsh regulations is almost instinctive, and adds urgency to Janet

Tyler's plight. The success or failure of her final operation is not simply a matter of correcting a deformity; in a world where individuality is abhorred and ultimately destroyed, the operation is the difference between social acceptance and rejection, and possibly even life or death.

Extremes of appearance are put to metaphorical use in assessing the value of the individual, and the juxtaposition of beauty and ugliness sets up the finale. Viewers are manipulated to expect the worst during the unmasking of a disfigured Janet Tyler, and those fears are confirmed when a shocked staff indicates that the operation has failed. Anticipating some hideous deformity, we are initially confused when Janet turns out to be strikingly beautiful. Before we have a chance to regain composure, however, the monstrous doctors and nurses are revealed, and our preconceived notions of appearance are rendered meaningless. Suddenly, in this place, we are all outcasts.

When first handed the "Eye of the Beholder" script, cast and crew alike reacted to the distinctive storyline. "I loved it," reveals associate producer Del Reisman. "Right from the start. I thought it was a marvelous idea, and I think that Rod just did a terrific job."

"I was so impressed with the quality of the writing," adds Maxine Stuart, the actress who portrayed the bandaged Janet Tyler. "It was a literate and challenging piece of work. *The Twilight Zone* always had good stories, but for me this was special."

A stellar script, however, does not automatically translate into a flawless episode. Many superior television scripts are weakened by lapses in quality during the various stages of assembly. In this case, however, all aspects of production converge and blend seamlessly to enhance the script. The credit for "Eye of the Beholder" starts with Serling but extends to the very talented *Twilight Zone* production staff.

Director Douglas Heyes and Director of Photography George T. Clemens pull off a tricky and essential bit of subterfuge by playing a meticulous game of hide-and-seek with the actors' faces. "The mechanical problems in that were extraordinary," says Reisman. "What Doug Heyes did—he was a marvelous director—was so skillful, but he tipped it. It is tipped, because the camera angles are so consciously avoiding the faces. So halfway through, when you've never heard of this or have seen it, you think, 'Hey, wait a minute, what's going on here?' Everything that Doug and George Clemens did, the corridors, the lighting of the corridors, that really strange otherworld feeling that they captured in that, it was very effective."

Douglas Heyes described the challenges of directing the episode in a 1982 interview for *Rod Serling's Twilight Zone Magazine*. "'Beholder' presented a problem of how to avoid the faces of the doctors and nurses—how to keep the secret. You could have done it all with inserts, but that would have made the audience suspicious. What I had to do was try to hold their attention and yet not let them see any faces. I was trying very hard to make it seem like I *wasn't* trying to do what I was doing!"

The surprise ending may have had a sharper edge in 1960, since today's media-savvy viewers are quick to spot the roving camera and hidden faces, but the camera's deception still serves to charge the show's atmosphere. "With the woman's face under the bandages, I tried to suggest that this was her vision," said Heyes. "She could only hear them around her. She isn't seeing, so we're not seeing them yet. And I think it worked visually. I'm very pleased with the way the camera enhances the effect I was after. By now, of course, everybody knows what the trick is."

The critical aspect of makeup was handled by MGM legend William Tuttle. Fresh from his creation of the ape-like Morlocks in George Pal's 1960 movie version of H.G. Wells' THE TIME MACHINE, Tuttle and Heyes decided on a similar look for the distorted faces of the "Eye of the Beholder" populace. Grotesque, misshapen facial arrangements—prominent brow, pig-like nose, swollen upper lip—were designed and molded in latex, then applied to the faces of various actors. These individual sections conformed to the features of the actors, something a mask could not do with any degree of realism. The results are shocking and unforgettable, giving form to Serling's description of dreadfully caricatured human beings.

"We had the problem of creating a race of people who were all similar in a way," commented Heyes. "One of the themes was that everyone should conform to an image—glorious conformity. So I talked to Bill about the Morlocks and said, 'Do something like them.' First I drew a man and said, 'Why don't you take these guys and give them some distinctive features, and then we have to distort them somehow—they have to look like mutants of some kind.'

"When designing that makeup, we were trying to make them grotesque but also not unsympathetic. When the characters do show up and you finally see them, they're not hideous-looking things, just kind of pathetic and strange-looking. They had sympathetic eyes, their real eyes. Bill was marvelous—a master. He could do anything you asked him to do."

The director's wife, Joanna Heyes, was cast as the reception nurse and Tuttle's facial appliances resulted in a laugh at her expense—courtesy of her husband. "When she came on the set with the full outfit on, all the makeup and everything, I glanced over and said, 'Hi, honey, shouldn't you be in makeup?' The day did not go well from that point forward."

Renowned composer Bernard Herrmann again supplies a score that perfectly compliments the on-screen action. Sparse and methodical to build tension early on, the score becomes a resonant force at the point of Janet Tyler's unmasking and accentuates her nightmarish run through the hospital.

Despite having to perform with her face buried in bandages, Maxine Stuart does an outstanding job as the concealed Janet Tyler. Her hand gestures animate an individual robbed of facial expressions, and her voice—which alternates between vulnerability and conviction—conveys the woman's emotional fragility. Stuart displays a great deal of range as her character's temperament evolves through stages of resentment, hope and anticipation. "It's easy to act when one's face is hidden," says Stuart. "Acting itself is a process of hiding."

"Under the bandages, I wanted a voice that suggested it could belong to an ugly person," added Douglas Heyes. "I wanted a voice with character, harshness, and timbre. So we used Maxine Stuart, a marvelous actress."

One facet of the role that Stuart did not appreciate was being replaced for the final scenes by actress Donna Douglas, who would gain fame two years later as the vapid Elly May Clampett in *The Beverly Hillbillies*. "For most of the script, my character is under bandages recovering from a surgical procedure designed to make her beautiful in conformity with the rest of the population. The actors playing those parts were made up to look like gargoyles and the drama was that the surgery had failed, for when the bandages came off, the woman looked lovely, and *not* like the gargoyles. Of course, for that scene they substituted Donna Douglas—a *great* beauty—for me.

"Now I certainly agree that I could not be considered a great beauty by any stretch of the imagination. However, I do feel that since this particular show dealt with conformity, they might have allowed for a less startling-looking woman and settled for reality!"

Stuart's point is valid, but it would not have worked on screen. Extravagant beauty is necessary to establish a contrast between Janet Tyler and her repulsive fellow citizens. When Serling describes the climactic scene in his script, he demonstrates his command of the visual medium of television. The stage direction says it all: *She raises her head. If she is not startlingly beautiful, we have missed our point entirely.*

Maxine Stuart is quick to point out that her disappointment was minor and did nothing to sour her *Twilight Zone* experience. "I certainly hope that my comments about the ending don't sound ungracious or ungrateful. I loved doing the show. It was a pleasure for me to act in such good material, and a gratifying and enjoyable task. I thought it was beautifully written."

One filmed scene—a detailed conversation between the doctor and nurse in a hospital lounge—is notably absent from Serling's script. The segment serves to soften the Doctor's character as he confesses his personal attachment to Janet's case and expresses his frustration with State mandates. The scene was a late addition and does not appear in any of Serling's personal script drafts.

Douglas Heyes described the rationale behind this humanization of the hospital staff. "The whole thing is almost a radio show. Up to a certain point late in the story, you're not seeing anyone's face, so the voices are going to be the most important thing. I had the idea that the voices of these monster people would be very sympathetic. Rod was surprised at that. He had not intended them to be that way, but he liked it.

"So I interviewed the actors for that show without ever seeing them. I sat in a room with my back to the door. They'd come in, and I'd read the part with them and listen only to their voices. I picked the people with the most sympathetic voices I could get. If we are going to believe that these people are the norm, then they have to sound like nice people.

"That was great fun. I look at it now and enjoy the camera work and the tricks that we did. In fact, I think that was my favorite of the ones I directed on *Twilight Zone.*"

Del Reisman describes an event that underscores the popularity and universal appeal of the episode. "A couple of summers ago, I was on a teaching seminar in France. All of the students were French but spoke some English. One of the students came forward and handed me two videocassettes of *Twilight Zone* episodes, so we played them. One was 'Eye of the Beholder.'

"Rod comes on in his usual host image, speaking beautiful French—Rod would have been just on the floor watching that—because they dubbed him. That show was a big hit to the class. I mean, they really applauded and were excited by it. It was wonderful. That was a terrific show. It's just so beautifully done."

The Twilight Zone

A MOST UNUSUAL CAMERA

Airdate: 12-16-1960

Manuscript Date: 10-14-1960

Dated 10-3-1960 with revisions dated
10-7-1960 and 10-14-1960

Script Six

Episode Forty-Six

THE TWILIGHT ZONE

Script Six

"A MOST UNUSUAL CAMERA"

by

ROD SERLING

Revised
October 3, 1960

"THE TWILIGHT ZONE"

"A Most Unusual Camera"

<u>SETS</u>

INT. FASHIONABLE ANTIQUE AND OBJETS D'ART STORE

INT. HOTEL SUITE

     (with bedroom)

EXT. RACETRACK RAIL

INT. RACETRACK BETTING

EXT. TOTE BOARD AREA

"THE TWILIGHT ZONE"

"A Most Unusual Camera"

CAST

CHESTER DIEDRICH......................Avaricious, tough, energetic;
a small-time criminal who
wants to graduate to the
biggest jobs.

PAULA DIEDRICH.......................Chester's wife and
partner-in-crime.

WOODWARD............................Paula's brother; a big oaf--
he wakes up in time to eat.

WAITER..............................A Frenchman with a shrewd
eye for the main chance.

ANTIQUE STORE OWNER..................A cultivated collector of
objets d'art.

OWNER'S WIFE.........................Also cultivated, considerably
more aggressive.

TOUT................................A racetrack habitue

DETECTIVE...........................

1.   STANDARD OPENING (WEB)   1.

     With propulsion into starry night, smashing into letters,
     then PAN DOWN TO OPENING SHOT OF PLAY.

2.   EXT HOTEL   2.

                                                   DISSOLVE THRU TO:

3.   INT HOTEL SUITE   LONG SHOT ACROSS THE ROOM   3.

     Of Paula Diedrich. She's one half of a team of con artists
     and she lounges on the bed reading aloud from a newspaper.

                         PAULA
               "Sometime during the morning, the
               rear door of the antique shop was
               jimmied open. The police surmise
               that the thief, obviously working
               with an accomplice, entered and
               began to remove items from the
               shelves. Mr. and Mrs. Jensen J.
               Brown, the proprietors of the
               shop, listed the following collector's
               items as among the goods stolen:
               'Six vases of the Ming Dynasty' -"

3A. WHIP PAN OVER TO SHOT OF CHESTER DIEDRICH ACROSS THE   3A.
     ROOM

     In front of him on the floor and all around him is the loot
     that Paula refers to from the newspaper. He holds up two
     vases and smashes them together, throwing the pieces over his
     shoulder.

                         DIEDRICH
               I don't know what Dynasty they're
               from -- but they ain't Ming's.
               They're from a rummage sale and
               they're worth a half a shuck a piece.

                                                   CUT TO:

3B. MED CLOSE SHOT   PAULA   3B.

                         PAULA
               Chester!

                         DIEDRICH
               Larceny. It's plain no good larceny.
               That's nothing but a list for
               their insurance company. Why
               those crooks.

                                                   CONTINUED

3B.   CONTINUED   3B.

                        PAULA
              An antique silver service for
              twelve. A Louis Fourteenth
              candlebra. A Queen Anne chest.

3C.   DIEDRICH   3C.

        As he points in turn to the objects.

                        DIEDRICH
              A phony Louis Fourteenth candlebra.
              A set of U.S. Navy surplus
              tableware...and a chest worth
              three dollars and fifty cents tops.

3D.   MED CLOSE SHOT PAULA   3D.

                        PAULA
              Three oil paintings by Picasso.

3E.   CLOSE SHOT DIEDRICH   3E.

                        DIEDRICH
              Three posters in frames. The guy
              who painted them thinks a Picasso
              is a foreign sports car!

3F.   OMIT.   3F.

3G.   PAULA   3G.

                        PAULA
                   (from across the room)
              "Two teakwood hand carved cigarette
              cases with platforms and --"

                        DIEDRICH
              Aw right, knock it off, knock it
              off!

3H.   DIFFERENT ANGLE THE TWO OF THEM   3H.

        Paula, rising from the bed, takes a camera off the floor.

                        PAULA
              They forgot this. An antique
              camera no less.

                                        CONTINUED

3H.   CONTINUED   3H.

                              DIEDRICH
                    (looking at it and then
                     very disparagingly)
                 Gorgeous!
                    (then looking over the
                     junk that surrounds him)
                 But it fits the rest of the haul.
                 Everything else for nothin'. So
                 it figures -- we get a camera
                 that's for nothin'!

He takes the camera from her hand and throws it on the bed.
We FREEZE FRAME ON DIEDRICH STANDING THERE ALONGSIDE PAULA.

                          SERLING'S VOICE
                 A hotel suite that in this instance
                 serves as a den of crime. The
                 aftermath of a rather minor event
                 to be noted on a police blotter,
                 an insurance claim, perhaps a
                 three inch box on page twelve of
                 the evening paper.

The CAMERA DOLLIES IN for a TIGHT CLOSE SHOT OF THE CAMERA
then WHIP PANS OVER TO SERLING standing across the room.

                              SERLING
                 Small addenda to be added to the
                 list of the loot. A camera. A
                 most unimposing addition to the
                 flotsam and jetsam that it came
                 with. Hardly worth mentioning,
                 really, because cameras are cameras.
                 Some expensive, some purchaseable
                 at five and dime stores.
                    (a pause)
                 But this camera...this one is
                 unusual, because in just a moment
                 we'll watch it inject itself into
                 the destinies of three people.
                 It happens to be a fact that the
                 pictures that it takes can only
                 be developed...in The Twilight Zone.

                                         DISSOLVE TO:

OPENING BILLBOARD
FIRST COMMERCIAL

FADE ON:

4.   INT BEDROOM   FULL SHOT THE ROOM   4.

As Diedrich once again picks up the camera, studies it,
shakes his head.

                    DIEDRICH
          Big deal. Twenty years ago you
          could have bought this in the
          drugstore for thirty nine cents
          and I've got to get it as part
          of a heist!
               (he holds it up)
          Look at this crummy thing. No
          place to insert film. No place
          to open it up. Just some crazy
          foreign lettering on it.
               (he looks through a
                sighting device)
          This must be the button here.
          Hold it, baby. Say cheese.
               (he pushes the button,
                pointing the camera
                at his wife, then he
                tosses the camera on
                the bed, surveys the
                mess that litters
                the room)
          Big deal! The whole haul is
          probably worth five dollars and
          eighty cents. A good fence'll
          give us a buck for it. You and
          your curio shops!

                    PAULA
          My curio shops? Who cased the
          place? Who fingered it? Who
          did all the planning?

                              CONTINUED

4.   CONTINUED   4.

                              DIEDRICH
                    (sits on the bed, lights
                    a cigarette then waves it
                    in her direction in a
                    grandly elegant fashion
                    as if introducing a
                    queen, with vast, biting
                    sarcasm)
          Listen to Miss Culture of 1960 over
          there! The patron of the arts!
          Never mind hock shops, she says. No,
          let's go up in life. Let's knock
          off a curio shop because curio shops
          have nothing but objects of art worth
          a fortune!
                    (then his face contorted
                    with anger)
          And who touted me? The art lover
          over there. Two weeks of planning,
          a whole night on the job, and what
          have we got, Paula?
                    (he makes a motion with
                    his hands surveying the
                    room)
          Four hundred pounds of junk. I
          Could have shot pool for a whole
          day and made more. Look, baby, the
          next hot idea you get about a heist -

He's suddenly interrupted by a clicking sound from the
camera alongside of him on the bed. A large snapshot has
just been ejected through the slot.

5.   CLOSE SHOT   DIEDRICH   5.

      Reacting.

6.   CLOSE SHOT   PAULA   6.

      Similar surprise showing.

7.   MED CLOSE SHOT   DIEDRICH   7.

      As he picks up the camera, examines it and tears off the
      picture. He studies it carefully then looks up in vast,
      speechless surprise.

8.   TWO SHOT   8.

                              PAULA
                    Well? How do I look?

                                        CONTINUED

8.   CONTINUED   8.

Diedrich just stares at her and looks back down at the
picture, then looks up at her again. He gulps, shakes his
head.

9.   TRACK SHOT   PAULA   9.

as she goes over to take the picture out of his hand.

10. CLOSE SHOT   PAULA   10.

as she smiles broadly.

                    PAULA
          Isn't that nice! And so clear,
          Chet. Can you imagine that? No
          lights or anything and look how
          clear it is.

11. TWO SHOT   11.

He rises off the bed and in a single motion swipes the
picture out of her hand. He stares at her then at the
picture then at her again.

                    PAULA
          What's the matter with you?

                    DIEDRICH
          What's the matter with me? Paula,
          go over to the mirror.

                    PAULA
          What?

                    DIEDRICH
          Go ahead. Look at yourself in the
          mirror.

They look at one another.

                    PAULA
          You missin' a coupla buttons?

Diedrich grabs her and propels her across the room toward
the dresser mirror.

                    DIEDRICH
          Go ahead. Look.

12. MED. SHOT   REFLECTION IN THE MIRROR   12.

                    PAULA
          So? What's to see?

CONTINUED

12. CONTINUED   12.

                              DIEDRICH
                    (slams the picture down
                     on the dresser)
                Now look at the picture.

She holds up the picture and studies it and shrugs.

                              PAULA
                So? There I am standing by the
                window wearing a...
                    (now her voice suddenly
                     becomes very tight and
                     startled)
                A fur coat!

She drops the picture like it was burning to the touch and
lets out a little scream, backing away from the dresser.

13. MED. CLOSE SHOT   PAULA   13.

                              PAULA
                Chester, what am I doing wearing a
                fur coat? I wasn't wearing a fur
                coat when you took the picture. I
                don't even own a fur coat.

14. LONG SHOT   ACROSS THE ROOM   14.

Diedrich looks down at the snapshot shaking his head from
side to side. He looks up, first at her reflection in the
mirror, then at her, then slowly his face relaxes.

                              DIEDRICH
                I got it. I got it!
                    (he points to the
                     camera on the bed)

                A gag camera. Strictly a gag
                camera. For laughs.

                              PAULA
                What do you mean?

                              DIEDRICH
                    (goes over to the camera,
                     picks it up)
                See? Inside they've got these ready-
                made pictures already developed. But
                the negatives already got a picture on
                them. The only thing this thing takes
                is the face.

                              (MORE)

                                                          CONTINUED

14. CONTINUED

                    DIEDRICH (CONT'D)
          You know - like in a carnival
          when you pose in front of those
          crazy cardboard things. Fat lady -
          driving a car - sailor - you know!
          And that's what this thing is.
                    (he looks at the camera
                     with admiration)
          Now that's not bad! That's kind of
          clever!
                    (he puts the camera
                     on the bed, rubs his
                     hands, looks around
                     the room again)
          Well, we might as well clear up the
          rest of this junk.

15. TRACK SHOT WITH HIM   15.

As he walks over to a small chest. He kneels down in front
of it, tries the latch and can't open it.

                    DIEDRICH
          Did a key come with this?

Paula, who has gone back to the dresser and is studying the
picture, looks up.

                    PAULA
          No. You'll have to open it in your
          own inimitable style.

He looks up at her, one hand still fiddling with the lock.

                    DIEDRICH
          Anybody ever tell you, you hadda
          lousy disposition?

                    PAULA
                    (bridling)
          If I have a nasty disposition, it's
          because I'm married to a nickel and
          dime heister who can't tell a real
          diamond from a baseball!

                    DIEDRICH
          Baby doll - this suite is twenty-eight
          bucks a day, delivered and paid for by
          Mrs. Diedrich's son Chester from profits
          collected during a potful of years
          when you weren't even in the picture!
          It so happens that I need you like I
          need a three-time conviction -

16. CLOSE SHOT   LOCK   16.

As it suddenly springs under his hand and the top clicks
open on the chest.

17. ANGLE SHOT   LOOKING UP AT HIS FACE   17.

From below the box. His eyes go wide. Her face appears
alongside of his. Her eyes go wide too, but more with
delight than fright. She reaches in as we
                                                      CUT TO:

18. TWO SHOT   THE TWO OF THEM   18.

Paula has picked up a gorgeous fur coat and in one shrug
has it on, goes immediately over to the mirror, oohing and
aahing as she walks over to the mirror to look at herself,
and then in the manner of a model, she walks back and forth,
then strikes up a pose near the window.

                         PAULA
          How do you like this? And don't start
          giving me any cheap pazazz about taking
          this to a fence. This is for little old
          Paula. And don't try to argue with me either.
                 (she suddenly stops abruptly, staring
                  at his face, frightened)
          All right, cue me! What's the matter?

Diedrich rises slowly and like a man in a dream, walks over to
the dresser. He picks up the picture. Paula slowly lets the
coat drop off her. She goes over to the dresser and the two
of them look down at the picture in his hand.
                                                      CUT TO:

19. EXTREMELY TIGHT CLOSE UP   SNAPSHOT   19.

There it is in all its detail. Paula in the fur coat posed by
the window in exactly the same pose as we've just seen her.
And then as if by direction, both of them turn to stare toward
the camera on the bed.

20. PAN SHOT ACROSS THE ROOM   20.

Winding up on a tight close up of the camera as it sits there,
just an uninteresting looking black object, but somehow
menacing beyond words.
                                                      DISSOLVE TO:

21. INT HOTEL SUITE BEDROOM   NIGHT   MED CLOSE SHOT   21.

Looking toward the window as a neon light from outside
flashes on and off and there's the distant sound of night
traffic. Intruding upon this is the sound of metal clicks
and drumming fingers.

22. FULL SHOT THE ROOM   22.

Paula is asleep in bed. Sitting on the chaise lounge across
the room is a sleepless Diedrich, in his bathrobe, fiddling
with the damera.

23. MED CLOSE SHOT PAULA   23.

as she awakens, looks across the room.

                         PAULA
              What are you doing? Come back
              to bed.
                   (and now, fully awake,
                    she props herself up
                    on her elbow and
                    stares across at him,
                    tiredly)
              Still with that?

                         DIEDRICH
              Shut up.

24. TWO SHOT   24.

Diedrich turns to look at her. He holds up the camera,
bounces it around a couple of times, wanting to say
something, then he puts it down, resignedly shakes his head,
totally nonplused.

                         PAULA
              So what do you care?

                         DIEDRICH
                   (trying to interrupt)
              You want me to let it go by, huh?

                         PAULA
                   (overlapping him)
              What do you care? So it's a crazy
              camera. So it takes dopey pictures
              that really aren't there.

                         DIEDRICH
                   (outshouting her)
              Sure it takes dopey pictures.
              Dopey pictures like things that
              haven't happened yet but do happen.

Paula gets out of bed, throws on a wrapper, angry now with
the anger of the frustrated sleeper.

                         CONTINUED

24. CONTINUED   24.

                         PAULA
                 So what's to do Chet? One lousy
                 kookie picture and you get
                 insomnia. It's a camera, that's
                 all. Look I'll show you.

She aims the camera to the other side of the room, and pushes
a button.

                         PAULA
                 There! See? Any lightning?
                 Drop it, why don't you? Let it
                 alone. Forget about it.

                         DIEDRICH
                 How can I forget about it? This
                 thing comes from...from witches
                 maybe. Or sorcerers. This thing
                 may be loaded with black magic.

25. SHOT OF PAULA   25.

As she strides across the room and grabs the camera out of
his hand.

                         PAULA
                 And what are you loaded with?
                 Do you see anything? Where is
                 the man with the horns who comes
                 in with the bargain for the soul?
                 It's a kookie camera, that's all!

She turns to look at him again and Diedrich is staring at the
camera in her hand. Paula herself now looks down at it,
suddenly ill at ease. There's a clicking sound as once again
a picture shoots out from it. Paula lets out a scream. The
camera drops from her hand and lands on the floor, the
picture protruding. Diedrich, trance-like, walks over, takes
the snapshot out and studies it, wets his lips and looks up
at her.

                         PAULA
                     (her voice tremulous)
                 Well?

He hands her the picture and she studies it, her eyes wide.
She looks across at Diedrich.

                                              CONTINUED

25. CONTINUED   25.

                         PAULA
                 (in a half whisper)
               It's my brother Woodward! Standing
               by the door!

                         DIEDRICH
                 (takes the picture
                  out of her hand,
                  nodding)
               That's who it is. It's that
               cheap, no-good brother of yours.

                         PAULA
               But that's crazy. He's in jail.
               Seven years for breaking and
               entering. And that was only a
               year ago. Oh no! No, Chester
               -- it's throwing us a curve.
               Maybe it's somebody who looks
               like Woodward.

                                        CONTINUED

25. CONTINUED   25.

He goes over to the dresser, takes a pack of cigarettes
and lights one, puts the picture down on the dresser.

                          PAULA
                    (in a still, small voice)
          Chester?

                          DIEDRICH
          What?

                          PAULA
          I'm scared!
                    (she clutches her heart)
          I'm palpitating.

                          DIEDRICH
                    (impatiently, but with
                    a bravado he obviously
                    doesn't feel)
          A little palpitating never hurt
          nobody! And what's to be scared
          about? The thing has obviusly gone
          tilt or something. Woodward's not
          here. Woodward can't possibly be
          here. Woodward won't be here.
                    (his voice warms now
                    to the logic of what
                    he's saying)
          Woodward is serving time. He's nine
          hundred miles away in a cell block
          and I don't care what that crazy
          camera shows us - whoever's in that
          picture isn't Woodward!

There's suddenly a sound from the living room outside.

26. FLASH CLOSE SHOT   PAULA   28.

Reacting.

27. FLASH CLOSE SHOT   DIEDRICH   29.

Reacting.

28. PAN SHOT ACROSS THE ROOM   28.

From where they're standing over to the door.

29. EXTREMELY TIGHT CLOSE SHOT   THE DOOR HANDLE   29.

As it moves. Pull back for a -

30. MED CLOSE SHOT   THE DOOR   30.

    as it opens. A big-headed, vapid faced idiot named
    Woodward is standing there with a Cheshire cat grin.
    He waggles his fingers at them.

31   CLOSE SHOT   31

                  PAULA
            (in a quavery whisper)
      Woodward!

32. MED. SHOT   32.

               WOODWARD
      Hello, Paula. Hello, Chester. I
      didn't want to wake you up so I
      just jimmied the door open. I've
      been sleeping on the couch.

    He looks from face to face.

33. TWO SHOT   PAULA AND DIEDRICH   33.

    As they just stare at him open-mouthed.

34. CLOSE SHOT   WOODWARD   34.

               WOODWARD
      I broke out. Me and another guy.
      Hid in the laundry truck.
          (a pause)
      That's nice, huh?
          (another pause)
      I didn't think you'd mind if
      I stayed with you a few days.
          (a pause)
      You don't, do you?
          (still silence at the other
            end. He looks a little
            disconcerted)
      I was thinking maybe if I was
      around you two wouldn't fight so
      much. You still all the time
      fightin'?

    He looks from one to the other, getting no response. His
    eyes slowly look down and see the picture on the dresser.
    He goes over, picks it up, studies it, looks up with a
    broad grin.

               WOODWARD
          (delightedly)
      Well, will you look at that! There
      I am standing right by the door.
      Wearing just what I'm wearing now!
          (then he looks at the
           two of them)

           (MORE)   CONTINUED

34. CONTINUED   34

                         WOODWARD (Cont'd)
              Ain't science wonderful? To be
          able to get a picture of --
                    (his eyes suddenly go
                    wide. He looks down
                    at the picture, then up
                    at them)
              Wait a minute. Wait a minute.
              Wait a minute.
                    (then a pause and his
                    voice comes out shrill)
          Like... How come?

                                              CUT ABRUPTLY
                                              TO BLACK

          END ACT ONE

ACT TWO

FADE ON

35.   INT HOTEL SUITE   LIVING ROOM   DAY   CLOSE SHOT CAMERA   35.

And behind it the three people, Paula, Diedrich and
Woodward. The shot remains on the camera while we
hear the other's voices.

> PAULA'S VOICE
> I still don't know how we can use
> it!

> DIEDRICH'S VOICE
> It's strictly for laughs. Try
> sellin' an item like that. They'd
> throw you out. They'd say you
> were off your rocker - or burn
> you at the stake, one or the other.

> WOODWARD'S VOICE
> (slow and halting,
> suggesting his one
> mile an hour brain)
> We could maybe sell tickets. Take
> pictures. Like at a carny. And
> then...
> (his voice trails off
> indecisively)
> Or maybe we could...or like that...

36.   FULL SHOT   THE ROOM   36.

Diedrich rises, walks across the room over to the window
and looks out. Then he turns toward them.

> DIEDRICH
> (intensely)
> Look I'm gonna lay it on the line
> now. What are we? I asked a
> question - what are we?

> WOODWARD
> What are we, Chet? We're people.

> DIEDRICH
> Sure, but what kind of people?
> We're three minor league heisters!
> Well now we finally got something
> that maybe might do something good
> for somebody else. Science could
> use something like this.

> WOODWARD
> Who?

CONTINUED

36.   CONTINUED   36.

                              DIEDRICH
                    Science. We got something here
                    for humanity.

                              WOODWARD
                    Who?

                              DIEDRICH
                    Humanity. The world. I'm not
                    so sure we shouldn't just give
                    this to humanity and do something
                    good for the first time in our
                    lives.

                              PAULA
                    You got a leak in your attic?
                    What's humanity ever done for us?

                              DIEDRICH
                         (looks at her, nods
                          knowingly and
                          points to her)
                    Sure, Paula, sure. That's what
                    I mean. Just what you said.
                    That's the way we are. Everything
                    for us -- not for anybody else.
                    Little! Petty! Selfish! Mean!
                    That's us.
                         (now his voice rises
                          dramatically, he
                          gestures flamboyantly,
                          he picks up the
                          camera)
                    Well I've risen above that now.
                    I say let's give this to the
                    world. Here, world. A gift from
                    Chester Diedrich and his wife.

                              WOODWARD
                    And me too, Chet. Don't forget
                    Woodward.

                              DIEDRICH
                         (with a sick little
                          look)
                    Yeah and Woodward.
                         (then he strikes
                          the pose again)
                    Here world. A gift for humanity,
                    a gesture that shows the size of
                    the heart of Chester Diedrich and
                    wife.

                                        CONTINUED

36. CONTINUED   36.

Woodward starts to make a motion.

                    DIEDRICH
          And Woodward.

                    WOODWARD
          Ay...that's better.

                    DIEDRICH
          Look isn't there something you
          want to watch on TV?

                    WOODWARD
          Eh?...Oh yeah there is.

He walks over and turns on the television set.

                    DIEDRICH
          Paula we don't know what medical
          science can do with this. There's
          no telling how valuable this
          thing will be as a scientific
          discovery. How do we know how --

He stops suddenly and listens to the television set.

37. OMIT.   37.

37A. SHOT OF WOODWARD AND TV SET   37A.

On the set we can see horses running, and o.s. voice of an
Announcer.

                    ANNOUNCER'S VOICE
          In the Los Tendros opener Hot
          Foot has just won it. Jerry's
          Flash second. Easter Baby third.
          This was Hot Foot's second win
          in three days. He paid twenty
          four ninety, fifteen eighty and
          six seventy. We now move into
          the second race here at Los Tendros.

38. MED CLOSE SHOT DIEDRICH   38.

                    DIEDRICH
          Shut that off.

Woodward shuts off the set. Diedrich turns and faces them,
his eyes wide with discovery and excitement. He looks at the
camera, then at the other two.

                              CONTINUED

38.   CONTINUED   38.

                              DIEDRICH
          I got it! I got it! I got it!!!

                              WOODWARD
          What, Chet?

                              DIEDRICH
                         (pointing to the
                          television set)
          This takes a picture of things
          that happen but haven't happened
          yet. It took a picture of Paula
          with a fur coat. Five minutes
          later she had the fur coat. It
          took a picture of that doorway
          with nobody standing there.
          And then Woodward was standing
          there. All right, boys and girls
          -- now get this! We take a picture
          of the winner's board at the race
          track before the race. The
          winner's board before the race!
          You get it?

                              WOODWARD
                         (a long beat, then
                          very dully)
          No I don't get it.

                              DIEDRICH
          Now do you get it?

                              WOODWARD
          Yeah, now I get it!

                              DIEDRICH
          Come on everybody, get your coats!
          Woodward grab one of mine. And
          put on a tie.

Paula grabs the fur, starts a hurry up primp at the mirror.
Woodward, lumbering, starts to pull his shoes on. Diedrich
flits around excitedly, prodding them.

                              DIEDRICH
          Come on. Come on. That was the
          first race. We can get there in
          time for the last six. How much
          dough we got?

                                        CONTINUED

                              PAULA
             I got a twenty and a ten.

                              DIEDRICH
             That's thirty.

                              PAULA
                    (offended)
             I know it's thirty.

                              DIEDRICH
             I got two tens and three twenties.

                              PAULA
             Come on...

                              DIEDRICH
             Okay and the old insurance my
             hundred dollar bill. That makes
             one eighty and thirty. You got
             anything Woodward?

                              WOODWARD
             Yeh, I got a ten.

                              DIEDRICH
             Two hundred twenty bucks.

                              PAULA
             Is that enough?

                                        CONTINUED

38. CONTINUED   38.

                              DIEDRICH
                 There's bound to be at least one
                 long shot. Why we can parlay
                 this into a million if we work
                 on it long enough. We can't
                 lose, Paula. We simply can't
                 lose. Come on! Everybody ready?

They start toward the door. Woodward stops abruptly,
turns to Diedrich, blocking him.

                              WOODWARD
                 Chet - Chest, what about Humanity?

                              DIEDRICH
                         (spitting it out)
                 Humanity? What did humanity
                 ever do for us! Go ahead!

He pushes Woodward through the door into the hall and the
three go out.

                                              DISSOLVE TO:

39-   39-
42   FILM CLIP   VARIOUS PARTS OF RACT TRACK   42

Ending on a long shot of the winner's board as the numbered
lights go out and it's blank.

                                              CUT TO:

43. MED GROUP SHOT   DIEDRICH, PAULA AND WOODWARD   43.

Standing at a railing. People go by back and forth behind
them and Diedrich is desperately trying to focus the
camera and being jostled by the spectators. Woodward,
close to him, keeps elbowing him like the excited idiot
that he is.

                              WOODWARD
                 Oh boy, Chet. Oh boy, you got us
                 an idea here. Oh boy, Chester.

                              CHESTER
                 My ribs aren't botherin' your
                 elbow, are they? Let loose of me
                 now. Let me get the picture.

He squints down to the camera then looks across at the
board.

                                              CUT TO:

44.   INSERT   THE BOARD   44.

                                        CUT TO:

45.   CLOSE SHOT   DIEDRICH'S HANDS   45.

As he pushes the button on the camera. CAMERA PULLS BACK
for a medium group shot the three of them as they just
stare at one another, almost holding their breaths. Then
the CAMERA BEGINS A SLOW PAN down to the camera again as
suddenly there's a click and the picture comes out. All
grab for it and Diedrich has to push both of them out of
the way as he himself rips out the picture and studies it.
His eyes go wide again.

                    PAULA
          Well?

                    DIEDRICH
          Look at it!

                    WOODWARD
          There's numbers on it now.

                    PAULA
          Six, three and eleven.

                    DIEDRICH
          And look what six pays. Forty-seven
          sixty to win.
                    (he looks down
                    at the racing
                    sheet in his hands)
          Number six. Number six. Number
          six...Tidy Too, that's number six,
          Okay, kids. We bet our money on
          number six.
                    (he holds up the
                    fistful of bills)
          Stay right here!

He turns and starts to fight his way through the crowd
toward the betting window.

46.   MED CLOSE SHOT   THE BETTING WINDOW   46.

As Diedrich arrives, throws the money down.

                    DIEDRICH
          Twenty-six dollars on number six.

The teller takes the money, hands him a ticket, a sport-
coated little tout stands near the window close to
Diedrich's elbow. The tout pulls at his sleeve.

                                        CONTINUED

46. CONTINUED   46.

                         TOUT
              Hey, Jack! A word to the wise, huh?

Diedrich turns to stare at him.

                         TOUT
                   (shakes his head)
              Not number six. That's Tidy Too.
              The last jockey that horse had was
              Paul Revere, but I mean the original
              Paul Revere. Really want to make
              some dough, I got a couple of goodies
              in my pocket here. The last two races
              and all I need is cash. You and me
              could go partners and we could really
              make ourselves a -

At this moment there's the sound of bells ringing, closing
the betting. Diedrich holds up the ticket.

                         DIEDRICH
              Number six. See you later...Jack!

Then he starts toward the railing again as we

                                        CUT TO:

47. FILM CLIP THE RACE STARTING   47.

                                        CUT TO:

48. MED GROUP SHOT DIEDRICH, WOODWARD AND PAULA   48.

At the railing wildly cheering the race as it goes on beyond
them.

                         ANNOUNCER'S VOICE
                   (over the loudspeaker)
              Rounding the far turn it's Tinky
              Beggar, Sir Midas, Pink Gloves, Bart
              Junior, Lady Deck! Coming into the
              stretch - Tidy Too coming up very fast
              on the outside. Now in the stretch
              Tinky Beggar, Sir Midas and Tidy Too
              is third. Tidy Too coming up very
              fast. Tinky Beggar and Tidy Too
              neck and neck. It's Tidy Too! It's
              Tidy Too all the way!

                                        CUT TO:

49. FILM CLIP CROWD SCREAMING AND APPLAUDING   49.

                                        CUT TO:

50. MED GROUP SHOT DIEDRICH, PAULA AND WOODWARD   50.

As they jump around hugging one another. There's a sudden
lull. They stop and turn toward the board.

                                          CUT TO:

51. LONG SHOT BOARD   51.

As the numbers appear on it. Six, three and eleven.

52. GROUP SHOT   52.

They all begin screaming again as Woodward takes the snapshot,
crumples it up and throws it up in the air. Then the three
of them head toward the window. CAMERA PANS DOWN to the
bent, torn photograph as people walk on it and finally kick
it off into the dust where it lies unnoticed.

                                          CUT TO:

53.   53.
to   to
56. MONTAGE   56.

First the board then the camera in Diedrich's hands taking
a picture of it. Then Diedrich's hands removing the
snapshot. Then Diedrich placing the bet. Then the horses
starting. The board lighting up. Then Diedrich collecting
money at the teller's cage. THis happens several times
as we

                                          DISSOLVE TO:

67. INT HOTEL SUITE LIVING ROOM NIGHT   67.

The CAMERA STARTS A SLOW PAN across the room taking in the
following items. First, several racing forms lying around
in profusion. Then several bottles of liquor in various
postures from standing to leaning to lying empty. Several
gift boxes open and disheveled, wrapping paper and ribbon
lying around in profusion. And then money! Money
everywhere. Money on the dresser. Money in chairs. Money
on the coffee table and in a suitcase lying open on the bed,
the bulk of the money stacked up and overflowing! The
CAMERA CONTINUES ITS PAN past the three people in the room.
Woodward, in a flaming, brilliant new sport coat that
shrieks discordantly at you, lies with his shoes off on
the couch eating a chicken bone that's come out of a silver
tureen. Across the room Paula tries on new hats, furs, et
al. The CAMERA CONTINUES on into the bedroom where
Diedrich is on the telephone.

68. MED CLOSE SHOT DIEDRICH   68.

                         DIEDRICH
                      (on the phone)
               Yeah, but when can I get
               delivery on something like that?
               No, no, no, no. I don't want a
               black one. It's gotta be yellow
               with black upholstery. Spoked
               wheels, continental kit on the
               back, dual exhausts, and everything
               powered. You get that? Now when
               can I get delivery? All right,
               then order it. That's right.
               No, no, no. I'll pay you in
               cash. You come over tomorrow
               morning with the papers and
               we'll settle it then. Now
               how much did you say that was?
               Eleven grand?
                      (there's a pause,
                       then hurriedly)
               No, no, no, no, no. I'm not
               backin' out. I was just
               thinkin'. Maybe I ought to
               get two. Well, you bring the
               papers over tomorrow morning.
               Fine. So long.

He puts the receiver down, studies the phone happily for
a moment. There's the sound of a knock on the door.

                         PAULA
               It's the waiter.
                      (as she crosses
                       to the door)
               Are you done with your snack,
               Woodward?

69. MED CLOSE SHOT WOODWARD   69.

As he puts the chicken bone aside and we can see the
remnants of a gigantic meal finished in front of him.

                         WOODWARD
               I guess that'll hold me till dinner.

70. FULL SHOT THE ROOM   70.

Paula opens the door. A middle aged French waiter enters
the room.

                         WAITER
               I came for the dishes, madam.

                                        CONTINUED

                         PAULA
               Right over there on the coffee
               table. Can you bring us a couple
               of bottles of champagne on your
               way back?

                         WAITER
                    (collecting the
                     dishes)
               Yes, ma'am, I can.

He covers up all the dishes with a table cloth, then spies
a couple of glasses on one of the book cases, goes over to
remove them and in doing so sees the camera near them. He
picks it up and looks at it for a moment.

                         WOODWARD
               Hey. Get your hands off that!

                         DIEDRICH
                    (coming in from
                     the bedroom)
               Let him look at it! Bet you never
               seen anything like that, Pierre, huh!

                         WAITER
               Mais non. Most unusual, sir.

                         PAULA
               Isn't it though! You don't know
               how unusual.

Then he takes the glasses, carries them over to the tray,
looks up.

                         WAITER
               But what do you do after your
               ten pictures? Is there any other
               way to get more film?

                         DIEDRICH
               Well, we've only had it for a
               little while and we -
                    (he stops, double
                     takes)
               What did you say?

                         PAULA
               Yeah, what did you say about
               ten pictures?

                         WAITER
               The inscription on the outside. It
               says deux a la proprietare. That
               means ten to an owner. I presume
               that means you may only take ten -

                                             CUT TO:

71.- SERIES OF FLASH SHOTS OF WOODWARD, DIEDRICH AND PAULA   71.-
73.   73.

74. MED LONG SHOT THE WAITER   74.

As he carries the tray across the room, talking as he does.

> WAITER
> It's so odd. The lettering is
> definitely French but I've never
> seen a French camera like that.
> As a matter of fact -

Woodward has propelled him out the door now and shut it
on him cutting off the sentence.

> DIEDRICH
> (turning to the others)
> All right, how many pictures have
> we taken? There was one of Paula!

> PAULA
> Then one of Woodward.

> WOODWARD
> How many pictures we take at the track?

> DIEDRICH
> (hurriedly recollecting)
> Six. We bet six races. That means
> we've taken -

> PAULA
> Eight. We've taken eight pictures.
> Chester, there's only two left.

> DIEDRICH
> (grabs the camera,
> studies the inscription,
> then he looks up)
> Ten. But how do we know what that
> means? Some frog waiter tells us
> it says ten so right away we think
> we only got two pictures left. How
> does he know what it means? I bet
> you we could take as many pictures
> as we want -

> PAULA
> (grabs the camera
> from him)
> But we don't know! Chester, we can't
> take any chances.

CONTINUED

74. CONTINUED   74.

                         WOODWARD
                    (lumbering over to
                     their side)
          No we can't.
                    (he grabs the
                     camera from her)
          You know what we should do.
          We should sell it!

                         DIEDRICH
                    (grabs it away from
                     him disgustedly)
          Who rattled your cage, ape!
          This don't even belong to you!
          You're strictly for charity,
          buddy! Now what we should do
          with it is to go to the track
          and bet two more races with it!

                         PAULA
                    (grabs the camera
                     from him)
          Are you both crazy? What you
          do with it is hang onto it!
          Save it for a rainy day!

                         PAULA
                    (grabbing the camera
                     protectively off the
                     floor)
          You stop it! You're going to
          break the camera!

                         DIEDRICH
          It took a picture! Now you made
          me waste a picture!

Now the three of them start to jabber at once. Woodward
screaming to sell it, Diedrich screaming to use it, Paula
shouting over both of them to hang onto it. In the middle
of the mad melee the camera is struck hard; lens pointing
to Paula. We hear a loud click.

                                        CUT TO:

75. CLOSE SHOT   THE FLOOR   75.

As the camera falls, its lens pointing toward Paula. We
hear a loud click as it takes a picture.

                                        CONTINUED

75.   CONTINUED   75.

                              PAULA
                    (then half closing
                    her eyes and
                    clutching her chest)
               Palpitations!

She slumps into a chair as Diedrich angrily goes to pour
himself a drink.

                              DIEDRICH
               You and your palpitations. Phony
               palpitations and a stupid brother.

                              WOODWARD
               Hey look, I don't have to take
               that guff from you.

                              DIEDRICH
               All right, all right. Have a
               drink.

76. TRACK SHOT WITH HER   76.

As with one hand on her heart and the other clutching the
camera, she walks over to the dresser. Just as she lays
it down -

                                                    CUT TO:

77. CLOSE SHOT   CAMERA   77.

A picture snaps out.

78. MED SHOT   PAULA   78.

Paula, more concerned with her heart than anything else
now, almost automatically reaches to rip the picture off
and looks at it in a sort of detached way.

79. CLOSE SHOT   PAULA   7   79.

Her mouth goes open as she stares at it.

                                                    CUT TO:

80. TIGHT CLOSE SHOT   THE PHOTOGRAPH   80.

It's an angle shot looking up toward Paula and it shows her
face contorted, mouth wide open, screaming.

81. MOVING SHOT   AS THE PHOTO CHANGES HANDS   81.

First to Diedrich then over to Woodward.   PULL BACK.

                         DIEDRICH
                  (in a very still voice)
            She's screaming!
                  (he looks down at the
                  picture again and then
                  up at Woodward)
            Why is she screaming in the picture,
            Woodward? I'll tell you why she's
            screaming. She's screaming because
            somebody's doing something to her
            husband. Some stupid ex-con with
            an idiotic idea about selling the
            camera and who doesn't care how
            he gets it either.

He slowly reaches into his pocket, pulls out a switch
knife and switches open the blade.

                                             CONTINUED

81.   CONTINUED   81.

                              WOODWARD
                    You better put that knife away,
                    Chester. If she's screaming
                    in the picture it's on account
                    of what some guy must be
                    doing to her loving brother.
                              (he takes a
                              step toward
                              him)
                    You better put that knife away.
                              (he holds up
                              both his big
                              hands)
                    You put it away or I'm
                    gonna take your skin
                    off.

He lunges at Diedrich who takes a swipe at him with
the knife and misses, throwing himself off balance
and falling across the room toward the window.
Woodward, holding tightly to him is carried across
with him.

                                        CUT TO:

82.   TIGHT CLOSE SHOT PAULA   82.

As she screams in exactly the same manner as the
photograph showed. There's a crashing, splinter
of broken glass and then dead silence. Paula's
hands slowly leave her face as she stares toward
the window.

                                        CUT TO:

83.   CLOSE SHOT THE WINDOW   83.

Broken glass littering the whole area and the two
men disappear.

84.   MED SHOT ROOM   84.

Paula closes her eyes and then like Lillian Gish in a
half-swoon, stumbles backwards into the room to
sit on the bed alongside of the suitcase with the
money in it.

                                        CONTINUED

84. CONTINUED   84.

                              PAULA
                    Oh, Chester! Chester, my poor
                    darling husband. And Woodward.
                    Woodward my brother, my flesh.
                    My own flesh¦
                         (she turns toward
                         the camera, clutching
                         her heart)
                    I'll die. I will simply just
                    die. There's nothing left for
                    me.

85. CLOSE SHOT HER HAND   85.

     As it brushes the money in the suitcase. PAN SHOT BACK UP
     TO HER FACE as one eye opens and she looks down at the
     suitcase.

86. CLOSE SHOT THE PILE OF MONEY IN THE SUITCASE   86.

     Paula's p.o.v.

87. CLOSE SHOT PAULA'S EYES   87.

     As they once again move across the room.

88. CLOSE SHOT THE FLOOR   88.

     Another stack of bills can be seen.

89. CLOSE SHOT PAULA

     Reacting.

90. CLOSE SHOT DRESSER   90.

     There's a pile of money there too.

91. CLOSE SHOT PAULA   91.

     As her eyes are wide open now. One hand reaches out to
     touch some of the money in the suitcase. She holds it
     out in front of her, staring at it.

                              PAULA
                         (softly)
                    However - we have to muddle through
                    these things. We have to live with
                    tragedy.
                              (MORE)

                                   CONTINUED

91.   CONTINUED   91.

                          PAULA (CONT'D)
                    (she looks out toward
                     the window)
                Poor Chester.
                    (then clucking)
                And poor Woodward. My heart is
                simply...simply too full to say
                any more! May you both rest in
                peace.
          She suddenly looks down at the camera, grins at it, turns,
          points it out of the open window, takes a picture.

                            PAULA

                    (with great reverence)
                For posterity, boys. Simply for
                posterity!

          Then laughing, tripping, humming jazzily, she jitterbugs
          across the room.

92.   TRACK SHOT WITH HER   92.

          As she puts the camera down on a table near the door then
          hurriedly begins to collect clumps of money and singing
          throatily she goes back and forth across the room tossing
          the money into the suitcase with great abandon and sheer
          animal delight. She then moves across to where the money
          is cascading out of the suitcase, starts to shut it. There's
          the sound of a door click and she suddenly straightens up.

93.   WHIP PAN OVER TO THE DOOR WHERE THE WAITER STANDS   93.

          He's holding a large laundry bag.

                           WAITER
                Pardon-moi, but I understand there
                is something in the way of laundry
                that I should take.

94.   DIFFERENT ANGLE THE ROOM   94.

          As he moves into it.

                           PAULA
                    (watching him with
                     a rising fear)
                You got the wrong room, jack. There's
                no laundry up here. I'm checking out.

95.   DIFFERENT ANGLE THE WAITER   95.

As he goes over and looks out the window.

                         WAITER
             And your two friends - they checked
             out already!
                    (he leans out of the
                     window looking down)
             Such a pity. Lying there in the
             courtyard. So young. One moment -
             full of life..vim, vigor..and the
             next moment -
                    (he snaps his fingers
                     as he turns to her)
             Ppppft!

He walks back to her, looks down at the suitcase, then takes
it out of her hand, opens it and starts to dump the money
from it into the laundry bag. She grabs his arm.

                         PAULA
             What do you think you're doing?

                         WAITER
                    (points to money)
             Doing? But madam...I told you, I
             was here for the laundry. I'm...
             how do you say..cleaning you out!

He gently but firmly removes her arm.

                         PAULA
             You're cleaning me out? And while
             you're cleaning me out, jack, what
             do you think I'll be doing? Well,
             I'll cue you, buddy.
                    (she turns and heads
                     toward the phone)
             I'm gonna be calling the cops.

                         WAITER
                    (laughs)
             The cops? You mean the police?
             Madam, you'll forgive me - but if
             you call the police..madam will get
             herself into - how do you say - one
             fantastic bind?
                    (points to money)
             This is - how you say - up for grabs.
             Dear lady, I know all about you now.
             I did some checking. Your husband, your
             brother and you...you're wanted.
                    (he shakes his head)
                       (MORE)

                                          CONTINUED

95.   CONTINUED   95.

                         WAITER (CONT'D)
                    And as for police - I would advise
                    you to get out while you can. When
                    they see what's in the courtyard down
                    there - they shall be up here sans
                    invitation. Translation - without
                    invitation. Uninvited. You ..how
                    you say....dig?

96.   TWO SHOT   96.

      As the waiter half bows, lifts up the bag.

                         WAITER
                    Now as to the laundry - this may be
                    back on Thursday.
                              (he makes a little
                              Gallic shrug)
                    Or maybe Friday....
                              (another shrug)
                    Or maybe never...

      He heads toward the door, pauses by the table near it,
      suddenly looks at the camera thoughtfully.

                         WAITER
                    But I am not a hog. This I will
                    leave with you!

      He cocks his head looking at it closer, then suddenly picks
      it up in his hands and stares at the picture that protrudes
      from it. He looks up surprised.

                         WAITER
                    Sacre nom! This is a picture of the
                    courtyard down below. And there are
                    more than two bodies.

      THE CAMERA ZOOMS IN FOR AN EXTREMELY TIGHT CLOSE SHOT
      OF HER FACE as her eyes bug.

                         PAULA
                    More than two bodies - !

98.   DIFFERENT ANGLE AS SHE TURNS   98.

      Races toward the window.

99.   CLOSE SHOT HER FOOT   99.

      As she trips.

100.   FULL SHOT   THE WINDOW   100.

As, screaming, she's propelled forward, unable to stop
herself, and goes headfirst out of the window. We hear
her scream very briefly on the way down then all is silent.

101.   OMIT   101.

101A. MED SHOT   THE WAITER   101A.

Still holding the picture. He shakes his head in a spasm
of compassion, walks over to the window and looks down.

                        WAITER
            Yes there are more than two bodies..

He turns, looks at the picture.

                        WAITER
            Just like the picture shows.
                 (counting)
            One...two..three....FOUR?

His eyes bug out as we CUT TO:

102.   FLOOR   102.

As the camera drops from nerveless fingers.

                     SERLING'S VOICE
            Object known as a camera. Vintage -
            uncertain; origin - unknown. But for
            the greedy...the avaricious..the fleet
            of foot who can run a four minute mile
            so long as they're chasing a fast buck--

THE CAMERA STARTS A PAN over past the window again, this
time there's no one in evidence in front of it, and then
up into the sky.

                     SERLING'S VOICE
            It makes believe that it's an ally,
            but it isn't at all. It's a
            beckoning, come-on for a quick walk-
            around-the-block...in The Twilight
            Zone.

                                        FADE TO BLACK:

                        THE END

The Twilight Zone

A MOST UNUSUAL CAMERA

Airdate: 12-16-1960

Manuscript Date: 4-23-1959

First Draft

Script Six

Episode Forty-Six

THE TWILIGHT ZONE

Script Six

"A MOST UNUSUAL CAMERA"

By

ROD SERLING

April 23, 1959

FADE IN:

1. EXT. SKY   NIGHT   1.

    Shot of the sky...the various nebulae, and planet bodies
    stand out in sharp, sparkling relief. As the CAMERA
    begins a SLOW PAN across the heavens -

                    NARRATOR'S VOICE (o.s.)
              There is a sixth dimension beyond
              that which is known to man. It
              is a dimension as vast as space,
              and as timeless as infinity. It
              is the middle ground between
              light and shadow - between man's
              grasp and his reach; between
              science and superstition; between
              the pit of his fears and the
              sunlight of his knowledge. This
              is the dimension of imagination.
              It is the area that might be
              called the Twilight Zone.

    The CAMERA has begun to PAN DOWN until it passes the
    horizon and is flush on the OPENING SHOT (EACH WEEK
    THE OPENING SHOT OF THE PLAY)

2. EXT. A SMALL CURIO SHOP   DAY   2.

    A handful of people cluster around the front door rubber
    necking as a police car pulls up in front. The policeman
    bulls his way through the crowd to go inside.

3. MED. LONG SHOT   THROUGH WINDOW OF SHOP   3.

    We see a flash bulb go off inside. A detective listens,
    bored and businesslike, to a somewhat harrassed looking
    store keeper who points out various items; a broken lock,
    a ransacked shelf, a broken display case glass. Over
    this pantomime is the Narrator's Voice.

                    NARRATOR'S VOICE
              Street scene - vintage 1959.
              Really a rather minor event to
              be noted on a police blotter, an
              insurance claim, perhaps a three
              inch box on page twelve of the
              evening newspaper.

    A pause. The CAMERA PANS in closer to the window past
    the rubble of broken glass, various bits of merchandise
    pushed aside by the thief, and finally winds up on an
    empty square in the window.

                                        CONTINUED

3.   CONTINUED   3.

                          NARRATOR'S VOICE (CONT'D)
              In this small square eight inches
              wide, thirteen inches long...was
              a camera! Minor item, hardly
              worth mentioning because cameras
              are cameras. Or so it is usually
              thought.
                    (a pause)
              But minor items have a way of
              injecting themselves into the
              destinies of men. This one does...
              or will, for this is a most
              unusual camera!

                                             DISSOLVE TO:

4.   INT. CURIO SHOP   4.

     The little balding owner is reading off an inventory
     to a laconic looking detective.

5.   MED. CLOSE SHOT   OWNER   5.

                          OWNER
              Two teak wood hand carved
              cigarette cases with platforms.

                          DETECTIVE
              Approximate value?

                          OWNER
              Fifty dollars.

                          WIFE
                    (almost over-lapping)
              Eighty five dollars.

                          OWNER
                    (pointing to broken
                     display case)
              A tray of rings. Three
              sapphires. Three rubies.
              Three emeralds.

                          DETECTIVE
              All genuine?

                          WIFE
              All genuine.

     She throws a warning look toward her husband.

                                             CONTINUED

5.　CONTINUED　　　　　　　　　　　　　　　　　　　　　　　5.

                    DETECTIVE
               (looks down at his
                list)
          I guess that does it, huh?
          Six vases. Five ceramics.
          Jewelry.
               (he looks up)
          Anything else? What about the
          stuff out of the window?

                    OWNER
               (walking over there)
          Oh, yes. Camera.

                    DETECTIVE
               (looking up)
          A camera?

                    WIFE
               (hurriedly)
          A very special kind of camera.
          Very unique.

                    DETECTIVE
               (jotting this down)
          Make?

                    OWNER
          Well, it didn't really have a
          make on it. At least we never
          could make it out. Had some
          sort of foreign lettering on it.
          But it was a very unusual looking
          camera. Never saw one like it
          before. It was here when we
          bought the shop -

                    WIFE
          But it was imported! Very
          rare camera. Must have been
          three hundred years old if it
          was a day.

                    DETECTIVE
               (sarcastically)
          What did it have - a beard?
               (then he turns to
                the owner)
          Anything else?

                              CONTINUED

5.   CONTINUED   5.

                         OWNER
              Let's see - some more vases, five
              or six of them -

                         WIFE
              Ming Dynasty.

                         OWNER
              Two antique children's chairs.
              A Louis the Fourteenth wash
              stand. Queen Anne chest -

                         DETECTIVE
              Containing what?

                         OWNER
              We don't know. We never could
              open it. Three oil paintings.

                         WIFE
              Originals.
                   (modestly)
              Early Picassos.

                         OWNER
                   (continuing to talk as
                    his voice fades off)
              A dining room chair, 1778 -

                                        WE LAP DISSOLVE TO:

6.   INT. HOTEL SUITE   TWO SHOT   CHESTER DIEDRICH AND   6.
     HIS WIFE PAULA

     They're in their thirties. A couple of well-groomed,
     attractive young people. In the hotel suite is a vast
     collection of antiques. Diedrich is reading off the
     list as his wife jots them down.

                         DIEDRICH
              Tray of rings. All paste.
                   (he walks through the
                    collection)
              Six vases, imitation Ming
              Dynasty. A phony Louis the
              Fourteenth wash stand. Two
              make-believe teak wood cigarette
              cases.

     Now he picks up the camera. It's a normal looking, rather
     old fashioned box-type with the lens and aperture, a slot
     in the back and that's it. Diedrich moves it around in
     his hands to examine it.

                                        CONTINUED

6.   CONTINUED   6.

                          DIEDRICH
           This camera.

                          PAULA
                     (looking up from the
                      notes)
           That looks antique.

                          DIEDRICH
                     (looking it over and
                      very disparagingly)
           Big deal. Twenty years ago you
           could have bought this in the
           drugstore for thirty nine cents.
           But I got to get it as part of
           a heist.
                     (he holds it up)
           Look at this crummy thing. No
           place to insert film. No place
           to open it up. Just some crazy
           foreign lettering on it.
                     (he looks through a
                      sighting device)
           This must be the button here.
           Hold it, baby. Say cheese.
                     (he pushes the button,
                      pointing the camera at
                      his wife, then he tosses
                      the camera on the bed,
                      surveys the mess that
                      litters the room)
           Big deal! The whole haul is
           probably worth five dollars and
           eighty cents. A good fence'll
           give us a buck for it. You and
           your curio shops!

                          PAULA
           Don't you yell at me.
                     (and then looking
                      pained and clutching
                      her heart)
           You know my heart.

                          DIEDRICH
           Oh, will you knock it off with
           your heart?

                          PAULA
           I'm a sick woman and you know
           it. And as to my curio shops,
           who cased the place? Who fingered
           it? Who did all the planning?

                                        CONTINUED

6.   CONTINUED   6.

                              DIEDRICH
                        (sits on the bed, lights
                         a cigarette)
                Oh, listen to the brain! The
                patron of the arts over there.
                Never mind hock shops. No.
                Let's go up in life. Let's
                knock off a curio shop because
                curio shops have nothing but
                objects of art worth a fortune.
                And who touted me? The art lover
                over there. Two weeks of planning.
                A whole night on the job. And
                what have we got, Paula?
                        (he makes a motion
                         with his hand surveying
                         the room)
                Four hundred pounds of junk.
                I could have shot pool for a
                whole day and made more. Look,
                baby, the next hot idea you
                get about a heist -

        He's suddenly interrupted by a clicking sound from the
        camera alongside of him on the bed. A large snapshot
        has just been ejected through the slot.

7.   CLOSE SHOT   DIEDRICH   7.

        Reacting.

8.   CLOSE SHOT   PAULA   8.

        Similar surprise showing.

9.   MED. CLOSE SHOT   DIEDRICH   9.

        As he picks up the camera, examines it and tears off the
        picture. He studies it carefully then looks up in vast,
        speechless surprise.

10.   TWO SHOT   10.

                              PAULA
                Well? How do I look?

                                            CONTINUED

10. CONTINUED   10.

Diedrich just stares at her and looks back down at the
picture, then looks up at her again. He gulps, shakes his
head.

11. TRACK SHOT PAULA   11.

as she goes over to take the picture out of his hand.

12. CLOSE SHOT PAULA   12.

as she smiles broadly.

                    PAULA
          Isn't that nice! And so clear,
          Chet. Can you imagine that? No
          lights or anything and look how
          clear it is.

13. TWO SHOT   13.

He rises off the bed and in a single motion swipes the
picture out of her hand. He stares at her then at the
picture then at her again.

                    PAULA
          What's the matter with you?

                    DIEDRICH
          What's the matter with me? Paula,
          go over to the mirror.

                    PAULA
          What?

                    DIEDRICH
          Go ahead. Look at yourself in the
          mirror.

They look at one another.

                    PAULA
          You missin' a coupla buttons?

Diedrich grabs her and propels her across the room toward
the dresser mirror.

                    DIEDRICH
          Go ahead. Look.

14. MED. SHOT REFLECTION IN THE MIRROR   14.

                    PAULA
          So? What's to see?

                              CONTINUED

14. CONTINUED   14.

                         DIEDRICH
                  (slams the picture down
                   on the dresser)
              Now look at the picture.

She holds up the picture and studies it and shrugs.

                          PAULA
              So? There I am standing by the
              window wearing a...
                  (now her voice suddenly
                   becomes very tight and
                   startled)
              A fur coat!

She drops the picture like it was burning to the touch and
lets out a little scream, backing away from the dresser.

15. MED. CLOSE SHOT PAULA   15.

                          PAULA
              Chester, what am I doing wearing a
              fur coat? I wasn't wearing a fur
              coat when you took the picture. I
              don't even own a fur coat.

16. LONG SHOT ACROSS THE ROOM   16.

Diedrich looks down at the snapshot shaking his head from
side to side. He looks up, first at her reflection in the
mirror, then at her, then slowly his face relaxes.

                         DIEDRICH
              I got it. I got it!
                  (he points to the
                   camera on the bed)
              A gag camera. Strictly a gag
              camera. For laughs.

                          PAULA
              What do you mean?

                         DIEDRICH
                  (goes over to the camera,
                   picks it up)
              See? Inside they've got these ready-
              made pictures already developed. But
              the negatives already got a picture on
              them. The only thing this thing takes
              is the face. You know - like in a
              carnival when you pose in front of
              those crazy cardboard things. Fat
              lady - driving a car - sailor - you
              know! And that's what this thing is.
                          (MORE)

                          CONTINUED

16. CONTINUED   16.

                          DIEDRICH (CONT'D)
                     (he looks at the camera
                      with admiration)
                Now that's not bad! That's kind
                of clever!
                     (he puts the camera on
                      the bed, rubs his hands,
                      looks around the room
                      again)
                Well, we might as well clear up
                the rest of this junk.

17. TRACK SHOT WITH HIM   17.

     As he walks over to a small chest. He kneels down in
     front of it, tries the latch and can't open it.

                          DIEDRICH
                Did a key come with this?

     Paula, who has gone back to the dresser and is studying
     the picture, looks up.

                          PAULA
                No. You'll have to open it in
                your own inimitable style.

     He looks up at her, one hand still fiddling with the lock.

                          DIEDRICH
                Anybody ever tell you you had a
                nasty little tongue?

                          PAULA
                     (bridling)
                If I have a nasty little tongue,
                it's because I'm married to a nickel
                and dime heister who can't tell a
                real diamond from a baseball!

                          DIEDRICH
                Baby doll - this suite is twenty-
                eight bucks a day, delivered and
                paid for by Mrs. Diedrich's son
                Chester from profits collected
                during a potful of years when you
                weren't even in the picture! It
                so happens that I need you like I
                need a three-time conviction --

18. CLOSE SHOT LOCK   18.

     As it suddenly springs under his hand and the top clicks
     open on the chest.

19. ANGLE SHOT LOOKING UP AT HIS FACE   19.

From below the box. His eyes go wide. Her face appears
alongside of his. Her eyes go wide too but more with
delight than fright. She reaches in as we

CUT TO:

20. TWO SHOT THE TWO OF THEM   20.

Paula has picked up a gorgeous fur coat and in one shrug
has it on, goes immediately over to the mirror, oohing and
aahing as she walks over to the mirror to look at herself,
and then in the manner of a model, she walks back and forth,
then strikes up a pose near the window.

                    PAULA
          How do you like this? And don't
          start giving me any cheap crud about
          taking this to a fence. This is for
          little old Paula. And don't try to
          argue with me either.
                    (she suddenly stops
                    abruptly, staring at
                    his face, frightened)
          Now what's the matter?
                    (she sits down, clutching
                    her heart again)
          If you're deliberately trying to
          frighten me into a heart attack --

Diedrich rises slowly and like a man in a dream, walks
over to the dresser. He picks up the picture. Paula
slowly rises and lets the coat drop off her. She goes
over to the dresser and the two of them look down at the
picture in his hand.

CUT TO:

21. EXTREMELY TIGHT CLOSE UP SNAPSHOT   21.

There it is in all its detail. Paula in the fur coat posed
by the window in exactly the same pose as we've just seen
her. And then as if by direction, both of them turn to
stare toward the camera on the bed.

22. PAN SHOT ACROSS THE ROOM   22.

Winding up on a tight close up of the camera as it sits
there, just an uninteresting looking black object but
somehow menacing beyond words.

DISSOLVE TO:

23. INT. HOTEL SUITE BEDROOM NIGHT MED. CLOSE SHOT   23.

Looking toward the window as a neon light from outside
flashes on and off and there's the distant sound of night
traffic. Intruding upon this is the sound of metal clicks
and drumming fingers.

24. FULL SHOT THE ROOM   24.

Paula is asleep in bed. Sitting on the chaise lounge across
the room is a sleepless Diedrich, in his bathrobe, fiddling
with the camera.

25. MED. CLOSE SHOT PAULA   25.

as she awakens, looks across the room.

                    PAULA
          What are you doing? Come back to
          bed.
                    (and now, fully awake,
                     she props herself up on
                     her elbow and stares
                     across at him, tiredly)
          Still with that?

26. TWO SHOT   26.

Diedrich turns to look at her. He holds up the camera,
bounces it around a couple of times, wanting to say
something, then he puts it down, resignedly shakes his head,
totally nonplused.

                    PAULA
          So what do you care?

                    DIEDRICH
                    (trying to interrupt)
          You want me to let it go by, huh?

                    PAULA
                    (over-lapping him)
          What do you care? So it's a crazy
          camera. So it takes dopey pictures
          that really aren't there -

                    DIEDRICH
                    (outshouting her)
          Sure it takes crazy pictures. Crazy
          pictures like things that haven't
          happened yet but do happen.

Paula gets out of bed, throws on a wrapper, angry now with
the anger of the frustrated sleeper.

                    PAULA
          So what's to do, Chet? One lousy,
          freak picture and you get insomnia.
          Drop it, why don't you? Let it
          alone. Forget about it.

                    DIEDRICH
          How can I forget about it? This
          thing comes from...from witches
          maybe. Or sorcerers. This thing
          may be loaded with black magic.

27. TRACK SHOT WITH HER   27.

as she strides across the room and grabs the camera out of
his hand.

                    PAULA
          And what are you loaded with?
          It's a camera. That's all. Look.
          I'll show you.
                    (she just, without
                     direction, aims the
                     camera to the other
                     side of the room and
                     pushes the button)
          There! See? Any lightning?
          Where's the man with the horns
          who comes in with the bargain
          for the soul? It's a freak
          camera, that's all!

She turns to look at him again and Diedrich is staring at
the camera in her hand. Paula herself now looks down at
it, suddenly ill at ease. There's a clicking sound as
once again a picture shoots out from it. Paula lets out
a scream. The camera drops from her hand and lands on
the floor, the picture protruding. Diedrich, trance-like,
walks over, takes the snapshot out and studies it, wets
his lips and looks up at her.

                    PAULA
               (her voice tremulous)
          Well?

He hands her the picture and she studies it, her eyes wide.
She looks across at Diedrich.

                    PAULA
               (in a half whisper)
          It's my brotherWoodward!
          Standing by the door!

                    DIEDRICH
               (takes the picture out
                of her hand, nodding)
          That's who it is. It's that cheap,
          no-good brother of yours.

                    PAULA
          But that's crazy. He's in jail.
          Seven years for breaking and entering.
          And that was only a year ago. Oh no!
          No, Chester - it's throwing us a curve.
          Maybe it's somebody who looks like
          Woodward.

                    DIEDRICH
          Nobody could look like Woodward.

He goes over to the dresser, takes a pack of cigarettes
and lights one, puts the picture down on the dresser.

                                        CONTINUED

27. CONTINUED   27.

                         PAULA
                    (in a still, small voice)
          Chester?

                         DIEDRICH
          What?

                         PAULA
          I'm scared.
                    (then clutching her heart)
          I can tell you right now I'm close
          to death. You should feel my heart.
          Oh, Chester, I'm so scared.

                         DIEDRICH
          Will you stop with that idiotic heart
          of yours? What's to be scared about?
          The thing has obviously gone tilt or
          something. Woodward's not here.
          Woodward can't possibly be here.
          Woodward won't be here.
                    (his voice warms now to the
                     logic of what he's saying)
          Woodward is serving time. He's nine
          hundred miles away in a cell block
          and I don't care what that crazy
          camera shows us -- whoever's in
          that picture isn't Woodward!

     There's suddenly a sound from the living room outside.

28. FLASH CLOSE SHOT PAULA   28.

     Reacting.

29. FLASH CLOSE SHOT DIEDRICH   29.

     Reacting.

30. PAN SHOT ACROSS THE ROOM   30.

     From where they're standing over to the door.

31. EXTREMELY TIGHT CLOSE SHOT THE DOOR HANDLE   31.

     As it moves. Pull back for a

32. MED. CLOSE SHOT THE DOOR   32.

     as it opens. A big-headed, vapid faced idiot named Woodward
     is standing there with a Cheshire cat grin. He waggles his
     fingers at them.

33. CLOSE SHOT   33.

                         PAULA
                    (in a quavery whisper)
          Woodward!

34. MED. SHOT   34.

                         WOODWARD
               Hello, Paula. Hello, Chester. I
               didn't want to wake you up so I
               just jimmied the door open. I've
               been sleeping on the couch.

He looks from face to face.

35. TWO SHOT PAULA AND DIEDRICH   35.

As they just stare at him open-mouthed.

36. CLOSE SHOT WOODWARD   36.

                         WOODWARD
               I broke out. Me and another guy.
               Hid in the laundry truck.
                    (a pause)
               That's nice, huh?
                    (another pause)
               I didn't think you'd mind if I
               stayed with you a few days.
                    (a pause)
               You don't, do you?
                    (still silence at the other
                     end. He looks a little
                     disconcerted)
               I was thinking maybe if I was around
               you two wouldn't fight so much. You
               still all the time fightin'?

He looks from one to the other, getting no response. His
eyes slowly look down and see the picture on the dresser.
He goes over, picks it up, studies it, looks up with a
broad grin.

                         WOODWARD
                    (delightedly)
               Well, will you look at that! There
               I am standing right by the door.
               Wearing just what I'm wearing now!
                    (then he looks at the
                     two of them)
               Ain't science wonderful? To be
               able to get a picture of --
                    (his eyes suddenly go
                     wide. He looks down
                     at the picture, then up
                     at them)
               Wait a minute. Wait a minute.
               Wait a minute.
                    (then a pause and his
                     voice comes out shrill)
               How come?

                              CUT ABRUPTLY TO BLACK

END ACT ONE

ACT TWO

FADE ON

37.   INT HOTEL SUITE LIVING ROOM DAY CLOSE SHOT CAMERA   37.

And behind it the three people, Paula, Diedrich and
Woodward. The shot remains on the camera while we hear
the other's voices.

                    PAULA'S VOICE
          I still don't know how we can use
          it!

                    DIEDRICH'S VOICE
          It's strictly for laughs. Try
          sellin' an item like that. They'd
          throw you out. They'd say you
          were off your rocker - or burn
          you at the stake, one or the other.

                    WOODWARD'S VOICE
                 (slow and halting,
                  suggesting his one
                  mile an hour brain)
          We could maybe sell tickets. Take
          pictures. Like at a carny. And
          then...
                 (his voice trails off
                  indecisively)
          Or maybe we could...or like that...

38.   FULL SHOT THE ROOM   38.

Diedrich rises, walks across the room over to the window
and looks out. Then he turns toward them.

                    DIEDRICH
                 (intensely)
          Look I'm gonna lay it on the line
          now. What are we? I asked a
          question - what are we?

                    WOODWARD
          What are we, Chet? We're people.

                    DIEDRICH
          Sure, but what kind of people?
          We're three nickel and dime crooks.
          Well now we finally got something
          that maybe might do something good
          for somebody else. Science could
          use something like this.

                                        CONTINUED

38. CONTINUED   38.

                         WOODWARD
          Who?

                         DIEDRICH
          Science. We got something here
          for humanity.

                         WOODWARD
          Who?

                         DIEDRICH
          Humanity. The world. I'm not so
          sure we shouldn't just give this to
          humanity and do something good for
          the first time in our lives.

                         PAULA
          You got a leak in your attic?
          What's humanity ever done for us?

                         DIEDRICH
                    (looks at her, nods
                     knowingly and points
                     to her)
          Sure, Paula, sure. That's what I
          mean. Just what you said. That's
          the way we are. Everything for
          us - not for anybody else. Little!
          Petty! Selfish! Mean! That's us.
                    (now his voice rises
                     dramatically, he gestures
                     flamboyantly, he picks up
                     the camera)
          Well I've risen above that now. I
          say let's give this to the world.
          Here, world. A gift from Chester
          Diedrich and his wife.

                         WOODWARD
          And me too, Chet. Don't forget
          Woodward.

                         DIEDRICH
                    (with a sick little
                     look)
          Yeah and Woodward.
                    (then he strikes
                     the pose again)
          Here world. A gift for humanity.
          A gesture is all, maybe. Just a
          little gesture, but it's just a gesture
          that shows the size of the heart of
          Chester Diedrich and his wife.

                                        CONTINUED

38.   CONTINUED   38.

Woodward starts to make a motion.

                         DIEDRICH
                And Woodward.
                    (he walks across
                     the room)
                How do we know how medical science
                can use this? How do we know how
                valuable this thing will be as a
                scientific discovery? How do we
                know how -

He stops suddenly and looks through the half open
door into the bedroom.

39.   LONG SHOT   DIEDRICH'S P.O.V.   39.

A television set in the bedroom. On it we can see
horses running and o.c. the voice of an announcer.

                       ANNOUNCER'S VOICE
                In the Los Tendros feature Hot Foot
                has just won it. Jerry's Flash
                second. Easter Baby three. This
                was Hot Foot's second win in three
                days. He paid twenty four ninety,
                fifteen eighty, and six seventy.
                We now move into the third race
                here at Los Tendros -

40.   MED CLOSE SHOT   DIEDRICH   40.

As he turns and faces them, his eyes wide with discovery
and excitement. He looks at the camera, then at
the other two.

                         DIEDRICH
                I got it! I got it! I got it!!

                         WOODWARD
                What, Chet?

                         DIEDRICH
                    (pointing to the
                     television set)
                This takes a picture of things that
                happen but haven't happened yet. It
                took a picture of Paula with a fur
                coat. Five minutes later she had
                the fur coat. It took a picture of
                that door with nobody standing in
                front of it. And then Woodward was
                standing in front of it. All right,
                boys and girls - now get this! We
                take a picture of the winner's board
                at the race track before the race.

                                              CONTINUED

                         WOODWARD
          I don't get it.

                         PAULA
          Wait a minute - you mean we
          take the picture then look at
          it -
               (then shrieking with
                excitement)
          Chester!

                         DIEDRICH
          See? When we take the picture we
          can tell the winning numbers on
          the board. We know what horses
          came in and what they paid. Come
          on, everybody. Get your coats.

Paula grabs the fur, starts a hurry up primp at the
mirror. Woodward, lumbering, starts to pull his shoes
on. Diedrich flits around excitedly, prodding them.

                         DIEDRICH
          Come on. Come on. That was the
          first race. We can get there in
          time for the last four. How much
          dough has everybody got?

Paula empties out her pocketbook on the coffee table.

                         PAULA
          Three...four...five and a half
          dollars.

                         DIEDRICH
          I got two tens. That's twenty
          five fifty.

                         WOODWARD
               (takes out two
                dollar bills)
          I got two.
               (then he looks up
                skyward toward the
                ceiling)
          Twenty five fifty plus two equals -

                         PAULA
          Twenty seven fifty. Is that enough?

                                        CONTINUED

40. CONTINUED   40.

                              DIEDRICH
                    There's bound to be at least one
                    long shot. Why we can parlay
                    this into a million if we work
                    on it long enough. We can't
                    lose, Paula. We simply can't
                    lose. Come on! Everybody ready?

They start toward the door. Woodward stops abruptly,
turns to Diedrich, blocking him.

                              WOODWARD
                    Chet - Chest, what about Humanity?

                              DIEDRICH
                          (spitting it out)
                    Humanity? What did humanity
                    ever do for us! Go ahead!

He pushes Woodward through the door into the hall and
the three go out.

                                        DISSOLVE TO:

41-44. FILM CLIP VARIOUS PARTS OF RACE TRACK   41-44.

Ending on a long shot of the winner's board as the
numbered lights go out and it's blank.

                                        CUT TO:

45. MED GROUP SHOT DIEDRICH, PAULA AND WOODWARD   45.

Standing at a railing. People go by back and forth
behind them and Diedrich is desperately trying to focus
the camera and being jostled by the spectators.
Woodward, close to him, keeps elbowing him like the
excited idiot that he is.

                              WOODWARD
                    Oh boy, Chet. Oh boy, you got us
                    an idea here. Oh boy, Chester.

                              DIEDRICH
                    My ribs aren't botherin' your
                    elbow, are they? Let loose of me
                    now. Let me get the picture.

He squints down to the camera then looks across at the
board.

                                        CUT TO:

46. INSERT THE BOARD   46.

                                          CUT TO:

47. CLOSE SHOT DIEDRICH'S HANDS   47.

As he pushes the button on the camera. CAMERA PULLS
BACK for a medium group shot the three of them as they
just stare at one another, almost holding their breaths.
Then the CAMERA BEGINS A SLOW PAN down to the camera
agains as suddenly there's a click and the picture comes
out. All grab for it and Diedrich has to push both of
them out of the way as he himself rips out the picture
and studies it. His eyes go wide again.

                    PAULA
          Well?

                    DIEDRICH
          Look at it!

                    WOODWARD
          There's numbers on it now.

                    PAULA
          Six, three and eleven.

                    DIEDRICH
          And look what six pays. Forty-seven
          sixty to win.
                    (he looks down
                     at the racing
                     sheet in his hands)
          Number six. Number six. Number
          six...Tidy Too, that's number six.
          Okay, kids. We bet our money on
          number six.
                    (he holds up the
                     fistful of bills)
          Stay right here!

He turns and starts to fight his way through the crowd
toward the betting window.

48. MED CLOSE SHOT THE BETTING WINDOW   48.

As Diedrich arrives, throws the money down.

                    DIEDRICH
          Twenty-six dollars on number six.

The teller takes the money, hands him a ticket, A
sport-coated little tout stands near the window close to
Diedrich's elbow. The tout pulls at his sleeve.

                                          CONTINUED

48. CONTINUED   48.

                              TOUT
                    Hey, Jack! A word to the wise,
                    huh?

Diedrich turns to stare at him.

                              TOUT
                         (shakes his head)
                    Not number six. The last jockey
                    that horse had was Paul Revere but
                    I mean the original Paul Revere.
                    Really want to make some dough, I
                    got a couple of goodies in my pocket
                    here. The last two races and all
                    I need is cash. You and me could
                    go partners and we could really make
                    ourselves a -

At this moment there's the sound of bells ringing,
closing the betting. Diedrich holds up the ticket.

                           DIEDRICH
                    Number six. See you later...Jack!

Then he starts toward the railing again as we

                                             CUT TO:

49. FILM CLIP THE RACE STARTING   49.

                                             CUT TO:

50. MED GROUP SHOT DIEDRICH, WOODWARD AND PAULA   50.

At the railing wildly cheering the race as it goes on
beyond them.

                         ANNOUNCER'S VOICE
                       (over the loudspeaker)
                    Rounding the far turn it's Tinky
                    Beggar, Sir Midas, Pink Gloves,
                    Bart Junior, Lady Deck! Coming
                    into the stretch - Tidy Too coming
                    up very fast on the outside. Now
                    in the stretch Tinky Beggar, Sir
                    Midas and Tidy Too is third. Tidy
                    Too coming up very fast. Tinky
                    Beggar and Tidy Too neck and neck.
                    It's Tidy Too! It's Tidy Too all
                    the way!

                                             CUT TO:

51. FILM CLIP CROWD SCREAMING AND APPLAUDING   51.

                                                      CUT TO:

52. MED GROUP SHOT DIEDRICH, PAULA AND WOODWARD   52.

     as they jump around hugging one another. There's a
     sudden lull. They stop and turn toward the board.

                                                      CUT TO:

53. LONG SHOT BOARD   53.

     As the numbers appear on it. Six, three, and eleven.

54. GROUP SHOT   54.

     They all begin screaming again as Woodward takes the
     snapshot, crumples it up and throws it up in the air.
     Then the three of them head toward the window. CAMERA
     PANS DOWN to the bent, torn photograph as people walk
     on it and finally kick it off into the dust where it
     lies unnoticed.

                                                      CUT TO:

55-68. MONTAGE   55-68.

     First the board then the camera in Diedrich's hands
     taking a picture of it. Then Diedrich's hands removing
     the snapshot. Then Diedrich placing the bet. Then the
     horses starting. The board lighting up. Then Diedrich
     collecting money at the teller's cage. This happens
     several times as we

                                                  DISSOLVE TO:

69. INT HOTEL SUITE LIVING ROOM NIGHT   69.

     The CAMERA STARTS A SLOW PAN across the room taking in
     the following items. First, several racing forms lying
     around in profusion. Then several bottles of liquor in
     various postures from standing to leaning to lying
     empty. Several gift boxes open and disheveled, wrapping
     paper and ribbon lying around in profusion. And then
     money! Money everywhere. Money on the dresser. Money
     in chairs. Money on the bed. Money on the coffee table.
     Bills of every denomination.

                              (More)

                                               CONTINUED

69. CONTINUED   69.

The CAMERA CONTINUES ITS PAN past the three people in the
room. Woodward, in a flaming, brilliant new sport coat
that shrieks discordantly at you, lies with his shoes off
on the couch eating a chicken bone that's come out of a
silver tureen. Across the room Paula tries on new hats,
furs, et al. The CAMERA CONTINUES on into the bedroom
where Diedrich is on the telephone.

70. MED CLOSE SHOT DIEDRICH   70.

                         DIEDRICH
                     (on the phone)
               Yeah, but when can I get
               delivery on something like
               that? No, no, no, no. I
               don't want a black one. It's
               gotta be yellow with black
               upholstery. Spoked wheels,
               continental kit on the back,
               dual exhausts, and everything
               powered. You get that? Now
               when can I get delivery? All
               right, then order it. That's
               right. No, no, no. I'll pay
               you in cash. You come over
               tomorrow morning with the papers
               and we'll settle it then. Now
               how much did you say that was?
               Eleven grand?
                     (there's a pause,
                      then hurriedly)
               No, no, no, no, no. I'm not
               backin' out. I was just
               thinkin'. Maybe I ought to
               get two. Well, you bring the
               papers over tomorrow morning.
               Fine. So long.

He puts the receiver down, studies the phone happily for
a moment. There's the sound of a knock on the door.

                         PAULA
               It's the waiter.
                     (as she crosses
                      to the door)
               Are you done with your snack,
               Woodward?

71.   MED CLOSE SHOT WOODWARD   71.

As he puts the chicken bone aside and we can see the
remnants of a gigantic meal finished in front of him.

                    WOODWARD
          I guess that'll hold me till
          dinner.

72.   FULL SHOT THE ROOM   72.

Paula opens the door. A middle aged waiter enters the
room.

                    WAITER
          I came for the dishes, madam.

                    PAULA
          Right over there on the coffee
          table. Can you bring us a
          couple of bottles of champagne
          on your way back?

                    WAITER
                 (collecting the
                  dishes)
          Yes, ma'am, I can.

He covers up all the dishes with a table cloth, then
spies a couple of glasses on one of the book cases,
goes over to remove them and in doing so sees the
camera near them. He picks it up and looks at it for
a moment.

                    WOODWARD
          Hey. Get your hands off that!

                    DIEDRICH
                 (coming in from
                  the bedroom)
          Let him look at it! Bet you
          never seen anything like that,
          Pierre, huh!

                    WAITER
          Mais non. Most unusual, sir.

                    PAULA
          Isn't it though! You don't know
          how unusual.

                              CONTINUED

72. CONTINUED   72.

Then he takes the glasses, carries them over to the
tray, looks up.

                    WAITER
          But what do you do after your
          ten pictures? Is there any other
          way to get more film?

                    DIEDRICH
          Well we've only had it for a
          little while and we -
                    (he stops, double
                    takes)
          What did you say?

                    PAULA
          Yeah, what did you say about
          ten pictures?

                    WAITER
          The inscription on the outside.
          It says deux a la proprietare.
          That means ten to an owner. I
          presume that means you may only
          take ten -

                                        CUT TO:

73.- SERIES OF FLASH SHOTS OF WOODWARD, DIEDRICH AND PAULA   73.-
75.   75.

76. MED. LONG SHOT   THE WAITER   76.

As he carries the tray across the room, talking as he
does.

                    WAITER
          It's so odd. The lettering is
          definitely French but I've never
          seen a French camera like that.
          As a matter of fact -

Woodward has propelled him out the door now and shut it
on him cutting off the sentence.

                    DIEDRICH
                    (turning to the others)
          All right, how many pictures have
          we taken? There was one of Paula!

                    PAULA
          Then one of Woodward.

                                        CONTINUED

76. CONTINUED   76.

                              WOODWARD
                    How many pictures we take at the
                    track?

                              DIEDRICH
                         (hurriedly recollecting)
                    Six. We bet six races. That
                    means we've taken -

                              PAULA
                    Eight. We've taken eight pictures.
                    Chester, there's only two left.

                              DIEDRICH
                         (grabs the camera, studies
                         the inscription, then he
                         looks up)
                    Ten. But how do we know what
                    that means? Some frog waiter tells
                    us it says ten so right away we
                    think we only got two pictures left.
                    How does he know what it means? I
                    bet you we could take as many pictures
                    as we want -

                              PAULA
                         (grabs the camera from
                         him)
                    But we don't know! Chester, we
                    can't take any chances.

                              WOODWARD
                         (lumbering over to their
                         side)
                    No we can't.
                         (he grabs the camera
                         from her)
                    You know what we should do. We
                    should sell it!

                              PAULA
                         (grabs it away from
                         him disgustedly)
                    Sell it! Oh, what an ape you
                    are. What we should do with it
                    is to go to the track and bet
                    two more races with it.

                              DIEDRICH
                         (grabs the camera from her)
                    Are you both crazy? What you do
                    with it is to hang onto it! Save
                    it for a rainy day.

                                                    CONTINUED

76. CONTINUED   76.

Now the three of them start to jabber at once. Woodward
screaming to sell it, Paula screaming to use it, Diedrich
shouting over both of them to hang onto it. In the
middle of the mad melee the camera is suddenly struck out
of Diedrich's hand.

                                        CUT TO:

77. CLOSE SHOT   THE FLOOR   77.

As the camera falls, it's lens pointing toward Paula.
We hear a loud click as it takes a picture.

                    PAULA
               (grabbing the camera
               protectively off the
               floor)
          You both stop it! You're going to
          break the camera and give me a
          heart attack. I can feel it
          coming on me now.

78. TRACK SHOT WITH HER   78.

As with one hand on her heart and the other clutching
the camera, she walks over to the dresser. Just as she
lays it down.

                                        CUT TO:

79. CLOSE SHOT   CAMERA   79.

A picture snaps out.

80. MED. SHOT   PAULA   80.

Paula, more concerned with her heart than anything else
now, almost automatically reaches to rip the picture off
and looks at it in a sort of detached way.

81. CLOSE SHOT   PAULA   81.

Her mouth goes open as she stares at it.

                                        CUT TO:

82. TIGHT CLOSE SHOT   THE PHOTOGRAPH   82.

It'a an angle shot looking up toward Paula and it shows
her face contorted, mouth wide open, screaming.

83.   MOVING SHOT   AS THE PHOTO CHANGES HANDS   83.

First to Diedrich then over to Woodward.   PULL BACK.

                         DIEDRICH
                  (in a very still voice)
            She's screaming!
                  (he looks down at the
                  picture again and then
                  up at Woodward)
            Why is she screaming in the picture,
            Woodward? I'll tell you why she's
            screaming. She screaming because
            somebody's doing something to her
            husband. Some stupid ex-con with
            an idiotic idea about selling the
            camera and who doesn't care how
            he gets it either.

He slowly reaches into his pocket, pulls out a switch
knife and switches open the blade.

                         WOODWARD
            You better put that knife away,
            Chester. If she's screaming in
            the picture it's on account of
            what some guy must be doing to
            her brother.
                  (he takes a step toward
                  him)
            You better put that knife away.
                  (he holds up both his
                  big hands)
            You put it away or I'm gonna take
            your skin off.

He lunges at Diedrich who takes a swipe at him with the
knife and misses, throwing himself off balance and
falling across the room toward the window. Woodward,
holding tightly to him is carried across with him.

                                        CUT TO:

84.   TIGHT CLOSE SHOT   PAULA   84.

As she screams in exactly the same manner as the
photograph showed. There's a crashing, splinter of
broken glass and then dead silence. Paula's hands
slowly leave her face as she stares toward the window.

                                        CUT TO:

85.   CLOSE SHOT   THE WINDOW   85.

Broken glass littering the whole area and the two men
disappear.

86. MED. SHOT   ROOM   86.

Paula closes her eyes.

                         PAULA
              Oh, Chester. Chester, my poor
              darling husband. And Woodward.
              Woodward my flesh. My own flesh -
                   (she turns toward
                   the camera, clutching
                   her heart)
              I will die. I will just die.
              There's nothing left for me.

One eye slowly opens.

87. CLOSE SHOT   A PILE OF THE MONEY ON THE DRESSER   87.

88. CLOSE SHOT   PAULA'S EYES   88.

As they turn in another direction.

89. A PILE OF MONEY ON THE BED   89.

90. CLOSE SHOT   PAULA'S EYES   90.

As they once again move across the room.

91. THE FLOOR   91.

As yet another stack of bills can be seen.

92. CLOSE SHOT   PAULA   92.

As her eyes are wide open now. One hand reaches out
to pick up some of the money. She holds it in front of
her staring at it.

                         PAULA
                   (softly)
              However - we have to muddle
              through these things. We have
              to live with tragedy.
                   (she looks toward
                   the window)
              Poor Chester.
                   (then clucking)
              And poor Woodward. May you both
              rest in peace.

Then she goes over, takes a suitcase out of the closet,
puts it on the bed, opens it up. She starts to shovel
money into it, collecting it in big clusters like leaves
and throwing it into the suitcase.

                       (MORE)

                                          CONTINUED

92. CONTINUED   92.

She starts to hum to herself. The hum turns into a
jazz rendition sung throatily and loud as she jitterbugs
back and forth across the room throwing money around
in abandon, some of it hitting the suitcase, some of it
missing. She goes over to the dresser to collect
brushes and things, sees the camera, winks at it, flicks
at it with her fingers in a little gesture. Then she
picks it up and holds it facing her reflection in the
mirror.

                    PAULA
          Only one left.
               (then she looks over
               at the suitcase with
               the money spilling out
               from it)
          So what? You've got all you'll
          ever need.
               (she turns back to the
               mirror)
          So this one's for you. Smile for
          the birdie, baby!

92. She pushes the button then puts the camera down laughing,
starts to pick up the stuff off the dresser and is
suddenly stopped by the click of the camera as a picture
comes out. She chuckles happily, rips the picture off
and looks at it.

                                        CUT TO:

93. HER REFLECTION IN THE MIRROR   93.

As she lets out a little gasp and, still holding the
picture, takes several backward steps over to the bed.
Her face now contorts in pain and one hand, shaking,
clutches at her heart. This time there is no subterfuge
or no deceit. This is a coronary and for real. She
starts to breath with great difficulty and then very
slowly sinks to her knees, her eyes half open and then
in a last moment of life, lets out one more gasp as she
falls forward on her face on the floor. A lifeless hand
falls forward holding the picture.

94. PAN SHOT ACROSS HER ARM   94.

Until it reaches the picture which falls from lifeless
fingers and lies face up on the floor.

95. DOLLY IN FOR EXTREMELY TIGHT CLOSE SHOT THE PHOTO   95.

It shows Paula lying lifeless on the floor in exactly
the same position she's in.

96. PAN SHOT ACROSS TO THE DRESSER   96.

To the camera. We stay on it for a long moment.

                                               SLOW DISSOLVE TO:

97. EXT. CURIO SHOP   DAY   MED. LONG SHOT   97.

Looking through the window on a shot of the camera sitting
there. We see the owner talking to a couple inside. The
man points to the camera. The woman looks skyward in
protest and disdain. We see the owner talking voluably
intermittently pointing to the camera. Then he picks it
up. THE CAMERA PANS over to the other window of the
store and we see him wrapping it up, the man pulling out
a wallet and paying him, the woman with many gestures
pointing to the package and to the man, shaking her head,
then throwing up her hands. CAMERA MOVES BACK for med.
long shot as the couple come out of the store. The man
carries the package. He pauses to light a cigarette.

                    WOMAN
          There's one born every minute,
          isn't it? Sweetheart, is it true
          you really did buy the Brooklyn
          Bridge one year?

                    MAN
          Will you knock it off? It's an
          antique camera. You heard what
          the guy said. This might be
          worth a lot of money.

                    WOMAN
          And what'll you use it for? What
          good is it?

98. CLOSE SHOT   THE PACKAGE   98.

As the man looks down at it in his arms.

                    MAN
          So give it a chance. Who knows
          what kind of pictures you might
          take with an old fashioned thing
          like this.

                    WOMAN
               (sardonically)
          Who knows is right! Come on.
          Let's go home.

                              CONTINUED

98. CONTINUED   98.

The man nods, takes her arm and they start down the
sidewalk away from the store. The CAMERA PANS slowly over
to the window shooting in toward the empty spot where
the camera was sitting. We hear the Narrator's voice.

                    NARRATOR'S VOICE
          Correct. Quite correct. Who knows
          what kind of pictures you might
          take with an old fashioned camera
          like that! Odd pictures. Bizarre
          pictures. Pictures that open up
          the curtain to the vast mysteries
          that lie beyond man's knowledge.
          Mysteries that best might remain
          unsolved...mysteries that should
          remain...in the Twilight Zone.

                                      FADE TO BLACK

          THE END

PHOTO FINISH

With tongue planted firmly in cheek, "A Most Unusual Camera" is an amusing romp that is fun right up until the end. Then it all goes, quite literally, out the window. Had it been played for serious drama this episode would have gone against tough competition; *The Twilight Zone* often made serious forays into the repercussions of greed and selfishness. Instead the script is given a clever, lighthearted treatment that serves it well.

The leads are perfectly cast. Fred Clark's smarmy hood and Jean Carson's gun moll seem like outcasts from some lost gangster movie. While the Woodward character is such an inane clod that his presence feels like tacked-on comedy relief, Chester and Paula compensate by chewing some scenery of their own. When they bicker and debate the camera's potential benefit to humanity, we know that high-minded, philanthropic pipe dreams will quickly fall victim to old-fashioned petty avarice.

"Rod Serling had seen me in a play I had done," recalls Jean Carson. "When I came to the [West] Coast after fifteen years of Broadway and live television, I wanted the New York people who had already come to know that I was here. So I did a play, *Mrs. Gibbon's Boys*. The next weekend I went to a party in Malibu, and Rod came over and told me he'd seen the play. He said, 'I'm working on an idea and it's just right for you.' About two years later I got a call that it was finally being done."

Director John Rich was a natural choice to helm the episode. Rich worked on many of television's top comedies, including *The Dick Van Dyke Show, All in the Family* and *Barney Miller*, over a nearly fifty-year career. He recalls a favorite memory while shooting the introduction for "A Most Unusual Camera."

"Rod really liked doing those introductions. He was very good at it, of course. He went through it this time and the script girl said, 'It's ten seconds too long.' So I said, 'Rod, you might want to go a little quicker.' He did another take and he went quicker but it was still about eight or nine seconds too long. I suggested cutting a word or two. He did and it was five seconds too long. We cut another word and it was eight seconds too long. Now he's starting to sweat a bit because I think he was truly embarrassed; he loved doing it so well and he was usually a 'take one' guy."

Serling then used levity to break the tension, referencing the clothing company that provided his trademark look—a dark suit—for much of *The Twilight Zone*'s run. "He looked at me and said, 'Hey John, what does the Kuppenheimer look like?' I said 'Your Kuppenheimer runneth over!' He laughed like hell and he got it on the next take."

Unfortunately, the problems with the episode extend beyond a difficulty in shooting the introduction. A French inscription on the camera is a curious and unexplained plot point. Obviously, Chester and gang must remain ignorant of the camera's limit on photos until the story's finale. But the introduction of a French waiter named Pierre who arrives on the scene primarily to translate the message is a bit too convenient.

Still, with bits like Paula's feigned "palpitations" and the delicious idea of abusing a racetrack as a moneymaking scheme, the minor bumps in the script can be overlooked. What cannot be ignored is the notoriously feeble and illogical conclusion.

"That was an episode," says associate producer Del Reisman, "that annoyed a lot of people because of the ending, which was kind of a trick ending, with everybody going out the window. No explanation; there's nobody in the room to push the last person out. It was a little bit of a device, a trick. I thought it was an okay show and not more than that."

Serling's earliest draft dates to April 23, 1959, over a year and a half before the finalized script and eventual airdate of the episode (both versions are included in this volume for comparison).

Aside from more subtle changes, this initial version contains an alternate ending that doesn't rely on the implausibility of Paula's accidental stumble out of the window or the waiter's mysterious off-screen plunge to the pavement. As originally conceived, the camera presents Paula with a glimpse of her own impending death and this self-fulfilling prophecy causes the distraught woman to die of a coronary.

This version instills the camera with a will and mind of its own as it exacts revenge after being forced to reward immoral and illegal behavior. This script also completes a circle that puts the camera back in the pawnshop from whence it came, awaiting another chance to bless or curse a new owner. This conclusion, while not perfect, is far superior and better suited to *The Twilight Zone*'s story structure. So why wasn't it used?

According to Jean Carson, Serling kept tweaking the script but could not satisfy the network. "CBS's Continuity Department," the actress asserts, "kept turning down Rod's endings to the show. Rod would call me now and then, or have his agent call me, and he would tell me that it was coming along, but that they still weren't 'punishing' us enough, according to CBS. It really took him about two years to get CBS to do that show. It's not for me to say this for Rod, because Heaven knows he knew it all, but I felt it was an arbitrary ending with us all jumping out of the window and dying."

When given the final shooting script, director John Rich took the issue to Serling. "I was a little concerned about the ending," says Rich. "It's a little ambiguous. But Rod liked that. I said, 'I think that's not going to play as well as you think' and I was right. I don't think it did play as well as it should have. I think it could have had a better finish because it's not clear.

"One of my favorite axioms came from Mack Sennett (creator and director of The Keystone Kops): 'The audience will not laugh if it is mystified.' It's a wonderful comment. I said to Rod, 'I think there's a little mystification going on here' and he said he kind of liked that. I'm not going to argue with a genius and he really was a genius."

"It was that hokey ending that really should have been fixed," adds Del Reisman. "For John Rich, who is really a very talented director, I think we didn't do right by him. I liked a lot of it, Marcel Hillaire was wonderful, but I think that's a script that should have gone in for another rewrite. I think another week of working on it and it would have been more effective."

Ironically, although Serling's first draft had been written eighteen months prior to shooting, the ever-evolving ending led to chaos and down-to-the-wire changes once production began. Reisman blames a tight production schedule for the shooting script's uncharacteristic lack of polish.

"Going back, trying to be honest about it, I think that was one of the rare times that *The Twilight Zone* was victimized by its weekly schedule. Anyone on a weekly schedule runs into that. You have to do the terrible thing of saying 'I'd like the script now, please,' and the writer says, 'No, I'm not ready.' And you have to say, 'Yes you are, you're ready.' Time constraints didn't hurt us on many because of Rod's speed but once or twice they got to us. I think that was one that could have taken another rewrite."

Regardless of the rough edges, the show left an impression with fans, and members of both cast and crew remember it fondly. "It was a delightful script," says John Rich. "It went well, it shot well. I enjoyed the fun of it and I had a very good cast. They were terrific."

"It was just a delightful shoot to do that show," adds Jean Carson. "It was up my alley and it was great for me to do. I still get a lot of fan mail about it."

The Twilight Zone

THE MIND AND THE MATTER

Airdate: 5-12-1961

Manuscript Date: 1-31-1961

Script Fifty-Five

Episode Sixty-Three

THE TWILIGHT ZONE

SCRIPT FIFTY-FIVE

"THE MIND AND THE MATTER"

by

ROD SERLING

January 31, 1961

THE TWILIGHT ZONE

"The Mind and The Matter"

<u>CAST</u>

Archibald Beechcraft................a frustrated man.

Office boy (Henry).................sincere and awkward

Rogers............................the office sub-executive who
                                   has the power complex

Landlady..........................like everybody's.

Host-Narrator.....................Rod Serling

THE TWILIGHT ZONE

"The Mind and The Matter"

<u>SETS</u>

Int. Subway Station and Subway Train

Int. Office Building, Lobby and Elevator -- small, to be packed
                                            with people.

Int. Crowded Clerk's Office

Int. Men's Room of Office Building -------- at washstands.

Int. Company Cafeteria -------------------- at food counter and
                                            table.

Int. Living Room ------------------------- a one-roomer, with
                                           door and corridor.

FADE ON:

1. STANDARD ROAD OPENING   1.

    With vehicle smashing into letters, propulsion into starry
    night then PAN DOWN TO OPENING SHOT OF PLAY.

2. INT SUBWAY STATION ANGLE TILT SHOT   OF THE SUBWAY DOORS 2.

    As people pull, yank, shove and in a spasm of what can best
    be described as an animal instinct for survival cram them
    themselves into a subway. In the middle of this group is
    Archibald Beechcraft, a small, clerkish little man who at
    this moment has had his glasses pushed askew, his hat almost
    pulled off his head, his clothing rumpled and yanked as,
    protesting, waving his arms innefectually, he shouts out a
    shrieking protest at his innundation by those around him.
    This is our first view of Mr. Beechcraft just as the doors
    shut and the subway train starts to move. The CAMERA THEN
    PANS OVER TO SERLING standing by the steps of the subway.

                        SERLING
            A brief, if frenetic, introduction to
            Mr. Archibald Beechcraft - a child of
            the Twentieth Century - a product of
            the population explosion and one of the
            inheritors of the legacy of progress.

                                        DISSOLVE TO:

3. ELEVATOR DOOR   3.

    As it opens, gourging out a morass of human beings that are
    swallowed up yet another morass of human beings in a lobby,
    then the elevator is immediately re-occupied by a seething
    mass of people pushing their way into it and carrying with
    them like a piece of flotsam one Archibald Beechcraft,
    already battered by his subway experience and now re-
    assaulted by this other attack on his sanity. THE CAMERA
    MOVES INTO A FULL SHOT OF THE ELEVATOR as the doors close
    and, elbow to elbow, rib cage to rib cage, it starts its
    ascent up the building. Beechcraft is in the center almost
    strangled and crushed to death. The CAMERA MOVES IN VERY
    TIGHT ON HIS FACE as he looks with agonized suffering at
    this other daily innundation. The CAMERA PANS OVER TO
    SERLING who is now in the back of the elevator.

                        SERLING
            Mr. Beechcraft again...this time act
            two of his daily battle for survival.
            And in just a moment our hero will
            begin his personal, one-man rebellion
            against the mechanics of his age. And
            to do so he will enlist certain aids
            available only.....in The Twilight Zone.

                                        FADE TO BLACK

OPENING BILLBOARD
FIRST COMMERCIAL

FADE ON:

4.   INT OFFICE   DAY   4.

A long, rectangular room flanked by two rows of desks occupied by electric typewriters, adding machines, tabulators, etc. Each person pounding out their own diminuative contribution to commerce.

5.   PAN DOWN THE ROW OF MACHINES   5.

For a stylized shot of racing fingers pushing keys, feeding in data, etc. At the far end is Mr. Beechcraft typing away furiously on an electric typewriter. An office boy carrying a tray of paper coffee cups goes by him just at the moment Beechcraft turns to get something out of a file close by. The two of them collide and one cup of coffee spills partially over Beechcraft's arm. He rises to his feet, his voice a fury..

                        BEECHCRAFT
             Why, you clumsy clod!

6.   TWO SHOT   6.

As the office boy kneels down and starts to wipe off the coffee from Beechcraft's sleeve.

                        OFFICE BOY
          (abject and white-faced)
      I'm sorry, Mr. Beechcraft. I wasn't
      looking where I was going.

                        BEECHCRAFT
      That's precisely your problem! I
      oughta send you the cleaning bill!

Then sullenly he turns away and goes back to his typewriter, but the spell has been broken. He closes his eyes, shakes his head, then reaches into his pocket for a bottle of pills, looks at them for a moment, then rises.

7.   TRACK SHOT WITH HIM   7.

As he walks down the length of the office to a men's room.

                                     CUT TO:

8.   INT MEN'S ROOM   DAY   8.

As Beechcraft goes over to one of the sinks, pours himself a glass of water, plops two of pills in his mouth and downs them with a swig of water. Then he just stands there with his head down, his thin, pigeon-chest breathing in and out, his sparse shoulders slumped.

                                 CONTINUED

8.   CONTINUED   8.

The door swings open and Mr. Rogers walks in, a small,
martinetish sub-executive who looks at Beechcraft with an
upraised eyebrow.

                    ROGERS
          Feeling ill, Beechcraft?

Beechcraft shakes his head. Rogers goes over to the sink,
rolls up his sleeves and starts to wash his hands in the
manner of a surgeon, casting an occasional glance toward
Beechcraft alongside.

                    ROGERS
          If you'll forgive an observation,
          you're not looking too well.

                    BEECHCRAFT
            (grunting)
          I'm all right, Mr. Rogers.

                    ROGERS
          You know keeping yourself fit is not
          only a personal obligation, Beechcraft
          - in a large sense, it's part of your
          responsibility to your job and to the
          firm that employs you.

                    BEECHCRAFT
            (looks at him tiredly)
          I'm not unaware of that, Mr. Rogers.

                    ROGERS
          Then why don't you pull yourself together,
          man. Get some sleep at night. Eat
          regular meals. Lots of milk and fresh
          vegetables. Greens. On you can't beat
          those greens for vitamins! I'm a lettuce
          and spinach man myself. I'd have them
          for breakfast if -
            (and then he grins sheepishly)
          Well, if....people wouldn't look at me
          a little tilt. But the power's in the
          greens, Beechcraft. The power's definitely
          in the greens!

He finishes washing his hands, goes over to a roller towel,
pulls it out several times before he permits himself the
luxury of choosing the absolute cleanest. Then he dries
his hands very meticulously and again looks over toward
Beechcraft.

                    ROGERS
          Not drinking, are you, Beechcraft?

                                        CONTINUED

8.   CONTINUED   8.

                          BEECHCRAFT
                     (starting to boil)
                 I don't drink, Mr. Rogers.

                          ROGERS
                 Well, if you don't drink and you don't
                 stay out late at night - are you
                 watching your diet?

                          BEECHCRAFT
                     (whirls around at him, his
                      eyes wide and angry)
                 If you'd really like to know, Mr. Rogers
                 ....if you'd really like to know precisely
                 why I'm so dead tired - you ought to try
                 coming to work on a 7:32 AM subway every
                 morning. Then jamming into an elevator
                 like part of a herd of cattle. Then working
                 in that -
                     (he jerks his head toward
                      the door)
                 In that cacophonous din that you call
                 an office! Then stand in line in that
                 so-called cafeteria during that so-called
                 lunch hour that is never more than forty-
                 two minutes. Then get trampled to death
                 in the 5:38 subway at night. Then stand
                 in line at a movie or concert or a greasy
                 restaurant. But always stand in line.
                 Always get shoved. Always get jostled.
                 Always get pushed around!

                          ROGERS
                     (white faced)
                 Take hold, Beechcraft. For goodness
                 sakes man, take hold.

                          BEECHCRAFT
                 I'll take hold, Mr. Rogers. I'll
                 take hold when I can achieve that
                 millennium...that absolute perfection
                 that comes with solitude. Understand?
                 Solitude. that means no-
                     (he spits this
                      out)
                 PEOPLE!! You read me, Mr. Rogers?
                 People. This is the ultimate sin -
                 people! And my problem is, Mr. Rogers,
                 that I can't get away from people. At
                 no time except during that wondrous
                 seven and half hours that I'm in my bed
                 at night. And even then - I hear them
                 outside. People!
                          (MORE)

                                              CONTINUED

8.   CONTINUED   8.

                          BEECHCRAFT (CONT'D)
                    Raucous, shrieking, shouting people!
                    Herds, droves, legions, hosts,
                    armies, bushels, bevies, flocks and
                    coveys of people. People, people,
                    people.
                          (he advances on
                           Rogers, shaking
                           his fist)
                    If I had my way, here's how I'd fix
                    the universe. I'd eliminate the
                    people. I mean cross them off.
                    Destroy them. Get rid of them.
                    Decimate them. And there'd only be
                    one man left -
                          (he pokes himself
                           in the chest)
                    Me! Archibald Beechcraft, Esquire!

         He starts past Rogers who gapes at him.

                          ROGERS
                    You're quite mad, Beechcraft. Do
                    you know that? You're either off
                    or enroute away from your rocker!

9.   DIFFERENT ANGLE   BEECHCRAFT   9.

         At the door. He whirls around to face Rogers, snaps his
         fingers royally in the air.

                          BEECHCRAFT
                    True? Well, if I am mad - I much
                    prefer the deranged product of my
                    day dreaming - to the so-called sanity
                    that surrounds me.
                          (then spitting it
                           out grandiosely)
                    People!

         He turns and goes out the door.

                                        DISSOLVE TO:

10. INT SECTION OF THE COMPANY CAFETERIA   LONG ANGLE SHOT 10.
     LONG ANGLE SHOT   LOOKING DOWN

         A line of tray-carrying lunchers and in the middle of
         them is Mr. Beechcraft, pushed and pulled at, his dishes
         sliding back and forth on the tray, the water spilling
         over from the top of the glass until he finally reaches
         the cashier, almost drops the tray reaching for cash, then
         hands the money to the cashier, takes the change on the
         tray and tries to ply his way through the mog of people,
         looking for an empty table.

11. LONG SHOT ACROSS THE CROWD OF THE OFFICE BOY   11.

Who rises from his table, wiggles a finger and shouts.

>   OFFICE BOY
>   Mr. Beechcraft! Oh, Mr. Beechcraft!
>   Here's a place for you, sir. I've
>   been saving it.

12. DIFFERENT ANGLE BEECHCRAFT   12.

As head down, like a very small fullback, he dives through
the line and finally reaches the empty stop. He wiggles
and squeezes his way in next to the office boy, turns to
him then somewhat grudgingly -

12.
>   BEECHCRAFT
>   I'm obliged, Henry.

>   HENRY
>   Think nothing of it, Mr. Beechcraft.
>   I was...well I was...trying to make
>   amends for this morning.

>   BEECHCRAFT
>   This morning?

>   HENRY
>   When I spilled coffee on your coat.
>   (then a shy smile)
>   I'm really sorry about that, Mr.
>   Beechcraft.
>   (then wetting his
>   lips)
>   A friend of mine works in a book
>   store around the corner. I went
>   there first part of the lunch break.
>   I got you this.

He takes a small book and slides it, still shyly, over
toward Beechcraft, who looks at it with upraised eyebrow.

13. CLOSE SHOT   COVER OF THE BOOK   13.

It reads: "THE MIND AND THE MATTER, How You Can Achieve
The Ultimate Power of Concentration".

14. TWO SHOT   14.

Beechcraft picks up the book, looks at it briefly and
reads from it.

>   BEECHCRAFT
>   "The Mind And The Matter, How You Can
>   Achieve The Ultimate Power of
>   Concentration." A little on the occult
>   side, isn't it, Henry?

                    CONTINUED

14.   CONTINUED   14.

                              HENRY
                          (eagerly)
               Maybe so, Mr. Beechcraft, but my
               friend is kind of a...well you might
               call him a student of the science of
               the mind. He swears by this book.
               He says to the best of his knowledge,
               it's the only one in existence.
                          (then looking around a
                           around a little
                           surreptitiously)
               Would you believe it, Mr. Beechcraft,
               I've seen him -
                          (he leans over,
                           speaking directly
                           nose to nose to a
                           chagrined and
                           discomfitted Beechcraft
                           who automatically
                           reacts to any
                           proximity)
               I've seen my friend cause a woman
               to purchase a chartreuse and orange
               scarf.

15.   CLOSE SHOT   BEECHCRAFT   15.

      As he stares at him blankly.

                              BEECHCRAFT
               How's that?

16.   TWO SHOT   16.

                              HENRY
                          (eagerly)
               That's right, Mr. Beechcraft. He
               was in a department store and he saw
               some woman picking over a table full
               of scarves that were on sale and he
               concentrated real hard on the
               chartreuse and orange one and, Mr.
               Beechcraft, as sure as I'm sitting
               here in the cafeteria of the United
               Tool and Die Company - that woman
               picked up the chartreuse and orange
               scarf.
                          (he slams his fist
                           excitedly on the
                           table, upsetting
                           Beechcraft's coffee,
                           shouting out)

                          (MORE)

CONTINUED

16. CONTINUED   16.

                          HENRY (CONT'D)
               It's the absolute, unvarnished truth.
                    (then he recoils
                     at the sight of
                     the coffee spilling
                     over on Mr. Beechcraft's
                     lap. He gulps, swallows
                     and looks positively ill)
               Oh, Mr. Beechcraft...I'm so sorry -

17. CLOSE SHOT   BEECHCRAFT   17.

     His eyes roll upwards. His face looks pinched and close
     to total collapse. He pushes his tray away, grabs the
     book.

                          BEECHCRAFT
               Thank you so much for the book, Henry.
                    (acidly)
               I'm indebted.

     He shakes his head at the absolute idiocy of the human
     beings he has to have intercourse with.

18. TRACK SHOT WITH HIM   18.

     As he starts to walk past the various crowded tables.

19. LONG SHOT OVER HIS SHOULDER   OF HENRY   19.

     Who has taken a bite of a sandwich, but suddenly remembers
     something, rises, waves wildly and through a full mouth
     gurgles out -

                          HENRY
               Mr. Beechcraft! Chapter three...
               that's the one on "Initial Phenomena
               Of Intense Concentration". Chapter
               three, Mr. Beechcraft -

20. CLOSE SHOT   BEECHCRAFT   20.

     Who shakes his head and closes his eyes then starts to
     walk again.

21. MOVING SHOT WITH HIM   21.

     As he looks down at the book, thumbs through it, starts
     to peruse it disinterestedly, but then is caught up by
     what he's reading. He stops abruptly, stands there and
     stares at the book, reading it now intensely to the point
     where he runs a finger down each line as he reads. Every
     few minutes he looks up in growing and deep-rooted interest.
     He mouths silently all that which he reads and then
     suddenly looks up to see a girl standing by a soft drink
     vending machine.

22.   CLOSE SHOT   OVER THE GIRL'S SHOULDER   OF THE VARIOUS   22.
     ASSORTMENT AND BUTTONS

     They run the gamut from Orange to Grape to Coffee Black
     to Hot Chocolate With Cream.

23.   CLOSE SHOT - BEECHCRAFT   23.

     As he bites his lower lip. His eyes look strangely dazed.
     He studies the book again then looks over toward the girl.

                           BEECHCRAFT
                    (under his breath)
            Grape. Pick grape. The grape is
            delicious. Pick the grape.

24.   CLOSE SHOT   THE GIRL   24.

     Who suddenly looks a little bewildered. Her finger is on
     the Orange, but it traverses the whole length of dials
     until it reaches the button marked Grape. This she pushes.

25.   WHIP PAN OVER TO BEECHCRAFT   25.

     Who looks amazed, a little startled and yet, with it all,
     strangely taken. He looks down at the book again and
     reads assiduously, then starts out of the cafeteria, his
     nose buried in his reading.

                                  DISSOLVE TO:

26.- SERIES OF DIFFERENT ANGLES OF BEECHCRAFT   26.-
30.   30.

     As he reads. First at his desk surrounded by machines
     and people as he continues to read oblivious to everyone.
     Then to the interior of the elevator as it goes down,
     mobbed to the gunnels with people all chatting volubly
     except Beechcraft who still reads from the book. Then into
     the lobby as the herd moves toward the swinging doors,
     carrying with them Mr. Beechcraft and his book which he
     still reads. Then into the subway car as the doors close,
     half crushing those people still trying to get on belatedly.
     Almost everyone has a newspaper, read at different angles...
     except Beechcraft who reads from the book.

                                  DISSOLVE TO:

31.   INT BEECHCRAFT LIVING ROOM   NIGHT   31.

     This is a small, somewhat aged brownstone apartment
     interior very much for the bachelor since the one room
     encompasses the Simmons Hide-a-bed, the dinky pullman
     kitchen, a door to a closet-like bathroom and also the
     living area. Beechcraft sits at a make-shift desk, still
     pouring over the book. He very slowly closes it and
     stares straight ahead of him, bits his lip in deep thought.

                                CONTINUED

31. CONTINUED   31.

                         BEECHCRAFT
                They're right! They're absolutely,
                unequivocally right. Concentration
                is the most under-rated, unknown power
                in the universe. A person could...
                well, a person could move mountains.
                     (then very thoughfully
                      as he walks toward the
                      window)
                There's really no limit to what a man
                could do using the power properly. No
                limit at all.

32. DIFFERENT ANGLE OF HIM   32.

     As he approaches the window and pulls it open. There is
     the blaring sound of traffic, crowds, music, et al. He
     hurriedly pushes the window down again.

                         BEECHCRAFT
                People!
                     (then a little
                      wildly)
                If I could just concentrate hard
                enough to get rid of the -

     He stops abruptly, turns and stares out the window again,
     takes a slow walk over to it and looks out.

33. FILM CLIP   NEW YORK   DOWNTOWN   33.

     At the high mid-evening traffic mark. It is absolutely
     jam packed with automobiles and pedestrians.

34. THE CAMERA DOLLIES IN FOR AN EXTREMELY TIGHT CLOSE SHOT 34.
     OF BEECHCRAFT

     As he looks off, his eyes almost feverish with excitement.

                         BEECHCRAFT
                Concentration! That's what it takes.
                Concentration. Concentrate on...
                on getting rid of people. No people
                at all.

35. MOVING SHOT WITH HIM   35.

     As he walks around the room.

                         BEECHCRAFT
                None. Nobody in the subway...nobody in
                the lobby...nobody in the elevator...
                nobody. Nobody in the office. Nobody in
                the cafeteria. Nobody on the street.
                Nobody.

                         (MORE)
                                              CONTINUED

35.   CONTINUED   35.

                          BEECHCRAFT (CONT'D)
                      (he stops, looking
                       up toward the ceiling,
                       in a spasm of exultation)
                   Nobody except Archibald Beechcraft!

                                          ABRUPT CUT TO:

36.   THE OUTSIDE OF BEECHCRAFT'S DOOR   36.

      Taking in the rear of his landlady who is pounding on his
      door.

                              LANDLADY
                          (shrieking)
                   Mr. Beechcraft? The rent is due,
                   Mr. Beechcraft.
                          (a pause and she
                           knocks again)
                   Mr. Beechcraft? Rent due? Mr.
                   Beechcraft -

                                          CUT TO:

37.   INT THE ROOM   37.

      As Beechcraft stares irritated at the door. He turns
      half sideways and sees the book on the desk.

38.   CLOSE SHOT   THE BOOK   38.

39.   BACK TO SCENE   39.

      He suddenly looks resolved and grim.

                              BEECHCRAFT
                          (in a whisper)
                   Go away. Disappear. Be extinct.
                   Go away. Disappear. Be extinct.
                          (then souting it)
                   Go away. Be extinct. Disappear.

                                          ABRUPT CUT TO:

40.   CLOSE SHOT   THE LANDLADY'S HAND   40.

      As it travels down in an arc, starting to knock again.
      The hand disappears and the knock never comes. There's
      the sound of footsteps from inside approaching the door.
      It opens. Beechcraft stands there. He looks tentatively
      left and right then this tentativeness is replaced by a
      look of absolute triumph. He slams the door.

41.   INT THE ROOM   41.

He stands in the center of the room like a small rooster.

                          BEECHCRAFT
            Concentration! Mind over matter!
            Today the landlady - tomorrow the
            world!

                                   FADE TO BLACK:

            END ACT ONE

ACT TWO

FADE ON:

42. INT SUBWAY STATION   ANGLE SHOT   LOOKING UP AT   42.
     BEECHCRAFT

     As he walks down the concrete steps. He pauses half way
     down.

                                        CUT TO:

43. LONG SHOT   HIS P.O.V.   43.

     Of a mob of people waiting for the subway train.

                                        CUT TO:

44. MED CLOSE SHOT   BEECHCRAFT   44.

     As his face looks grim and determined. He shuts his eyes
     for a long, long moment, then suddenly there is no more
     sound in the place. He opens them and stares.

                                        CUT TO:

45. LONG SHOT   HIS P.O.V.   45.

     Of the subway platform. It is absolutely empty. After a
     moment we hear the subway train arriving.

                                        CUT TO:

46. MED CLOSE SHOT   BEECHCRAFT   46.

     As the lights of the train play on his face.

47. ANGLE SHOT LOOKING DOWN AT HIM   47.

     As deliberately, slowly and with almost royal mein, he
     walks down the steps into the subway car.

                                        CUT TO:

48. INT SUBWAY CAR   48.

     He insouciantly lies down on one complete seat, propping
     up his head with the back of his hands. After a moment
     he turns toward the open doors, rather nonchalantly lifts
     a limp hand, snaps his fingers.

                          BEECHCRAFT
                 All right, let's get going!

49. CLOSE SHOT   THE DOOR   49.

     As they slide shut on direction and the train takes off.

                                        DISSOLVE TO:

50. INT LOBBY   DAY   LONG SHOT ACROSS THE FLOOR   50.

Of the swinging front doors as Beechcraft comes in totally
alone. He walks over nonchalantly past the newsstand, takes
a paper, starts to fish in his pocket for a coin, then
chuckles, puts the coin back.

51. TRACK WITH HIM OVER TO THE ELEVATOR DOORS   51.

He pushes the button and looks up at the floor indicator.
The arrow starts down to one and the doors open.

52. PULL BACK FOR A SHOT OF BEECHCRAFT   52.

As he takes a deep enjoyable breath, slowly saunters into
the elevator and with a rather grandiose gesture, pushes
a button with his pinky.

53. INT ELEVATOR   53.

As it ascends. He takes out a cigarette, starts to light
it, then looks up at a sign which reads: "No smoking,
please."

                                          CUT TO:

54. INSERT SIGN   54.

55. BACK TO SCENE   55.

He makes a gesture of distaste and goes back to lighting
the cigarette, taking deep and luxurious drags.

                                          CUT TO:

INT OFFICE LONG SHOT LOOKING DOWN THE TWO ROWS OF
DESKS

As Beechcraft comes in, hands in his pockets, whistling.
He pauses briefly by the time clock, takes the cigarette
out, butts it against the clock, then lets it drop to the
floor. He saunters over to his desk and sits down, puts
    feet up on the top of the electric typewriter, exhales,
looks around like a cheshire cat, smiles broadly and just
sits there enjoying himself. After a moment he rises, walks
to the window and looks out.

                                          CUT TO:

57. FILM CLIP OF AN ABSOLUTELY EMPTY CITY   57.

58. BACK TO SCENE   58.

As Beechcraft turns and goes back to his desk, sits down
again, looks up at the clock on the wall that ticks loudly
and persistently.

59.   CLOSE SHOT BEECHCRAFT   59.

As he points to it.

                    BEECHCRAFT
          That'll be just about enough of that!

                                        CUT TO:

60.   CLOCK   60.

As the hands stop and all noise ceases.

61.   SHOT OF BEECHCRAFT   61.

He puts his hands behind his head and leans back in the
chair, takes out a cigarette and is about to light it when
he suddenly looks very, very pensive. He blows out the
match, throws the cigarette away and just sits there for
a long, silent moment. Then he takes off his glasses and
rubs his eyes, putting the glasses on the desk.

                    BEECHCRAFT
          Hmmph. Hmmph. All well and good. All
          well and good, to be sure. But what's
          to do? How does one occupy his time?

                                        CUT TO:

62.   SHOT OF THE GLASSES   ON THE DESK   62.

We see his reflection in them.

                    REFLECTION IN GLASSES
          Too much of a good thing?

                    BEECHCRAFT
          I wouldn't say that.

                    REFLECTION IN GLASSES
          But you're thinking it.

Beechcraft shrugs, rises, walks a few feet away from the
desk, looks at his reflection in the mirror on the opposite
wall.

                    REFLECTION IN MIRROR
          Bored to death, aren't you?

                    BEECHCRAFT
          Let's just say that...let's just say
          that I'm temporarily somewhat accessible
          to suggestions as to how to occupy my
          time.

                              CONTINUED

62. CONTINUED   62.

> REFLECTION IN MIRROR
> (laughs)
> Let's face it - you're bored to tears.
> Solitude is one thing, but loneliness
> - loneliness is quite another.

> BEECHCRAFT
> (with a sloughing gesture
>   of his hand)
> Loneliness nothing! I despise people.
> I loathe them. And I....Archibald
> Beechcraft, have done away with them.
> For good and all, mind you. For good
> and all.

63. TRACK SHOT WITH THEM   63.

As he walks over to a coffee machine at the far end of the
office.

> REFLECTION IN MACHINE MIRROR
> Thought about any alternatives?

> BEECHCRAFT
> (irritated)
> Alternatives to what?

> REFLECTION IN MACHINE MIRROR
> (with a shrug)
> Alternatives to this. You're bored.
> You don't have idea one how to occupy
> your time. People are bad enough -
> but inactivity's even worse.

Beechcraft jams a coin into the machine and withdraws a
cup of coffee. He carries this back to his desk and sits
down.

> REFLECTION IN GLASSES
> How about it? Think of any alternatives?

> BEECHCRAFT
> (puts the glasses aside)
> Don't talk nonsense. I'm content. I
> am honestly and truly content for the
> first time in my life. I have rid myself
> of the worse scourge there is - the
> populace!

                                                    CONTINUED

63. CONTINUED   63.

He reaches over, takes his glasses and puts them on, squirms
in the chair for a moment, drums with his fingers, lights
a cigarette, then scratches his head.

                    BEECHCRAFT
          Although if the truth be known...I
          would like,...well, I would appreciate
          a little diversion of some sort. Any
          kind of diversion.
               (his eyes look brighter)
          Like an earthquake!

64. FULL SHOT   THE ROOM   64.

As it trembles. Glass cracks. Desks move.

                    BEECHCRAFT
               (shouts)
          No, no, no, not that. Perhaps a
          nice electrical storm!

From outside there's the sound of thunder and lightning.
The lights in the office flick on and off. Beechcraft goes
over to his desk, sits there glumly for a moment as nature
boils around him. He closes his eyes, puts his fingers
against them, waves toward the window.

                    BEECHCRAFT
          Forget it!

                                        CUT TO:

65. SHOT OF THE WINDOW   65.

As the rain stops abruptly and it's daylight outside.

66. DIFFERENT ANGLE BEECHCRAFT   66.

As he rises, walks the length of the desks toward the door,
pauses by the door, turns, stares at the empty desk.

                    BEECHCRAFT
          I believe I've had it for the day.
          I'll go home and nap.

67. CAMERA PANS OVER TO HIS REFLECTION IN THE MIRROR   67.

                    REFLECTION IN MIRROR
          Alone, of course.

                                        CONTINUED

67. CONTINUED   67.

                              BEECHCRAFT
                         (a little forlornly)
                    Of course, alone. Who else is there
                    ....except me!

                                        DISSOLVE TO:

68. SERIES OF SHOTS OF BEECHRAFT   68.
thru   thru
72. Alone in the elevator, a little disconsolate, leaning   72.
     against the wall. Then in the subway sitting alone in
     the car as it comes to a stop. The doors open. He walks
     out to an empty platform. He may over to a young woman on
     a poster, draw a mustache and then throw away the pencil in
     a kind of strange despair.

                                        DISSOLVE TO:

73. INT BEECHCRAFT LIVING ROOM   73.

     As he sits alone in the center of the room, hands clenched
     together staring off at nothing. He takes off his glasses,
     rubs his eyes tiredly.

74. PAN DOWN TO CLOSE SHOT THE GLASSES AND HIS REFLECTION   74.

                         REFLECTION IN GLASSES
                    What about it?

                              BEECHCRAFT
                    Why don't you let me alone!

                         REFLECTION IN GLASS
                    Haven't you about had it?

                              BEECHCRAFT
                    You know I can break you to pieces
                    as easily as look at you!

                         REFLECTION IN GLASS
                         (laughs)
                    Without a doubt! But where'll that get
                    you? Uncorrected astigmatism!
                         (then a pause)
                    What do you think you're going to do?

                              BEECHCRAFT
                         (turns away)
                    I really don't know.

                                        CONTINUED

74. CONTINUED   74.

                    REFLECTION IN GLASS
            Preying on you now, isn't it? I mean
            the quiet...the emptiness.

                    BEECHCRAFT
                (whirls around to
                 face the glasses)
            The thing of it is - it's just that,
            while I don't much care for people -
            it's difficult not having anyone!

                    REFLECTION IN GLASSES
            Why not get someone.

                    BEECHCRAFT
                (pettishly)
            That's the point! Someone is
            everyone and I can't stand everyone
            or anyone for that matter! There
            frankly isn't a breed or a specie
            of human being that I can stomach!

                    REFLECTION IN GLASSES
            Ever thought of a cocker spaniel?

                    BEECHCRAFT
                (a little sadly)
            I never cared much for animals, either.

He suddenly stares at the glasses and holds them up, looking
deep into them. And then he whirls around, rises, runs into
the bathroom, stares at his reflection in the mirror. He
turns from the mirror, facing the camera, his eyes bright and
excited.

                    BEECHCRAFT
            Of course! Of course! Why didn't
            I think of it before?

The CAMERA MOVES UP SLIGHTLY so that it is shooting over his
shoulder toward his reflection.

                    REFLECTION IN MIRROR
            Think of what?

                    BEECHCRAFT
                (snaps his fingers)
            People...people who I can stand.
            People like...people like myself.
                    (MORE)

                                        CONTINUED

74. CONTINUED   74.

                              BEECHCRAFT (CONT'D)
                         (he whirls around
                          to stare at the mirror)
                    That's what I'll do. I'll create
                    people....but they'll be like me!

                              REFLECTION IN MIRROR
                    A world full of Archibald Beechcrafts!
                    Now that's a thought!

                              BEECHCRAFT
                    You bet your life it's a thought.
                    You bet your sweet life!

75. TRACK SHOT WITH HIM   75.

     As he walks back toward the center of the room.

                              BEECHCRAFT
                    That's what I'll do. I'll will it.
                    I'll concentrate and I'll will that
                    from now on everyone I see will be
                    like me! It's really quite simple!

76. CLOSE SHOT   THE GLASSES   76.

     That he's laid back on the desk and the reflection in them.

                              REFLECTION IN GLASSES
                    And when is this new era ushered in?

                              BEECHCRAFT
                         (looks down at glasses)
                    Tomorrow morning! Tomorrow morning....
                    I'll re-people the earth!
                         (he grins, stretches
                          yawns luxuriously,
                          goes over and lies
                          on the sofa, hands
                          behind his head
                          staring up, sleepy-
                          eyed at the ceiling)
                    That's what I'll do. First thing in
                    the morning. I'll re-people the earth.
                         (he yawns)
                    Nothing but my kind of folks.
                         (then he closes his
                          eyes and seems about
                          to drift off into sleep
                          when one eye opens and
                          he looks up at the light
                          in the ceiling)
                    All right - you've had it!

He snaps his fingers sluggishly and the light goes out.

                                             DISSOLVE TO:

77. INT SUBWAY STATION   DAY   77.

It is totally devoid of anyone and is blanketed with silence.
A SLOW PAN OVER to the steps as Beechcraft appears at their
top. He looks down toward the empty platform, wets his lips,
looks a little grim and determined, closes his eyes, mouths
a soundless collection of words and half way through, we
suddenly hear the shrieking, shouting noise of people along
with the approaching roar and rattle of a subway train.

78. CLOSE SHOT   BEECHCRAFT   78.

As he slowly opens his eyes and looks. He reacts, reaches
for the railing for support and starts to walk down the
steps.

                                        CUT TO:

79. SHOT FROM BEHIND HIM   79.

As he suddenly is innundated by people scrambling for the
subway car door which has just opened. Each time he gains
a foot he is pushed back two, until finally everyone has
been packed into the car except him. The doors close and
he stands alone on the platform. The car starts up.

                                        CUT TO:

80. CLOSE SHOT   BEECHCRAFT   80.

As the passing light of the subway train crosses and
recrosses his face, a white, staring, incredulous face.

81.- SERIES OF CLOSE UPS   OF FACES IN THE WINDOWS   81.-
85.   85.
As the train passes. Each one is Beechcraft himself in
different costume, different look, different stares, different
pose, but each one undeniably Beechcraft.

                                        DISSOLVE TO:

86. MED CLOSE SHOT   THE SWINGING DOORS LEADING INTO HIS   86.
OFFICE BUILDING LOBBY

The swinging door slowly moves and Beechcraft enters,
sticking his head into the lobby and looking around
surreptitiously.

87. MOVING SHOT   WITH HIM   87.

As he walks. He stops by the newsstand.

88. DIFFERENT ANGLE OF HIM   88.

As he picks up a paper a little absent mindedly.

                        A VOICE
                    (from behind him)
            People! It isn't enough that they're
            just a mob! They are a dishonest mob.
            Kindly deposit ten cents for the
            purchase or shall I call the police!

89. CLOSE SHOT   BEECHCRAFT   89.

As he whirls around to stare toward the news vendor. It is
Beechcraft himself in a turtle neck sweater and cap.

90. DIFFERENT ANGLE   BEECHCRAFT   90.

As he flings the paper aside and sprints across the lobby.

91. ANGLE SHOT   LOOKING DOWN AT HIM   91.

As he plows through the open elevator door.

                                            CUT TO:

92. INT ELEVATOR   THE CAMERA BEHIND THE ELEVATOR'S OCCUPANTS 92.

Looking toward the door as it closes. In the midst of this
group is Beechcraft who slowly looks left and right and
finally turns to face the camera, biting his lip, his eyes
wide and almost disbelieving. The elevator doors open
again and the elevator operator turns to the group.

                        ELEVATOR OPERATOR
            Fifteenth floor. Kindly get off,
            please.
                    (then shaking his
                    head, witheringly)
            Sardines!

And the elevator operator is Beechcraft himself in uniform.

                                            CUT TO:

93. DIFFERENT ANGLE   OF THE HALL   93.

As seen from the open elevator. We are on the backs of the
people as they leave, but each in turn looks over his
shoulder and again each in turn is Beechcraft.

94. MED CLOSE SHOT   ELEVATOR   94.

As Beechcraft walks out and the doors shut immediately behind
him. He stands there in the empty corridor, takes out a
handkerchief, leans against the wall, mops his brow.

95. TRACK SHOT   WITH HIM   95.

As he takes a slow, unsteady walk over to his office door
and opens it.

                                        CUT TO:

96. CLOSE SHOT   THE DOOR   96.

As it opens, framing a picture of the long rectangular room.

97. PAN SHOT   DOWN EACH DESK   97.

And each occupant in turn is Beechcraft. As we PAN DOWN the
Beechcrafts, each has a small aside.

                    BEECHCRAFT ONE
          The noise. The miserable noise. I'll
          go out of my mind. I'll go out of my
          ever lovin' mind.

                    BEECHCRAFT TWO
          A sty - that's what it is. Nothing but
          people. And people are pigs.
               (then looking ceilingward)
               me, pigs. No offense.

                    BEECHCRAFT THREE
          People, people, people, people. Is
          there no respite? Is their no relief?

                    BEECHCRAFT FOUR
          Herds, droves, legions, hosts, armies,
          bevies, coveys of people! Deliver me.
          Please deliver me.

                                        CUT TO:

98. CLOSE SHOT   BEECHCRAFT   98.

As he steps back into the corridor, closing the door. He
slowly turns to face the camera and then very slowly looks
down at his feet.

                                        CUT TO:

99. ANGLE SHOT   BEECHCRAFT'S P.O.V.   HIS REFLECTION IN THE 99.
POLISHED MARBLE FLOOR

Looking up at him.

                    REFLECTION IN FLOOR
          Had it?

                    BEECHCRAFT
          Undeniably.

                    REFLECTION IN FLOOR
          Coming through to you, huh?

                    BEECHCRAFT
               (nods)
          Without a doubt. A lot of me is just
          as bad as...as a lot of them.

                    REFLECTION IN FLOOR
          So what's to do now?

100. CLOSE SHOT   BEECHCRAFT   100.

As he takes a long, deep breath.

                    BEECHCRAFT
          I'll just put it back the way it was.
               (then looking up)
          Just the way it was.

He heaves a deep sigh, closes his eyes, concentrates, then
opens the door.

                                        CUT TO:

101. LONG SHOT   THE OFFICE   101.

It's just as we remember it. A lot of people and machines,
but each person a separate entity.

102. MOVING SHOT   BEECHCRAFT   102.

As he enters and almost the second he reaches his desk,
Henry, the office boy, hurriedly passes with a tray full of
coffee cups, slams into him and once again the coffee spills
over his sleeve.

103. CLOSE SHOT   HENRY   103.

His face white and stricken.

                    HENRY
          Oh, Mr. Beechcraft...please, sir,
          forgive me.

104. CLOSE SHOT   BEECHCRAFT   104.

His first instinct is to react in precisely the violent way
he always reacts, but then looking into the boy's white,
stricken face, something happens to him. He grins, winks.

                    BEECHCRAFT
          Forget it, Henry. Nothing serious.

He passes the now amazed office boy and sits down at his
desk. He looks up to see the office boy still standing
there.

                    BEECHCRAFT
          Yes?

                      HENRY
          I was just wondering, sir... the book
          I gave you. Get anything out of it?

105. CLOSE SHOT   BEECHCRAFT   105.

As he looks down at the desk. The book is sitting there.

106. CLOSE SHOT   THE BOOK   106.

As he picks it up.

107. BACK TO SCENE   107.

He looks at it for a moment, then hands it back to the office
boy.

                    BEECHCRAFT
          Not really, Henry. Frankly... I think
          it's a lot of pap.
               (he shakes his head)
          Interesting, but...totally unbelievable!

He hands the book back to the boy as the CAMERA STARTS A
SLOW PAN past the chattering, screeching machines. We hear
Serling's Voice in narration.

                  SERLING'S VOICE
          Mr. Archibald Beechcraft, a child of the
          Twentieth Century, who has found out
          through trial and error...and mostly
          error...that with all its faults...it
          may well be that this is the best of all
          possible worlds. People not withstanding
          - it has much to offer. Tonight's case
          in point...in The Twilight Zone.

                              FADE TO BLACK:

                    THE END

THE POWER OF
NEGATIVE THINKING

In "The Mind and the Matter," Rod Serling doles out a gift of absolute power in the form of focused concentration. The recipient of this formidable talent is, playfully enough, a misanthrope who proceeds to rid the world of humanity.

Shelley Berman is flawless as the cantankerous yet somehow likeable lead character. It's no accident that the role is well-suited to Berman's deadpan delivery and comedic timing. A Grammy winner (for Best Non-Musical Recording) and the first stand-up comedian to appear at Carnegie Hall, Berman was cast as Archibald Beechcroft as the script was being developed. Rod Serling tailored the Beechcroft character to fit Berman's whiny and grumbling comedic persona.

"Rod Serling approached me and said he'd like to write an episode for me," says Shelley Berman. "I jumped at the idea. At that time I was guesting on many other types of television shows. Being a comedian, I might have been considered for more offbeat roles in offbeat shows.

"I regarded getting to appear on *The Twilight Zone* as having been granted a special adventure. I believe most actors knew how good it would be to get a role on the show. It was immensely popular and we welcomed the exposure as well as the opportunity to work with a truly original script. At the time, of course, I had no idea *The Twilight Zone* would become a classic series."

Jack Grinnage portrays Henry, the jumpy young coworker who introduces the title tome to Beechcroft. The actor was no stranger to comedy or episodic

445

television when the episode was filmed. Already thirty years of age, Grinnage's boyish looks allowed him to fashion a career playing clumsy and youthful characters. He went on to play another prissy office worker as Ron Updyke, straight man to Carl Kolchak in the cult series *Kolchak, The Night Stalker*.

"Playing Henry was fun," says Grinnage of the character who accidentally douses Beechcroft with a beverage on three separate occasions. "I usually played the typical young man, the 'office boy' type. I played nineteen while I was thirty-eight. I like playing those nervous sort of people who don't understand what they're doing and drop everything. Most of the things I had done prior to *The Twilight Zone* were light comedy."

When he discovers the power of concentration, Beechcroft engages in antics that are clever and fun. It's easy to side with the frustrated curmudgeon when he uses his newfound skill in ways that would tempt us all. What big-city commuter hasn't daydreamed about wishing away throngs of fellow travelers to ride an empty subway in quiet repose? Who wouldn't like to control the weather, or dismiss a rent collector with a flash of thought? The secret Beechcroft trapped within each of us marvels at the endless possibilities.

"The character," explains Berman, "has no special powers. He was simply an unhappy office worker who, through circumstances he could not explain, was granted a fervent wish; that everyone would be like himself."

A precursor to this script, and a possible influence on Serling, is the 1937 film THE MAN WHO COULD WORK MIRACLES. Based on a short story by H.G. Wells, the film tells introduces three gods who debate the effects of granting complete and absolute power to a human being. George McWhirter Fortheringay, the recipient of this "gift," attempts to use his power to help others but finds that his well-intentioned efforts often backfire. The film puts a comedic spin on the Wells story in much the same fashion as Serling's "The Mind and the Matter."

The moral code of *The Twilight Zone* would normally demand strict punishment for such a blatant attempt at playing God, but because the episode is a comedy, Beechcroft is given a pass. This is one of the reasons why the script works so well with a lighthearted approach. A straightforward exploration of such complete power would be difficult to stage and simply not as interesting. Freed from all physical boundaries, a serious main character would merely create a perfect personal existence from the outset. But Archibald Beechcroft thinks small. He tends to his petty, momentary concerns, failing to see the big picture, and viewers get to indulge in a bit of vicarious wish fulfillment.

Pardoned at last from a world packed with the humanity he despises, our malcontent anti-hero proceeds to haunt himself. Beechcroft is not devoid of a conscience and Serling brings it out in a literal sense. As the monotony of solitude weighs on him, Beechcroft's alter ego—in the form of an interactive reflection—visits repeatedly. The results are amusing as Berman's character is forced to keep company with himself and face his own shortcomings.

The dual exposure and split-screen work in these scenes is handled beautifully. Berman's reactions to his own character were filmed separately and added in at a later point, during post-production. The timing, lighting and synchronization of details such as eye contact all hit the mark, combining to give the illusion that Beechcroft really is talking to an alternate self.

"They had difficulty with the reverse shots," remembers Jack Grinnage, "and where he was looking when he played himself in the mirror. So where he needed to look, to the right of the camera or the left of the camera, that was a problem."

When Berman acted opposite his nonexistent doppelganger, it was Grinnage who fed him the lines of the reflected image to maintain timing and rhythm. "When he was playing to himself, I was him," laughs Grinnage. "He'd say to me, 'No, no, no, I wouldn't read the line that way.' And the director would say, 'No Shelley, it's okay, *you're* going to do the line.' Shelley would come back with 'But *I* wouldn't give it that inflection.'"

Although Henry appears on screen only in sporadic bursts of ham-fisted nervousness, Grinnage was hired for the entire shoot. "I was there every day. Because of the size of the part I ordinarily wouldn't be, but I played Shelley's scenes and I ran lines with him. Both ways, Beechcroft's actual character and Beechcroft's reflection. It was fun because I was on the whole extent of the show."

The cranky conversations with his duplicate should have caused Beechcroft to realize that he simply cannot live with himself. But he fails to take the clue and instead decides to repopulate the world with clones of the one person he thinks he can stomach: Archibald Beechcroft, Esquire. So begins the final act and Beechcroft's ample helping of humble pie.

A city full of Archibald Beechcrofts leads to encounters that are predicable, but entertaining and well-coordinated. One particularly successful shot tracks a progression of griping, petulant workers—all Berman, of course, as both male and female facsimiles of Beechcroft—as they mumble their grievances to and about the surrounding office personnel.

"The most interesting shot I remember," recalls Grinnage, "was when Shelley appears and the camera pans, and he's at this desk, then he's at this desk, then he's at this desk. They had to chain the camera down. They actually chained the camera to the floor with big chains. Shelley would do his stuff, they'd stop, he'd get up and go change, sit back down and the camera would continue."

Far less successful was the attempt to incorporate several Beechcrofts within a single camera frame. To avoid using costly and time-consuming optical effects, makeup legend William Tuttle crafted latex masks of Shelley Berman's face that were worn by extras.

"For me," Berman says, "the strangest experience was the business of everyone having to look like me. A life mask was made of my face and head. My entire head was covered with Plaster of Paris. Drinking straws were fitted into my nostrils so I could breathe. It was a slow, claustrophobic process.

"Ultimately, the rubberized masks of my head and face were utilized in various scenes. One was in the subway where a slew of extras wearing the masks, looking like me, piled into the train and moved off. It was the eeriest thing I'd ever seen. The masks were not perfect. The faces were immobile, rather inhuman. Even worse," Berman jokes, "up until that shooting day I had no idea how homely I was."

"I thought the masks were dreadful," Grinnage adds. "Now they have great masks you go buy at the store, but these didn't have much definition in them. They were slit in the back and the hair was molded on them. The people just put them on their heads and looked through these eyes that didn't even match."

For all the effort and expense to produce the masks, they were used only briefly, undoubtedly due to the disappointing appearance of the effect. This single flaw is hardly fatal, however, and does little to detract from the charm of the episode. Both Jack Grinnage and Shelley Berman praise the show and the series as a whole.

"I was delighted to do a *Twilight Zone*," Grinnage says, "because it was the top show at the time. It was very pleasant. Shelley was nice and friendly. I saw Rod filming his intros, a very dynamic person. Buzz Kulik was really wonderful. Everyone was extremely nice."

"It was a great script," Berman notes. "During the shooting Rod remained pretty much out of the way, allowing his director Buzz Kulik to do his job. The three of us met on the first day of shooting and one more time to discuss a writing change. It was a wonderful show to appear on. I worked with fine actors and with an excellent director. I recall the experience as one of the most delightful of my career."

The Twilight Zone

THE DUMMY

Airdate: 5-4-1962

Manuscript Date: N/A

Adapted from an original story by
Leon Polk

Episode Ninety-Eight

THE TWILIGHT ZONE

"THE DUMMY"

Written by

Rod Serling

Adapted from an
original story

by

Leon Polk

"THE DUMMY"

FADE ON:

1.   STANDARD OPENING: "SATELLITE TOP" DISAPPEARING INTO   1.
      DISTANCE; TWILIGHT ZONE LETTERING APPEARS AND THEN
      DISINTEGRATES.

      PAN DOWN TO OPENING SHOT OF SHOW.

2.   INT. SMALL NIGHT CLUB   2.

      as seen from a dinky upraised stage looking out at
      what is the first tier of tables spotlighted by the
      stage lights. Sitting on the bare platform on a chair
      with a DUMMY on his lap, is JERRY ETHERSON - a tall
      man, attractive, in his middle thirties. He has the
      very careful nonchalance of a professional entertainer,
      and this image is only imperceptively marred by the
      perspiration and a very small sense of tension that
      permeates the give and take between himself and the
      little wooden creation on his knee.

3.   CLOSE ANGLE   JERRY AND WILLY   3.

      on his lap.

                         JERRY
                Well, we're certainly happy to be
                here tonight -

                         WILLY
                (brash, bright,
                ridiculous)
                Speak for yourself, jerky -

                         JERRY
                That's Jerry -

                         WILLY
                (looking at the crowd
                and winking)
                Every dummy to his own taste.

                         JERRY
                (grabbing him and
                shaking him)
                Now, cut that out!

      They continue the colloquy, and it stays underneath as
      the CAMERA starts a PAN AROUND the first tier of tables,
      winding up on a SHOT of SERLING sitting alone at one
      of them.

3. CONTINUED   3.

                          SERLING
              You're watching a ventriloquist
              named Jerry Etherson - a voice
              thrower par excellence. His
              alter ego, sitting atop his lap,
              is a brash stick of kindling
              with the sobriquet, "Willy".
              In a moment, Mr. Etherson and
              his knotty pine partner will
              come up with some gags not to
              be found in a script; some
              straight lines that are less
              a part of a night club then a
              nightmare, for Jerry Etherson
              and Willy are about to be booked
              into one of the out-of-the-way
              bistros - that small, dark,
              intimate place known as...
              The Twilight Zone.

                                        FADE TO BLACK:

OPENING BILLBOARD
FIRST COMMERCIAL

ACT ONE

FADE ON:

4.   INT. NIGHT CLUB   ANOTHER ANGLE SHOT   4.

looking down on Jerry and Willy as they continue toward
the end of the act.

                    WILLY
          Awright...awright...let go of the
          suit - I'm getting out of here!

                    JERRY
          Now, Willy...please, Willy...
          control yourself. Really - you
          can't go now. That's impossible.
          Now, look - I apologize. Whatever
          I did, I didn't mean it.

                    WILLY
               (goggling at the
               audience)
          Oh, no? Oh, no? Just tell me
          this, wise guy. You did admit
          you were superstitious, didn't
          you?

                    JERRY
          Well...on occasion -

                    WILLY
          But you don't throw salt over
          your shoulder or cross your
          fingers or anything like that -
          now, do you?

                    JERRY
          Well...no...

                    WILLY
          No, wise guy. Tell me what it is
          you do.

Jerry looks around, shrugs, and then taps Willy on
the head.

                    JERRY
          I knock wood!

There is much laughter from the audience.

                    WILLY
               (exploding in anger)
          There! You did it again!

4.   CONTINUED   4.

He makes a motion as if leaving the lap, and Jerry has
to pull him back.

                        WILLY (CONT'D)
              I'm through! I resign!   From now
              on I'm a single. As for you...you
              can turn in your lap!

                                            CUT TO:

5 to 7.   SEVERAL DIFFERENT SHOTS OF THE AUDIENCE   5. to

as they laugh.

8.   ANGLE SHOT   8.

looking up over the footlights toward the entertainer.
This is perhaps the first time that the dummy's face,
as seen from this angle, is devoid of any humor. The
glaring over-large eyes, the grimacing mouth, the
absurd tuxedo, carry with them a special grotesquery.

                        JERRY
              Now, listen, Willy. I mean...
              be reasonable about this...think
              about it some. What in the world
              could you do without me?

                        WILLY
              Well, for one thing - I could be
              a better ventriloquist. Watch this!

At this moment Willy shuts his mouth and Jerry opens
his, and it is Willy's voice that floats out.

                        JERRY
                   (as Willy sings)
              I can do anything better than
              you can - I can do anything
              better than you.

                        WILLY
                   (as Jerry sings)
              No you can't.

                        JERRY
                   (as Willy sings)
              Yes I can.

They continue the refrain of the song, each picking
up the other part.

                                            CUT TO:

9 to 11.   SHOTS OF THE CUSTOMERS   9 to 11

   as they eat this up. At the end of the song, the o.s.
   orchestra hits a note of finality. Jerry rises with
   Willy in his arms and both bow to a massive round of
   applause.

12.   TWO SHOT   JERRY AND WILLY   12.

                    JERRY
          Willy...I think it would be very
          nice if you would say goodnight
          to all these wonderful people.

                    WILLY
               (blinks at him and
               then at the audience)
          You can do anything I can do better?
          Awright, wise guy - can you do this?

   He turns his head around completely, to the delight
   of the audience, then goggles at them again.

                    WILLY (CONT'D)
          Come around tomorrow night, folks.
          I'll be alone. Just you and me -

                    JERRY
               (with an obviously
               strained smile)
          Come on, little pal - we're
          cutting out.

                    WILLY
               (ignoring the ventriloquist)
          Let me tell you something, folks.
          When I shake this busher and get
          me a real act - you're gonna see
          some class.

13.   CLOSE SHOT   JERRY   13.

   The smile remains fixed.

                    JERRY
          Let's go, Willy. We don't want
          to overstay our welcome.

                    WILLY
               (throws back his head and
               lets out a peal of idiotic
               laughter)
          What welcome, jerk?

14.   CLOSER ANGLE   JERRY   14.

   The sweat pours down his face. He grabs the dummy more
   tightly and starts to back into the curtains.

14. CONTINUED   14.

                              JERRY
                    Goodnight, everyone - thanks for
                    being such a wonderful -

                              WILLY
                         (shouting)
                    Help! I'm being kidnapped! Call
                    my lawyer - call my doctor! Never
                    mind - just get me to the nurse
                    on time.

15. CLOSE TWO SHOT   15.

     as they reach the fold in the center of the curtain.
     Just as Jerry backs through he claps his hand over
     Willy's mouth, shutting the dummy off, while the
     audience applauds and cheers.

                                        CUT TO:

16. SHOT OF THE STAGE   16.

     behind the curtain.As Jerry backs in, he lets out a
     stifled shout, pulls his hand from the dummy's mouth,
     looks briefly at a STAGEHAND surveying him, then
     hurries off to the right toward his dressing room.

                                        CUT TO:

17. INT. DRESSING ROOM   17.

     as Jerry enters and slams the door shut. He deliberately
     keeps his eyes away from Willy, puts him down on a chair
     near the door, then crosses to a small makeup table and
     mirror. He sits down heavily, closes his eyes, then
     slowly lifts up his hand and stares at it.

                                        CUT TO:

18. TIGHT CLOSE SHOT   HIS PALM   18.

     There are two rows of teeth marks.

                                        CUT TO:

19. SHOT OVER JERRY'S SHOULDER   19.

     into the mirror. We SEE his reflection and that of
     Willy's, sitting in the chair, his eyes fixed on the
     back of the ventriloquist. The CAMERA ARCS AROUND so
     that it is SHOOTING directly into Jerry's face. He
     takes some tissue and starts to wipe away the makeup,
     but every moment or two his eyes travel right to stare
     at the reflection of the dummy.

                                        CUT TO:

20. ANOTHER SHOT OVER JERRY'S SHOULDER   20.

     into the mirror. He finishes removing the makeup,
     again stares at Willy's reflection in the mirror.

21. EXTREMELY TIGHT CLOSE SHOT   JERRY'S REFLECTION   21.

     in the mirror, staring. PAN ACROSS the mirror to:

22. CLOSE SHOT OF WILLY'S REFLECTION   22.

     as the eyes of both figures meet and lock. It is
     Jerry who has to break away.

23. ANOTHER ANGLE   DRESSING TABLE   23.

     as Jerry, his hand shaking, pulls open a bottom drawer,
     takes out a bottle of whisky, takes a long thirsty
     compulsive gulp, then sits up straight, puts his head
     back, breathes deeply and for a moment seems to relax.
     Then his features set and once again his eyes move up
     to the mirror where once again we SEE the dummy staring
     at him. Again there is a battle of wills and finally
     Jerry, defeated and close to a breaking point, whirls
     around, knocking a cold cream jar onto the floor.

                                        CUT TO:

24. A SHOT OF HIM   24.

     across the room, as seen from the now open door, as
     his agent, FRANK GAINES stands there and then hurriedly
     closes the door behind him. Frank looks around the room,
     spots the cold cream jar on the floor, the liquor bottle
     on the dressing table, then the dummy sitting in the chair.
     He crosses over to a couch and sits down, lighting a
     cigarette.

                         FRANK
               What do you say, maestro?

                         JERRY
                    (nods)
               How did it look, Frank?

                         FRANK
               Not bad. Small audience, but a happy
               one. There weren't any complaints.

     He leans across and chucks the dummy under the chin.

                         FRANK (CONT'D)
               What do you say, boobie -

     Jerry jumps to his feet, his voice icy.

                         JERRY
               Frank, I've told you not to do that!

                         FRANK
                    (turns to him, his
                    smile fading)
               You still on the bit, huh?

                         JERRY
                    (turning away
                    from him)
               Knock it off, Frank.

                         FRANK
               Still with your heebie-jeebies -
               still with your bottle -
                    (he shakes his head)
               - still mistaking a little white
               lightning for some black magic.
                    (he points to the
                    bottle, meaningfully)
               You know, palsie, I've seen some
               fast skids in this town. One day
               they're headliners and comes the
               dawn, they're some soggy has-beens
               that live out of scrapbooks. Now,
               I thought we'd talked about this.
               I thought you gave me a solemn
               promise you were gonna do your
               drinking out of soda pop bottles
               and coffee jugs. What's it take,
               Jerry, to get you wise?

                         JERRY
               I'm tired, Frank, and I don't feel
               well. Give me a break and clear
               the area, will you?

                         FRANK
               First I'd like to clear the air.
                    (he rises)
               Palsie, I don't know where you
               manufacture all your illusions,
               but you're not Edgar Bergen and
               you're not Shari Lewis. At the
               moment, you're a second rate night
               club entertainer -and if you stay
               on that bottle, you're gonna lose
               even that rating.

                         JERRY
                    (sitting at the table)
               I'll put the bottle away, I promise.
               Just pull out.

          Frank moves a step closer to him.

24. CONTINUED (2)

>   FRANK
>   I've only got about two minutes
>   of dialogue left. I don't even
>   know why I waste my time. Ten
>   per cent of you is grief, and
>   it's always been that way. Maybe
>   it's just because I've got a soft
>   spot in my heart for people who
>   commit suicide eight hours a day.
>   (his tone changes and
>   there is more compassion
>   now)
>   Jerry...it doesn't have to be this
>   way. You give in to some bad hooch
>   and then you have bad nightmares.
>   It's as simple as that. Take away
>   the hooch - and you take away the
>   nightmares. Now, do you need a
>   college degree to figure that out?

Jerry whirls around at him, his voice shaking.

>   JERRY
>   You've got the chronology wrong.
>   First it's the nightmares...then
>   it's the bottle. I wouldn't drink
>   if I didn't need to, and I wouldn't
>   be a second rate night club hustler
>   if that filthy, miserable little -

He rises and points a finger toward Willy. His hands
shake and he forces them down to his sides. He turns,
again facing the mirror, shuts his eyes tightly, and
it's a moment before he can speak again.

>   JERRY (CONT'D)
>   Frank...I keep telling you. I've gotta
>   get rid of him. I have to get rid of him.

Frank looks briefly at the dummy, then back to Jerry.

>   FRANK
>   The stick of wood? The fugitive
>   from the fireplace? How many
>   psychiatrists do you have to see,
>   Jerry? How many hours on the couch
>   does it require? How many twenty-
>   buck-an-hour visits?

>   JERRY
>   (half shouting)
>   I can't help it -

>   FRANK
>   (out-shouting him)
>   You can help it. You know what
>   it is. You've been told!

24. CONTINUED (3)   24.

                        JERRY
                (sitting down, half
                burying his face in
                his hands, through
                gritted teeth)
        Often. Endlessly. Up to my cr? ↗
        and overflowing. Schizophrenia.
        I know it by heart. "Patient feels
        helpless and manipulated by forces
        beyond his control".
                (he slams his fist
                down on the table)
        I could give it to you backwards,
        forwards, sidewards, and in three
        different languages. It's like a
        well-rehearsed off-color joke. So
        the "patient makes the step between
        himself and his lifeless dummy, but
        is then unable to separate himself
        from that dummy".
                (he's on his feet
                again)
        Now, that's all very psychiatric
        and erudite - and it's worth about
        two and a half bucks a word.
                (then, screaming)
        But that's not it, Frank! I told
        them and I've told you - it isn't
        schizophrenia or paranoia anymore
        than it's athletes foot and a head
        cold.

He grabs Frank, pulls him to him. Now his voice is
quieter but intense, almost to the point of breaking.

                        JERRY (CONT'D)
        Willy is alive, Frank! I tell you,
        he's alive -

Frank slams his own hands down to break Jerry's grip.

                        FRANK
        Willy is a dummy! He's a piece
        of wood!

Frank whirls around, grabs Willy off the chair and
holds him out at an arm's length.

                        FRANK (CONT D)
        Look at him! Does this thing look
        alive to you?
                (he shakes the dummy)
        Twenty four inches of lumber and
        you're shoveling yourself into a
        grave over it!

24. CONTINUED (4)   24.

He throws Willy back on the sofa, turns to face Jerry.

                    FRANK (CONT'D)
          Now, listen to me, Jerry. I've
          gone along with you. I've held
          your hand and I've sung you lulla-
          bies and I've patted you on the
          back. I've also covered for you
          the hundred and ten times you've
          run out on a performance. I've
          thought up excuses that haven't
          even been invented yet. I've
          gone without sleep and without
          commission, because I thought I
          had a talented article here who
          eventually was going to crawl out
          from under a bottle and hit it big.
          Well, I don't think you're such a
          talented article anymore, Jerry.
          Or, , let's put it this way. Maybe
          I think you could be - but you're
          never going to. I think you're a
          self-indulgent sot with an overactive
          imagination, and the only thing you
          like better than scotch is sympathy!
              (he turns and walks
              toward the door)
          Well, I'm just gonna give you just
          twenty four hours to straighten out.
          Get rid of the bottle and get rid of
          that crazy obsession that you're
          battling a dummy!

25. CLOSE SHOT   JERRY   25.

His mouth and features work. His eyes look haunted,
wild and paranoiac.

                    JERRY
              (in almost a whisper,
              as he moves across
              the room)
          Frank...Frank...Frank...it isn't
          just a dummy.
              (then, shouting)
          I tell you, it isn't just a dummy!

He whirls around and goes over to a trunk. He unbuckles
it fiercely, wildly - kicks the top open and pulls out
a ragged little hillbilly FIGURE wearing glasses.

                    JERRY
          This is his replacement. This
          takes the place of Willy.

26. CLOSE SHOT   FRANK   26.

      who stares at it, then over at Willy, then up to Jerry.

                          FRANK
                  Go on.

                          JERRY
                  That's it. I'm gonna scrap -
                      (he points toward
                      Willy)
                  I'm gonna get rid of him. I'll
                  do a whole new routine.

                          FRANK
                  A whole new routine takes time.
                  You've got another show in a
                  half hour.

                          JERRY
                  I won't be able to go on for the
                  late show. Tell 'em...tell 'em
                  I'm sick or something.

                          FRANK
                  I've told them you're sick or
                  something. The trouble is, they
                  know it's something. And they
                  know something is bottled in bond.
                      (he opens the door)
                  You be out on that stage when you
                  hear your music. I don't care
                  which dummy you bring, but you
                  be out there. This is one I'm
                  not covering for!

      He walks out and slams the door behind him.

27. MOVING SHOT   JERRY   27.

      as with tight sporadic motions he moves back over to
      the trunk, reaches down and picks up the other dummy.
      He carries it over to the dressing table, props it up
      against the mirror, then stares at it.

28. SHOT OF THE MIRROR   28.

      We SEE both "Goofy" and his reflection. And beyond
      him, lying on the couch where he's been thrown, the
      figure of Willy.

28. CLOSER ANGLE OF JERRY   28.

      as he starts to apply makeup, looks over at the other
      dummy.

28. CONTINUED   28.

                         JERRY
                 (shakily and obviously
                 improvising)
         Say...ah...say, Goofy Goggles, why
         don't you have your glasses fixed?
                 (then as Goofy)
         Are you kidding? I don't have to.
         My eyes are better now.
                 (then as Jerry)
         Goofy...you're talking to the
         band leader. I'm over here.
                 (then as Goofy)
         Keep talking - I'll find you.

He puts Goofy on his lap and concentrates on him.

                         JERRY
                 (as Goofy)
         Say, Etherson, I've been meaning
         to tell you. You put too much
         starch in my collars.
                 (then as Jerry)
         Too much starch in your collars?
         Listen, Goofy, I'm not your laundry
         man.
                 (then in a different
                 tone - intense, suggest-
                 ing a resolve that has
                 been dredged up from
                 a pit)
         We're going to make it! You and me...
         nobody else. Just you and me.

Still cradling Goofy in his arms, he rises and is about
to turn to move across the room when his eyes turn in
the direction of the mirror. His face goes white, his
mouth opens. He lets out one short frantic gasp. WHIP
PAN OVER to the mirror. SHOT of Willy's reflection.
He is no longer lying down but is sitting up against
the back of the couch, hands in his lap, his strange
painted little eyes glitter brightly, staring back
at Jerry. PULL BACK FOR:

29. SHOT OF JERRY   29.

as he whirls around facing Willy. His voice sounds choked.

                         JERRY
              You _moved_! _YOU_ _MOVED_!

A SLOW PAN OVER to Willy. One painted wooden eye
slowly winks.

30.   CLOSE SHOT   JERRY   30.

        as he turns away, slamming against the dressing table.
        The force of his body pushes the table hard and breaks
        the center mirror. He looks down at one large fragment
        of glass propped up against the wall. CAMERA ZOOMS IN
        for a SHOT of the glass and the reflection of Willy
        inside of it, sitting there, staring malevolent, accusing -
        and at this moment, strangely human.

                                        FADE TO BLACK

        END OF ACT ONE.

ACT TWO

FADE ON:

31.　INT. BACKSTAGE　　NIGHT　　　　　　　　　　　　31.

STAGEHANDS and CHORUS GIRLS move back and forth as
the CAMERA MOVES IN on a SHOT of Jerry's dressing
room door. It opens and he comes out carrying Goofy.
TWO CHORUS GIRLS, seeing him, stop and move toward
him. Noreen grabs hold of the other girl.

                    NOREEN
          Margie - listen to this - this'll
          knock you out.
               (to Jerry)
          Make me talk, Jerry. Go ahead.
          Watch this, Marge.

                    JERRY
               (tiredly, his face
               showing the strain
               through the makeup,
               his eyes haggard)
          I'm due on in a couple of minutes,
          Noreen. How about after the show?

                    NOREEN
          Aw, c'mon. Watch this, Marge. He
          makes me sound just like Willy.
          It's real crazy. Go ahead, Jerry.

She makes a gesture, chucking him under the chin.
He pulls away from her, and at that moment we HEAR
Willy's VOICE from inside the dressing room.

                    WILLY'S VOICE
          Knock it off, babe - that tickles.

                    JERRY
               (whirling around,
               shouting at the
               closed door)
          Cut that out!

The two girls convulse in laughter.

                    NOREEN
          What did I tell yuh, huh? What
          did I tell yuh? Isn't he wild?

At this moment there is the SOUND of an orchestra
playing an introductory fanfare.

                    A VOICE (o.s.)
               (calling)
          Etherson - you're on.

31. CONTINUED   31.

Jerry pushes his way through the two girls and on toward
the wings.

32. CLOSE TWO SHOT   NOREEN AND MARGE

as Noreen crooks her finger at Marge, then opens the door
to Jerry's dressing room.

33. SHOT THROUGH THE TEN INCH OPENING   33.

We SEE Willy sitting on the sofa staring straight ahead.

DISSOLVE TO:

34. INT. NIGHT CLUB   NIGHT   34.

PAN SHOT AROUND the room as a fairly noisy little crowd
divides its attention with drinking and conversation
along with a rather perfunctory reaction to the ventriloquist on the stage.

CUT TO:

35. TWO SHOT   JERRY AND GOOFY   35.

who blinks through his idiotic spectacles.

                    JERRY
          Now, listen, Goofy. I think it's
          about time you had your glasses
          fixed. I really do.

                    GOOFY
          I don't have to. My eyes are much
          better now.

                    JERRY
          Goofy, you're talking to the band
          leader - I'm over here.

Goofy half rises out of Jerry's lap, staring around
wildly.

                    GOOFY
          Keep talking - I'll find you.

There is mild laughter from the crowd.

                    JERRY
          You know something? I think you ought
          to have an eye test.

                    GOOFY
          An eye test?

                    JERRY
          That's right - an eye test.

GOOFY
(blinking at the
audience)
I'm at your disposal.

JERRY
Okay.

He pulls out a big card with an enormous "E" on it.

JERRY (CONT'D)
Now, what does this say?

GOOFY
Where?
(he turns his head and
runs smack into it)
Oh...that thing...uh...how about
a hint?

JERRY
(looking helplessly at
the audience)
Come on, Goofy. It's right there
in front of you as plain as day.

GOOFY
Just give me a hint.

JERRY
Okay. It's a letter that's between
"D" and "F".

GOOFY
(rolling his eyes up,
making extravagant
gestures, finally
pounces on it)
I've got it! It's "E".

JERRY
I don't know how you did it!

GOOFY
I cannot tell a lie. I saw that
card before and I memorized it!

JERRY
(with a look at the
audience and responding
to the sporadic laughter)
Oh, for goodness sake! Just finish
your song and let's get out of here.

> GOOFY
> (clears his throat and
> then starts to sing
> "I Only Have Eyes For You")
>
> "You are here...so am I...maybe
> millions of people go by...and
> they all disappear from view..."

> JERRY
> With that voice it's no wonder
> they're disappearing...for the
> exits!

> GOOFY
> I'll make the jokes - you just
> move your lips.

He continues to sing as the CAMERA MOVES OVER to
Frank and the owner of the night club, GEORGIE,
who stand in the shadows near the bar.

36.   TWO SHOT   FRANK AND GEORGIE   36.

> FRANK
> (with a forced smile)
> Cute act, isn't it, Georgie?

> GEORGIE
> (looks at him fix-eyed)
> What's cute about it? Besides that -
> I like the old dummy better. Why did
> he change it?

> FRANK
> (improvising)
> You know - brighten it up a little bit -
> gives it some novelty.

> GEORGIE
> Novelty? With a ventriloquist?
> Frankie - you've seen one, you've
> seen 'em all. Every dummy looks
> the same -and if just once they'd
> change the jokes, I'd have a coronary.
> What's with Etherson anyway?

> FRANK
> (playing it dumb)
> What do you mean?

> GEORGIE
> (lighting a cigarette)
> Well, usually the acts will go mix
> with the trade. You know...you know...
> walk out on the floor and do a little
> drinking with the customers. This

> (MORE)

36. CONTINUED   36.

                              GEORGIE (CONT'D)
                    guy plays it like Greta Garbo.
                    Locks himself up in his room and
                    he's a prima donna.

                              FRANK
                         (still forcing a
                          smile)
                    Oh, he's a little nervous tonight,
                    Georgie . You know, he hasn't been
                    well and this is his first time out
                    in a month or so - but he'll warm
                    up for you.

                              GEORGIE
                         (as he moves away)
                    You tell him to. Tell him to bring
                    the dummy out and walk around the
                    tables after the show. It's psycho-
                    logical, Frankie - makes people
                    thirsty.

          He moves away now, leaving Frank alone as the CAMERA
          MOVES BACK OVER to the stage as Goofy just finishes
          his song.

37. TWO SHOT   JERRY AND GOOFY

          Jerry rises and bows along with Goofy to some perfunctory
          applause. The band strikes up a few closing chords as
          Jerry moves back and then through the rear curtains.

                                             CUT TO:

38. FULL SHOT   BACKSTAGE   38.

          as Jerry walks past the line of SIX CHORUS GIRLS,
          Noreen leans over and gives Goofy a kiss, then giggles
          as Jerry yanks him away and continues toward his
          dressing room.

                                             DISSOLVE TO:

39. INT. DRESSING ROOM   39.

          Jerry has his makup off and is just putting on a top
          coat. Goofy sits on the couch limp and lifeless.
          Jerry walks over and looks into the trunk. CAMERA
          ARCS OVER his shoulder to stare down toward Willy,
          who lies at the bottom of the trunk. Willy is
          obliterated by the trunk lid closing.

40. ANOTHER ANGLE   JERRY   40.

          as he stares down at the closed trunk. He makes a
          couple of hesitant gestures then takes the big
          leather strap and buckles it securely around the trunk.

41. ANGLE SHOT LOOKING UP AT HIM   41.

His features work.

> JERRY
> Rest in peace, Pinoccio. Your next
> booking is going to be in a fireplace.

He turns, walks across the room and picks up Goofy.
He stares at the dummy's face, touching it as if
examining the texture, adjusting the idiotic glasses,
and then obviously is satisfied and throws another
look at the closed trunk, smiles grimly, nods, turns
to start out of the room when the door opens. Frank
stands there.

> FRANK
> (pointing to Jerry's
> top coat)
> You leaving?

> JERRY
> What's it look like?

> FRANK
> It looks like you're leaving. I
> waited for you after the last show.
> Georgie was hoping you'd mix with
> the customers.

> JERRY
> You tell Georgie I'm a ventriloquist,
> not a shill!

42. CLOSE SHOT   FRANK   42.

There is a silence.

> FRANK
> Why don't you tell him?

43. CLOSE SHOT   JERRY   43.

who looks up a little startled.

> JERRY
> And that means?

44. TWO SHOT   FRANK AND JERRY   44.

> FRANK
> That means that I'm resigning
> from the club. You keep your
> ten per cent - and I'll keep
> my self respect. Also my sense
> of humor, my regular meals, and
> my normal office hours. You and
> I have had it, Jerry. I have
> (MORE)

44. CONTINUED   44.

                         FRANK (CONT'D)
          gone the route and then some.
               (he shakes his head)
          You don't need an agent. You
          need some medical help. I think
          it's reached that now.

                         JERRY
          You never believed me, did you?

                         FRANK
          I believe you have obsessions. I
          believe that these obsessions are
          eating you up alive. But I also
          believe, Jerry, that you're letting
          them.

Jerry moves in closer to him.

                         JERRY
          Frank, he talks when I don't talk.
          He moves when I'm not looking. He
          tells jokes I've never even heard
          of. He steps all over my lines.
          He throws me bum cues, and then
          drowns out my gags.

He grabs Frank with his free hand and yanks him to him.

                         JERRY (CONT'D)
          Frank, he's real. He's alive.
          That's why I've had to stick
          him in that trunk. That's why
          I've had to lock it. I'm going
          to take Goofy and catch a plane
          outta here. I'll go down to Miami
          or maybe to Los Angeles. Frank,...
          what was that place in Kansas City
          that we did so well in -

Frank slowly releases Jerry's hand.

                         FRANK
          The place in Kansas City was the same
          as Miami, which is the same as Los
          Angeles, which is the same as Sioux
          City, Iowa, which is also the same as
          any town south, west, and north of here.
          They're all the same, Jerry. You're not
          gonna be able to leave Willy by hopping
          on a plane, train, taxi, or a one-horse
          shay. This thing you lick right here.
          This thing you lick at the source.
               (he shakes his head,
                his voice is quieter)
          This thing you just don't run away from.

45. CLOSE SHOT   JERRY   45.

     His lips tremble, his face is taut. He holds Goofy
     closer to him.

                         JERRY
               We'll see.

     He walks across the room past Frank and to the doorway
     and turns.

                         JERRY (CONT'D)
               We'll see, Frank. We'll just see.

     He turns and goes out the door.

                                        CUT TO:

46. INT. BACKSTAGE   MOVING SHOT   JERRY   46.

     as he walks toward the exit door. His face is grim,
     purposeful, resolved, and it's not until he reaches
     the door that suddenly his eyes go wide. He stops,
     whirls around, stares toward the curtains.

47. CLOSE SHOT   THE CURTAINS   47.

     They hang limp and motionless.

48. CLOSE SHOT   JERRY   48.

     as he frowns, wets his lips, closes his eyes and blinks
     for a moment, then turns and starts toward the door.
     An old grizzled DOORKEEPER looks up from reading a
     newspaper.

                         DOORKEEPER
               Goodnight, Mr. Etherson.

                         JERRY
               Goodnight.

     He turns his hand on the knob, starts to open the door,
     when he HEARS Willy's voice.

                         WILLY'S VOICE
                    (filtered)
               You're not going to leave me in this
               stuffy old trunk, are you?

49. CLOSER ANGLE   JERRY   49.

     as he whirls around, wide-eyed.

50. ANGLE SHOT OVER HIS SHOULDER   50

     toward the doorkeeper, who looks up.

50. CONTINUED   50.

                        DOORKEEPER
            Something was there, Mr. Etherson?

                        JERRY
            Did you...did you just say something?

                        DOORKEEPER
            I just said goodnight, that's all.

                        JERRY
                  (nods, his voice
                   strained)
            Sure. Sure. Goodnight.

He walks out.

                                    CUT TO:

51. EXT. ALLEY   NIGHT   51.

      as Jerry comes out the backstage exit, still carrying
      Goofy. He walks down the concrete steps, pauses for
      a moment, reaches into his pocket and takes out a
      pack of cigarettes, lights one, leans against the
      railing of the stairway. Again he HEARS Willy's voice.

                        WILLY'S VOICE
            Oh, c'mon, old sport. I wouldn't
            lock you in a trunk.

52. CLOSE SHOT   JERRY   52.

      as again he whirls around to stare toward the door.

                        JERRY
            Where are you?
                  (then, screaming)
            Willy, where are you!

                                    CUT TO:

53. SHOT OF STAGE DOOR   53.

      as it opens. TWO CHORUS GIRLS come out, walk down the
      steps.

                        GIRL #1
            Goodnight, Jerry.

                        JERRY
                  (breathing heavily)
            Goodnight...goodnight.

The girls look at one another a little strangely then
continue to walk on down the alley. Jerry watches them
for a moment then, still lugging Goofy, he starts to
follow them.

                                    CUT TO:

54.   LONG ANGLE SHOT   54.

looking down, as he walks.

CUT TO:

55.   CLOSER ANGLE OF HIM   55.

walking.

CUT TO:

56.   SHOT OF HIS FEET   56.

Suddenly mixed in with the SOUND of his own footsteps
is the SOUND of yet another set. Jerry's feet stop.
CAMERA PANS UP for a SHOT of him as he listens, whirls
around again and stares down the alley.

57.   SHOT OVER HIS SHOULDER   DOWN THE ALLEY   57.

It's completely empty and dark save for the single
yellow light over the stage door.

58.   CLOSE SHOT   JERRY   58.

as he shuts his eyes tightly.

                       WILLY'S VOICE
              Hey, Garabaldi! Didn't you forget
              someone? Didn't you forget Willy?

Again Jerry whirls around. He looks left and right
and up and down, then shuts his eyes again tightly,
fiercely.

59.   ANGLE SHOT   59.

as he starts to walk more briskly out toward the alley.
After a moment the walk becomes a dead run. Again,
suddenly he stops abruptly, whirls around and stares.

60.   ANGLE SHOT OVER HIS SHOULDER   60.

The wall of the building alongside. There, in silhouette -
massive and enveloping, is the shadow of Willy playing on
the wall.

61.   CLOSE SHOT   JERRY   61.

as he opens his mouth as if to scream, then clamps his
teeth down on his lower lip, cutting it off. At this
moment there are footsteps approaching. He backs into
the shadows, the light falling across his eyes. They
look like fathomless pits of fear as the footsteps get
closer.

CUT TO:

62. ANOTHER ANGLE OF THE ALLEY   62.

     as we SEE Noreen, the chorus girl, walking alone toward
     him. She stops and peers into the darkness, then looks
     relieved.

                          NOREEN
               Jerry?

     Jerry steps out into the partial light. His features
     show a massive relief. It is obvious now that at this
     moment he is totally unable to face things by himself.

                          JERRY
               Noreen...Noreen...I was waiting
               for you. Yes, that's right. I
               was waiting for you.

                          NOREEN
                    (smiles at him)
               The line is - this is so sudden. And
               in this case, it happens to be sudden.
                    (she peers into the
                    darkness)
               Is that Willy with you?

                          JERRY
                    (his voice shaking)
               No, no, no - it's not Willy. I
               thought maybe...I thought maybe
               we could go get a drink together
               or a sandwich maybe.
                    (he takes a step
                    toward her, his move-
                    ments convulsive,
                    nervous, his voice
                    still shaking)
               You know, I've been meaning to tell
               you...I've been meaning to tell you...
               you're a nice looking kid. You're
               a real pretty girl. I'm not kidding
               you. You're a wonderful looking girl,
               and I was thinking we could have a
               drink or -

63. CLOSE SHOT   NOREEN   63.

     staring at him. The smile fades, an eyebrow goes up.

                          NOREEN
               What's the matter with you, Jerry?
               Are you sick?

                          JERRY
                    (the words spewing out
                    of him)
               What do you mean, sick? I just like
               your looks, that's all. I like to
               be with you.
                          (MORE)

63. CONTINUED   63.

                              JERRY (CONT'D)
                         (he moves closer
                         to her)
                    I just thought we could have a drink
                    or something.
                         (his voice breaks
                         wide open)
                    Noreen...Noreen...I can't be alone
                    now. He's bugging me. His voice
                    is coming out of everywhere. I
                    even see his shadow.
                         (then, screaming)
                    That Willy is bugging me!
                         (he grabs the girl)
                    Noreen, you've got to help me.
                    You've got to stay with me now.
                    I can't be alone now. I tell
                    you, that Willy -

The girl pulls away from him, frightened, and starts
to run. He starts after her, screaming.

                              JERRY
                    Noreen...Noreen...please...

He stops, whirls around.

64. LONG SHOT OVER HIS SHOULDER   THE STAGE DOOR   64.

He runs away from the CAMERA toward it.

                                             CUT TO:

65. INT. BACKSTAGE   65.

as Jerry comes in through the stage door. He stumbles
up the steps to the stage level, flings himself through
the curtains and winds up on the stage facing a totally
empty room.

                              WILLY'S VOICE
                    What do you say, stranger? You
                    slumming?

Jerry whirls around to stare at an empty chair on
the stage.

                              WILLY'S VOICE (CONT'D)
                    Funny thing happened to me on the
                    way over to the club tonight. I
                    was out in front of the Savoy Hotel -
                    that's where I live - out in front
                    of the Savoy Hotel.
                         (he breaks off into
                         a cackling laugh)

66.   CLOSE SHOT   JERRY   66.

      as he looks for the voice, goes back through the curtains.

67.   MOVING SHOT   67.

      as he stumbles through the backstage corridor to his
      dressing room, kicks open the door and moves inside.
      Willy's laughter continues sporadically. First it
      seems to come from one corner then the other - first
      behind the sofa then behind the open door.

68.   FULL SHOT   THE ROOM   68.

      as Jerry flings furniture, opens and shuts closets,
      throws things left and right, then stops and stares
      at the trunk.

                         WILLY'S VOICE
                    (cackling)
           Come out, come out, wherever you are!

      With feverish hands, Jerry unstraps the belt around
      the trunk, flings it open, dives inside with both hands.

69.   CLOSE SHOT   THE DOOR   69.

      as it swings shut, cutting out the corridor light.
      Inside, Jerry wrestles with the thing in his arms.
      We SEE him fling it to the floor, stepping on it a
      half dozen times and then after a moment it is quiet.
      Panting, half sobbing, he goes over to the door and
      opens it. A shaft of light from the corridor plays
      on the smashed remnants of the dummy on the floor.

                                  CUT TO:

70.   CLOSE SHOT   THE REMNANTS   70.

      and alongside of them, Goofy's cracked glasses. Jerry
      sinks to his knees and INTO THE FRAME, fingers in his
      mouth, stifling what is a sob, a scream, a protest.

                           JERRY
          The _wrong_ _one_. How could I get
          the wrong one?

                       WILLY'S VOICE
          Maybe you need glasses. Why
          don't you take the eye test?
          Now, what am I holding out in
          front of you? I'll give you a
          hint. It's between "D" and "F".
          Don't peek.

      Jerry slowly looks up and across to the couch. Willy
      sits there, his eyes gleaming balefully.

70. CONTINUED   70.

                           WILLY
                What do you say, partner? What do
                you say we get down to business.

71. REVERSE ANGLE   71.

    looking toward Jerry, Willy's POV.

                           JERRY
                     (in a whisper)
                How? How? You're a dummy. You're
                made of wood. Somebody built you.
                How can you be real?

72. CLOSE SHOT   WILLY   72.

    He throws back his head and laughs, rolls his eyes.

                           WILLY
                You jerk! You made me real.
                You spanked me to life. You
                gave me a brain. You poured
                words into my head. You moved
                my mouth. You stuck out my
                tongue. You jerk - don't you
                get it? You made me what I am
                today, I hope you're satisfied -
                from the song of the same name.

    He starts to laugh again as the CAMERA PANS DOWN to
    Jerry, who collapses on the floor crying.

                                     A SLOW DISSOLVE TO:

73. INT. NIGHT CLUB   NIGHT   73.

    A spotlight goes on pointing toward a small stage.
    An M.C. comes out.

                           M.C.
                And now, direct from New York City -
                the funniest pair of cuckoos you'll
                ever see - here in Kansas City or
                anyplace else....Jerry and Willy!
                Let's bring them on big, folks, and
                show them they're welcome!

    The crowd whistles and applauds as we

                                     CUT ABRUPTLY TO:

74. SHOT OF THE CURTAINS   74.

    parting. We're looking on the backs of a man and a
    dummy as they step into the light from backstage.
    The ventriloquist bows, as does the dummy, and then
    we HEAR the voices. Willy's voice is human, Jerry's
    voice has the hollow falsetto sound of the traditional
    dummy.

                    JERRY'S VOICE
          How do you do, folks - how do you do.
          Funny thing happened to me on the way
          over to the club tonight. I met this
          broad -

                    WILLY'S VOICE
          Now, c'mon, Jerry. You don't mean
          broad - you mean lady.

                    JERRY'S VOICE
          You just make the jokes - I'll deliver
          them.

The audience laughs as we PAN AROUND until we're looking at
Willy, the ventriloquist, and on his lap - distorted, grotesque
a dummy that looks like Jerry. They launch into the typical
colloquy of the second rate night club act as the CAMERA starts
to MOVE AWAY.

                    SERLING'S VOICE
          What's known in the parlance of the
          times as the old switcheroo. From
          boss to blockhead in a few uneasy lessons.
          And if you're given to nightclubbing on
          occasion, check this act. It's called
          "Willy and Jerry" and they generally
          are booked into some of the clubs along
          the gray night way known as...The Twilight
          Zone.

                    - THE END -

WOODEN PERSONALITY

A fear of anthropomorphic dolls—especially those endowed with supernatural life and a malevolent personality—is deeply rooted in the human psyche. The cuddly Teddy Bear or the slightly creepy clown doll that comes to life in order to perform horrific acts of murder and mayhem is a common childhood nightmare. Horror tales—old and new—tap into this universal phobia. "The Dummy" is neither the first nor the last entry in the "possessed ventriloquist dummy" sub-genre of horror, but it is a well-crafted and chilling drama.

The ventriloquist dummy, a grotesque human caricature that often seems at odds with the person who manipulates it, provides fertile ground for a "loss of identity" tale. The typical ventriloquist act involves a playful, almost schizophrenic power struggle between man and mannequin. Only a small leap of faith is required to accept the innate horror of a dummy imbued with a life of its own waging a mental war to wrestle control from its human counterpart.

Stories of this type usually adhere to one of two distinct approaches: the mad ventriloquist or the preternaturally possessed dummy. Either the ventriloquist is an off-kilter, socially repressed psychotic who lives vicariously through an inanimate dummy, or it is the puppet itself that has come alive, unbeknownst to all save for the puppeteer. Serling's version, based on an unpublished story by Leon Polk, blends both of these tactics to fine effect.

Viewers are given early clues that could support either approach. Jerry Etherson is depicted as a recluse who shuns interaction with nightclub patrons. His obsession with Willy is no secret; Etherson has frequented a psychiatrist yet still insists that his dummy is alive. He also drinks to excess in order to escape

483

Willy's grip, calling into question his tenuous hold on reality. Yet we see the teeth marks from Willy's bite, and given the very nature of *The Twilight Zone* we already suspect that there's more to Willy than a master with a persecution complex.

While it doesn't take long for Willy to confirm our suspicions by moving and talking on his own, we are also left with a persistent, nagging feeling that perhaps we are viewing events through Etherson's skewed point of view. After all, no matter how real Willy seems to be, Etherson is the only true witness to his dummy's antics. No one else hears Willy's taunting voice, and the dummy's final speech could indeed be a manifestation of the ventriloquist's split personality. During the climactic scene, Serling even goes so far as to depict Willy as a shadow—an archetype of Jungian psychology—to symbolize the dualism of the ventriloquist.

This paranoid, isolated fear keeps Jerry Etherson, and the viewer, off balance. Are we viewing reality, or merely one man's psychotic delusions? Only when hit with the shock ending do we realize, quite unequivocally, that Willy is alive and well and in complete control of his "master."

The movie that seems to have directly inspired this *Twilight Zone* episode is 1945's DEAD OF NIGHT, a quintet of supernatural stories that culminates in a creepy segment entitled, simply, "Ventriloquist's Dummy." This battle of wills is a precursor to "The Dummy" in several aspects, including distorted camera angles, an alcoholic ventriloquist, and a scene in which the dummy's bite yields vivid impressions of its teeth. 1964's THE DEVIL DOLL would later unleash another living puppet while MAGIC (1978) would go the route of the psychotic-killer ventriloquist.

Serling's writing is taut and maintains a crisp pace. The show's success, however, is largely due to two factors: Cliff Robertson's nuanced lead performance and the eerie visual air supplied by director Abner Biberman and *Twilight Zone*'s director of photography, George T. Clemens.

Future Academy Award winner Cliff Robertson is riveting as the tortured ventriloquist. Frank Sutton offers able support as Etherson's manager but it is Robertson who shoulders the load. His initial on-stage scenes with Willy depict a man who clearly has lost control of his act. Later, Robertson convincingly shows the frustrations of a man who is progressively losing a battle with an improbable enemy. As much as Etherson would like to believe that his problems are in his mind, he simply knows better and sticks to his conviction that Willy is alive. Robertson does a particularly splendid job near the finale, when Etherson, desperate for an end to his madness, cracks and submits to Willy.

"Don't listen to that dummy," jokes Robertson about his wooden co-star. "Shooting the episode was a remarkably enjoyable experience. *The Twilight Zone* showed so much imagination. They had a puppeteer make my dummy directly from a photo. And Rod Serling was not only an incredible writer but a wonderful guy."

"That was the first time I had met Cliff Robertson," notes actor George Murdock, who makes a brief appearance as Willy in human form. "He was a nice guy and I was impressed and intimidated by his work and by him. It was early on in my career; I had just come from New York. At that time—I was so frightened of everything—I was fortunate enough to get a role in the show, and I worked hard and tried to give it my best. I was in such awe of everything around me in those days. I remember being so impressed, feeling so lucky, so happy."

Murdock has enjoyed a long, diverse career and is perhaps best known as Lt. Ben Scanlon in the hit comedy series *Barney Miller*. "The Dummy" marked his first television appearance. "There was such activity on that lot at that time," recalls Murdock of the MGM studio. "It was an incredible experience. A couple of months or so ago I was there and—as I am wont to do on many occasions when I've been on the lot—I walked past the location where we did the final scene. It used to exist but now that they've renovated so many of the streets, they've destroyed that particular area. It made me very sad that they had taken away a little of my history."

Actor and director Abner Biberman—making his *Twilight Zone* debut behind the camera in "The Dummy"—would go on to helm a total of four episodes. Born in Milwaukee, he migrated to Philadelphia to establish an acting career on the stage and eventually became a Broadway director. Biberman's shifty appearance eased his transition to the big screen, where he often portrayed ethnic villains. His roles include a fanatical East Indian in GUNGA DIN (1939), a small-time Italian hood in HIS GIRL FRIDAY (1940), and countless turns as a renegade Native American Indian.

As evidenced by shows such as *The Untouchables* and *The Outer Limits*, Biberman's directorial work favored the *film noir* feel of early black-and-white television, and "The Dummy" showcases his use of stark lighting and shadow. Intricate detail is also on display during the early dressing room scene, when prominent use is made of mirrors and reflected images as metaphors for Etherson's duality.

Perhaps more influential to the feel of the episode, and indeed the look of the series as a whole, is director of photography George T. Clemens. Plying his craft in such classics as DR. JEKYLL AND MR. HYDE (1931) and HOLLYWOOD BOULEVARD (1936), Clemens came out of retirement to work on *The Twilight Zone* and filmed the vast majority of the show's 156 episodes. In Robertson's climactic scene—the final battle with Willy—Clemens' camera twists and spins to impart a feeling of disorientation and loss of control. This distortion of the camera was a Clemens trademark and added to the warped, nightmarish look of a number of the series' most memorable shows. Rod Serling wasn't the only member of the *Twilight Zone* creative team to win the prestigious Emmy Award in 1961; Clemens also took home a statue for Outstanding Achievement in Cinematography.

"George was just marvelous," says *Twilight Zone* associate producer Del Reisman. "He had a sense of an 'other world' kind of situation, particularly in lighting. You always felt you were in another part of the forest. You were somewhere else. He was brilliant. He was very tough on the set, by the way. He was a real, wonderful veteran cameraman—as they were called in those days, a cameraman—and he knew what could be done. He knew the time that it would take to set up and light. He knew what his schedule was and Buck [Houghton, producer] was very strong on scheduling. Clemens was really a great strength on the set. He had a wonderful combination of old movie-making savvy and art."

Cliff Robertson's most vivid memory regarding "The Dummy" is an astonishing true story about his commute from New York. "I've never talked about this," the actor confides, "but I've been very lucky in life, in more ways than one, and one was dealing with that particular show. They said—as they are wont to do in Hollywood—that they wanted me out on a Friday night. It's the old 'Hurry up and wait.' And I looked at the schedule, and I called a few people, and they said, 'You know, they're not going to need you for about five days.' I didn't want to come out early and hang out.

"I called a friend of mine and I said, 'Listen, I don't want to argue with these people but they won't need me until at least Monday or Tuesday and I'm canceling the flight.' He said, 'Cliff, you're gonna catch hell.' I said, 'Well, there's nothing in the contract that says I have to be there and I think it's ridiculous.'"

At this point, Robertson's tale becomes worthy of its own *Twilight Zone* episode. "They had a reservation for American Airlines, Flight Number One, Friday morning, and I called up and I cancelled it. Flight Number One took off Friday morning as scheduled, right on time, got over the Great Jamaica Bay and the chief pilot had a heart attack. Everybody perished."

ACKNOWLEDGEMENTS

To Carol Serling, for support and encouragement every step of the way, and for sharing Rod Serling's work with the world.

To the colleagues and admirers of Rod Serling who graciously took the time and effort to share recollections and opinions for this volume: Denise Alexander, Richard L. Bare, Shelley Berman, Jean Carson, Ivan Dixon, Jack Grinnage, Kim Hamilton, Buck Houghton, Ron Masak, Richard Matheson, George Murdock, Rockne S. O'Bannon, Del Reisman, William Reynolds, John Rich, Cliff Robertson, William Self, Robert Stack, Maxine Stuart and Fritz Weaver.

To my friends and associates, old and new, for contributions and assistance with the myriad details involved in assembling this collection: Bridget Bower, Dorthea Christiansen, Evelyn Crystal, Christopher Conlon, Bill Devoe, Dwight Deskins, Barry Hoffman, Wanda Houghton, Earl Hamner, George Clayton Johnson, Harry O. Morris, Marc Moser, Andrew Polak, Andrew Ramage, Steve Schlich, Stewart Stanyard, Bill Walker, and fellow Board members of the Rod Serling Memorial Foundation.

And to the many others who have contributed to and assisted in the production of *The Twilight Zone.*

Special thanks to:
Christopher Conlon for his recurrent guidance and editorial counsel.